ONLY THE GOOD

A Jack Hart Mystery

Rosemary Reeve

Cover designed by Cover Designer
Cover Photograph by pexels.com / Used as authorized by Creative Commons Zero License
Back cover photograph by Busath Photography / Used by digital and print license to Rosemary Reeve

Rosemary Reeve
Please visit my author's pages at amazon.com/author/rosemaryreeve
and https://www.goodreads.com/goodreadscomrosemary_reeve

Printed in the United States of America

First Printing: May 2018
Independently Published

ISBN - 9781982989217

To my dad,
Reed Reeve,
who told the best stories.

CHAPTER 1

If I hadn't had dinner with my clients before I left Bellingham, the police would never have known I was in town. But after being crammed together in a conference room for three days of depositions, you get chummy with your clients. When they suggested drinks and dinner at a nice restaurant called *il fiasco* - which sounds like pretty poor advertising but actually means "flask" in Italian - it seemed churlish to decline.

For a bunch of insurance executives, my clients were sort of fun. In-house counsel Leah Batson was tall and ramrod-thin, with masses of frizzy brown hair and an explosive laugh. Claims manager Jerry Franks was as short as Leah was tall, a dapper, fussy little man with a droll wink and a much-consulted pocket watch. And senior vice president Carl Moore was tall, distinguished, and soft-spoken. Over pasta, the four of us dissected the days' deponents.

Leah turned to me just as I plopped a forkful of capellini in my mouth. "Jack, correct me if I'm wrong, but didn't that guy you deposed this morning pretty much admit that the paper mill knew their processing chemicals were leaking into Bellingham Bay?"

I swallowed hastily. "Yes, he did," I said. "But he claimed it was an accident."

"An accident that the mill happened to commit every other day for twenty years?" Carl asked, leaning back skeptically in his chair.

"Yes," I confirmed. "A *prolonged* accident."

"So where do these deps leave us, Jack?" Jerry Frank peered at me over the rim of his wine glass.

So much for dinner. My clients wanted legal advice. In this case, that meant a deep dive into *scienter*, or state of mind. That's what their coverage exclusion turned on, and that's what the deps had established.

"They could turn out to be vital," I said, abandoning my pasta. "Under the mill's policy with you, American Fidelity has no obligation to indemnify or defend the mill if the mill knowingly dumped the chemicals. From what we've heard over the last couple of days, clearly, the mill knew that chemicals were escaping during paper processing. They said it was an accident, but they still knew. I think that gives you a strong case for summary judgment that you have no obligation to pay for the environmental cleanup. Because you guys write your exclusions so well, we don't have to prove intentional pollution, which would be a lot harder on these facts."

There were satisfied nods around the table. Good enough. A happy client pays their bills. Now for the caveats.

"But we should consider filing right away. If the mill goes into bankruptcy – and they might, given their financials – then it's not just the superior court that's going to be assessing your coverage exclusion. It's potentially the bankruptcy court as well, and all the environmental agencies that might be looking for a deep pocket."

The satisfied nods subsided. I nipped a quick forkful of pasta into my mouth. "How soon could you get a summary judgment motion together, Jack?" Leah asked.

I swallowed fast. "We'll have to wait a couple of days to get transcripts of the deps, but once they're in my hand, I can draft the motion, the memorandum, and the supporting declarations and shoot it all down to L.A. for your review within a week. Assuming you're OK with everything, we can file by the end of October."

"Good." Carl seemed pleased. "Let's plan on that, Jack. By the way, you've done a great job on this case. I was a little worried when Dan Bradford told us he was delegating most of the work to a senior associate, but you're more on top of things than Dan."

A chimp with attention deficit disorder was more on top of things than Dan, but I didn't tell them that. "Thanks," I said, uncomfortably aware that the tips of my ears were red. "It's been great working with you. If we can get you out on summary judgment, I'll be psyched, but I'll miss you guys."

"Don't worry," Leah assured me, swirling the melted wax in the cornice-shaped candleholder. "We'll be back on your doorstep before you know it. We get sued all the time."

Talk around the table soon veered from legal matters to more personal topics. I asked as many open-ended questions as possible to draw them out and give myself a chance to eat. Even though they were based in Los Angeles, all of them had ties to the Northwest. Leah Batson was married to a Vancouver investment banker. She and her husband spent every other weekend together in Seattle, a convenient meeting place between Canada and California. Leah blushed as she talked about her husband, and Jerry Franks gallantly interrupted her and agreed that Seattle was the ideal place for a romantic rendezvous. He and his then-wife had conceived their twin daughters in Seattle, he confided with a twinkle in his eye, during an unforgettable visit to the 1962 World's Fair.

"It was the Space Needle," Jerry said. "It inspired me."

As for Carl Moore, I learned to my surprise that he was from Seattle - just like me. Unlike me, however, Carl had moved to California in the late-1980s, just as half the state of California seemed to be moving to Seattle. He had sold his Laurelhurst house for a grossly inflated sum to a Los Angeles transplant, then paid bottom dollar for a nice place the Hollywood Hills.

"Like they always say, 'Buy low; sell high,'" Carl said, smiling. "How about you, Jack? What's your story?"

"I'm a Seattle kid, born there and never left," I replied. "I'm what's known as a Double Dawg. I played two seasons of college ball for the University of Washington. I got hurt, so I ended up at the U-Dub law school instead of having a shot at the NFL. Ever since law school, I've been at Piper Whatcom & Hardcastle."

"Is your family still in Seattle?" Carl asked. He had no idea how complicated a complete answer would be. I gave him the abbreviated version.

"Unfortunately not. My mom and little brother just moved to Spokane. My mom's getting remarried."

More accurately, my mom was getting married. Married, as in for the first time. Married, as in hooking up with a guy who wasn't the father of either of her sons - me or my adorable, almost-five-year-old half-brother, Jimmy. Married, as in community property, joint filings, and all that financially advantageous good stuff.

My mom had met a comfortable, balding, recently widowed owner of a trucking company at a bar called The Stumble Inn. Forty-eight hours later, they were engaged. I had been sure that the poor guy would come to his senses after he saw my mom in natural light, but it had been two weeks, and he still seemed crazy about her.

I had helped him pack up her stuff, and he hadn't turned even one of his remaining hairs at the sight of my mom's crystal balls, magic candles, and fully articulated small animal skeletons.

"Jack," he had said to me as we shoved the last box onto one of his trucks, "your mother is one hell of a woman."

"Bill," I had replied, "you don't even know how right you are."

"Jack?" Leah's voice nudged me. "Are you OK?"

"Yeah. I'm sorry," I said hastily. "Just a little tired."

"Thinking about your mommy?" Jerry teased.

"Yes," I confessed, and they all laughed. If they only knew, I thought.

I turned the conversation to safer topics. The World Series. The Seahawks. Bellingham's new museum, which was opening in the old city hall. All in all, it was a pleasant way to conclude three grueling days. I grabbed the check – client development – but yawned a little too obviously as we headed for the door.

"Are you sure you want to drive back to Seattle tonight?" Carl asked. "You've been putting in 18-hour days as it is. We'd be happy to pay for you to stay at the hotel tonight and drive back to Seattle in the morning."

"That's really nice of you," I said, stifling another yawn. "But I need to get home."

"Eager to see your girlfriend?" Jerry said, fluttering a lecherous eyebrow.

"Well, yes, actually, but my girlfriend's in Japan right now. Mostly, I'm eager to see my dog."

"Ah, a dog fancier," said Leah, who was partial to cats. "I guess we shouldn't even try to talk sense into you, then. Just drive safely, OK, Jack?"

"You got it," I said, shaking hands. I opened the door for all of them to leave, and continued to hold it for a bevy of chic, sixtyish ladies to waft into the restaurant.

One of them gave me a haughty, condescending smile of thanks, then blinked, gasped, and exclaimed, "Jack Hart! What in the world have you done to yourself?"

Through no fault of my own, I had been involved in a couple of high-profile murder cases. Every now and then, people recognized me from the newspaper or TV.

I had learned what to do. I stuck out my hand and said, "Yes, ma'am. But I don't think I've had the pleasure of meeting you before."

The lady in the doorway made no move to take my hand. She looked me over, from my straight, blond-brown hair to my bulging shoulders and big hands. She shook her head.

"No," she said, sounding flustered. "I'm terribly sorry. I thought you were someone else. Please excuse me." Then she pushed past me into the restaurant.

Carl gave me a quizzical smile as I joined them on the sidewalk. "An adoring fan, Jack?"

"Hardly. Mistaken identity, I'm afraid." I thanked them for their time, promised the summary judgment motion ASAP, gassed up the trusty old Buick, and headed out of Bellingham to I-5.

The interstate was dark, wet, and boring. If I had left right after the last deposition, I would have taken the scenic route down Chuckanut Drive, where even on late, rainy afternoons you could watch the sun slipping into Samish Bay and feel like you could touch it. But even though the unexpected dinner at *il fiasco* had consigned me to I-5, I was glad I had taken the time with Leah, Jerry, and Carl. I figured it could only help me in terms of client development.

A long, dark drive is such an isolating thing. I kept my mind on my dog, on the rush of warmth I always felt when I opened the door and Betsy leapt to greet me, barking madly and wriggling as if her joy at my arrival was just too big for her skin. I wanted to see my roommate, too. Mark Oden had shared my house near Green

Lake for about six months, but we had first lived together as foster kids, almost twenty years earlier. He and Betsy always made it fun to come home.

I was so focused on getting back to Seattle that I didn't spare a single thought for American Fidelity, or the flustered lady in the dark restaurant, or the paper mill that had accidentally dumped processing chemicals into Bellingham Bay for the past twenty years.

I had no idea that I was about to lose American Fidelity as a client, that the flustered lady actually had a very good reason for recognizing me, and that the paper mill would soon become a lot more to me than your average, garden-variety environmental despoiler.

I had no idea that behind me, somewhere up I-5, that paper mill was on fire.

CHAPTER 2

I let myself sleep late the next morning. It was a cold and rainy Saturday. Betsy sacked out beside me, her thick orange fur almost luminous in the dark room.

At 10 or so, I dragged myself out of bed, showered, and dressed to head into work. In deference to the weekend, no tie. I had to get a jump on the stuff that had piled up while I was in Bellingham, and I wanted to start the summary judgment motion for American Fidelity. I could nail down the legal issues and be ready to drop in the factual admissions as soon as I got the transcripts.

But first, breakfast. It seemed like a long time since *il fiasco*.

I fed Betsy and looked around for something for myself. Whenever Harmony was in Japan, Mark and I were somewhat less than self-sustaining. I reread the note he had left on the fridge:

> Welcome back! I got called into work. See you tomorrow night.
>
> M.
>
> P.S. I did the grocery shopping.
>
> P.P.S. Did we need anything besides beer?

When you have roommates, you learn that there are multiple definitions for household chores. My fridge contained a six-pack of beer, an empty pizza box, the apparently mandated baking soda, and half a bag of coffee.

I made coffee, very strong. There were some elderly graham crackers over the sink. Not bad if I dunked them. I was working on my to-do list when I realized that Betsy's nose was inching toward a coffee-soaked cracker. A caffeinated Betsy might get us both arrested. I tossed her my last dry cracker.

She caught it, crunched it – then dropped it and bolted for the front door, barking. Betsy's leaving a treat could mean only one of two things: either we were being invaded, or someone Betsy liked was on the other side of the door. I reached the entryway just as the door swung open.

Betsy leapt up to welcome Mark, then sat down in mid-woof. I took a step back and looked at my roommate. Usually, Mark was perfectly groomed and extremely handsome in an Elvisy way. But not today. Today his dark eyes were bloodshot, and his black hair was matted with the rain.

"Are you OK?"

"*I'm* OK," he said, putting a strange stress on the first word. "But we need to talk to you, Jack."

"Who's we?" Then I looked over his shoulder and saw Detective Anthony C. Anthony, Mark's partner at the police department.

"Hi, son," Anthony said, putting his hand on my shoulder. "Can we come in?"

"Of course." I ushered them into my living room, but their manner chilled me. They were my friends, but suddenly so formal. It struck me that having two homicide detectives just drop by is generally a not a good sign.

"I have bad news, Jack," Anthony said.

All I could think about was my girlfriend. Mark and Anthony knew how much Harmony meant to me. They knew how happy I was that we were dating.

"Harmony -" I blurted, but Anthony stopped me.

"Not Harmony," he said.

My mind leapt to another horrible thought just as Anthony added, "Not your little brother or your mother, if you were going to ask about her."

I shook my head. I wasn't going to ask about her. "Well, then what's going on?" I asked.

"It's your father, Jack. He died last night."

My father. *My father*. The first thing I could feel was relief: relief that it wasn't Harmony or Jimmy or even my mom who was dead; relief that it was just my father, just my father who was dead. But then I heard this noise, a noise that I would have sworn was real. I heard a door slam shut. I could hear it closing. I could feel it closing. I could hear the echo. I could hear nothing but the echo. All my relief, all the good things of the world, were suddenly locked away from me, locked behind that door.

"I'm so sorry, Jack."

I took a deep breath. With difficulty, I met his eyes. "There's nothing to be sorry for, Detective Anthony," I said. "He left when I was five, and I never saw him again. I didn't even know him."

Anthony waited a moment before he said, "That's something to be sorry for, Jack."

I couldn't think of any response to that. I just took another deep breath and tried to jerk myself to my feet. "Thanks for coming over to tell me, you guys," I said. "I appreciate it, but I've got to get to work."

Anthony put up his hand. "There's more."

I waited. What more could there be?

Anthony clearly didn't want to say what he had to say. He hmmmed a few times before explaining, "Your father's death is suspicious in some ways, Jack. That's why we're involved. We're not in charge of the investigation, but we've been asked to get some information from you. Mark and I thought you'd rather talk to us than anyone else."

"You mean where was I last night? Who was I with? Who saw me? That sort of information?"

Anthony nodded.

"Was my dad murdered?"

"We don't know yet. But possibly."

"Am I a suspect?" I couldn't keep the indignation out of my voice. Even in death, my father was ruining my life.

"You're not a suspect."

"Am I a person of interest?" I demanded, using the police jargon for someone who is well on his way to becoming a suspect.

"Not to us. But the people in charge of the case are interested in you. We told them they were nuts. But we can't get them to lay off you until we have the information they want. OK?"

I was suddenly so tired that I just wanted to get it over with. "OK." I gave them a complete account of my movements the day before. I had been in depositions from 8 until 5:30. My presence would be proven by the sworn transcript. I had spent lunch and bathroom breaks consulting with my clients or wrangling with opposing counsel. Then I had had drinks and dinner with the good people of American Fidelity. I had left Bellingham around 9:30.

"Did you stop for gas?"

"Yeah. On my way out of town." I dug through my Day-Timer and handed him the receipt.

"What were you wearing?"

"My lucky blue suit, a white shirt, a red tie, and wingtips."

"Have you washed any of that since you've been home?"

"Are you kidding? It's hanging on the exercise bike."

"Do you mind if we take your clothes for a few days?"

"No. But I'll need the shoes back pronto."

"We'll expedite it. How long did it take you to drive home?"

"I'm not sure. It was raining, and there was a lot of traffic. About two hours, probably."

"Did you see anyone or talk to anyone after you left the gas station in Bellingham?"

"No. I just got home, saw Mark's note that he had been called into work, and went to bed."

I had known better than to ask Detective Anthony for information until he had finished questioning me. He couldn't have told me anything that would have tipped me off. I didn't really want to know, but I had to ask. "What's suspicious about the way my dad died?"

Anthony gave me a sympathetic look. "He died in a fire, Jack," he told me. "They don't know yet how it started."

I shuddered. One summer, I had almost been caught in a brush fire in Eastern Washington. The fire had jumped the road right ahead of me. It went so fast that I didn't see the flame. I saw only the sudden expanse of black - black, twisted, smoking stubble that seconds before had been a grassy field. No matter what my dad had done to me or hadn't done for me, he hadn't deserved to die like that.

"What about my dad's body, Detective Anthony?" I asked, feeling the fear even as I said the words. "Do they want me to identify him? Because I can't. It's been twenty-four years since I've seen him."

"Don't worry about that," Anthony said. "You don't have to identify him. His daughter made a positive ID this morning -" He broke off and blinked with concern and surprise at my face. "Jack, what's the matter?"

I didn't trust myself to speak. After a moment I got out, "His *daughter*?"

"Yes. His oldest. She's going to take care of all the funeral arrangements, too. His wife's not well enough to handle it, but they have four girls."

I could feel things crumbling inside me. I didn't know what they were, but I knew that they were important things, imperative things, and that I was losing them.

The first flush of the hurt passed, although I was still hot with the pain. I tried to explain myself. "I'm sorry," I said. My voice sounded flattened, like it was coming from somewhere far away. "I didn't know that my dad had another family. I've always just assumed that my dad left us because he didn't want a family. That's always been how I explained it to myself. But if he's got a wife and daughters somewhere else -" I couldn't complete my sentence.

Finally I said, "I guess it's not that he didn't want a family. I guess it's just that he didn't want *me*."

Betsy whimpered and licked my chin. Anthony spoke quietly but distinctly:

"If that's true, Jack, then he was a fool."

CHAPTER 3

"I've already interrogated him, Lee," Anthony said into the telephone. He was trying to convince the cop investigating my dad's death to leave me alone. From the edge of irritation in his voice, it sounded like he wasn't having much success. He was silent for a long time, just listening to the officer on the other end of the line, drumming his fingers on my kitchen counter, and fuming.

"Look, Lee," Anthony said in exasperation, "the boy wasn't alone for five minutes until after 9:30 p.m. One of his neighbors heard him arrive home around 11 or 11:30. You know that doesn't fit in with your time frame for the fire. He's got no motive and no opportunity. He didn't even know his dad. He's cooperating, he's shaken up, and he's a good kid. I can vouch that he's a good kid." Anthony fell silent again. He looked over at Mark and rolled his eyes.

"No, we haven't searched the place yet," he said wearily into the phone. "You don't have a warrant, you won't be able to get a warrant, and I haven't asked him to consent." He listened a moment, then retorted, "Because it would have been a colossal waste of everybody's time, that's why." He put his hand over the mouthpiece and turned to me. "Jack, will you give us permission to take a look around your house and examine your car?"

I knew it was routine. I knew that Anthony was doing everything he could for me. Harmony and I had stood by Mark when he had been involved in a shooting earlier that year, and I had learned how much cops value loyalty. But I felt like a walking open wound. More bitterly than I intended to, I said, "You don't need my consent. Mark lives here. He can let you search anywhere you want."

Anthony shook his head. "Lee already asked Mark for permission to search the place, Jack," he told me. "Mark told him to spin on it."

I looked over at my roommate. Being a cop was more important to Mark than anything else. I couldn't imagine that Mark would mouth off to another officer like that.

"You told this guy to spin on it?" I demanded.

"Not quite in those words," Mark said. "But that was the gist of it."

"Why?"

"Because it's your house, Jack. I just live here. I think you should give us permission to search, and I think you will give us permission to search, but I didn't want you to feel like you had a spy under your roof. I'm not giving consent to anybody. They can go get a search warrant for all I care."

I turned to Detective Anthony, who was waiting patiently, his hand still over the phone. "You can look anywhere you want," I told him. "Just don't let anybody scare Betsy."

It turned out that Betsy was far from scared of the officers and criminalists who arrived to search my house. It was quite obviously the other way around. Betsy wasn't trying to be intimidating, but she was 95 pounds of muscle and teeth. She was also a curious, intelligent dog, and she was fascinated by the search.

"I'm sorry. She thinks she's being helpful," I explained to a young, jumpy officer, who had yelped in alarm when Betsy had suddenly charged between his legs. "She loves to find things."

The jumpy officer was not comforted by my reassurances, and Betsy and I ended up playing keepaway in the back yard while the police sifted through my belongings. At least, we tried to play keepaway. I did not feel up to romping in the rain right then. Neither, apparently, did Betsy. After a few dutiful turns around the lawn, we just sat together on my sodden deck.

I rubbed Betsy's ears and tried to remember anything about my dad. I could dredge up only three clear memories.

I remembered him dragging me through a grocery store or a shopping mall, my hand swallowed up in his vast, hard grasp. I remembered sitting beside him on the couch one night and hearing him call Howard Cosell a horse's patoot. And I remembered the morning after the night he left. He hadn't even said goodbye. I remembered looking around the apartment for him, for any evidence of him. That was it. That was the sum of my relationship with my dad. I couldn't even picture him.

That was not to say that I hadn't thought about him over the years. I had. When I was eight, my mom had put me in foster care so she could take up with a guy who didn't want kids. In that first, horrible foster home, I had spent hours concocting elaborate fantasies of my dad coming to rescue me. I knew what kind of car he would drive - a red Mustang convertible with one of those bobbing-head critters on the dash. I knew what he would wear - a really sharp tan suit with wide lapels, not the tight turtlenecks and T-shirts favored by my case workers and foster dad. And I knew what he would say: "At last, I've found my boy." And if my foster father or my foster mother or any of those damned case workers got in his way, I knew that my dad would punch them right in the nose.

It would have been one hell of a touching reunion. There was only one problem. It never happened. I had spent a blur of time in a home somewhere in Ravenna, where I was usually hungry and always scared. Then my case worker had shipped me down to Tacoma, where my foster father beat me up for all manner of infractions - real and imagined - but where I met Mark Oden. There were other homes after that - one after another - but my father had never come to rescue me. No one had ever come to rescue me. I had spent ten years as a ward of the State, and by the time I had turned 18, aged out of the foster system, and struck out on my own, I didn't have fantasies about my dad anymore. I didn't have fantasies about anything.

"You OK?" Mark sat down next to me.

"No."

"They're almost done in there. Go inside and get dry."

Actually, it felt kind of good to sit out there on my deck in the steady Seattle rain. I was cold and wet and fast approaching numb. There was nothing wrong with being numb.

Mark said, "At least take pity on Betsy." On cue, she sneezed. I let him pull me up and shepherd me and Bets into the living room. The police had already searched there. I moved things around on my desk to reestablish my sense of ownership and control. Mark watched me without trying to interfere.

"Better?" he said, after I had picked up my telephone, debated a moment, and replaced it in the exact same spot.

"Yeah," I said. "At least I know I was the one who put it there." The phone rang, and Mark and I both jumped. When I hesitated, Mark picked up the receiver.

"Hello?" He listened, then cocked an eyebrow. *Dan Bradford*, he mouthed at me.

Geez. Dan Bradford was an overgrown, snickering frat boy who also happened to be Piper Whatcom's managing partner. The mantle of authority didn't fit Dan at all, but he had seized control of the firm the year before, when the rest of Piper Whatcom's senior partnership seemed to be either dead or in jail.

It was unheard of for Dan to call anyone at home on a Saturday, not because Dan was courteous or considerate of associates' time, but simply because Dan himself never worked a single weekend. I could think of only two reasons for Dan to call: either I was in deep, deep trouble, or Dan had a new dirty joke. I prayed for the joke.

"Jack! You sly bastard, you. You really had me going there for a while. But I knew it wasn't true."

Dealing with Dan was like doing the daily Jumble in the newspaper. "Knew what wasn't true?" I ventured.

"Sounds like the deps went well up in Bellingham," Dan went on without answering my question. "American Fidelity's very pleased with you. They'll be delighted to hear you're still among the living. As am I, of course, Jack. For one horrible moment, I thought I might have to take back that dog of a case I dumped on you." He snorted with laughter.

The hair prickled on the back of my neck.

"Hey, Jack, I was only kidding, you know," Dan said, in a tone that was the verbal equivalent of an elbow in the ribs. "I really was worried about you. Jack? Jack? Are you there? Hellooo, Jack."

I said, as calmly as I could, "Let me just make sure I know what's going on. Did you hear a news bulletin or something saying that a Jack Hart had died in a fire last night?"

"Well, I didn't hear it, but Leah Batson sure did. She was so worried that she tracked me down at the tennis club. I'll call her back and let her know that it was a false alarm."

"It's not exactly a false alarm, Dan," I said. "A Jack Hart did die in a fire last night. Just not this Jack Hart."

Dan said sharply, "He wasn't a relative or anything, was he?"

"Yes," I said. "He was. He was my father."

I don't know what I expected Dan to say. Something awkward, something uncomfortable, maybe even something grossly inappropriate. I wouldn't have been surprised if he had tried to make a joke of it. A dirty joke of it, even. But what he said knocked the wind out of me.

"Your father? What the hell do you mean, 'your father'?"

I was too stunned to reply. Dan ranted on: "And just how the hell did your father end up dead in the fucking paper mill that you're fucking well supposed to be investigating up there in fucking Bellingham?"

I let the phone slip from my fingers. I could hear Dan's roaring voice ebb to a furious squeak as the receiver clattered to the floor.

Mark picked up the telephone. "This is Detective Mark Oden of the Seattle Police Department," he said sounding like nothing on earth could rattle him. "Mr. Hart will call you back, Mr. Bradford." He paused just a second, then added, "I *said,* Mr. Hart will call you back."

The phone clicked into the cradle. I sank onto my couch and looked up at him.

"You and Anthony neglected to mention that my dad died in Bellingham."

He flinched and shook his head. "We couldn't tell you what we knew until we had collected all the evidence. It would have tainted everything you had to say. I'm sorry. We weren't trying to trick you."

He paused. "But now you know why the Bellingham police are so interested in you. Someone who knew your dad from high school spotted you in the restaurant where you had dinner. When she heard about your dad on the early news, she thought she had seen his ghost. She got so hysterical that her husband called the police. It didn't take them long to put things together. They called around to all the hotels in the area and found out that a Jack Hart from Seattle had checked out yesterday. They called down to the department demanding that we arrest you."

I didn't respond.

"But don't worry, Jack. Everything's going to be fine. I kept an eye on the search. Anthony already called the Bellingham police back and told them that there isn't anything linking you with the fire."

I made myself inhale. Then I made myself exhale. Before I had left for Bellingham, I had told Mark that I was going up there to take some depositions, but I hadn't told him who I was representing or who I was going to be deposing.

If my dad had been involved in any way with the paper mill, then I had had an undisclosed conflict of interest in defending American Fidelity. At the very least, I would be off the case. At the most - well, I didn't want to think about the most. Dan Bradford was not one for assuming innocence.

"Where in Bellingham was the fire, Mark?"

"Some old mill down by the bay. It's by a cement plant."

"What's it called?"

"Does it matter?"

"Yeah, it does. It matters a lot."

"Just a second then. I'll find out." He slipped out of the room. I could hear him calling for Detective Anthony. While I waited for them, I stared at the ceiling and wondered just how much trouble I was in.

"You need to know something, Jack?" Anthony had entered the living room so silently that even Betsy hadn't stirred.

"What's the name of the mill where my dad died?"

Anthony hesitated a second before replying. "It's called SPP - Squalicum Paper Products."

Just the day before, I had deposed two estimable representatives of Squalicum Paper Products. I had been fighting SPP for months, ever since the mill had sued American Fidelity for refusing to pay for the state-ordered cleanup of Bellingham Bay. I swallowed. "And what was my dad's relation to SPP?"

Anthony sat down across from me.

"Well, until last night, Jack," he said, "he owned the place."

CHAPTER 4

Considering the circumstances, Dan Bradford was the soul of restraint when I phoned him back and broke the bad news. He used the F-word only five times, called me a stupid bastard only twice, and threatened to fire me only once.

"What in the hell were you thinking, Jack?" he demanded, sounding tight and strangled, like he was going to have a massive coronary right then just to emphasize the magnitude of my infraction. "What possessed you to think you could defend a lawsuit by your father's company?"

"I didn't know, Dan."

"Didn't know what, Jack?" he shot back. "Didn't know that everybody - especially the good folks on the Bar Ethics Committee - would frown on your representing American Fidelity against a suit by your daddy?"

"I didn't know that my dad was involved with Squalicum Paper Products. His name didn't show up on any of the documents or the pleadings. He wasn't on the conflicts check. He's not on any of the org charts. I had no idea that he owned the mill."

"You expect me to believe that bullshit?" Dan exploded. "What, you and your dad just don't communicate very well, Jack?"

I was silent a moment. Except for my girlfriend, who retained only a tangential relationship to the firm, no one at Piper Whatcom knew about my rocky childhood. You can't show any weakness at a law firm. If there's any reason to discount, overlook, or denigrate you, other lawyers will lock onto it, like sharks on blood in the water. But if it was going to come down to a choice between being ostracized and being disbarred, then I would rather be a pariah with a Bar card than a pariah without.

"My dad and I didn't communicate at all, Dan," I said. "He abandoned me when I was five, and I never saw him again. It's been twenty-four years since I've had any idea where he was. If I had known he was involved with SPP, I would have told you. But I didn't. I didn't know he was in Bellingham. I didn't know he was in Washington. I didn't even know he was still alive."

That shut Dan up for a moment. But only a moment. "Surely your mother knew where he was," he insisted. "Or did your mom abandon you, too?"

The sarcasm in his voice stung me into divulging more than I had intended to. "As a matter of fact, she did."

"Oh." Dan suddenly sounded tired. "I'll call you back, Jack. I've got to call Leah and try to explain this whole big shitty mess." He hung up without saying goodbye.

I sank down on my couch and rubbed my temples. Detective Anthony was still sitting across from me. "How did it go?"

"About as well as could be expected."

"They can't be mad at you for not knowing that your dad was involved with SPP."

"Oh, yes, they can. Besides, I doubt Dan believes that I didn't know. I doubt the Bellingham police believe it, either."

"I believe it, Jack."

"I know. Thanks."

Anthony pushed his fingers through his close-cropped grey hair. "Mark's going to stay home with you today. I really ought to be going. We found a body down by the Kingdome last night, and I need to follow up on some leads."

"I'll be OK, Detective Anthony," I said. "Thanks a lot - for everything."

He nodded at me, said, "It's going to be all right, Jack," and headed for the door. He exchanged a few quiet words with Mark, and then he was gone.

Mark had put in a load of laundry and ordered a pizza while I had been wrangling with Dan Bradford.

"I must really look pathetic," I said.

"I've seen dead bodies that looked better." He handed me a beer and a plate. "Eat," he ordered.

The pizza smelled great, but I wasn't hungry anymore– much to Betsy's delight. She had finished my piece and was pushing her nose into the box when Mark shooed her away. "Save some for Harmony, Bets."

"Harmony's coming?" I said, perking up. I had deliberately denied myself the comfort of calling her. I didn't want her to feel like she had to drop everything and rush home from Japan.

"Of course Harmony's coming. Anthony and I phoned her as soon as we got the call from the Bellingham police. She's on her way right now. She should be here when you wake up in the morning - provided you oversleep long enough, of course."

"What about Higuro?" I asked.

For the purposes of public identification, Higuro Yamashita was Harmony's godfather. He was actually her biological father, but she was still working through how she felt about that. The man who had raised her had been killed the year before, and as much as Harmony wanted to know about Higuro, she did not want to be disloyal to Humphrey Piper.

After Humphrey's death, Higuro had tried to find a place in Harmony's life. He offered her a job as his general counsel. He had helped her rebuild the confidence Piper Whatcom had lost with our Asian clients. Thanks to Harmony and Higuro, Piper Whatcom had been able to rehire all their staff and associates. They had even rehired *me* – even though some of the partners still seemed offended by my rank disloyalty in refusing to be murdered in our law library.

Higuro was not so eager to find a place in my life – or to have me find a place in Harmony's. Over the summer, Harmony and I had been thinking of hanging out our own shingle as Piper & Hart, a boutique civil litigation firm. Somehow Higuro had gotten wind of our quiet excursions to office space around the city. He had suffered what Mark and I referred to between ourselves as an "aneurism of convenience," and Harmony had rushed back to Japan to help him. She had been gone for weeks.

"What *about* Higuro?" Mark's caustic rejoinder cut across my thoughts. "Higuro's faking it, Jack," Mark said. "All three of us know that, even though Harmony doesn't want to admit it. Don't you think so?"

If Mark had asked me that question a few hours earlier, before I had known about my father, I would have agreed. But I was suddenly much less sure of myself. "I don't know," I said slowly. "It was just a year ago this month that Humphrey Piper died. And now, supposedly, Higuro is sick. Really sick. In Harmony's mind, it must seem like everything's repeating itself. It must seem like she's losing her dad all over again."

I fell silent, thinking over what I had said. I had lost my dad twice. Once when I was five, when the wound had never quite healed because I had always nurtured the possibility, the faint but wonderful possibility, that he might come back. And once that morning, when Anthony had told me unequivocally that he wasn't ever coming back. I wondered how many more times I would have to lose my dad before just the thought of him didn't hurt.

"Jack?" Mark was standing beside me, the phone in his hand. I hadn't even heard it ring. "Do you want to talk to Dan Bradford, or should I tell him to call back?"

Dan Bradford was the last person I wanted to talk to, but I knew I had to get it over with. "Hi, Dan," I said.

Dan sounded impossibly jaunty. "Hey, Jack," he said. "Thanks to me and my golden tongue, you don't need to worry about a thing. I got you off the hook."

Relief swept over me. At least I wasn't going to lose my job and my dad on the same day. "You mean Leah believed that I didn't know about my dad's connection with SPP?"

"Leah believed it, Jerry believed it, and even Carl believed it. They were a little skeptical at first, but once I explained about your tragic youth, they were pretty sympathetic. So put together a status memo about the SPP case and have it on my desk first thing Monday. I'm going to reassign SPP to Cory Corliss, and we'll construct a Chinese wall to prevent you from having anything to do with SPP or any other American Fidelity matter in the future."

I was confused. Dan was talking about creating what ethnically sensitive people referred to as an ethical screen, a firm-wide division that prevented people working for one client from divulging relevant information to people working for another. I could understand why American Fidelity would not want me to continue working on the SPP defense. Even though I hadn't known that my dad was on the other side, Leah, Jerry, and Carl might well question whether I could calmly and dispassionately defend against a lawsuit by my late father's company. But there wasn't any reason to bar me from other American Fidelity cases in the future. I tried to explain that to Dan without insulting his intelligence. No dice.

"Jack," he interrupted, "I understand the rules of professional conduct. Believe me, I do. It's not the ethics rules that I'm worried about. I just think it would be better if you didn't work for American Fidelity again."

"But why?" I pressed, still confused. "Are they mad at me?"

"No, they're not mad at you, Jack. They feel sorry for you, actually. But you're not exactly the type of lawyer they're used to. Cory Corliss will be a lot more their speed. He'll be the senior associate in charge of their cases from now on."

Cory Corliss was one of my classmates, a preening little pipsqueak of a fifth-year associate. He had been two years behind Harmony at Harvard, and he persisted in calling her "Monie," as though they were old school friends. The chummy nickname was a pure sham. Harmony had never laid eyes on Cory until he showed up at the firm, but as she had pointed out, philosophically, it was better to be called "Monie" than it was to be called "Harm."

Modesty aside, I couldn't think of one reason for American Fidelity to prefer Cory Corliss over me. I had more litigation experience, I worked a lot harder, and I didn't pad my hours. "Why?" I demanded, unwisely. "Why will Cory Corliss be more their speed?"

"It's nothing personal, Jack," Dan said, as if he were explaining something to a four-year-old. "It's just that American Fidelity is a very Brahmin, white-shoe Eastern company. Even most of the executives in their L.A. office are transplants from Boston or New York. They're just not used to dealing with people with your, um, *colorful* background. Cory comes from a prominent family. His father used to be a congressman, and his mother and Carl Moore's wife were Regents at the U-Dub together before the Moores moved to California. He's just what they're looking for."

"You mean I'm not the right sort of people?" I hissed into the phone. "My blood's not quite blue enough?"

If Dan had any sarcasm receptors, they weren't functioning that day. "Exactly," he said, as if he were proud of me for catching on. Then he added, "But don't worry, Jack. It's no reflection on your value to the firm. We've got plenty of cases where we need a junkyard dog."

A junkyard dog. Three words, and I was blindly furious. I knew what he meant. He meant that some cases required belligerence, and some cases required finesse, and that I was welcome to shed my and anyone else's blood any time the firm needed naked aggression. Never mind that I was easily the softest-spoken, slowest-tempered guy at the firm. Never mind that I had handled hundreds of sensitive, delicate matters and dozens of high-strung, pedigreed clients during my five long years at Piper Whatcom, without anyone's ever questioning the purity of my breeding or the color of my blood. Just because I had grown up rough, Dan - and Leah, and Jerry, and Carl - assumed that I was rough, that I was so radically different from them that I couldn't even be trusted to handle the relatively indestructible instrument of civil litigation.

I expected Dan to be an idiot. I expected him to say crass, stupid, reckless things. It was his calling. It was his one true talent. But I had - I had thought - hit it off with Leah, Jerry, and Carl. I had worked so hard for them, and they had seemed to appreciate it. They had seemed to appreciate *me*. I shook my head in astonishment at my own ingenuousness. They had seemed so friendly that I had treated them like my friends. I had forgotten that I was just their hired gun. Or their junkyard dog.

Dan was silent on the other end of the line, clearly waiting for my abject expression of gratitude. I longed to tell him what he could do with American Fidelity, SPP, and particularly, Cory Corliss, but junkyard dogs can't be too proud when it comes to their next meal. As politely as I could, I said, "Dan, thanks for taking care of all that. I'll get the status report to you Monday morning. But right now I've got to go. The police are here again." Then I hung up the phone, let out a long sigh, and looked around for something to throw.

Fortunately for my furniture and my homeowners' insurance premium, the police were there - in the person of my roommate. I told Mark what happened.

Mark went right to the bottom line: "Jack, you have to get out of that shithole once and for all. You quit - or I guess you were fired, but the point is, you left - after Humphrey's murder, but then you went back. They know they can treat you like shit because you let them treat you like shit. Just quit for good."

Mark's change of subject was abrupt. "And while I'm doling out advice, I think you should get some sleep. You've had a bitch of a day."

"I was going to give Betsy a bath. And with Harmony coming home, one of us needs to do actual grocery shopping. For actual food."

He rolled his eyes at me. "I'll give Betsy a bath tomorrow. And you know whatever food you buy, Harmony will get something else. So why bother?"

He had a point.

"Just go to bed," he said. "The worst day is over."

CHAPTER 5

Maybe the worst day was over, but the worst night still loomed before me. I lay on my back and stared at the ceiling. Betsy licked my arm until it was dripping. Then she inched up beside me and panted heavily in my face. She really did need a bath. I eased upwind, then stroked behind her ears until she fell asleep. Slowly and carefully, so as not to wake her, I maneuvered her toward the foot of the bed. It was like trying to pull the cloth off a table without disarranging the dishes - but in reverse. Then I got back into bed and stared at the ceiling once again.

Soon the house was quiet. Mark had turned in early too. I remembered belatedly that he had been up all night investigating that murder down by the Kingdome. So had Detective Anthony. It made their patience with me even more remarkable. Maybe I didn't have a dad - maybe I had never really had a dad - but I had wonderful friends.

And I had a wonderful girlfriend. I treated myself to a moment of excitement at the thought of Harmony's arrival. Harmony was such an interesting mix. She had Higuro's thick, straight black hair and her mother's Scandinavian features, skin tone, and deep blue eyes. But her blue eyes were almond-shaped, and her cheekbones were dauntingly high. She was an extraordinary lawyer - firm, careful, and courteous, but with an almost frightening ability to see the whole sweep of a case without losing the details.

But even though she was one of the best lawyers I had ever met, it wasn't the career she would have chosen. Humphrey Piper, the man she would always think of as her dad, had pressured her into going to law school and practicing at Piper Whatcom. Harmony had resented the pressure while she was growing up, but after Humphrey died, the thought of it made her sad. She could see that Humphrey had been trying to find some connection with her. Pushing her into a legal career had provided tangible proof - to himself, to the world - that Harmony was just like her dear old dad.

I stared at the ceiling and thought about my dad. Did I take after him at all? Apparently, I looked enough like him to give the elegant lady in the restaurant some serious willies when she had heard about his death. Mark had said she had known him from high school. Had they dated? Had she had a crush on him? Had he been a ladies' man, or had she once been the love of his life, however temporarily? I tried to picture her as she must have been in high school. In my mind, she was tall and blonde, dating the captain of the football team. I just assumed that my dad had played football. It was my one innate talent, the one thing I hadn't had to struggle for, and I knew I hadn't inherited it from my mom.

I thought some more about the woman in the restaurant. Maybe she would be willing to tell me about my dad. Or maybe not. As I screwed up my eyes in the darkness and tried to picture her face, it seemed to me that her expression had not been entirely welcoming. Maybe my dad had run out on her, too.

Then I shook my head in surprise. The lady in the restaurant was elegant and fashionable, but she had to be over sixty. My mom was only in her mid-forties, though she looked older. If my dad had gone to high school with the *il fiasco* lady, then he must have been a dirty old man as far as my mom was concerned. No wonder she always referred to him as The Biggest Mistake of Her Life.

I wasn't used to thinking of my mom as a victim. As far as I was concerned, my mom was a born predator. If she hadn't fogged her mind with drink and drugs, she would have made a great lawyer. She never gave an inch, and she had an uncanny sense of where other people were vulnerable. She would find your soft spots and press them until you gave her what she wanted. The only person she loved was my little half-brother, Jimmy. She didn't love me; she didn't even like me. And I was sure she didn't love Bill, the man she was going to marry. Bill was just a meal ticket, and she was marrying his bank balance, his Overbluff home, and his 401(k), not really him at all. I wondered if she had loved my dad, even a little bit. Odds were, she hadn't.

The hours crawled by. I regretted petting Betsy to sleep. Even smelly company was better than no company at all. I don't remember sleeping, but I must at least have drowsed. I didn't hear the cab drive away or the door open, but I did hear Harmony's voice in the darkness, so soft that I almost thought I imagined it.

"Jack?"

I rolled up on my elbow. She was silhouetted against the faint grey glow from my bay window. "Are you awake?"

"I'm awake." I fumbled for her hand and pulled her close. "How did you get here so fast?"

"Higuro sent me home in the company jet."

"He what?"

"He's worried about you. And he's feeling better. He told me to tell you how sorry he was."

I repented of every single bad thought I had ever had about Higuro. I repented even more vehemently as Harmony took me in her arms and kissed me.

"How are you holding up?"

"OK, I guess," I said, trying to sound rational. "It's not like I've lost someone I loved or who loved me. I wouldn't have recognized him if I had fallen over him in the street." I stopped. She stroked my hair. I demanded, "So why does it hurt so bad, Harmony? Why does it hurt so bad to lose something I never even had?"

I hadn't expected her to answer, but Harmony was a lawyer. When you asked for her opinion, you got it. "I think you've always planned on reconciling with your father," she said. "Maybe you haven't been aware of it, but I think it's always been there. I mean, you worked things out with your mother. There's sort of an uneasy truce between the two of you. I think you've always planned on reaching the same sort of accord with your dad."

I thought that over, holding her theory against the pain to see whether it would fit. It fit better than I was willing to accept. "So why didn't I look for him? He's been up there in Bellingham for the past twenty-four years. He got married and had four daughters. He owned a paper mill. If I had so much as run a LEXIS FINDER search, I would have stumbled across him. Why didn't I try to find him, Harmony?"

"I don't know, Jack," she whispered to me. "Maybe because he apparently didn't try to find you, either."

She had me there. Without knowing it, probably without even meaning to, Harmony had touched the place that hurt the most.

For all her faults, my mother had tried to find me. True, all she had wanted from me was money, and true, she had waited until I was fully grown, employed, and able to give it to her before she had approached me. But even if she didn't want me, at least she had needed me. I had always just assumed that someday my dad would need me, too. I had always pictured him as a broken, asocial loner - maybe a fisherman, maybe a day laborer - who would need me desperately as he grew older and his body or his will gave out. But I had been wrong. I had been so, so wrong. He hadn't wanted me. He hadn't needed me. There was just nothing there.

I had a sudden vision of my law school graduation. I had been second in my class and one of the speakers. It had been a grim year. We were all graduating into the teeth of one the worst recessions ever for young attorneys. Across the country, firms were laying off hordes of associates. Only about twenty percent of my class had jobs lined up for after the bar, so I had talked about the opportunity we had to pursue the law on its own merits, undazzled by huge salaries, untempted by prestige, unshackled by the accoutrements of profit and success. We were the first law school graduates in years, I told them, who objectively could determine whether being a lawyer - *by itself* - was worth it.

It had been a pretty good talk. The Washington State Bar News had picked it up, and the National Law Journal had reprinted it. But while I was giving it, I was struck by how alone I was in the world. Meany Hall was packed with people - parents, siblings, spouses, children, and friends - all craning to see around me, all looking away from me, all trying to spot their child, their brother, their sister, their spouse, their parent, their friend there in the crowd of graduates. Everyone was looking for someone else. No one was looking for me.

"Jack?" Harmony's face was right next to mine. "Jack, are you OK?"

She held me, cushioning my head between her breasts. That was the closest I had ever been to Harmony, and I was too torn up and miserable to enjoy it. I just clung to her and closed my eyes.

For the first time since I was a little, little kid, I cried myself to sleep.

CHAPTER 6

The next few days passed in a haze. On Sunday, Mark bathed Betsy so thoroughly that her fur shone like gold. Betsy minced around the house - dainty and sweet-smelling - taking care not to disarrange her lovely self. On Monday, I went to work long enough to pound out a thirty-page status report on SPP v. American Fidelity. As I was describing witnesses and summarizing depositions, I scanned every document for any mention of my dad. Nothing. He wasn't listed as an owner. The chart of the mill's current hierarchy revealed no one by the name of Jack Hart. My father must have either retired from active service or always been an absentee owner.

I spent the rest of Monday puttering around my house. Since I had been yanked off SPP, I didn't have much to do at work, and I was still smarting from being called a junkyard dog. I changed into my grubbiest clothes and tiled the floor in my basement bathroom. Mark and I were building him a bachelor pad down there, and there was something soothing about placing exactly the right tiles in exactly the right places. As the pattern came together - creamy center tiles bordered by an intricate edging of black and green - I felt the satisfaction of watching a giant jigsaw puzzle take shape under my hands.

On Tuesday, two floral arrangements arrived. The bigger one had spears of gladiolas sticking out of it like the Statue of Liberty's hat. It was from Piper Whatcom, which contracted with a PR consultant to make it look like a generous, warm-hearted place. On the card, the consultant had written, "We are all so sorry." I wondered how much she charged the firm for coming up with dynamite stuff like that.

The other arrangement was from the Seattle Police Department. More accurately, it was from all my friends in the Seattle Police Department. It was a bunch of poppies and autumn leaves. The officers wrote me notes on a big, floppy sympathy card. My favorite message was from Detective Brewster, who had been Mark's boss on undercover drug investigations. He wrote: "Hang in there, kid.

We're all pulling for you. Your friend, Brewster." Then he added underneath: "P.S. Poppies are narcotic. Dispose of them carefully. If I find out you made opium tea out of them, I'll kick your butt."

I stuck the sympathy card on my fridge and put the flowers in a place of honor on top of my bookcase, carefully out of reach of Betsy. She was the only member of the household who might decide to consume the poppies. Once Betsy had inhaled the duct tape I was using for some fix-it job around the house. I had looked away for a moment. When I turned around, the roll of tape was hanging out of her mouth. She was chewing it like gum.

On Wednesday, I went back to work. I spent the morning scrounging little scut projects to fill the time I had cleared for SPP. Because every attorney has to meet a yearly quota of billable hours, you can't feel comfortable taking a day off, even when there's nothing to do. You know you'll have to account for that day by working evenings, nights, and weekends later in the year. So even though my dad had just died and I had essentially nothing going on, I had to make the rounds and ask for odd jobs to "fill my plate."

It is just like panhandling. Attorneys whose plates are full treat a request for work with only slightly less icy condescension than they would a plea for a quarter on the street. They figure that it's your own fault that you don't have work, that you either mismanage your caseload or are such a screw-up that no one else trusts you with their projects. After two hours of being told, "No, I don't have anything for you today, Jack, but I'll keep you in mind," I was exasperated. It's bad enough to have to deal with the stressful, contentious, life-shortening bullshit of civil litigation. It's intolerable to have to beg for it.

To make my day even more pleasant, the firm was buzzing with gossip about me and my dad. Sidney Leath, the associate with the wickedest mouth in Seattle, dropped by my office around lunchtime, "just to chat." Her sorrowful expression couldn't hide the greedy gleam in her eyes.

"I heard about your father, Jack," she said, with a bloodthirsty leer she probably meant to appear sympathetic. "And about the problem with SPP. I'm sure it's the last thing you want to talk about, but as a fellow litigator, I'd really appreciate your perspectives on what lessons we can all take away from this case. I mean, is there something we should be doing to make sure this doesn't happen again?" She leaned forward and actually licked her lips.

Sidney was digging on so many levels that I was almost impressed. She wanted to know whether I had screwed up, how I had screwed up, and whether I was in trouble. And if I let slip any juicy personal details along the way, I'm sure she would have snapped those up, too.

I longed to tell her that the only lesson I had learned from the experience was that, if at all possible, one should avoid being abandoned by one's father. Instead, I pretended I was thinking it over. I was about to fob her off with some blather about piercing the corporate veil on conflict checks when my telephone rang. It was an outside call, and I picked it up gratefully.

"Jack?"

It was Detective Anthony. I held my index fingers about a foot apart, conveying to Sidney that the conversation was going to be long, and that she should leave. She shrugged her shoulders and didn't budge. She wasn't going to give up that easily. I kept widening the gap between my fingers, but she still wouldn't go. I asked Detective Anthony to wait for a moment and covered the receiver with my hand. "Sid, I really need to take this call in private," I said. "I'll catch up with you later."

She left, most reluctantly, although I had the distinct impression that she was loitering just outside. I closed my door and returned to Detective Anthony. "I'm sorry. I had a spy in my office."

"I don't know why you stay in that cesspool," Anthony replied. He had gotten an up-close and unflattering look at my firm the year before, when he had investigated Humphrey Piper's murder and Harmony's kidnapping. "Cesspool" was the nicest thing I had ever heard him say about it.

"Believe me, Detective Anthony, if I had so much as the smell of another job, I would walk out of this place right now."

"How about the Fan Belt Inspectors? They're always looking for lawyers. You'd be a natural."

He meant the FBI. It's a rare local policeman who has anything more than a grudging tolerance for the feds. "I don't know about that," I said. "There's just something wrong with giving a lawyer a gun. It seems like a genuinely bad idea to me."

"Well, they like accountants, too."

I tried to picture the few accountants I knew wearing shoulder holsters and carrying badges. "That's even more disturbing," I told him.

"Somehow, Jack, I'll get you out of there," he said. "But I didn't call to talk to you about that right now. I called because I just spoke to Sergeant Lee from the Bellingham Police."

Sergeant Lee was the guy who seemed determined to pin my father's death on me. I tried to sound casual as I asked, "What did he say?"

"Well, the good news is that you're not a person of interest anymore."

"They caught the guy who killed my dad?"

"Not exactly. They did the autopsy. Lee thinks your dad either committed suicide or accidentally got caught in the fire as he was trying to destroy some documents."

Anthony's careful attribution put me on guard. "*Lee* thinks so?" I asked

"Yes."

"But you don't think so?"

Anthony sighed. "There are some things that don't make sense to me. But I'm not the investigating officer, and Lee's a good cop. If he says it's suicide, I'm willing to respect that. Apparently, your dad's business was struggling. It was facing bankruptcy, and Lee thinks your dad might have had a hard time accepting that. The mill has been a going concern for years. It's an important employer up there, and your dad and his other family lived pretty well off it. Lee thinks the thought of losing it might have pushed him over the edge."

I swallowed hard. I knew why my dad's paper mill was having such a hard time. I knew why it was facing bankruptcy. It was having a hard time and facing bankruptcy because American Fidelity had refused to pay SPP for the state-ordered cleanup of Bellingham Bay. And American Fidelity had refused to pay for the cleanup because I had advised them not to. And I had advised them not to because of the clause in the policy that excused American Fidelity from having to pay for environmental cleanup costs if SPP knowingly allowed the contaminants to escape.

For months, I had been fighting my father's company, trying to prove that SPP had known about the dumping. And on the day that I had actually established corporate knowledge of dumping, my father had killed himself - either intentionally or accidentally - in the very mill I had imperiled. Maybe Sergeant Lee had been right the first time. Maybe I really had been responsible for my father's death.

"Jack?" Anthony sounded worried. "Jack, are you still there?"

It hurt too much to tell him what I was thinking. I just asked, "What documents was my dad trying to destroy?"

"I don't really know," Anthony replied. "Not much survived the fire. From what Lee said, they were just old bits of things: purchase orders for processing chemicals, formulas for pulping, proportions for bleaching and additives, stuff like that. Why do you ask?"

"Because all those documents would have been responsive to my requests for production. The mill has been giving me the runaround for months. First they said the documents were trade secrets. I stipulated to a protective order. Then they said it would be too burdensome to produce them. I offered to review their files at American Fidelity's expense. Then they said the documents didn't exist anymore. I filed a motion to compel discovery the day I arrived in Bellingham." I paused, choked with guilt and anger. "So *I'm* the reason my dad was trying to set that fire, Detective. And *I'm* the reason the mill has been having such a hard time. And *I'm* the reason my dad's been so despondent about his business. *I'm* the reason - *I'm* the reason - *I'm* the reason that he's dead."

"Jack, no -" Anthony protested, but I cut him off.

"Detective Anthony, I can't talk about this anymore," I said, hating the way my voice cracked at the end of the sentence. "I just can't."

"All right, son. But you didn't do anything wrong. Whatever happened, it was not your fault." When I didn't answer, he continued, "I'll call you tonight, Jack. But think about what I said."

I sat looking with a fresh horror at the crumbs of work I had been able to beg and beseech during my rounds that morning.

One partner wanted me to bring an unlawful detainer action to evict some tenants who had been squatting in one of our client's condos.

I had been evicted before. It wasn't fun. So why the hell was I even considering evicting somebody else? I was sure that legally, the tenants shouldn't be there. Legally, they should either pay their back rent or get out. But suddenly, that didn't seem like a good enough reason to evict them.

Legally, my dad's company was liable for dumping chemicals into Bellingham Bay. Legally, American Fidelity shouldn't have to pay a dime for the cleanup or the mill's defense. And legally, my dad should have turned over the documents I had requested within 30 days of my request for them, not played footsie with me for five months. But even though legally, everything I had done was correct, necessary, and even required, somehow that didn't seem to account for much against my dad's life.

I thought about my dad's wife and his four daughters. His girls had to be pretty young. He had left my mom twenty-four years ago, so probably at least a couple of his daughters might still be in their teens. I wondered how on earth I could explain to a teenage girl that her father had killed himself because legally, one clause in one contract was going to destroy his whole business.

Then an even worse thought crossed my mind. If my dad's death was ruled a suicide, American Fidelity might not pay under any life insurance policies. Had he left his family with enough other assets to tide them through? The girls wouldn't be able to get much money out of sale of the mill, not considering the fire and the cleanup costs. And if my dad had set the fire intentionally – even if his death was ultimately an accident – American Fidelity might not pay any casualty claims on the mill. Somewhat understandably, insurance companies are sticklers for arson exclusions.

I shook my head in sympathy. It's hard enough to be poor your whole life. It must be unbearable to go from riches to rags.

I don't know how long I would have sat there feeling sorry for four half-sisters I had never met if Rob Browning, a partner in our creditors' rights section, hadn't walked into my office without knocking.

"Hey, Jack," he said, ruffling his sleek hair. "I hear you're looking for work."

I nodded.

"I've got a seminar coming up on repossessions and foreclosures. I need you to put together my speech and my written materials." He tossed the seminar brochure on my desk. "That will give you the theme of what I need. OK?"

I looked down at the brochure. The title was "Taking What's Yours."

I almost groaned aloud. Not only did Rob want me to prepare a speech on the fine points of dragging away people's cars and kicking them out of their homes, but he wanted me to do it all on my own time. Doing other people's nonbillable work is like digging your own grave. It wears you out and runs you down, while you just get farther and farther behind on your billable hours. Suddenly I was so tired I could barely raise my head.

"OK?" Rob was waiting for my assent.

It wasn't OK, I thought. Nothing was OK. Nothing had been OK since Saturday morning, when Anthony had told me that my dad was dead. Nothing was ever going to be OK again.

"I'm sorry, Rob," I said. "I can't do this."

Rob bristled. "I thought you said you were looking for work."

"I was." I got up and pulled my coat off the hanger on my door. "But I can't do this anymore."

I picked up the seminar brochure and slapped it back into his hand.

"I quit."

CHAPTER 7

"How was work today?" Mark was digging in the refrigerator for something, and his voice was muffled.

"I quit."

"Come again?" Mark straightened up so fast that he hit his head.

"I quit," I repeated, still a little surprised at myself. "At lunchtime. I spent the afternoon bumming around downtown. I bought a sandwich at the Sound View Cafe and looked out at the water for a while. Then I went to the library. I downloaded some lawyer jokes, and I read a Spanish novel. And then I came home." I looked around the room, as if I expected to find the explanation for my behavior somewhere in my kitchen. "And here I am."

"Are you all right?"

"No, probably not," I conceded. "But I'm better than I was before I quit."

"Well, then, congratulations, Jack," Mark said, giving me a high five. "I'm proud of you. I really am. I'm kind of amazed, but I'm happy for you. Does Harmony know?"

"Harmony knows," Harmony said from the entryway, locking my front door, taking off her coat, and kissing Betsy hello on the forehead in one smooth, fluid movement. She wrapped her arms around my waist and held me tight. "Where have you been? Dan Bradford called me in a lather about three hours ago. He said, and I quote, 'Harmony, Jack has flipped his lid.' I've been driving around trying to find you ever since. But you weren't at the 211 Club or Green Lake or Ray's Boathouse or any of your usual haunts."

I explained about spending the afternoon at the public library. "I'm sorry, Harmony," I said, giving her a squeeze. "I didn't realize that you'd be looking for me. It didn't occur to me that Dan would call you. It's just that the library seemed like an economical place to go."

"Have you flipped your lid?" It wasn't a challenge. It was merely a question.

"I don't think so. I feel rational enough. I just couldn't take it anymore. Why? Do you think I've lost my mind?"

"Not necessarily," Harmony said. "I think leaving Piper Whatcom is, standing alone, a clear sign of mental health. If you've actually decided that you don't owe them anything and that you don't need them, then I'm delighted. But if you're just reeling from your dad and pushing everything away, then I'm worried about you. So should I be worried about you?"

I paused, trying to figure out why I had suddenly walked off the job I had held for almost five years, even though I had only minimal savings, a sizeable house payment, and no prospects whatsoever of another position. Once again, I was saved by the bell. "Hi, Detective Anthony," Mark said into the phone. "Did you hear that Jack quit today?" He listened, grinned, and held the phone out to me.

"Well, you're an impressionable kid, I'll say that for you," Anthony grumbled at me. "Are you OK?"

"I'm OK," I said to both Harmony and Detective Anthony. "You don't need to worry about me."

"Do you want me to call my friends in the FBI?"

I thought about it. I couldn't imagine myself carrying a gun and arresting people, but for that matter, I couldn't imagine myself doing civil litigation anymore, either. So what the hell? "I guess so," I said.

"Are you sure you're OK?" Anthony asked. "I mean, I feel responsible for this. When we talked this afternoon, I didn't have any idea that you were so close to walking out the door."

"Neither did I," I told him. "And it's not your fault."

"That's my line, Jack," he replied. "How are you holding up otherwise?"

All the freedom and euphoria I had felt after quitting suddenly flickered and dimmed. "I still can't talk about that," I said after a pause.

"I'm sorry." Anthony was quiet for a moment. "Look, Jack, I don't know whether you even want to know this, but your father's funeral is tomorrow at noon up in Bellingham. Do you want the address?"

Did I? I couldn't tell. When I didn't answer right away, Anthony said, "Let me give Mark the address. That way, if you get up tomorrow morning and want to go, you can go. If not, then you don't need to worry about it. OK?"

It made sense. I handed the phone to Mark and, for the rest of the evening, surrendered to Betsy's and Harmony's attentions. They both fussed over me until I felt almost guilty about it. Betsy even brought me her favorite toy, a squeaky rubber newspaper called The Daily Growl. Whenever I tried to return it to her, she nosed it back into my hand and wagged her tail.

I worried all night about whether or not I should go to my father's funeral. Toward morning, I fell asleep, exhausted by indecision. If Betsy hadn't suddenly jumped onto my bed and licked my face at 9:30, I probably would have slept until noon.

Harmony was wearing black. That, in itself, meant nothing, as Harmony often - even usually - wore black. It went perfectly with her shiny black hair, and it set off her pale, clear complexion and her deep blue eyes. But this was some serious black. It took me a moment to figure out why she looked so somber. Then it hit me: Harmony was wearing the black wool dress she had been kidnapped in the year before. The police had finally gotten around to returning it. She flushed slightly under my gaze.

"It just seemed appropriate for today," she said, smoothing the skirt. "And all the rest of my black clothes are really too business-like for a funeral."

"Does this mean we're going?" I asked.

"This means that if you want to go, I'm ready," she said.

"I still don't know whether I want to go," I said, standing there in my pajamas and feeling like an idiot. "I really, really do, and I really, really don't."

"Do you want me to make the decision, or do you just want me to make a suggestion?"

"Yes," I said.

"I'm sorry. That was a compound question. Let me make a suggestion. You get dressed, and we drive up there. Any time along the way, you can decide you don't want to go to the funeral. You say the word, and we'll keep going and have an early dinner in Vancouver. Or we could have lunch somewhere on Chuckanut, or we could just spend the day together doing anything you want."

"*Anything* I want?"

"*Almost* anything. Good plan?"

"Great plan," I said. We were on the road by 10.

On the way up I-5, Harmony and I compared our reactions to the deaths of our respective fathers. Harmony had heard a wild, animal-like scream when Detective Anthony had come into her hospital room and told her that Humphrey Piper was dead. I had heard - and actually had felt - a door slam shut. Harmony had spent more than a month in a grim, suffocating mist that seemed to prevent her from doing anything healing or constructive. I had been walking around in a haze for days. Harmony had withdrawn her name from partnership consideration and become of counsel - a very tenuous of counsel - to the firm. I had quit outright.

"So when does the pain go away, Harmony?" I asked.

"It doesn't, Jack," she said. "It just becomes more and more a pain you suffered in your past. But I still miss my dad like you wouldn't believe. I kept a bottle of his aftershave, and when things are really bad, I open it up and pretend he's there. It's like Dad-In-A-Bottle, I guess." She looked out the passenger window for a moment. "I still feel like an orphan."

I put my hand on hers as we approached the exit to Old Fairhaven Parkway. We didn't speak until we were at the mortuary, a huge, turreted mansion that looked like it was trying to be haunted. A nightmarish Cadillac hearse was parked out front. I turned off the engine and tried to convince myself to get out of the car.

"You don't have to do this, you know," Harmony said.

"Yes, I do. It's the only opportunity I'm going to have to know anything about my dad."

"I could go in alone, take notes, and tell you everything they say."

That made me laugh. "You are a very good girlfriend," I told her. "Let's go."

If possible, the mortuary looked even more desperately spooky inside than out. We passed through two rooms heavy with velvet draperies, glowering paintings, and gilt wall sconces. A brilliantined man in a black suit tried to steer us into "the greeting area," but I resisted. I was not up to trying to exchange pleasantries with my dad's other family. Instead, Harmony and I sat and waited at the very back of the funeral home's chapel, which was surprisingly light and modern. Huge windows looked out on a thicket of trees, alive with fluttering red and yellow foliage. The room's carved wooden pews and podium gave the impression of a church, but it was relentlessly ecumenical. I wondered whether my father had been a religious man. I didn't remember ever going to church as a child. Or as an adult, either, for that matter. Harmony was Presbyterian, and Mark was Catholic, but I was just a generic, God-fearing good person.

People started trickling into the chapel. A few glanced back curiously at me and Harmony, but most diverted their attention to the flowers that were wedged, blossom to blossom, at the front of the room. My father must have been either loved or feared, I thought, calculating the cost of all those wreaths and arrangements. People were either very, very sad or very, very happy he was dead.

I was concentrating so hard on the flowers that I didn't even notice when Anthony and Mark sat down next to me. Harmony had to squeeze my arm and say, "Look who's here," before I snapped back to reality.

"I didn't know you were coming," I said, surprised and touched.

"You didn't think we'd let you go through this alone, do you?" Anthony smiled at me. Then he nodded toward a greying, bullet-faced man who had just entered the chapel. "That's Sergeant Lee."

Lee acknowledged Anthony and Mark with the slightest possible bob of his head. He looked me over as if he were mentally frisking me for weapons. Even from across the room, his face seemed skeptical and unimpressed. He turned away with what sounded like a harrumph.

"He still thinks I did it," I said, almost involuntarily.

"No, he doesn't," Anthony replied. "Lee just hates to be wrong."

When the chapel was almost full, the funeral director with the glistening hair asked us all to stand. Two dark-suited men wheeled in my father's casket. It was topped with a bouquet of red roses, and it was big. I stood about 6' 4'' and weighed considerably more than 200 pounds, but I could have fit in that coffin with space to spare. A sudden memory of trying on shoes as a child came back to me. I remembered someone - maybe my father, maybe the salesman - pressing down on the tops of my shoes without hitting my toes: "Room to grow on."

A tiny, white-haired woman in a wheelchair followed my father's coffin up the aisle, propelled by a plump, pretty woman in her forties. My grandmother and my dad's wife, I guessed. I hadn't even considered the possibility of having grandparents. After the wheelchair trotted two adorable little girls, wearing matching blue and green plaid dresses and black velvet bows in their hair. I almost whistled in sympathy. The older one couldn't have been more than ten. The younger looked about six, not much older than I had been when I had lost my dad - for the first time. I looked in vain for the other two girls. They must have been too young to attend. I started to regret my decision to quit my job. My dad's poor little family was going to need all the help it could get.

A woman with long, straight blond hair followed the little girls. Her face was innocent of makeup, and she was wearing a crinkly, black, gauzy affair that seemed oddly festive given the circumstances. She got the two little girls settled while the pretty, plump lady tended to the woman in the wheelchair. Then two other women walked up the aisle to the family pew. One was cuddling a red-faced, drooling, and very angry baby, who glared at me malevolently over her shoulder. The other was arm-in-arm with an ineffectual-looking man with a droopy mustache and tweed jacket. They all sat down, and the funeral began.

The man with the glistening hair read the eulogy. He had a stupefying drone of a voice, but I strained to hear the details. John Henry Hart was born sixty-four years earlier, in Bellingham, Washington. His father had had to sell the family pulp mill during the Depression. His mother was a teacher, and John - or Jack, as he was known - wanted to follow her into that profession. He served in the Army, graduated from the University of Washington in history, and returned to Bellingham to teach high school social studies and coach the football team.

He married the former Virginia Carlson - here the droning man nodded, astonishingly, to the tiny woman in the wheelchair - and fathered four beautiful daughters. The mortician nodded to each one of the women in the pew as he read off their names: Marianne, Emily, Sarah, and Beth.

When Jack left teaching, he bought the pulp mill that his father had had to sell during the Depression, and modernized it to make high-quality paper products on-site. He was a good and generous employer. He took early retirement to care for his wife after her debilitating stroke, and the mill suffered without his daily supervision.

He died in his old office at the mill, the place he loved second only to his Edgemoor home.

He was survived by his loving wife, his four delightful and accomplished daughters, his son-in-law, Gary Kendall, and his three darling granddaughters, who ranged in age from nine to nine months, and whom he adored.

"And his darling son, Jack," Harmony said, not quite under her breath enough. A few people turned to look at us, then looked quickly away.

I didn't blame them. I couldn't believe that I had come. My father hadn't wanted me when he was alive. How could I have thought that anything would have been different after he was dead? I was too baffled and stunned to try to shoehorn myself into my father's life, let alone his death. Clearly, my dad's marriage and daughters predated whatever had gone on with my mom. At most, my mom must have been nothing more than an extra-marital fling. At most, I must have been nothing more than a complication. No wonder I barely remembered him. If there had been any way of getting out of there without trampling on people's feet and drawing attention to myself, I would have split. I was split, between fury and – there was no denying it – shame.

Harmony took one of my big hands in both her little ones. I sat in misery during the rest of the funeral. I could barely pay attention. Someone who had worked with my father at the mill talked about what a good boss he had been. Whenever one of his employees was having family troubles, he gave them time off with pay to sort it out. He had run the mill like a business and had done well, but he always had time for friendly greeting or a sincere chat. Everyone at the mill had missed him terribly since he retired. There was a murmur of assent. Somebody said "amen." The speaker rubbed his hand over his forehead. "Now," he said, "we'll miss him even more."

The lady I had seen at *il fiasco* sang some sort of complicated, lugubrious aria that seemed to go on forever. She started crying at the end - or at what became the end - and the tweedy, ineffectual-looking man proved himself at least competent enough to put his arm around her and lead her back to her seat. Then the woman with the malevolent baby - one of my sisters, I assumed - got up and started talking about "Daddy." She was tall and solid. She had shoulder-length blond hair and shiny pink cheeks. She didn't introduce herself; she didn't even put down the baby. She just stood there and talked about what it was like growing up with my father as her dad.

"Daddy loved dogs," she said. "The bigger, the better. When I was a teenager, we had a Great Dane named Pilate. As in Pontius. Pilate was bigger than Mama, he was bigger than me, and he was bigger than every single date I ever had. When boys would come to pick me up, Daddy would insist that they let Pilate sniff their hands. Then he'd say, 'I want to make sure Pilate can find you if Sarah isn't home on time.'

No one ever, ever brought me home late. When I told Daddy he had almost ruined my social life with his dogs and his threats, he said, 'Almost? What do you mean, *almost*? I'm going to have to get a gun.' And that made me laugh, and I couldn't be angry at him anymore. When we stopped laughing, he put his arms around me and said, 'I just want to make sure you're safe, Sarah. That's all.'"

Sarah stopped and pretended to fuss over her baby. She cleared her throat a few times before she continued: "I always felt safe with Daddy there. Sometimes, when I was a little girl, I'd even pretend to fall asleep on the couch so Daddy would have to pick me up and put me to bed. It felt so good to have him carry me up the stairs and tuck me under the covers. Whenever we were sick, he'd smuggle us big bowls of strawberry ice cream. It didn't matter what disease we had. Unless we were actively vomiting, Daddy was always sure that strawberry ice cream was what we needed. And he was usually right. After Jennifer was born -" she bounced the now-sleeping baby in her arms - "I was just dropping off to sleep in the hospital when Daddy came in with a strawberry ice cream cone hidden under his coat. He ended up eating most of it, but it really did make me feel better."

Sarah shifted Jennifer onto her other hip. Suddenly, the baby seemed too heavy for her to hold. The ineffectual-looking man once again went to the rescue, relieving Sarah of Jennifer and returning to his seat. "After Scott was killed," Sarah began, and stopped. A hum of sympathy rose from the chapel. She swallowed and tried again. "After Scott was killed, my doctor thought I was going to lose the baby. Daddy moved me back into my old room at home. Anything I wanted, he got for me. He even insisted on going into the delivery room with me. I wasn't absolutely sure I wanted him in there, but Scott was gone, and Mama wasn't well enough. Daddy was just wonderful. He held my hand and kept telling me, 'You're doing great.' I didn't even know what I was doing - I was just pushing as hard as I could - but Daddy kept squeezing my hand and telling me I was doing great. And ever since Saturday morning, ever since I found out he was gone, that's all I've been able to think about: about how much I'm going to miss having someone who always thinks I'm doing great."

I pretty much stopped listening after Sarah returned to the family pew. It was all too much to absorb. I think somebody played the flute, and somebody else talked interminably about SPP's prominence in the community. He was the mill's vice president of something or other, and it turned out - surprise! - that he was running for Congress. And then it was over. The funeral director asked us to stand again, and the pallbearers shouldered my father's coffin and struggled down the aisle and toward the door, panting and bowlegged under its weight. Then the family parade reversed itself in following the coffin.

My youngest sister - Beth, I guessed - led the way, arm-in-arm with the brilliantined mortician and looking small and fragile in an austere black velvet dress. Close behind her was Sarah, pink-cheeked and red-eyed, holding Jennifer in front of her like a shield. Jennifer was wide awake and looking around. She wasn't screaming anymore, and she was actually a very pretty baby when her face wasn't distorted with howls. As Sarah drew close to the last pew, Jennifer caught a glimpse of me.

She cooed and gurgled. She stretched out her sticky hands to me, and she started pumping her bootied feet, as if she would run to me if Sarah would put her down - and if she knew how to walk. Sarah glanced indulgently at her squirming daughter, then followed Jennifer's gaze toward me. She stopped so quickly that her gauze-clad sister - Emily, I guessed - crashed into her back.

"Oh," Sarah cried. She was staring at me as if she didn't know whether to scream for help or hug me. Her eyes closed in a long, tremulous flutter. Both Harmony and I instinctively stepped forward to catch Jennifer in case Sarah fainted. At our footfall, Sarah's eyelids snapped open, and she snatched Jennifer away. There was no ambiguity in her expression. "Don't touch her," she screamed.

I did not know what to do. When I managed to wrench my eyes away from Sarah's stare of frozen horror, I saw the entire congregation gaping at me, their necks twisted around and livid, as if they were being wrung. If I had wanted to ruin my father's funeral - which I hadn't - I could not have gone about it more effectively.

I cursed my father, my mother, and myself - especially myself - for stranding me in this predicament. I was about to apologize profusely and scuttle, head bowed, to the exit, when I heard the screech of tires outside. Mark and Anthony automatically reached for their guns, but not before two explosions - an enormous one swallowing the echo of the smaller - suddenly jolted the quiet chapel.

Wreaths and vases pitched and crashed, one of the huge picture windows cracked from head to sill, and Jennifer screwed up her reddening face and got ready to shriek in protest. Before Jennifer or anyone else could let loose, however, Mark, Anthony, and Sergeant Lee started shouting and pushing people to the ground.

"Police! Get down! Get down on the floor and cover your heads! Police!"

"Get down, man. Get down and stay down," Mark hissed in my ear, as a wave of people screamed and hit the floor. I covered Harmony with my body and bade farewell to any thought of ever joining the FBI. Mark, Lee, and Anthony were heading toward the door, guns drawn and guarding one another, moving carefully and purposefully toward what might be a swift and inevitable death.

I could hear sirens in the distance, but the chapel itself was silent except for Jennifer's muffled wails. From my vantage point, all I could see were bodies. Jennifer's whimper was excruciating, as if she were the lone survivor of a bloodbath. As the sirens screeched ever closer, I poked my head up just enough to try to spot Mark or Anthony coming back.

My father's widow was still sitting in her wheelchair, looking around the body-littered chapel in terror. She obviously couldn't move herself, and she was either physically unable to summon help or unwilling to jeopardize her daughters and granddaughters by asking them to get her out of her chair. I couldn't leave her like that. In her wheelchair, her head was well above the sill of the vast expanse of glass. If someone armed was in that thicket of trees, they could have picked off my father's widow like a pumpkin in the window.

"Stay down, babe," I whispered to Harmony. "I'll be right back."

I slid off Harmony and scooted over my sisters' bodies, pivoting around their arms and legs as if we were playing Twister. I inched past my pretty little nieces, who were sprawled side by side like discarded dolls.

When the tiny, white-haired lady saw me coming toward her, she started shaking her head in alarm. I couldn't tell whether she thought I was a ghost or whether she knew full well who I was and would, on balance, have preferred a supernatural visitation. It didn't really matter.

"It's OK," I said, raising myself just enough to take her by the waist and ease her onto the floor. "I'm going to help you down."

My father's wife flopped over in my arms as if she had no strength in her body. Her bones seemed as light and fragile as a bird's. I put her on her stomach on the carpet, brought her arms up over her head, and turned her face to the side so she could breathe. "OK?" I whispered.

"Yes." It was the smallest squeak of a response. I patted her shoulder and was about to squirm my way back to Harmony when Mark and Anthony walked into the room. "It's all right. You can all get up now," Anthony commanded. "The police have the place surrounded. It's all right. Just follow the officers' directions, and we'll get you out of here."

I pulled myself to my feet, scooped my father's wife back into her wheelchair, and threaded my way back to Harmony. She was standing between Mark and Anthony, and the three of them were watching me approach. "Good work, Jack," Anthony said, nodding toward the wheelchair. "I wondered if anyone would help the old lady down."

"What happened?" I asked, folding Harmony into my arms.

"We'll show you," Mark said. "But first we have to clear the area."

The "we" in that sentence apparently meant the brotherhood of law enforcement because Mark and Anthony didn't budge from me and Harmony during the time it took the Bellingham Police to usher my father's shocked, terrified, grieving family one way and all the other clamorous mourners another.

Finally, the chapel was empty, and Mark and Anthony led us through a warren of rooms. Harmony and I followed them closely. In a mortuary, even more than most places, you really do not want to make a wrong turn.

We emerged into the weak October sun. Mark and Anthony took us around to the front of the funeral home, and Harmony and I both sucked in our breath. It was easy to see why Mark and Anthony hadn't taken us out the front door. There wasn't a front door anymore. In its place were a few charred and gaping beams. Beyond the wreckage from the door, the mortuary's opulent entryway was demolished. Nothing was left except a blackened lump that had been a rosewood table and a sodden strip of gold-flocked wallpaper. When we turned around, we saw the hulk of the hearse, smoking, steaming, hissing, and listing at the curb on its half-melted tires. The back door was buried up to its window in the mortuary's front lawn. The door from the driver's side was nowhere to be seen.

Anthony grimaced at our stunned expressions. "Two pipe bombs," he said. "One in the hearse, the other in the front door of the funeral home. It was propped open so the pallbearers could carry out the casket." He paused and rubbed his hand over his short, grey hair. "If the pallbearers had been ten feet farther down the hall, we would have lost a few of them. It's just a good thing that your father was so heavy, Jack."

Sergeant Lee's approach saved me from having to reply. He and Anthony faced each other on the glass-strewn path. The awful, wounded house was on one side of them, the gutted hearse on the other. Anthony looked to his right, then his left.

"Well, Lee," he said, without challenge or condescension, "do you still think it was suicide?"

CHAPTER 8

"If it was murder," Lee returned evenly, "why would the killer call attention to himself like that? If someone killed poor old Jack, what on earth would the murderer gain by firebombing his funeral? He couldn't kill him again."

"Unless it's someone with a grudge against him, someone who wouldn't be satisfied with the murder itself," Anthony pointed out. "Have you checked to see whether the gravesite was desecrated?"

"No. No, that is a good idea, though. I'll send someone over to Bayview to take a look. But you know, Anthony, the only person with a grudge against Jack was -" Lee caught sight of my face, stopped, and looked away. "- Was at the funeral," he finished. I couldn't tell whether the ellipsis was out of kindness or suspicion.

Anthony tactfully diverted Lee's attention away from me. "So if the late Mr. Hart wasn't the target, who was?" he asked.

"Well, two of the pallbearers are running for office. Clark Swanson's up for reelection as a Port commissioner, and Mike Saunders is trying to get into Congress. They've both had hot campaigns, and their ties to the mill have opened them up for potshots by the environmentalists. And Gary Kendall - that's Jack's son-in-law - has had some scuffles with students over at Western Washington University."

"What about?" Mark asked.

"Damned if I know. I honestly can't explain anything that happens over there. But Gary - who's the meekest little cuss you'll ever meet - is the oppressor of the year to the campus crowd. I think we're dealing with some sort of wigged-out protest group. To a big part of this town, it's always 1969 and the morning of the revolution."

Anthony stuck out his hand. "Good luck, Lee. Unless you need us to stay, I think we'll be heading home."

"Sure. I mean, thanks, you two. But actually, I would like a word with the son before you go. In private."

I saw Anthony stiffen. "It's OK, sir," I said. Some things were just inevitable. I had a feeling that if I didn't talk to Lee then, I was going to talk to Lee later.

Lee apparently thought so, too. "To your left, kid," he said, jerking his thumb toward a molting oak tree. "Might as well get it over with."

Lee's jaw was tight, but his weather-beaten skin sagged over the prow of his nose like a battered tarp on a broken boat. When we were out of earshot, he suddenly turned on me. There was such venom in his voice that it was all I could do not to take a step back.

"I don't know what you've got on Anthony, kid, and I don't know if this was a one-shot thing, or whether this is how Marta raised you, but I am going to give you a word of advice: You got away with it once. That doesn't mean you'll get away with it again. You try anything with Jack's family, and I'll personally make sure I have your ass. I don't care if you're best friends with the damned chief of police; I'll drive down to Seattle and make a citizen's arrest if I have to. You understand?"

"No," I said. "I don't understand anything right now."

"Then understand this. Your father's widow is one of the finest women alive. She stuck with Jack no matter what. She even took him back after he ran off with that tramp of a mother of yours. She is old and ill and in pain. She doesn't have much time left. There is no way in hell that I am going to humiliate her by arresting you for killing your dad. There is no way in hell that I would put her through the agony of having everyone in town know that Jack was unfaithful to her, that he ran out on her, that he had a son with some chippy from his 10th grade civics class. She's too fragile to go through that again. So you just keep in mind that the only thing between you and a jail cell is Virginia Carlson. If anything happens to her, kid, you're toast." He glared at me. "You got it now?"

I counted to ten. It wasn't enough. I was still so hurt and so furious that I could have punched him. I forced myself to picture him as a particularly unreasonable and loathsome opposing counsel, someone I needed to defuse and deter without taking anything he said to heart.

"Sergeant Lee, if you think my father was murdered, then you had better keep looking for his killer," I said. "Because you've got the wrong guy. You seem really pissed at my father for running around on his wife, but that doesn't have anything to do with me. I may have been the result of it, but I wasn't the cause. If you want to protect Virginia Carlson's feelings, that's your business, Sergeant, but you've got no reason to protect her from me."

I walked away. I held my hand out to Harmony and pulled her close. "Will you drive back with Mark and Anthony?"

She looked at me sharply. "I will, but why?"

"Because I am going to use words you don't even know all the way home."

"What happened?"

"I'll tell you later. But right now I need to blow off some steam, and I don't want you in harm's way when I do."

"I don't mind being in harm's way," Mark interrupted, slipping between us. "And I guarantee you that I know more bad words than you do, Jack. Harmony, why don't you drive back with Detective Anthony? That way, Jack and I can cuss together all the way home."

Reluctantly, Harmony acquiesced. She kissed me and searched my face for any clue about what was going on. I was too upset to allow her even a glimpse inside. Mark took my keys out of my hand and marched me over to my car. My last view of the funeral home was of the brilliantined man standing on the sparkling, glass-strewn path, shaking his shiny head at the charred maw of the house. Just for something to think about, I wondered where my father's coffin was.

Mark and I didn't speak until we were southbound on I-5. "You're not cussing," he observed.

"I am inside."

"You just want to sit there and stew?"

"No."

"Then tell me what Lee said. What did he want?"

It took me until Marysville to calm down enough to recount my eventful conversation with Sergeant Lee.

Mark shook his head.

"I'm sorry, Jack. Anthony and I didn't know Lee was going to try anything like that. We weren't trying to lead you into a trap. Honest."

"What do you mean?"

"I mean that Lee was probably just prodding you. It's good cop/bad cop, but he was playing both sides. If he had had anything on you, he would have arrested you right there - Virginia Carlson's tender feelings be damned. Lee's too good a cop and too aggressive a cop to let a suspect walk, for any reason. He was trying to make you blow up or start bragging or something. If you had let something slip, you'd be in the Whatcom County Jail by now."

I was stunned. "Do you play games like that with suspects?"

Mark grinned, self-consciously. "Don't ask embarrassing questions, Jack," he said. "Of course I do. I do whatever I think will work. If someone's trying to snow me or intimidate me, I can be a real pain in the ass. Anthony usually plays the clean-cut veteran who goes by the book. I usually play the cocky hotshot who might - just might - go over the line."

"Wow." This was a side of my roommate that I hadn't seen before. "Don't ever pull that on me, OK?"

"Yeah. You're pretty good about not lawyering me. Besides, what you have to watch for is when Anthony suddenly decides to play bad cop. That's when the shit approaches the fan."

I was quiet a moment, reaffirming my decision not to pursue the FBI. "So what did Lee want to get from me?" I asked. "Does he still think I did it, or was it just a shot in the dark?"

"My guess is it was a shot in the dark. But I also think that Lee isn't all that convinced that your dad killed himself. There are some things that don't make sense."

"What things?"

"It's not my case, Jack, but from what Lee's told us, it doesn't feel like a suicide. No one kills themselves by bashing themselves over the head and setting the place on fire. His head wound bled, which means he got it before he died. There wasn't any smoke in his lungs, and his body wasn't twisted or curled. Usually, if someone dies in a fire, the body goes back to the fetal position, or the arms come up, like a boxer's. It's possible that your dad deliberately set the blaze, that it went up faster than he expected, and that the ceiling came down, hit him on the head, and killed him before there was a lot of smoke. But it's also possible that someone bludgeoned your dad to death and set the fire to cover it up."

A shudder went through my body.

Mark apologized immediately. "I shouldn't have told you all that."

"I asked for it," I said. "I guess I just haven't wanted to think about the way my dad died." I pretended to rub my eyes as if I were tired.

"What did you think of the funeral?" I asked, in a relatively normal voice.

"I thought your dad sounded like a nice guy," he said. "Actually, he sounded a lot like you."

"He's nothing like me!" The objection burst out before I could think about it. Ignoring Mark's stunned expression, I raved on, words streaming out like ants, unwelcome and unending. "How can you say that? I wouldn't run around on my wife. I wouldn't have an affair with one of my students. I wouldn't ever, ever abandon my son." If we hadn't been rushing toward Seattle at precisely 73 miles per hour, I would have launched myself out of the car. "Dammit, Mark. Is that what you think of me?"

"No, of course not, Jack. But the dogs. And it sounded like he was good to his employees. Even though it's not the style in your firm – it's not even really acceptable in your firm – you're decent to everyone there. I don't know why he messed up so bad with you. I'm sorry."

I thought that over. "I know. I'm sorry I flew off the handle. I'm a little confused right now."

"That's OK. You want to talk about something else?"

"Yeah."

We discussed my front yard during the rest of the ride home. More precisely, we discussed different ways of killing the slugs that had taken over my front yard. Over the summer, Mark had planted some flowering cherries and hostas around my front door. Hostas are apparently the equivalent of pizza and beer for the charismatic banana slug. Welcome to the Beautiful Northwest.

Mark and I had been home for a while, pacing out where we would install the copper flashing to deter our new wildlife, when Detective Anthony drove up. He dropped off Harmony, said, "One of us was speeding," pointedly to Mark, gave me a one-armed hug, and told me he would be in touch about the FBI. I didn't have the heart to tell him that I had changed my mind. My body was such a wreck after ten years in foster care and two years of college football, though, that maybe I just wouldn't pass the physical.

It wasn't until I was getting ready for bed that I noticed the light blinking on my answering machine. Two messages. I almost left them for the next day, but there's something insistent about that pulsing light. It's hard to ignore. I guess it's for the same reason that I open even my junk mail: You never know when you're going to get something good.

The first message was from Dan Bradford, my managing partner. He sounded improbably subdued. He had talked to Harmony, he said, and he was worried about me. He knew I was going through a hard time, and he didn't want me to make any rash decisions. The firm would consider me to be on indefinite, unpaid personal leave. Any time I wanted to come back, I could. "After all, Jack," he said, "you are a very valuable - I mean valued - member of the firm."

I was still gritting my teeth when the second message started to play. At the first word, the hair rose on the back of my neck. The voice was familiar in a skewed, startling way. I cringed as if I were hearing my own voice and wincing at the way I sounded. But it wasn't my voice. It wasn't even a man's voice. It was a woman's voice, and even though I had heard it just that afternoon up in Bellingham, it was somehow way too intrusive to have that voice talking in my bedroom. I almost yanked out the plug of the answering machine to stop it.

As it was, however, my hand froze inches from the cord. No matter how disturbing it was, I had to hear what my half-sister had to say. I sat on my bed, rewound the tape, and let the message play:

> Jack, this is Sarah Duncan. Sarah Hart Duncan. I got your number from directory assistance. Sergeant Lee told me who you were. Are. I'm calling, well, I'm calling for two reasons. One, I am just really, really sorry about the way I

> behaved this afternoon. I had been looking at old photographs of my - our - father this morning, trying to figure out what to say at the service. When I saw you standing there at the back of the chapel, I didn't know what to make of it. You look a lot like Daddy did when he was young. And when I figured out that you weren't a ghost, that somehow seemed even worse. We all knew that Daddy and Mama had separated when we were little, but none of us knew the extent of it. None of us knew about you. But you had a perfect right to be there, and I shouldn't have embarrassed you like that. It was just a really hard day, and I didn't know what to do.

Join the club, I thought. As if Sarah read my mind, her message continued:

> I could tell that you didn't know what to do, either. But when I thought about it later, I could see how hard you had tried not to make us uncomfortable. You shouldn't have had to sit in the back like that, and I'm sorry you didn't feel welcome enough to come to the interment. I suppose that was my doing. If you had come to the cemetery, I would have apologized to you there. But you didn't, so I'm apologizing to you now. Anyway, Jack, we've all talked it over, and we'd like to meet you. Meet you properly, I mean. We're all at sixes and sevens right now, but the house is just stuffed with food from people in the neighborhood. Mostly ham, I think. If you don't mind eating ham and let's see –

There was the unmistakable sound of a refrigerator door opening.

> - jam and pickles and something that looks like a chicken casserole, then we'd like you to come

> up for dinner. Like Saturday, maybe? If you want to. Why don't you call me and let me know? If you just want to leave a voicemail, that's OK. We're not really answering the phone much at the moment. I'm kind of glad that you're not there right now. I mean, I know that you'll be there when you listen to this, but sometimes it's easier to talk to a machine than a person, you know? By the way, your voice on your answering machine sounds nice. You sound a lot like Daddy.

She left her number and hung up. Her goodbye was hurried and breathless, as if she was about to cry.

I listened to the message one more time, making sure I hadn't hallucinated it. Then I snapped off the light, dropped onto my bed, and pulled the covers over my face.

I had had enough. I didn't know whether I was going to call Sarah back or not, but I did know that I couldn't deal with it right then.

I was just beginning to agonize over the decision when my brain said to hell with it and I fell asleep.

CHAPTER 9

I woke in the middle of an eerie dream about pale flowers fluttering in the darkness outside my door. Then two thoughts hit me in rapid succession. One, my father was dead. Two, I had to decide whether or not to call my sister. I hadn't even opened my eyes, and already, my day was shot.

I took Betsy for a run through the close, wet morning, her orange fur flickering like a flare in the glare of headlights. A little girl in a yellow slicker asked to pet her, and she obliging dropped her head and let the child rub her ears. "She's wet," the child protested, giggling and squealing as Betsy suddenly shook herself, creating her own little rainstorm there at the curb. Betsy and I ran until the sun was up and the clouds hung at half-staff over the lake, a roiling black mass capping a layer of clean, pink light.

Back at home, I dried Betsy's fur, fixed her breakfast, and listened to Sarah's message again. Mark had already left for work, but Harmony was there, sitting on my living room floor with papers spread out around her.

"Hey," I said, threading my way through stacks of purchase-sale agreements. "Can I have .2 of your time?"

Harmony and I had met as associates at Piper Whatcom, where we had limited our breaks to twelve minutes - two otherwise billable tenths of an hour.

"Sure," Harmony said, putting aside the box of documents she had been reviewing. "For you, maybe even .3. What's going on?"

"I've got a hypothetical for you."

"Shoot."

"If Higuro had died before you knew that he was your biological father, and if he had a son from a separate personal entanglement, and if the son contacted you and wanted to meet you, what would you do?"

"I take it Sarah called."

Not much got by Harmony. "She called, all right. She left me a five-minute message on my answering machine. She invited me up for dinner on Saturday."

"Well, do you want to go?"

"Don't fight the hypo, Harmony. The question is, would you go?"

Harmony considered that for a moment, tapping her fountain pen against her lower lip. "Yes," she said. "I couldn't resist it. I'd go. If it was horrible, I'd never have to see him again, and if it was great, then I'd be happy to have a brother. The only danger would be the possibility of discovering something that I would have preferred not to know."

"I already know that my dad was a two-timing, student-corrupting, chemical-dumping coward," I said, feeling strangely disloyal. "What else can there be for me to discover?"

"*A lot.*"

I knew Harmony pretty well. I knew her well enough to pick up on the quiver in her reply. "Is something going on with Higuro?"

She gave me a tiny, startled smile - half congratulatory, half abashed. "Apparently," she said. "Higuro is very, very successful and very, very wealthy. He didn't get that way by being nice. Or even by being ethical. As I get deeper into his companies, I'm finding deals and schemes and strategies that I don't much like. He never crosses the line, but he never moves away from it, either. Everything is always a battle, and he always wins."

"Have you talked to him about it?"

"Oh, yes. We've had numerous heart-to-hearts on the company jet."

"Was he receptive?"

"He's always receptive to what I say. But he always uses it as another tether to keep me working for him. Whenever I'm concerned with something, he gives me full authority to make it right. Since I'm the one who brought it up, I feel obligated to see it through. And while I'm fixing a little corner of one thing, I always find something else that bothers me. Then he tells me to fix that. But he hasn't stopped the way he does business. He hasn't stopped planting spies in other people's companies or luring talent away from his competitors or gobbling up - and then spitting out - anyone he thinks might have a good product or a good idea. He hasn't stopped keeping dossiers on the personal lives of his employees, and he hasn't stopped making lavish and conveniently timed gifts and contributions to politicians - including the President's reelection campaign. He hasn't stopped, and he's not going to stop." She sighed and cocked an eyebrow at me. "Is he?"

"He might stop for you, Harmony. I think Higuro would do anything for you."

She shook her head and hugged her knees to her chest. "No, what he'd do is make me his compliance officer and tell me that he needed me to redirect his companies' ethics. He'd trot me all over Asia so I could audit and reeducate every company and every office. He'd be incredibly supportive and enthusiastic. And after years of reviewing policies and doing touchy-feely training sessions, I'd finally realize that nothing had changed - except that I would have made a *de facto* move to Japan and that my boyfriend would have married someone else while I was away."

"That last bit is not going to happen, Harmony," I told her. "Even if you do make a *de facto* move to Japan." I pulled her close to me and worked my fingers into her lovely hair. "At least Higuro sent you home on the company jet."

"Only because I out-lawyered him."

It was entirely possible. "What did you do to that poor man?"

"When Mark and Anthony called me about your father, I went in and told Higuro that I had booked the first flight out of Narita. He didn't like that. He said, 'But Jack didn't even know his father.' And I replied, rather testily, I'm afraid, 'So? I didn't even know you.'" She sighed again. "I was on the company jet in 45 minutes."

"What about his aneurism?"

"What aneurism? When I got there, he was off playing golf. I heard him come home; he was humming and whistling. His assistant told him I had arrived, and the next thing I heard was a pitiful moan from his room. He's a good enough actor that I wondered whether something might actually be wrong with him: an intermittent aneurism or something. But he's fine. I found out that the day before he allegedly fell ill, he had had dinner with the owner of one of the executive suites we looked at for office space. I think he was just trying to block our going out on our own."

Ouch. "How come he hates me so much?"

"He doesn't hate you. If you were Japanese, he'd be OK with our getting married. If you were Japanese and rich, he'd be happy about our getting married. And if you were Japanese, rich, and influential, he'd marry you himself." She cocked her head and looked up at me. "How is it that we began talking about your father, and we ended up talking about my father?"

"Your father is more interesting."

"I rather doubt that." She stroked my hair back from my forehead. "Do you want me to go with you up to Bellingham to meet your sisters?"

"I would like to have you there. I would like to have you, and Mark, and Detective Anthony, and Betsy, and several bomb-sniffing dogs. But I think this is something I have to do by myself."

"So you've decided to go?"

I blinked at her. "You tricked me," I protested.

"I didn't mean to. I just got my questions out of order." She kissed me very tenderly. "Do you want privacy to call your sister?"

Amazingly, I did want privacy to call my sister. As a general rule, I loved having Mark, Harmony, and Betsy around, but calling Sarah was going to require courage and concentration. I couldn't decide whether I wanted to call from the bedroom, the kitchen, or the living room. Even after I settled on the bedroom and closed the door behind me, I couldn't decide whether I wanted to stand, sit, or lie on my bed. I listened to Sarah's message a few more times before I was ready to call. Then I punched in the number and shut my eyes as the rings unfurled across the distance.

If I had known where that call was going to lead me, I don't know whether I would have done it. But all I knew at the time was that Sarah and my other half-sisters were opening a door for me that I had never known existed. It wasn't the door that my father's death had slammed shut, but it was close, somehow. And I was in such pain where I was that it didn't seem to matter where the phone call might lead. Barring any mishap to Harmony, Mark, Jimmy, Betsy, or the Anthonys, I couldn't imagine that I could feel worse.

When Sarah answered the phone, I nearly lost my nerve. I veered between hanging up and saying hello. I croaked, "Sarah?"

There was an electric silence on the other end of the line. "Jack?" she eventually responded.

"I got your message. It was too late to call back last night. I - um, I -" What in the hell was I going to say? *Thrilled to see you Saturday night? Can I bring anything, darling? Kiss-kiss?* "- I thought you said you weren't going to be answering the phone," I finished lamely.

"Would you like me to hang up so you can call back and get our voicemail?" Sarah asked. She sounded genuinely apologetic for taking my call.

"No, no. It's OK. It's just really awkward."

"I know."

"Saturday night," I started, then stopped. "Are you sure you want to do this?"

"We're sure. Ever since Daddy died, we've all been searching our desks and looking through our bookcases for cards he gave us or books he wrote in. We've been trying to hoard as much of him as we can. Even though we didn't know about you, you're part of him, Jack. And we want you. We at least want to meet you." She paused, and I heard someone fussing in the background. Jennifer, I suspected. My niece. I had a niece. Three nieces. My life was expanding so rapidly, it was hard to keep count. "So will you come up tomorrow?"

Tomorrow. It had seemed a lot farther away when I had thought about going there on *Saturday*. "Would you rather we meet somewhere neutral?" I ventured, sounding like we were negotiating a prisoner swap. "We could go somewhere between Bellingham and Seattle - The Sisters in Everett or Pacioni's in Mount Vernon, maybe. That way, we could all get away fast if things don't work out."

"We thought about that, too. But I really can't leave Mama or Jennifer." There was a long pause. "Unless you absolutely don't want to come to the house, I'd rather we meet here."

"OK," I said. "I'll come to the house. What time?"

"Is six too early? With the kids and everything, we can't let dinner wait too long."

"Six is fine," I said. "How do I get there?"

She told me the address and gave me directions to Edgemoor from the freeway. We discussed whether or not spouses, children, and significant others should be invited. Except for Jennifer, who was breast-feeding and therefore difficult to dispatch, we decided that they should not. Then, out of sheer anxiety, I made the mistake of asking whether there was anything I could bring.

"Do you have any pictures of Daddy?" Her voice was so wistful that I couldn't be angry at her, but her question hit me like a fist to the gut. So that was why my sisters were inviting me to dinner. They didn't care about me. They just wanted to figure out what I had of their father. It really was going to be like a prisoner swap.

"I don't have any pictures," I said, a little too quickly. "I don't have anything - of him or from him. If that's what you want, then we may as well call it off now. There's nothing I can give you."

I don't know how I expected Sarah to respond. I wouldn't have blamed her if she had hung up on me right then. After all, she was trying to do what at least appeared to be a nice thing - extend a hand of friendship to her illegitimate half-brother. I had no business questioning her motives. And I wouldn't have been at all surprised if she had gotten mad, or cried, or agreed with me that there was no point in pursuing this detente. But her response was so unexpected that it disarmed me.

"Poor little Jack," she said, as if she had known me all her life. "I'm putting together an album of pictures of Daddy. That's why I asked. I'm making copies for all of us. I'll make a copy for you, too. It won't be ready by tomorrow, but maybe that's good. It will give us another excuse to meet."

I didn't respond. I couldn't. Sarah seemed unperturbed. "We'll see you tomorrow at six then," she said. "I'm glad you called back." And then she was gone.

I could not decide what to wear up to Bellingham. Such fashion agonies were extremely unusual for me. I was too big to be stylish. I just wore whatever fit. But I had first-date-type jitters like you wouldn't believe. I wanted to be the best-looking, best-dressed, best-smelling person I could be, so I enlisted Mark and Harmony - both of whom always looked like they were just about to have their pictures taken - to outfit me for the occasion. After inspecting every inch of my closet and dresser, they hit on their favorite combination: drab, almost military dark green pants and an eggplant sweater over a white shirt.

I took the designated clothes to the cleaners, polished the designated shoes, washed my car - which Mark had long before christened the BetsyMobile - and scrubbed the nose prints off the inside of its windows and vacuumed the orange fur off its seats. I listened to the weather report. "No rain tomorrow," the meteorologists predicted, "although there will be showers throughout the Puget Sound region." I was a Seattle native. It made sense to me.

Throughout my preparations, I kept calculating how long I had until I was going to meet my sisters. First I had 24 hours, then 20, then, as I was going to bed, 18. I couldn't tell whether I was anticipating it or dreading it. It was like waiting for a simultaneous birthday party/root canal.

Before I knew it, it was time to go. I was dressed in my designated clothes, wearing my polished shoes, and bracingly scented with Mark's aftershave, which smelled better than my aftershave. I put on my brown leather jacket - a birthday present from Harmony - and the two of them debated whether I should zip it all the way, halfway, or not at all. I settled for halfway and gave Harmony a lingering kiss goodbye.

"Are you sure you don't want us to come with you?" Harmony asked, squeezing me hard.

"You can't. Except for the baby, we agreed it would just be the five of us."

"We could follow you up there and park a ways down the street," Mark offered. "We'd keep an eye on the house, but your sisters wouldn't know we were there."

The idea of Harmony and Mark doing surveillance on my father's house was so entertaining that I almost took them up on it.

"I'll be OK," I said with more confidence than I felt. I hugged them both, gave Betsy a brief but intense ear-rub, and took off, feeling like I was leaving a lot more behind than I could ever hope to find ahead. During the long drive, I repeated over and over what had been my mantra for the prior twenty-four hours: If it's bad, I can go. I prudently gassed up before I headed into Bellingham itself, just in case I needed to burn the hell out of town.

At quarter to six, I cruised into Edgemoor, a newish, opulent Bellingham neighborhood, and marveled up and down the twisting streets until I pulled up in front of my father's Shoreview house. Mansion, I should say. I couldn't tell whether it was a restored mansion or a new mansion, but it was a Mansion with a capital M. It was red brick with white accents, but there was nothing homey-looking about it. It had columns and arches, balustrades and bay windows. Screened from the street by an evergreen hedge, it had the air of an ornate hotel. There was no obvious driveway, so I parked on the street and waited. I was going to arrive precisely at six.

At three minutes to, I combed my hair, ate a LifeSaver, and brushed myself off. I took my time strolling up the immaculate path to the house. At six exactly, I rang the doorbell. No one answered, even though the place was ablaze with lights.

I waited thirty seconds and rang again, feeling like I had been set up. I was about to head for my car when I heard hurried, heavy footsteps and the door suddenly swung open.

Sarah was standing there, barefoot and wearing blue jeans and a stained sweatshirt. My first reaction was to feel overdressed. My second reaction was to gape at the nature of the stain across her shirt. It was bright red, it looked sticky, and it sure as hell wasn't jam.

"Is that blood?" I blurted.

Sarah looked down at her chest. "Well, I'll be damned," she said.

Then she lifted her hand and stared with almost offended silence at the crimson slick across her skin. She looked from her hand to me and back again - and then she fainted right into my arms.

CHAPTER 10

Some things you pick up just from living with a cop. My first priorities were to stabilize and protect Sarah. My second priorities were to determine whether anyone else was injured and take care of them. My third priorities were to secure the area and preserve the evidence. So much for looking and smelling good.

I lowered Sarah to the hardwood floor and checked her over. She was breathing normally, and her pulse was strong and steady. The only wound I could find was a slash across her palm.

The cut was long but not deep, and it looked like it was already beginning to clot. I had no idea how the house was laid out or whether anyone else was there. Moving sideways, so I could keep glancing back to Sarah, I followed the trail of blood spatters down a long hallway. The blood ended at a sort of glassed-in area at the back of the house. It was massed with lush plants that Mark, the mad gardener, would have loved, and I spotted a granite-topped table and some comfy-looking leather chairs amid the foliage. I also spotted a hubcap-sized hole in one of the floor-to-ceiling windows. The parquet floor sparkled with shards of glass, a broken brick was ensconced in one of the comfy leather chairs, and Jennifer was crawling toward the wreckage from a carpeted room off to the side.

I picked my way across the glass and intercepted Jennifer. At least, I tried to intercept Jennifer. She saw me coming, turned around, and started crawling as fast as she could the other way.

If she had been a puppy, I would not have been in the least afraid to pick her up. A baby, however, posed a different sort of challenge. I didn't want to hurt her or scare her. I especially didn't want Sarah or one of my other sisters to walk in and find me wrestling with a howling child.

I cornered Jennifer near a massive stone fireplace. We examined each other warily, while I tried to figure out how she was constructed and where exactly I should grab her. Finally, I just scooped her up like a football and held her firmly against my chest. She didn't cry, but she braced her little hands against me and leaned back. Her eyes were huge, and she didn't move them one inch from mine. Then she suddenly wrapped her chubby arms around my neck and buried her face in my sweater.

Feeling chosen and immensely flattered, I tore off a few meters of paper towels and hurried back to Sarah. She was rubbing her head and trying to sit up. Still clutching Jennifer, I wrapped Sarah's hand with paper towels and pressed down hard on the wound. When she opened her eyes and saw me leaning over her, Sarah blushed beet red.

"I am so embarrassed, Jack. I've never been able to stand the sight of blood."

"Well, don't look down the hall, then," I told her. "You left a trail the whole way." She blushed again, and I changed the subject. "Where's your telephone? We need to call the police."

"No. No police," she protested.

"Sarah, someone threw a brick through your window. This is serious. You cut your hand trying to pick up the glass, and Jennifer would have crawled right into it if I hadn't grabbed her."

Sarah looked stricken and held out her good arm for the baby. "Jennifer, you climbed out of your high chair again," she chided, in an indulgent tone that was nonetheless freighted with worry. "What is Mommy going to do with you?" She nuzzled her daughter, rubbing her nose and forehead against the baby's. Jennifer cooed and patted Sarah's cheeks with delight.

Sarah glanced up at me. "She's our little escape artist," she explained with a certain amount of pride. "Her pediatrician even recommended that I tie her into her high chair to get her used to the idea of staying in one place. It worked only once. After that, Jennifer would take a deep breath whenever I tied the ribbon around her waist. Then she'd suck in her tummy and wiggle right out. She's our little Houdini."

"The police," I prompted, trying to return Sarah's attention to the gravity of the situation. "We need to report the broken window and have someone look at your hand."

"My hand is OK," Sarah said. "And we don't need to report the window. I already know who broke it, and there's nothing we're going to do about it. Except fix it."

"Why not?" I demanded, unwisely blundering into something that was none of my business.

"Because it was my little sister who threw the brick. It's the second window she's smashed this week. She's really upset about Daddy, and she -" She broke off, suddenly uncomfortable. I started to apologize for prying, but she interrupted. "Beth is developmentally disabled. She doesn't talk much, and she doesn't cry, and she doesn't ever tell you when things are bothering her. But when she gets upset, she throws things. And right now, she's really, really, really upset."

"Where is she?"

"Probably still in the backyard. I didn't hear her come in. She'll come in when she wants to. If you go out and try to find her, she'll hide from you."

I thought about Beth, and how heartbreakingly fragile she had looked wearing her black velvet dress at my father's funeral. The thought of her hiding in the dark backyard gave me the creeps. I don't think I shuddered, but my face must have betrayed my discomfort. Sarah hung her head and sighed.

"I'm sorry, Jack. You must think I've invited you up to a madhouse. I had such good intentions. Marianne was going to cook the dinner - which meant that there was a fighting chance that it would have been sort of edible; Emily was going to put together a centerpiece of all the flowers we've received; and I was going to play the piano with Beth so she'd be all calm and ready to sit down to eat. But one of Marianne's little girls sprained her ankle in a soccer game this afternoon, so Marianne won't be here until later. Emily flaked, and Beth - well, you know what happened with Beth. She fled about an hour ago, and like a fool, I went looking for her. So, in other words, Jack, dinner isn't ready, my sisters are missing, and you're stuck with me, Jennifer, and hole in the window for an indeterminate period of time."

She looked so forlorn that I felt desperate to make things right. I helped her up, bandaged her hand, swept up the glass, and mopped up the blood. I settled her into the flowered loveseat in the corner of the huge kitchen, made her some tea, and put Jennifer within easy reach in her playpen. "OK, Chief," I said, fishing around until I found a sufficiently plain and manly apron. "Tell me what to do. What was Marianne going to make for dinner?"

"Damned if I know, Jack. All I know is that it had something to do with ham."

I retrieved the most plausible-looking ham from the refrigerator, wrapped it in foil, and plopped it in the oven. "Do you mind if I poke around a bit?" I asked. "I'm pretty good at finding stuff to eat."

Sarah gave me free rein to look anywhere and use anything I wanted. There was a bag of rolls on the counter. I spread them with butter and garlic salt, wrapped them in foil, and put them in the oven. There were potatoes and onions in a bin. I rifled through the drawers until I found a somewhat rusty knife, chopped them up and threw them in a skillet that I found in the dishwasher. I pulled five crumpled half-bags of lettuce and other greenish things out of the fridge and tossed them into something that credibly resembled a salad.

"Sarah, dinner smells delicious -" Marianne broke off as she rounded the corner and saw me standing behind the granite-topped island. "Oh, my. You're not Sarah," she said, flustered.

"I'm Jack," I said helpfully.

She gave me an abstracted smile. "I figured. Welcome. But I think the idea was that you be our guest, not our cook. Where is Sarah?" She jumped as Sarah pulled her coat from behind.

"I'm right here, Marianne. I had a little accident. Beth threw another rock through the window, and I cut myself on the glass. Jack was kind enough to pick up the slack. And me, actually."

I busied myself at the wine rack while Sarah and Marianne conferred in tense whispers for a few minutes. After the briefing, Marianne bustled around, perspiration beading on her pretty face. First she called her husband, the ineffectual-looking college professor, to tell him that another window would have to be replaced. Then she marched into the backyard to find her sister. I was secretly relieved. The thought of Beth lurking out there in the darkness had set my nerves on edge. While Marianne was gone, I opened the wine that Sarah had selected as being "ham-compatible," and carved the critter into thick, juicy slices.

When I turned around, I saw a woman with long blond hair standing in the kitchen doorway. She was wearing a ruffled skirt over a black leotard. She gave me a slow, deliberate, dazzling smile.

"Jack Hart, I presume?"

"Yes, ma'am."

"I'm Emily. Emily the Tardy. Emily the Tardy and in Trouble." She tugged a lock of Sarah's hair. "I'm sorry, sweetie. I fell asleep. But it looks like everything is in good hands." She wafted over to the granite island. "That all smells pretty damn appetizing for something that's chockful of fat, growth hormones, and carcinogens."

"Emily!" Sarah reproached.

"Are you a vegetarian, Emily?" I asked, wondering why in the world Sarah hadn't warned me.

In response, Emily picked up a particularly juicy and inviting slice of ham, tipped back her head, and slowly and rapturously lowered it into her mouth. It would have been a sensuous if not provocative gesture if she hadn't been my sister. She licked her lips, lowered her lashes, and smiled at me again. "Not today, darling," she said.

Marianne chose that moment to usher a wet but unrepentant Beth into the kitchen. She sat her down, dried her off, and wrapped a thick, fluffy sweater around her, all the while talking to her in an even, exhausted tone that bespoke unbounded patience and even more unbounded hopelessness that she would ever be understood.

"You see Sarah's hand, sweetheart? Sarah got hurt because of that rock you threw. I know you didn't mean to hurt Sarah. But when you throw things, and when you won't come out of the backyard, someone is going to get hurt." Beth didn't acknowledge her sister's lecture. She didn't even look up when Marianne tried to introduce me.

"This is Jack, Beth. Jack is our little brother."

I held out my hand, but Beth didn't respond. After what seemed like an eternity, I reached down and took her hand. It was ice cold. "How about something to warm you up?" I asked. I handed her a garlic roll hot from the oven. Then I quickly moved the ham and the rest of the food to the table, and we all sat down to eat. After a few minutes, I noticed, Beth stopped just clutching the roll and began to nibble at it. She didn't raise her head, but she seemed to like the roll.

In fact, everyone liked the rolls. Everyone liked everything. My sisters exclaimed over everything. "You know, I think Mama would like this," Marianne said. "She hasn't had much of an appetite lately, but she used to love good food. Jack, do you mind if I take a tray up to her?"

"It's your house, Marianne."

"But it's your dinner," she replied, laughing. Marianne took a plate upstairs. "What's the matter with your mother?" I asked Sarah.

"A lot of things," she replied. "She had her first stroke about ten years ago. That's when Daddy retired from the mill. She's been in and out of a wheelchair ever since. About six months ago, she was diagnosed with cancer. It's in her spine and her liver. It's inoperable, and the radiation is just slowing a little, not getting rid of it. So the prognosis isn't good."

"I'm so terribly sorry," I said, shooting an uneasy glance at Beth, who, fortunately, showed no sign of having heard. "I shouldn't have asked."

Sarah gave me such a brave little smile that my heart twisted. "Of course you should have asked. That's the purpose of this dinner, remember? We've got a lot of catching up to do."

Marianne returned with the happy news that her mother was actually eating, and the rest of us tucked in with renewed vigor. Even fragile, pencil-thin Beth could really pack it away, picking up the bite-sized pieces of ham that Marianne had cut for her and nibbling them like a squirrel. "So, tell me about yourselves," I said, looking around the table.

"What do you want to know?" Emily teased, somehow making the question sound flirtatious.

"Anything you want to tell me. Anything you don't want to tell me. I don't even know where you live."

Marianne was the oldest, so she started off. She and her husband Gary lived on Bellingham's South Hill, in a 101-year-old Victorian house that they were painstakingly restoring. Gary was a professor of economics at Western Washington University. Marianne was active in Junior League, PTA, and the Faculty's Club. She had taught kindergarten for a while, then quit about ten years ago when Tessa and

Nichol were born. Tessa played soccer and was feeling much better after a quick trip to the emergency room that afternoon. Nicky liked to swim and to dance. Marianne spent most of her time chauffeuring her daughters to and from swimming lessons and soccer games. While her children were at school, she stayed with her mother and Beth so Sarah had some free time to devote to Jennifer.

"And that's pretty much my life in a nutshell," she said, blushing a little. "I went first because I'm such a good warm-up act for Emily."

Emily stretched delightedly at the introduction. "She's only saying that to prevent you from digging into her checkered past," she said, with a sly but somehow loving wink at her older sister. Emily had attended Smith College, where she had studied "some sort of poetry, I think." After Smith, she had backpacked across Europe, followed the Grateful Dead in a VW bus, lived on an Israeli kibbutz, and considered joining the Peace Corps.

"I didn't though," she said, "because that's when I went through my period where I thought I was a lesbian. And it was such a great scene there for a while. I went to these great womyn's festivals - womyn with a 'y,' not an 'e,' you understand - and there'd be this great music, these great speeches, and this great feeling of love and sisterhood. Everyone was really into their energy and their past lives. In fact, one festival I went to had a special program for Native American women. They had to put up a sign: 'Native Americans: This Life Only.'"

She laughed and shook her long, straight hair. "So it was wonderful because it was just intrinsically wonderful, and it was wonderful because it really drove Daddy nuts. He just did not understand it. But that was good, too, because at the same time he was setting his dogs on Sarah's dates and telling Marianne that she could do a lot better than Gary, he was thrilled with every single guy I brought home. He was just so happy to see me with a man."

Emily gave me another one of her slow, dazzling smiles, this one tinged with tenderness. "Daddy was great, you know, Jack." She looked away and recovered her insouciance. "Anyway, it turned out that I wasn't a lesbian, which actually, was just as well. I mean, can you believe how pissed I would have been if I had spent four years at Smith without realizing I was a lesbian? What a waste!"

"What are you doing now?" I asked.

"I work for a non-profit environmental foundation. Daddy didn't like that either - not at all. But, you know - different strokes." She reached over and patted Sarah's hand. "Your turn, sweetie."

Sarah looked startled. "Jack already knows me."

"No, he doesn't," Marianne said. "Tell him about yourself."

"I'm a widow," Sarah said, bluntly and somewhat testily, as if she resented having to perform at her sister's command. "My husband died just over a year ago in an accident at the mill. Jennifer was born about three months afterward. I have my teaching certificate, but I haven't worked since I was married. I live here, and I take care of Mama, and I take care of Beth, and I take care of Jennifer." She threw me a look I couldn't read. "And that's all."

She stroked Beth's drying, fine, golden hair. "Beth, do you want to tell Jack about yourself?" With a restraint that I admired, Sarah paused for a suitable interval to let Beth reply. Then, as if Beth had declined, Sarah patted her back and said, "OK, I will for you. Beth lives here, too. She goes to school two days a week, and she's very good at playing the piano and tatting."

I was not familiar with the word. "Tatting?"

"Lace-making," Sarah explained. She turned to her sister, who - for the first time - seemed to be listening. "Beth, Jack's never seen tatting before. Do you want to show him the handkerchief you've been edging?"

Beth shot a dubious glance at me. Then, to my surprise, she got up, opened one of the maple cupboards near the flowered loveseat, and pulled out a blue velvet bag. She spread the velvet out on the loveseat and arranged the beginnings of a lace-trimmed handkerchief on top of that. I bent over it to take a closer look. I had never seen anything so painstaking. Around the perimeter of the thin, white fabric was a design of tiny loops, scrolls, and circles. As I bent closer, I could see that they were formed of fine, white thread, knotted so carefully and precisely that the lace seemed to grow out of the weave of the handkerchief.

"That is just beautiful," I told Beth, who was standing right beside me, keeping an anxious eye on my big, clumsy hands. "You are so talented. Will you show me how you do it?"

Too far. Beth blushed a hideous red, snatched up her handiwork, and rushed out of the room. Emily followed her.

I looked helplessly from Marianne to Sarah. Before I could apologize, Marianne put a comforting hand on my back. "You didn't do anything wrong, Jack," she said. "Beth is delighted. Really. She's just shy. It was so nice of you to pay attention to her like that."

"I wasn't being nice," I said. "I meant it. It's beautiful. Where did she learn how to do it?"

"From Mama," Sarah replied. "Before her strokes, Mama tatted all the time. Even while she'd be watching TV, her hands would be flying along. She tried to teach all of us except Beth. She didn't want to make Beth sad or frustrated, but it turned out that Beth's the only one of us who picked it up. Mama couldn't figure out why her tatting seemed to be going so much faster than it used to. Then she found Beth digging in her sewing box one day, and that explained it. Whenever Mama laid her work aside and went to bed, Beth would pick it up and imitate what Mama had been doing. She doesn't make up her own patterns, but she can copy anything."

Sarah broke off as Beth came back into the room, looking pink and pleased. She didn't acknowledge me, but there was a tiny smile on her thin face. I was just starting to dish the mint chocolate chip ice cream - my favorite kind - when Emily strolled in with the tray that Marianne had taken up to her mother.

"Hey, Jack, look at this!" she said, holding up a plate that betrayed no evidence of dinner. "You are going to have to come and see us more often. This is the first time in six months that Mama has cleaned her plate. It looks like she licked it. Before you leave, she wants you to step upstairs. She wants to give her compliments to the chef."

I glanced at my watch. It was already a quarter to eight, and I had at least a ninety-minute drive ahead of me. "I'd better be going now," I said, not expecting the clamor of protest that greeted my announcement. Even Beth shook her head.

"No, you can't go," Emily insisted. "You haven't told us anything about yourself yet. All we know is that you're a great cook. That's hardly enough to gossip about during my next book group meeting. We might have to talk about the book. Unacceptable. So come on, Jack. Spill it."

Marianne squeezed my hand. "I think you're trapped, Jack," she said, smiling. "We're all dying to know about you. Tell us all about yourself before you go up to say hello to Mama. And then we'll decide whether or not we'll let you leave."

I knew when I was licked. I gave them the same abbreviated life history I had recited for Leah, Jerry, and Carl just a week before at *il fiasco*: Two years of college football at the U-Dub, where I had earned my marketing B.A. and J.D. Going on five years at Piper Whatcom & Hardcastle, where I was a civil litigator and practiced mostly corporate defense. I shrugged and lifted my palms. "That's it," I said.

"Bullshit," Emily returned. "What about your personal life? Do you have a girlfriend?"

"I have the best girlfriend in the whole world," I told them truthfully.

"What's she like?" Sarah pressed.

I didn't want to remind them of what had happened at the funeral, so I didn't mention that Harmony had been standing beside me as the family had filed out of the chapel. I just pulled out my wallet and showed them one of the pictures I always carried. It was of Harmony, Mark, Betsy, and me, gathered around my fireplace on Christmas morning. Harmony was wearing a black silk kimono, a present from Higuro, and she looked utterly stunning. I passed the wallet around and listened in pride and amusement to my sisters' reactions.

"My, she's gorgeous," Marianne gushed.

"She's beautiful," Sarah agreed. "Look at her, Beth. And the doggie is beautiful, too."

"Who's the hunk?" Emily demanded. "Who is he, and is he married?"

"Mark is my roommate," I said, laughing. "And he is not married."

"Is he gay?"

"He is not gay."

"Are you sure?" Emily examined the picture carefully. "He is way too handsome not to be gay."

"He'll be flattered to hear that."

I was feeling very comfortable right then. I was feeling warm, accepted, and well-fed. I thought my sisters were very kind and understanding. I thought that Sergeant Lee must have filled them in on all the bad stuff about my past, but that they were being tolerant enough to overlook it. That's my only excuse for what I did next.

Still gazing at Mark's picture, Emily prodded, "How did you meet him?"

I responded, without thinking about it, "Oh, we were foster brothers when we were kids."

You would have thought that I had confessed to being a serial killer. Emily dropped my wallet, as if afraid that it carried some contagion. Sarah snatched up Jennifer. Marianne and Beth just gaped. Sarah said, "You were in a foster home, Jack?"

I was in too deep to back out. "Yes," I said. I thought - but didn't add - *I was in a lot of foster homes.*

As if she read my mind, Sarah pressed, "For how long?"

"Ten years," I said reluctantly. There were gasps around the table. I had ruined the dinner party just as thoroughly as I had ruined my father's funeral. I was already apologizing and standing up to make my escape when Marianne put her arms around me and held me fast.

"Oh, poor Jack," she said. "What about your mother? Where was she?"

"I don't know. She dropped me off at Child Protective Services when I was eight. I didn't see her again until I was in my twenties."

"Oh, no," Emily said. All the teasing artifice was gone. She patted me awkwardly on the cheek. "Oh, you poor little thing."

She hugged me so hard that I felt the ache in my ribs. "Jack, if we had known for an instant that you were in a foster home - if Daddy - if any of us - had known that you needed us, we would have been down there in ten seconds demanding you. I mean it, Jack. There's no way we would have let them put you in a home." She kissed me on both cheeks and made a great show of rubbing her lipstick off my skin, even though, as far as I could tell, she wasn't wearing any. There were tears in her eyes as she turned around to her sisters. "Wouldn't it have been great to grow up with Jack as our baby brother?"

"We would have put doll clothes on you," Marianne said.

"And we would have braided your hair," Sarah added.

"And painted your nails." Emily's teasing tone had returned, even though her eyes still glittered with tears.

"And tried out our makeup on you," Marianne agreed. "You would have been much, much better than a Barbie."

"Are you trying to make me feel better about being in a foster home?" I demanded, blustering a little.

I couldn't believe their reactions. Seconds before, I had expected to be tossed out of the house. I hadn't expected my sisters to cluster around me and try to comfort me. But - astonishingly - that was what was happening. Marianne and Sarah had their arms around my shoulders; Emily was hanging on my neck, and even Beth sidled up to me and slipped her cold little hand into mine. They held me tight, as if I were something rare and precious, something not to be jeopardized by letting go.

Emily said, in a tone approaching her earlier delighted drawl, "You know, girls, we could give Jack a manicure right now."

"No, no, no," I said, breaking free of their grasp. "There will be no manicures this evening. Or ever. There will be no hair-braiding, no dress up, and no makeup. You guys had your chance." I was busy evading their playful attempts to keep hold of me when we heard a bell ringing somewhere upstairs. The effect on my sisters was amazing. All the tomfoolery ceased in an instant.

"That's Mama," Marianne said, suddenly dropping my hand. "I bet she wants a chance to see Jack before she goes to sleep." She turned to me. "Jack, do you mind stepping upstairs and saying goodnight to our mother?"

I pocketed my wallet so my sisters couldn't look at the other picture in it while I was gone. It was a photo of Mark and my four-year-old half-brother, Jimmy, and I didn't want my sisters to figure out that my mom had been extremely young - fifteen, to be exact - when she had me. They might have been touched by the fact that I had been in foster care since I was eight, but I figured that they would not be quite so sympathetic to learn that their father - our father - had been messing around with a fourteen-year-old girl.

I wasn't apprehensive as I followed Marianne up the lovely, curving staircase. The evening had gone so well, and my sisters seemed so nice. I couldn't imagine that their mother would be any less welcoming. Besides, I still labored under the delusion that age, illness, and impending death have a way of putting resentments into perspective.

I can't believe that I was that naive, but I was. So I followed Marianne meekly and went willingly, innocently, into the comfy, overstuffed bedroom that my father had shared with the white-haired, blue-eyed little lady who was perched on a stack of pillows and wearing a pink satin jacket.

"Mama, this is Jack," Marianne said, patting me on the back as I leaned over to shake Virginia Carlson Hart's thin, ringed hand. She acknowledged me with a nod and indicated a frilly, flowered chair next to her bed.

"Sit there, dear," she said.

I sat.

Virginia turned to her oldest daughter. "Marianne, I think Jack and I probably have some things we'd like to discuss in private. Why don't you give us a few minutes alone?"

Marianne threw me a doubtful look, but unfortunately, I still didn't have the good sense to be scared. Noticing her hesitation, Virginia said, "Don't worry, dear. I won't keep him long. You and the rest of the girls will have him back before you know it."

With that assurance, Marianne withdrew. At the click of the door behind her daughter, Virginia seemed to expand before my eyes. Her back grew straighter, her jaw tighter, her eyes colder. When she spoke, she didn't mess around, and she didn't waste time calling me "dear."

"So," she said. "We meet at last."

CHAPTER 11

I didn't respond. I was afraid. Very afraid. I looked around the room for an escape route. Dark wood paneling lined the walls, and the bed was draped with lace and red velvet. It was like being trapped inside a cherry chocolate.

Virginia was undeterred by my silence. She fixed her cold, blue eyes on me like a hunter getting a bead on a deer. "How is your mother?" she demanded.

It was not an idle inquiry. She was watching me closely, as if the question were a test. I couldn't untangle her motives. Did she just want to get the goods on her competition? Or was she trying to figure out how close I was to my mom? I decided to play it safe. "She's OK, I guess."

For some reason, my answer seemed to relax Virginia. She settled back on her pillows, as if mollified. "What is she up to these days?"

I didn't like my mother. She had lived off me for years, and now she was sponging off poor old Bill in Spokane. Part of me wanted to dish with Virginia. Part of me wanted to tell her about my mother's drinking, drugging, and witchcraft. Part of me wanted to tell her how infuriating she was, how dishonest she was, and how much grief she had brought into my life over the decades. But I didn't. For one thing, she was my mother, after all. For another, I didn't like Virginia Carlson any more than I liked my mom. Even from the little I had seen, I already sensed that my dad had had appalling taste in women.

Still treading carefully, I replied, "My mother moved to Spokane a while ago. She is getting married in December."

I wasn't expecting the cackle of laughter that broke from the old lady's throat. "*Married*? Your mother?" She gave me another hard, piercing look. "Mary Boyden is getting *married*?"

"Well, yes," I said, shifting uncomfortably on the flowered chair. Out of sheer nervousness, I added, "She doesn't go by Mary anymore, though. Her name is Marta Boyden now."

Virginia glared at me for a moment. Her eyes seemed to burn into mine. Then she looked away and suddenly patted her forehead with a wispy handkerchief. It was bordered, I noticed, with tatting. She stared straight ahead, not seeing me, not seeing anything really. I started to take my leave, but she stopped me with an imperious wave of her hand.

"Sit."

I sat.

"We're not done," she said. "We haven't even started." When I didn't answer, she gave me a grim smile. "Don't worry. You're safe, Jack. I asked you up here for two reasons. One, I wanted to thank you for lifting me down during the attack on Jackie's funeral."

Jackie. I had never thought of my dad as being called *Jackie.* "You're welcome," I said.

"And two -" she swallowed. "And two, I wanted to ask a favor of you."

If she was angling for a favor, she had one hell of a weird way of ingratiating herself. Before I could ask her what she wanted, she said, "What do you think of my girls?"

I noted that proprietary "my." "I think your daughters are wonderful," I said truthfully.

"They're good girls," she agreed. For the first time, there wasn't any subtext to what she was saying. "Even Emily, although she'd be insulted at the thought. But they're going to need some help, Jack. They're going to need you, and sooner than you think."

"I'm sorry. I don't understand," I said.

"Jackie was very protective of the girls. And much as I love them, they do need protecting. Not one of them has ever stood on her own two feet. Marianne has Gary, and he's a nice fellow, but they would have gone under a hundred times if Jackie hadn't bailed them out - over and over again. He even bought their house for them. And Emily, well, she's a will-o'-the-wisp if there ever was one. She claims to work at that dreadful environmental place, but she doesn't get paid for it. She writes an article here and there, and sometimes they get published, but for peanuts, you know? And then there's Beth, of course. Beth will need care for the rest of her life." She fell silent.

"What about Sarah?" I prompted. She had seemed pretty level-headed to me.

"Sarah has more on the ball than the rest of the girls, but she's been dealt a hard hand. She and Scott were a good pair. Scott wasn't educated, but he was smart. Sarah's educated, but she's not always savvy. Since Scott was killed, Sarah has just been lost. If she didn't have Jennifer, I don't know whether she'd even get up in the morning."

Virginia Carlson Hart didn't seem like a dragon any more. Her shoulders drooped, and her eyes were pale and watery. She looked like a sad, sick old lady who was worried to death about her girls.

"I like your daughters a lot," I said. "I'll do whatever I can to help them. But I don't have any money. I won't be able to support them."

"Just promise me that you'll do what you can for them," she insisted. When I didn't answer quickly enough to suit her, she demanded, "*Promise me.*"

I promised. Again, I tried to leave. Again, she restrained me. This time, however, it was with an imploring, not an imperious, hand.

"Jack, you are going to hear a lot of tales about me and your father during the next few weeks. The rumors are already flying. I'm surprised someone didn't try to bend your ear at the funeral. I'd rather you hear it from me first. And if you hear something that makes you angry - and you will - all I can ask is that you be angry only at me, not at the girls."

"Why should I be angry at you?" I asked. It seemed far more likely that it would be the other way around.

She met my eyes with difficulty. "There are reasons." She mopped her forehead and continued, "Jackie and I separated when the girls were small. Everyone assumed that he was at fault, and I let them think so. But in reality, I'm the one who walked out on him."

From what I had heard of my dad, leaving him didn't seem like much of a sin. But clearly, it was bothering Virginia Carlson. I was getting curious in spite of myself. "Why did you walk out?"

She shook her head and looked at her handkerchief. "It was a horrible time for us. Beth was two, and it was like having a wild animal in the house. I couldn't talk to her. I couldn't control her. Most days, I couldn't even get her to eat. She fought me every day of her life. She had no remorse, no understanding of consequences. Everything seemed to be backwards with her. She'd run at full speed into a wall or gash her head open on a cupboard and not shed a single tear, but when I would give her a little pat or a kiss, she'd arch her back and twist away from me, as if I was hurting her. I begged Jackie to let me get some kind of help for her - a nurse, a therapist, even an institution if we had to. He wouldn't hear of it. But," she added bitterly, "he wasn't the person who had to stay home with her all day."

I didn't know what to say. I could only imagine how thoroughly Beth could turn a household upside down. "She seems -" I paused, trying to figure out what word to use - "better now."

"She is better now. She's also drugged into a stupor half the time. The medicines help her function, but there's a real price. When she was fighting, scratching, and biting, at least she'd be there. The drugs calm her down, but most of the time she seems like she's a hundred miles away."

Virginia looked a hundred miles away herself, lying there in her satin bed jacket and mopping her brow with a trembling hand. Her rings glinted dully in the half-light. With an effort, she turned back to me. "Anyway, by the time Beth was two and a half, I had had enough. I was tired of scrimping and saving and fighting. My family had money, and my parents wanted to help us - at least to help us with Beth. But Jackie was terribly proud. The six of us - not to mention his insane dogs - were living in a two-bedroom, tumbledown house that doesn't even exist anymore. We had four children under the age of nine, we were trying to make do on a high school teacher's salary, and Jackie was always gone. I know he was just trying to bring home a little bit extra to help out, but I needed him there. When he wasn't teaching, he was coaching, and when he wasn't coaching, he was tutoring, and when he wasn't tutoring, he was singing at weddings and funerals all around town."

"My dad *sang*?" I was incredulous. I couldn't fit singing into my memories of him. As far as I had been concerned, there had been nothing melodious about him.

"He sang beautifully. He had a gorgeous baritone voice. He and Ida - the woman who sang at his funeral - used to perform duets together." Ida, I deduced, was the lady from *il fiasco*. "Ida's an incredible scatterbrain, and she loathes me, but she and Jackie did sound good together."

"Why does she loathe you?"

"Because Jackie married me instead of her, of course." She almost preened, and for just a moment, I had a glimpse of what a pretty girl she must have been. "Ida and her boyfriend used to double date with Jackie and me, and she was always flirting with him: dropping her hankie, brushing past him, pretending to straighten her seams when she wasn't even wearing stockings. Jackie was such a great big, good-looking son of a gun." She shot me an accusing glance. "Just like you. I used to tell him that if I died before he did, he'd probably end up taking a date to my funeral."

That hit a little too close to home. We both hmmmed uncomfortably and looked at the velvet curtains for a moment, then Virginia sighed. "So it was my fault, Jack. I moved out. I moved back home, just like my girls keep doing with me. My father hired a full-time nurse for Beth, and for the first time in what seemed like decades, I was able to sleep through the night. We never divorced, and Jackie still came to see the girls, but I told him that we couldn't get back together until he could support us. It was a cruel thing to say. Jackie was so proud, and he worked so hard. But I was just so tired, Jack. I was so tired of the diapers and the screaming and the barking and the macaroni and cheese. And I was angry at Jackie for putting me through that just because he was too vain to let my parents help us. So I threw him out, and that's, apparently, when he took up with your mother. He went down to Seattle to get his master's degree so he could make a little more money as a teacher. I assume that's when it happened. When you happened, I mean."

I was confused. Sergeant Lee had said my mother had been in my father's civics class. "So my mother wasn't one of his students?"

"Oh, Marta was one of his students all right. I knew her by reputation."

"Reputation?"

"As in bad. I went to his classroom once to get his keys or something. Marta was wearing white go-go boots and a miniskirt and sitting in the very front row. You could see London, and you could see France."

The image was excruciatingly disturbing. I passed from it as quickly as possible. "So how did my mom end up in Seattle with my dad?"

"I don't know, Jack." Virginia's voice was almost gentle. "You'll have to ask her."

Touché. "I don't see why you thought I'd be angry at you," I said, trying to change the subject. "Whatever happened between you and my father is your own business. Just because you left him didn't mean he had to go chasing after one of his students."

I immediately regretted what I had said. Virginia's thin, lined face bore the same convulsed expression I had seen earlier on Sarah's - although Virginia looked a lot closer to tears than laughter. She pressed her handkerchief to her face and waved away my apologies. "There's more," she said, her voice muffled by the cloth.

I waited. After a moment of daubing her eyes, Virginia had recovered sufficiently to continue. "Do you know why your father came back to me?" she asked.

I shook my head.

"My father died. My mother and I had never had anything to do with the finances, and both of us were caught off guard. My parents always seemed like they had money. They lived in a glorious home, and Daddy always had a new car. But when he died, it turned out that they had almost nothing left. Just a lot of debts. I guess Daddy thought that if you acted rich, you would be rich. But it didn't work that way in his case. Mother sold their home, and we all moved into a little apartment. Somehow Jackie heard about it. I would have been too proud to tell him, but all of a sudden, there he was. He managed to convince the landlord to let him in, and one morning I woke up and found him there on the couch. Jackie just took charge. There was a little money left from my father's house, and somehow Jackie managed to swing a deal to buy his family's old mill. He worked twenty-four hours a day to make it go. And it wasn't because he wanted to be in the pulp and paper business, Jack. Jackie loathed that mill. It was just the only way he could think of to support us. We couldn't survive on a teacher's salary - not even the salary for a teacher with a master's degree."

She paused and coughed. It was a deep, dry, rattling cough. The lace-draped room was close and hot, but she pulled her satin jacket around her as if chilled by a sudden wind.

I didn't speak for fear I'd interrupt her train of thought. Soon she continued: "Jackie didn't know the first thing about papermaking, but he knew how to run a business, and he knew how to sell. He said he learned it in the classroom. You have to be good at putting your ideas across. He was ahead of the game on recycled papers. He could tell that timber supplies were getting tighter, so he modernized the mill to make recycled products on-site. They caught on, and in five years, we owned our own home. In ten, we owned this place. The mill made money until Jackie retired. That new fellow they put in his place - the one who's running for Congress -"

I searched my mind for the name that Lee had mentioned. "Mike Saunders?" I ventured.

Virginia snapped her fingers and pointed at me. "Odious man. He's been busily running the mill into the ground for the last ten years. Every so often, Jackie would have to intervene and save his bacon, but mostly he just left them alone. He was so happy when Sarah married Scott, though. He let Mike Saunders know in no uncertain terms that Scott should be the new COO. It's quite a leap from foreman to chief operating officer, but Scott was quite an impressive man. It just destroyed all of us when he was killed." She shot me a tremulous glance. "One of the big rolls of paper - the 900-pounders - somehow fell off its stand and crushed him. They didn't find his body until the next morning."

Poor Sarah. Poor Jennifer. No wonder Virginia was so worried about them.

"I still don't see why you were afraid I'd be angry at you," I said. "It was my dad's decision to leave us and come back up here. You didn't make him go. You didn't even tell him that you needed him. I might want to punch my dad right in the nose, but I'm not angry at you and the girls."

Virginia didn't seem to have heard me. She just looked at me with her watery, pale blue eyes. "Every month, he sent money down to Marta for you," she said. "At first it was just a few dollars, but that didn't last long. By the time the mill was five years old, he was sending her $500 a month."

Sheer rage surged through me. By the time the mill had been five years old, I would have been at least ten years old - and would have been in foster care for at least two years. With difficulty, I managed to keep my voice under control. "I don't think I ever saw any of that," I said, feeling like throttling my mother. "Mostly, we lived with my mother's boyfriends, and there never seemed to be any money around. My mom -" I paused, trying to tell the truth without giving anything away. "My mom isn't very good with money," I said.

Virginia was not fooled. "I imagine Marta is very good with money," she replied with a raised eyebrow.

"Well, she's not very good at keeping it around."

"She wasn't very good at keeping you around, either, was she?"

The question took the wind out of me. My sisters, clearly, had had no idea that I had been in foster care. But Virginia Carlson had not only known that I existed, but apparently had known that my mother had abandoned me. My scalp prickled. If she knew, then my father must have known, too.

"How did you know about that?" I demanded.

"Jackie found out. For years, Marta wouldn't let him see you. She told him that he upset you too much, so he stayed away. But one day he was in Seattle on business, and he just had to see you - even if only from a distance. He went to Marta's apartment and talked the landlady into letting him in." She had a ghost of a smile on her face. "Jackie could be very, very persuasive. He found Marta passed out in the bedroom and some hippie with long hair and tattoos sprawled there next to her. But you weren't there. He couldn't rouse Marta, so he talked to the landlady. She told him that Marta had never had a child living with her, that as far as she knew, Marta didn't have any kids. It took a while, but eventually he tracked you down. You were somewhere in Tacoma, as I understand it."

My heart was pounding. I was incandescent with rage. I suddenly surged to my feet. The frilly chair went crashing into the wall, and I bonked my head against a low-flying, Tiffany-looking lamp. The pain just made me even madder. "He knew?" I exploded. "He knew that I was in a foster home? He knew and he just left me there?"

Virginia Carlson may have been a lot of things, but a coward wasn't one of them. She looked up at me from her fluffy white pillows, set her jaw, and said, "He wanted to take you. He wanted to bring you up here with me and the girls."

"And the State wouldn't let him?" I demanded. Those damned rule-bound, unthinking, bureaucratic paper-pushers, I thought. My hatred of social workers in general and my caseworkers in particular boiled up again. I wondered what other atrocities they had committed under the guise of protecting my best interests.

Virginia didn't answer immediately. She seemed to be steeling herself. Then she looked me right in the eye and said, firmly, "No. I wouldn't let him."

Her answer knocked me back as if she had slapped me. "*What*?"

"I wouldn't let him bring you up here. He begged me. He cried. He had never cried before - not even when I left him, when we found out about Beth, or when his mother died. I told him that if he brought you anywhere near Bellingham, he would never see me or the girls again. I told him I would divorce him, I would ruin him, and I would make sure everyone in town knew about him and your mother. My family was still respected enough that we had been able to hush up most of the gossip, but I told him I would blow the whole scandal sky-high if he ever tried to get you out of that home. And I would have done it, too."

I had been too stunned to interrupt her. All I could think about were the years I had spent in foster care. I still bore a formidable collection of scars - inside and out.

One foster father had smashed my nose. Another had beaten me until the strap broke across my back. Still another had thrown me down a flight of concrete stairs.

But more than any of the beatings, what I remembered was how it felt to be superfluous, to be shuffled from one sad, cold, shabby home to another, to be left to the tender mercies of people who had to be paid to look after me. To be abandoned.

For years, I had dreamed about my father coming to rescue me. For years, I had looked for him in shopping malls, on busy streets, in every televised crowd. For years, I had waited for a Christmas card, a birthday card, for anything that would show me that even if he couldn't take care of me, he still cared about me. Nothing. Ten long years of nothing. Eternity to a child.

I struggled to get myself under control. All my usual tactics failed. I couldn't count to ten because a shriek of pain and fury rang in my ears, drowning out everything else. I couldn't take deep breaths because I had, inexplicably, ceased to breathe. I couldn't picture Virginia Carlson as an obstreperous opponent because she wasn't an obstreperous opponent. She was a mean, selfish, cold-hearted, manipulative, jealous old bitch, and it was all I could do to keep from striking her.

"Do you have any idea what you did?" I hissed at her. My voice sounded strangled and broken. "Do you have any idea what you put me through? Do you even have a clue of what it's like to be in a foster home?"

"I couldn't let him bring you up here," she replied, never taking her eyes from mine. "I couldn't let him put a boy I didn't know - a boy *he* didn't know - in with my girls. Especially with Beth."

"You were afraid of me?" I snapped at her. "You were afraid of a ten-year-old boy?"

"I was afraid of you and for you."

"*For me*?"

She was shaking, but her voice was firm. "I taught kindergarten for six years, Jack. I had never met a child I didn't like. But the thought of you - the thought of having you here day after day, of having to make your lunch and wash your socks while I knew everything that had gone on between Jackie and your mother -" She broke off and took a deep breath. When she looked back at me, there were tears in her eyes. "I was afraid I would hurt you."

For some reason, that just stoked the fires inside of me. I was not going to let her weasel out of what she had done by claiming that she had been worried about my welfare. I took a step toward her, and she clutched her bell in alarm. Without a struggle, I took it out of her hands. She cowered against her pillows. If I had sat on her, I would have killed her. I probably outweighed her by a hundred pounds. I got right in her face, and I made my voice stop shaking.

"Well, there were plenty of people who did it for you," I said.

I pushed up my sleeve and thrust my arm under her nose. The skin was puckered by a round, hollowed, unmistakable scar. "That's a cigarette burn," I hissed. "My foster father held me down, and my foster mother burned me because I was late for dinner." I made her look at my broken nose. I made her look at the gash above my eye. I told her about my busted ribs and my busted jaw and my dislocated shoulder.

"I'm sorry," she stammered. "I'm sorry, Jack."

I jerked back and towered over her. I let her take a good look at how big I was and how strong I was and how easily I could have hurt her. I had never hated anyone as much as I hated her right then.

"That's not enough," I said. Then I turned on my heel and strode out of the stifling bedroom.

I was halfway down the hall before I realized that I had gone out the wrong door. I had entered from the landing, but the door where I had exited led to a long corridor. There was no way in hell I was going to go back into Virginia Carlson's room, so I had no choice but to follow the hallway to its conclusion.

It concluded in a massive, messy bedroom overlooking the dark backyard and the glimmering sheet of Bellingham Bay. A mahogany chest of drawers was cluttered with keys, Kleenex, spare change, pens, breath mints, reading glasses, receipts, and scribbled notes - all the detritus that accumulates in a man's pockets every day and on his dresser every night. One drawer was open, and a single black sock was hanging out. Sheets, pillows, and a down comforter trailed from a rumpled brass bed.

A leather chair sat next to a magnificent roll-top desk, its pigeonholes crammed with dog-eared and curling papers. The seat of the chair was smooth and shiny. So was the center of a leather-upholstered bench at the foot of the bed. I could imagine the occupant of the room sitting there every morning, putting on his socks, then his pants, then his shoes. I could imagine my father sitting there.

Separate bedrooms. When I gashed my head on the lamp, I should have realized that a man my father's size could never have survived in Virginia Carlson's poisoned confection of a bedroom.

I wondered: Separate bedrooms because of her illness? Separate bedrooms because of their comfort? Separate bedrooms because they were rich enough to not give a damn? Separate bedrooms because they had remained, in a sense, separated, even though he had left my mother and returned to her? I looked around the well-worn, manly mess.

Just eight days before, my father had risen from his bed, pulled on his clothes, and left his room for the last time. I was eight days too late. I was too late to see the man I had waited for for ten years and hated for ten more. I was too late to let him explain himself to me, to apologize to me, to make me understand that he had wanted me, that he had always wanted me, but that he had had to choose the welfare of four daughters over the welfare of one son. To make me understand the greater good.

I don't know how long I stayed in my father's room. I seemed powerless to leave. Sarah found me sitting on the leather bench at the foot of his bed, my head in my hands. I heard the relief flooding into her voice as she walked into the room.

"There you are! We've been looking all over for -"

I raised my head, and she stopped at the sight of my face. She was beside me in a flash.

"Jack, what is it? What's the matter?"

I could only shake my head.

"Did something happen with Mama?"

I nodded.

"Can you tell me what it was?"

I shook my head again. I could muster no words to explain it to her. I couldn't even explain how I had ended up uninvited in her father's bedroom.

I said, "I'm sorry I came in here. I took a wrong turn. I'm lost."

Sarah put her arms around me and pulled me right against her. I could feel her heart thudding next to mine.

"No, you're not, Jack," she whispered to me. "You're not. You're not lost."

CHAPTER 12

That night I dreamed about my dad. I dreamed I was in his house again. This time, however, he was alive and well upstairs, and I was moving quietly around below, trying not to disturb him. I walked down the long hallway toward the back of the house and saw the parquet floor sparkling with shattered glass. I saw the brick that had smashed the window. I saw the plants, the flowered loveseat, the fireplace, the bright maple kitchen. As I neared the granite island, something tilted in my mind, and I started as if I could catch it. I woke with the distinct impression that I had seen something out of place at my father's house.

It was dark outside, but there was a glow across the hall. Harmony was up and talking on the phone. Was she speaking Japanese or English? I couldn't tell. Given the time - almost 6 a.m. - she could be saying good night to Higuro. He didn't like to go to sleep without hearing her voice.

"Jack?" Harmony had appeared at my doorway. I didn't need to hear anything else to know that something was wrong. Her voice was small and taut, and there was a little gasp or a crack in it that gave my name two syllables, maybe even three. I started up, bed clothes and all, and put my arms around her.

All I could think of was Higuro. I was so sure that something had happened to him that I just stared at her in confusion when she reached up to me and said, "Jack, that was Detective Anthony. You've got to get dressed. Someone tried to kill Virginia Carlson last night. She's in a coma, and the Bellingham Police want to talk to you. If you don't go up there voluntarily, they're going to get a warrant for your arrest."

I was so stunned that I just obeyed. While I pulled on my clothes, Harmony tried unsuccessfully to reach David Mann. David was the best criminal defense attorney in Seattle. He was also recovering from a massive heart attack. His doctor had ordered him to relax, and David had undertaken the task with the same blinding intensity that had given him the heart attack in the first place. Harmony tracked him and his family as far as Chesterman's Beach in British Columbia, but after that, they just disappeared. The Manns had left the country.

I sat on the couch and petted Betsy while Harmony bustled around putting her toys and snacks in an overnight bag. We were going to leave Betsy with Mrs. Anthony, Mark informed me carefully, in case we had to stay a few days in Bellingham.

"You mean in case *I* have to stay in Bellingham," I corrected him.

"If you stay, we all stay," he replied, as if that should have been obvious. We were on the road by half-past six.

I drove up with Detective Anthony, with Mark and Harmony following in her little red car. After a few miles of silence, Anthony cleared his throat.

"I know you know all this stuff, Jack. But since David's not around, and since you just woke up, it never hurts to be clear. You know you don't have to say anything to anyone. But whatever you do say, they can use against you."

Detective Anthony was sort of giving me the Miranda warnings. I was simultaneously touched and insulted. He really thought I was in trouble.

"It's OK, Detective Anthony," I told him. "I didn't do anything."

There was another silence while he thought that over. Then he nodded, and for the rest of the drive, filled me in on the little he knew about the assault on Virginia Carlson. Virginia's bedroom had been trashed, and she had scratches and bruises around her throat. Sarah had found her at 5:30 a.m., broken and insensible at the bottom of the stairs. I winced at the thought of Sarah, of her fear, her shock, her pain. Hadn't she been through enough already?

Then Anthony said something that made me shudder: "Your youngest sister was sitting next to her mother. Sarah told Lee she was trying to wake her up."

We pulled up in front of my father's Edgemoor estate. I had expected Anthony to take me straight to the police station, but Lee had requested my presence at the house instead. The scene of the crime, as he had put it. Both Anthony and Mark rocked back a little on their heels at the sight of the house, which looked even larger and more resplendent in the thin, grey morning light. Harmony didn't even seem to notice. She just took my hand and squeezed it tightly as we walked up to the door.

Inside, the hallway was thick with aftershave and the squeaky sound of policemen wearing too much leather. We couldn't get near the staircase, but I was relieved to see no apparent bloodstains on the shiny floor below. Maybe Beth really had thought that her mother was just asleep. Anthony said to a passing officer, "Please tell Sergeant Lee that Jack Hart is here."

Everyone in the hall suddenly shut up and swung toward me. Even the squeaking stopped. Six or seven police officers looked me over with undisguised suspicion. It seemed like a full minute passed before one of the officers broke ranks and approached me. He put his hand on my back in a proprietary fashion and propelled me around the assembled policemen and down a few slate steps beyond the main staircase. "This way," was his only explanation.

The moment I passed through the arched doorway, I understood why Sergeant Lee had elected to question me at my father's house. The room was vast and comfortable, but it was the painting over the fireplace that caught my attention, that held me fast.

It was a life-size painting of my dad, or someone I assumed to have been my dad, standing with his hand on the neck of a fawn-colored Great Dane. He was bending over a bit to pat the enormous dog, which meant he had to have been at least as tall or even taller than I was. He was wearing blue jeans and a brown leather jacket - as was I, I realized with a start. He had thick, straight, silver hair and bright and humorous blue eyes.

The dog was looking up at him, his head to one side, regarding him not with awe but with something akin to benign conspiracy. The two of them looked like they were enjoying a hell of a good private joke, out together for a romp on a crisp fall day.

"Is that him?" I asked the policeman, who was guiding me to a seat right in front of my father's portrait.

The officer threw me a scornful glance - "*as if you didn't know*," it said - but replied evenly, "That's Mr. Hart and Pilate. One of Mr. Hart's employees painted it for him after Pilate died."

I sat where the officer told me to and stared at the picture. I didn't even realize that Sergeant Lee had entered the room - until he plopped down in front of me and said, almost sorrowfully, "You just don't listen, do you, kid?"

It took me a moment to refocus from my father to the greying, bullet-faced sergeant. "Excuse me?"

"I warned you," Lee said. "I told you what would happen if you laid a finger on Virginia Carlson."

"I didn't lay a finger on Virginia Carlson," I replied, aiming for the same even, emotionless tone as the policeman who had ushered me into the room.

Lee glared at me before answering. "Well, every time you come to town, something awful happens to this family. I can spot a pattern when I see it."

With that, he snapped his head around and addressed the others in the room: "Who saw Jack come home last night?"

Mark and Harmony raised their hands, like they were in school. Lee dispatched Mark to give a statement to the uniformed officer, while he turned his attention to Harmony. She briefly outlined the events of the night before: I had arrived home around 12:30, soaking wet from fixing a blowout on the highway. After I had dried off and warmed up, I had spent about an hour telling her and Mark about my dinner with my half-sisters. Harmony had tucked me into bed at a quarter to two and stayed with me until I fell asleep. Then she had gone back to her own room, where she worked on a merger for Higuro until Detective Anthony called shortly before six. She had kept her door open, so Betsy could pad back and forth among the three of us, and she was sure I hadn't left my room at any time. She had checked on me twice during the night, and I had been asleep.

Sergeant Lee was skeptical. "So your story is that Jack never went anywhere during the night?" he challenged her.

"Yes."

He gave her a dangerous smile. "In my long experience of dealing with witnesses, Ms. Piper, you wouldn't be the first young lady to lie to keep her boyfriend out of trouble."

"Nothing in your long experience has prepared you for dealing with me, Sergeant," Harmony said.

He looked away from her and focused back on me: easier prey. After some initial wrangling over whether I was in custody and whether I had a right to have Harmony present as my attorney, Lee leaned forward and started questioning me.

He began with the chronology. I told him everything that had happened during and after dinner with my sisters. I told him about my eventful conversation with Virginia Carlson. I told him about taking the bell out of her hands.

"What time did you leave Bellingham?"

"Around 10:30."

"Why did it take you so long to get home?"

"I had a flat tire just before Edmonds. It took me a while to change it."

"Why didn't you limp into Edmonds and go to a gas station?"

"I know how to change a tire, Sergeant Lee," I said.

"Did anyone stop to help you?"

Two State Patrol troopers had pulled up right as I was replacing the hubcap: just after the nick of time. I told him that, and he immediately responded, "Did you get their names?"

"No. They just asked if I was all right and sent me on my way."

"*How convenient*," Lee sneered, in a tone that stirred Anthony to intervene.

"Can you describe the troopers, Jack?" Anthony asked.

I shut my eyes and did my best to picture them. It had been dark and rainy on the highway, but the troopers had been visible in the glare of their headlights. I described them as best as I could: one thin, younger man with a long, sad face, and one dark-haired, mustachioed man with a fleshy neck and the bearing of a proud and competent walrus.

"They all look something like that," Anthony said. "But let me make some calls." Anthony slipped out of the room as Mark slipped back in.

"Where's the flat tire now?" Lee asked me.

"In my trunk. Here." As I handed him my keys, Lee saw the gash where the jack had slipped and dug into my palm. He all but wriggled with excitement.

"How'd you get that?"

I explained. He didn't buy it. He handed my keys to the one of the uniformed officers. "Bag the jack, too," he instructed.

"I'll help you," Mark offered, rising from his seat beside me. "The trunk sticks a bit."

I almost smiled. The trunk didn't stick at all. Mark was going to supervise collection of the evidence, just to make sure nothing was added to or subtracted from what was actually in the car.

Lee turned his attention back to me. For what seemed like hours, he led me back and forth through the chronology of events, asking the same questions over and over, asking different questions in different contexts, trying to prod me to change my story. If I had been lying, he would have gotten me hopelessly confused. As it was, I breathed deep with relief when Lee dropped his head back and shrugged, as if in defeat. I was letting myself relax when someone moved in the still room, someone just out of my range of sight.

His shadow preceded him as he strolled to the fireplace. For one incredible moment, I thought he was my dad. He had the same height, the same build, as the man in the picture. But his hair was sparse and white instead of thick and silver, and his face was square instead of round. He stood there at the fireplace, half-smiling at me. Mark and Anthony, back from their various errands, tensed beside me. Harmony was motionless across the room, turned toward the man so I could see her only in profile. With her hair up and her eyes wide with surprise, she looked like she belonged on an ancient coin.

The man glanced up at my father's portrait and gave me the kindest look I remembered seeing from a stranger. He ambled over to the coffee table and sat down right in front of me. We were nose to nose. In as gentle a voice as could come from a great big, barrel-chested guy, he said, "Jack, did you ever think about hurting your dad?"

With that one question, I knew I was in the hands of a master. If I said no, I would be lying, and he would make me admit that I was lying. Of course I had thought about hurting my dad. You try being abandoned sometime, and you see whether popping your dad really hard in the nose doesn't cross your mind once or twice. But if I said yes, the man in front of me would treat it as a dangerous admission. I had thought about hurting him, after all. So when the opportunity presented itself to do just that, why wouldn't I have put my plans into practice - even to the point of murder?

I just looked at the smiling man in front of me. He repeated his question, and I braced myself. I lie only when it's truly unavoidable.

"Yes," I told him. "I've thought about hurting my dad."

Something flickered in the man's eyes, although his smile never faltered. "How were you going to hurt him?" he asked.

Another mind-bender of a question. The man had moved my admission one step further, from thinking about hurting my father to planning on hurting my father.

"I never got that far," I told him, truthfully.

"Why not?"

"Sorry?"

Another kind half-smile. "I know a little about you, Jack," the man said. "Your dad left you and your mother when you were five. Your mother put you in foster care when you were eight. And there you stayed until you were eighteen. That's no life for a little boy, Jack. No life at all. And then you come up here and you just happen to stumble across your dad. Living in a mansion. Coddling his daughters. Taking early retirement so he could look after his other family, when he couldn't be bothered even to call you on your birthday. It was your birthday last week, wasn't it, Jack?"

I nodded. I had celebrated my twenty-ninth birthday by taking a full day of depositions for American Fidelity. Leah Batson, the company's in-house counsel, had brought me a cupcake with one candle in it during a break. Harmony had called me from Japan, and Mark had called from home to wish me happy birthday. He had ticked off all the people who had sent me birthday cards: friends, clients, the Anthonys, miscellaneous police officers, former classmates, one of my football coaches, my favorite law school professor. My parents had been conspicuously absent from the list.

"Was it an accident, Jack?" The large man brought me back to the present.

I blinked at him in real confusion. "Was what an accident?"

"I don't think you meant to kill him. I don't think you had any idea how hard you hit him. You were just shocked, and hurt, and upset, and you let him have it. And when you realize you'd killed him, you panicked, and you had to make it look like he had been caught in a fire trying to destroy documents. But I don't for a minute think it was premeditated, Jack. Unless you force our hand, we're not going to go for first-degree murder."

Big of you, I thought. I sighed and stretched. "Look, I haven't seen my dad for twenty-four years. I'm not even sure I would have recognized him if I had seen him. I didn't know he was up here. I didn't know he owned the mill. I didn't know he had another family. And I didn't kill him. I didn't touch him. I didn't even know him."

I was ready to end the discussion right there, but the man in front of me had other ideas. He started reading back the notes of the conversation I had recounted with Virginia Carlson, making me listen to all those barbs and slights again. I flinched when he got to the part about Virginia's forbidding my dad to bring me up to Bellingham.

"So she made sure you stayed in foster care?"

I nodded.

"And she made sure your father stayed away from you?"

I nodded again.

"But you're telling us that you didn't try to hurt her?"

I nodded once more.

"OK, Jack," the large man said, "after hearing all that from her, after realizing after all those years that she was the reason you went through so much, how did you *keep* from hurting her?"

I thought that over. Aside from football and the odd clearly provoked defense, I had never been closer to hurting another person than I had the night before. Every bit of me had ached with the violence inside. Even in the cold light of day, even knowing that I was the prime suspect in her attempted murder, the thought of Virginia Carlson made my heart race with anger. "I'm not sure," I said, making my voice sound as even as possible. "I just wasn't going to let her take anything else away from me."

The large man was quiet, waiting for me to fill the cavernous room with nervous babble. I was not going to fall for that trick, which I had learned at Piper Whatcom under Harmony's tutelage. I just looked back at him and let the silence build.

When Anthony's cellphone rang, every one of us jumped. Anthony answered, asked a couple of questions, and handed the phone to Sergeant Lee. Then he turned to the large man opposite me and said, "That's the State Patrol. The troopers logged Jack's blowout. They remember him, and they back up his story. Jack was changing a tire just outside of Edmonds at midnight."

Lee was hissing into the phone - "Are you sure? How can you be sure? Why are you so sure?" - but the large man seemed unperturbed. "So?" he said to Anthony.

"So, you told me yourself that Sarah took her mother some pain pills at midnight. Now you've got two unimpeachable witnesses who say that at midnight Jack really was on his way home like he said he was, that he was all the way to Edmonds. It's at least an hour's drive from Edmonds to Bellingham, even if you speed. And you've got two more witnesses and several of Jack's snoopy neighbors who say that Jack got home at 12:30 and didn't leave again. There was no time for Jack to get back here and attack Mrs. Hart. No time at all." He put his hand on my shoulder and started to rise. "I think we'll be going now."

The large man opened his mouth, but whatever he was saying was drowned by the arrival of my sisters. Three of them, at least. Marianne, Emily, and Sarah suddenly clattered into the room from a doorway near the fireplace. Marianne took one look at me and burst into tears. She threw her arms around my neck and collapsed into my arms. Emily was right behind her, although she - somewhat tactically, I suspected - collapsed into Mark's arms. Sarah just stood on the other side of the coffee table, head bowed and hands slunk deep in her pockets. She looked across at me and said, "Thank you for coming, Jack. Thank you so much."

My sisters' display of affection served only to antagonize the two policemen. The large man lost his kindly look, and Lee seemed ready to explode.

"This isn't exactly a condolence call, Sarah," the large man snapped. "Jack's here to see me, not you. And not by choice, either. If the Seattle Police hadn't brought him up here, we would have gotten a warrant to arrest him."

"*Arrest* him?"

All three of my sisters were momentarily shocked out of their grief. Even Emily forgot to cling to Mark, who capitalized on the moment by seating her on the couch and stepping a few feet out of reach. Without seeming to notice that Mark was gone, Emily demanded, "Arrest him for what?"

"For the murder of your father and the attempted murder of your mother," Lee said. The last word was almost lost in my sisters' gasps.

"That's ridiculous," Marianne insisted, keeping a tight hold on me. "Jack's a sweetheart. He's darling. He wouldn't hurt a fly."

"He couldn't have done anything anyway," Sarah chimed in. "He left at 10:30, and Mama was fine at midnight. I told you so myself."

"And besides, what possible reason could Jack have for killing Daddy? Or attacking Mama?" Emily spoke from the couch. "It doesn't make any sense."

The large man and Lee exchanged a look of triumph. "I'm afraid it does, Emily," Lee said, almost gloating. "We talked to your parents' lawyer this morning. Your father apparently never got around to telling you this, but he and your mother divided up their community property about eighteen months ago. Your mother's will leaves everything she had to the four of you, in equal shares. But your father's will leaves everything he owned - everything, Emily: the mill, the lodge, even the house - to none other than Jack Hart Junior."

"*What*?" This time, I joined my sisters' exclamations. We were all staring open-mouthed at Lee, who nodded with grim satisfaction.

"You heard me," he said. "Everything goes to Jack. Your mother can stay in the house for as long as she lives, but after last night, that's not likely to be very long." He jerked his head toward me. "Thanks to that little sweetheart over there, Marianne. One of Jack's law school classmates is an associate in the lawyer's office. We think that's how Jack found out about the will. He knew he was coming into money, all right. Your father wasn't even buried when Jack suddenly quit his job."

Marianne dropped her arms from my neck. She looked from Lee to me and back again. The shudder that went through her threatened to knock her off her feet, but when I stepped forward to catch her, she sprang back in alarm. Marianne was still staring at me in horror when Emily attacked me from behind. Her elbow ground into the back of my knee as she launched herself off the couch. She started smacking my arm and shoulder, punctuating each slap with sobbing, angry accusations:

"You killed him. You killed Daddy. And then you came up here and you pretended -" Her voice failed in a wave of sobs. "You made us like you, but you killed him. And Mama. You tried to kill Mama. Were you going to kill us, too? Or did you just want to laugh at us, Jack? The whole time we were hugging you and eating with you and being so glad we found you, you were just playing with us."

Emily hit me one last time, a vicious, stinging slap that probably hurt her a lot more than it hurt me. Then she stumbled out of the room, her hands over her face, as if she couldn't bear to look at me. Marianne followed her, still stony with shock. She didn't even glance at us as she left.

I made myself turn to Sarah. She was ashen and shaking. She folded her arms across her chest, as if she were trying to hold herself together. She didn't take her eyes off mine. It was like she was searching for something I couldn't give her. Then she turned around and headed out of the room. I kept waiting for her to stop, to turn around, even to look back over her shoulder. But she didn't. She just kept on going. I heard her footsteps on the stone stairs, on the wood floor, on the thick carpet. I heard her footsteps going away.

There was a long silence after Sarah's footsteps finally faded. Mark, Harmony, and Anthony were staring at me the way you look at a falling glass right before it hits the floor. I turned back to the policemen, who were red and radiant, barely able to contain their glee at how effectively they had alienated me from my sisters.

"Don't leave town, Jack," the large policeman said. "Anthony will tell us where you're staying, and we'll be checking on you. You try to get away, and you'll be a guest of Whatcom County before you know it." With that, he and Lee sauntered from the room.

I took a deep breath. It seemed to snag on all the shards inside me. "Let's get out of here," I said.

Harmony hugged me and kissed me. "It's going to be OK, Jack," she whispered in my ear. Mark patted me on the back, and Anthony put his arm around me. I stole one last look at my father's portrait and let Anthony guide me out of the big, comfortable cave of a room. We were almost to the front door when I heard Sarah's voice behind us. "Jack?"

She was about ten feet from me, leaning against the staircase as if she didn't dare come any closer. But she said, "Jack? Can I talk to you?"

Mark, Harmony, Anthony, and I all stepped forward. My bodyguards. Sarah dropped back and put up her hand. "I can't take all four of you right now," she said. "Just Jack."

Alone in the nicest mudroom known to man, Sarah faced me, chin out, eyes blazing, arms still folded tightly across her chest. Her voice was low and broken, but her gaze never faltered.

"Did you kill my father?" she demanded.

"No, Sarah, I did not."

"Did you attack my mother?"

"No, Sarah, I did not."

Again that searching stare, scouring me for something I didn't have. Then I saw the tears rise in her eyes, and she choked and ducked her head. Some women look fetchingly helpless when they cry. Sarah was not one of those women. Her eyes were red, her nose was pink, and she snuffled into her sleeve. Hesitantly, and protecting my midsection in case she too decided to attack, I raised one hand and patted her shoulder. She groaned and snuffled harder, but she didn't pull away.

"If you're lying -"

"I'm not lying."

"If you're lying," she tried again, "then just take anything you want, Jack. Take the house, take the money, take everything. Just take it and leave us alone. Because I can't stand to lose anyone else. Losing Scott was bad enough. And we knew Mama was coming to the end, but not like this. And Daddy - Daddy -" She couldn't finish. She sobbed a dreadful, rasping sob and rubbed her hands over her face. "I can't stand to lose you, too."

I pulled her to me and rested my chin on top of her head.

"You're not going to lose me," I said into her hair. "And you don't have to be afraid of me. Sarah, I'm for real."

CHAPTER 13

Let me state right here that I was a civil litigator. I did no transactional work, I did no tax law, and heaven knows I did no estate planning. In fact, I knew just enough about trusts and estates to pass the Washington state bar exam. That meant I knew nothing whatsoever about trusts and estates.

Harmony was also a civil litigator, but she had the advantage of a lifetime as a trust fund baby and a year as in-house counsel of a multi-national conglomerate. After reviewing the documents Sarah produced from the family safe and calling the Washington Secretary of State, we were pretty sure of only one thing: I was in medium-deep shit.

When he bought the company, my father had formally incorporated the mill. That's why he hadn't shown up on any of the discovery. As far as the mill had been concerned, my dad and his family had just been shareholders of the closely held corporation. Unfortunately, since my dad had retired, the people running the place had paid little attention to niceties like corporate governance. A corporation needs care and feeding, like any other critter. Without that, the corporation dies. Several years back, the state of Washington had dissolved the mill's incorporation for unpaid license fees and failure to file annual reports.

All that meant several things, all bad. One, as heir to my dad's interest in the mill, I was now directly adverse to American Fidelity in the lawsuit against which I had been defending them. Two, even worse, I was now in the chain of title of the mill - and therefore potentially liable for the environmental damage it caused. And three, to make matters even more complicated, my father had named me trustee of my sisters' interests in the mill. I had 50%; they had 50% between them - but I controlled their votes.

I mentally estimated the value of my inheritance: the Edgemoor mansion, a vacation lodge in the San Juan Islands, several boats, and an interest in a paper mill that was hemorrhaging money and teetering on the brink of bankruptcy.

I knew the kind of numbers involved in the mill's share of the environmental cleanup of Bellingham Bay. You could throw a couple of million dollars at the problem and, literally, have the impressive impact of spitting in the ocean. All told, it looked like it could be a lot worse than a wash.

A squeak from the other side of the table roused me from my calculations. Sarah laid down the will. "So he did leave you the house," she said. "When do you want us to move out?"

I started to explain about probate and life estates and all the other legal reasons she didn't need to worry. Then I looked into her eyes and saw the fear that craves assurance, not analysis.

"I've got a house, Sarah," I said. "I don't need yours."

"But it's not ours anymore. Daddy wanted you to have it."

"Your dad drafted this will when you and Scott were living over on Fairhaven and Emily had her own apartment," I reminded her. "He just never got around to updating it after Scott died and you moved home. There's no way he would have passed your house out from under you."

"But he did." I could hear the ache of betrayal in her voice. With everything she learned about her dad, she was losing him again and again, losing what she had believed about him, losing what she had believed about herself. I had lost my father twice, and that was bad enough, but Sarah had had so much more of him that now she had so much more to lose.

I couldn't stand the pain in her face. "It will be OK, Sarah," I told her, squeezing her hand. "I won't do anything to hurt you. I promise."

She squeezed back and seemed a little comforted, even allowing me to shepherd her and Jennifer upstairs so they could get some rest. I caught a glimpse of Virginia's room as we turned onto the landing. The door was open, and the interior dazzled under unnaturally bright lights. In the stage-like glare, uniformed officers and criminalists were painstakingly dismantling and collecting the wreckage that just the night before had been Virginia's stifling but tidy bedroom. Crushed red velvet curtains seeped obscenely across the tangled white bedclothes, drawers stood empty and upended like headstones, and shards of glass covered the floor between the bed and the door.

Here and there I recognized bits of the crystal bell that I had taken from Virginia's hands so I could yell at her without interruption. Despite myself - despite my innocence - I couldn't keep my eyes off the glass on the floor. I wondered whether any of those shards were big enough to bear my fingerprints.

Sarah invited us to stay at the Edgemoor house, but the air was so heavy with shock and suspicion that we went looking for a bed and breakfast on South Hill. We almost ended up in the old town brothel - a large Victorian affair that still bore the purple paint once used to attract sailors docking in Bellingham Bay. But right across the street was a white clapboard house with lace curtains, a lavender hedge, and a brass door plaque that read, "Beware: Spoiled Rottweiler Lives Here." After making friends with said Rottweiler - a wonderful slobbery fellow named Bear, who wore a red bandanna and liked grapes - I showed the B&B owner a picture of Betsy and provided her with a carefully edited description of Betsy's charms.

Karen, the owner, seemed enthusiastic about the thought of hosting Betsy, and I called Mrs. Anthony with the happy news. She would bring Betsy up after school the next day, she assured me, and take Detective Anthony home. Someone had to investigate that suspicious death down by the Kingdome. Until they cleared the case, Detective Anthony and Mark would take turns staying with me in Bellingham.

Bear the Rottweiler and I crashed in the upstairs bedroom overlooking the dark, glittery bay. I fell asleep almost immediately. Images of bombs and dogs, fire and glass, rain and flowers gradually shifted and solidified into the same dream I had had that morning.

I dreamed I was in my father's house, moving quietly so as not to bother him, knowing that he was alive and well upstairs. I passed the open door, my cold, blood-stained sister, the glass-strewn parquet floor. So much glass. As I neared the granite island, something caught my eye, twisted me, took me out of the dream. I woke with the same impression - even stronger this time - that I had seen something out of place at my father's house.

I stared up at the ceiling, my arm around the dog, unwilling to risk that dream again, unwilling to risk going back inside that room. My thoughts chased each other, tumbling over each other. Whether he meant to or not, my father's will stranded me in a corporate and ethical tangle. The mill's only hope of survival was to force American Fidelity to pay for the state-ordered cleanup. As trustee of my sisters' interests in the mill, I had a fiduciary duty to press the lawsuit. But I also had an ethical duty never to be adverse to a former client on the matter for which I had represented them. Ethically, I couldn't continue the suit against American Fidelity, and ethically, I couldn't let it go. No matter which way I turned, I was breaking a fiduciary obligation. I could get suspended from practice. I could get disbarred.

I flopped over in bed, much to Bear's annoyance. *Did my dad know he was handing me the biggest mess of my life?* I wondered. *Did he even care? Was he just dumping on me, or did he want to have something to give me when his wife died and it was safe for him to contact me?*

I tried to think myself back into my dad's state of mind when he made the will, tried to visualize what he was trying to do. It had been so easy when I had comforted Sarah that afternoon, so easy for me to tell her that her dad couldn't possibly have intended for her to lose her home. But now I couldn't even picture my father, let alone fathom what he must have been thinking about me. There were just too many dads for me to keep straight. The person I knew, or thought I knew - an impatient man who had an affair with a student, left his kid with a drug-addicted teenager, and took off - was rapidly receding. I couldn't square him with the man who adored his daughters and granddaughters, who sent my mother $500 a month back when $500 really was $500, who begged his wife to let him bring me up to Bellingham, who cried when she refused.

Somebody was lying. That was the only conclusion I could reach. But who it was and why and what escaped me. I closed my eyes and felt Bear creep closer as I relaxed.

The next morning, after Mark and Detective Anthony set out to talk to as many cops as possible, Harmony and I sat in the car and tried to figure out what to do. After waiting several minutes for me to turn the key, she took my hand.

"You can just walk away, you know," she said.

"You mean disclaim the inheritance?"

She nodded. "I think you can disclaim in whole or in part. So you could pass on the mill and take the rest of the assets, although the mill's creditors might have a claim on you for contribution to the environmental cleanup. Or you could just disclaim completely. You never would have been in the mill's chain of title. You'd have no environmental liability. Your sisters couldn't complain of breach of fiduciary duty, and American Fidelity couldn't accuse you of conflict of interest."

She was right, of course. The best way to get out of a box is not to go into the box in the first place. And if someone's trying to put you in a box, you can always say no. At least, you can if you don't desperately want what's in that box.

When I didn't answer, Harmony put her hand on my knee.

"We have plenty of money, Jack," she said.

The "we" in that sentence was a bit premature. She was the timber heiress, not me. And we'd only been dating two months. "It's not the money, Harmony. Not just the money, anyway. It's just that -" I stopped and swallowed, not sure I wanted to tell her what I was thinking, what I had been thinking since I heard about the inheritance in the first place. "It's just that I want to have something from him. I deserve *something.*"

"You deserve a lot more than that."

"And, it's also - it's like he wanted me to do something for him. Like he was entrusting things to me - the house, the mill, my sisters. It's like all of a sudden I'm the head of the family."

"Do you want to be head of this family? This family may be a bit of a handful."

I looked out over the steering wheel at Bellingham Bay, oyster-colored under a dove-grey sky. Lummi Island was barely visible, a misty hummock on the horizon. Only a slight darkening of the fog betrayed the existence of the other San Juan Islands, where my father had left me a vacation lodge. I thought how easy it would be to start the car and drive back to Seattle, assuming I didn't get arrested on the way. I could go back to my little Green Lake house; I could go back to work at Piper Whatcom; I could ask Harmony to marry me. I could have the life I knew, the life I wanted, the life I knew I wanted. Sarah and I could exchange Christmas cards each year until one or both of us forgot. I would never know - never have to know - what was out there in that fog.

"I want a family, Harmony," I said, and the minute the words left my mouth, I felt the sureness of them. "I don't necessarily want to be the head of the family, but I want a family. I want Sarah and Marianne and Emily and Beth as my sisters. I want to help them through this. They're in the chain of title for the mill, too. I don't want them to lose everything they own. I don't want them to face this by themselves. I don't want them to be so sad and afraid."

I took a deep breath and rubbed my eyes. "I want to fix this," I told her. "I want to make this better."

Harmony leaned over as far as her seatbelt would allow and kissed me. Her lips barely brushed mine before the seatbelt pulled her back. I had the sudden, strange sensation of losing her too. "Well, then," she said, "we had better get to work."

We headed downtown, discussing strategy along the way.

Fact-finding first. The plan was to call on each of the mill's executives and sound them out about their plans for the American Fidelity litigation. Unfortunately, Kirk Carder shut the door in my face. We waited for an hour outside Clark Swanson's office at the Port of Bellingham - pretending to be fascinated by an architect's model of a new waterfront hotel - until his secretary told us he was tied up all that day and the rest of the week. By the time we arrived at Mike Saunders' campaign storefront on Commercial Street, I was choking down the exasperation.

When the tiny blond secretary - who was barely visible behind her "Vote Mike" button - protested that Mr. Saunders could not be disturbed, I informed her that I was demanding my legal right to examine the books, records, and minutes of Squalicum Paper Products. To turn up the heat, I handed her a ferociously legal-looking document, which Harmony and I had created at the public library not ten minutes earlier - full of whereases and heretofores and frightening cites to the Revised Code of Washington. We were in Mike Saunders' office within 30 seconds.

Mike had the easy, practiced smile of a man who has faced one too many television cameras. His teeth were very fine: white, straight, and expensive. He flashed them like punctuation marks at the end of every sentence, as if cued by an invisible producer.

"Jack, you can't imagine how much I would like to be able give you that information," he said, smiling broadly, "but what with the fire and everything, I just can't."

"Are you saying that SPP's records were destroyed in the blaze?" I asked.

Mike's smile flickered. "Well, no," he admitted.

"Then I need to see them," I pressed.

"Jack, you've got to realize what's been going on around here lately." He shot me such a sincere look that I almost believed him. Mike Saunders was going to be one hell of a politician. "People are shocked and grieving; our old offices are a shambles; and even in our new place - which is where we keep minutes and the rest - some stuff got soaked by the firehoses. Our folks are moving boxes back and forth, we're trying to sort things out, but Jack, I'll level with you: we can't meet your request right now."

"I see," I said. "So essentially, everything's just such a mess that you know you've got the records, but you don't know what condition they're in or where they are."

"Exactly." Mike beamed, grateful that I was smarter than I looked.

"All right." I tapped my fingers together. "Thank you for your time, Mike. You don't need to scare up the records for me."

Mike beamed even more brightly. Soon he would be rid of us and back in the thick of the election. He had votes to garner, speeches to make, babies to kiss.

He was half out of his chair and starting to say how much he looked forward to working with me when I added, "I'll just go look for them myself."

Now Mike was completely out of his chair. All pretenses of smiles were gone. I felt Harmony tense beside me. Getting in a fight with Mike over the mill's records had not been our original plan. We just wanted access so we could talk to him about the lawsuit. "No, Jack, you absolutely cannot do that."

"Why not?"

"Well, it's not safe, for one thing."

"You just said that your 'folks' were moving boxes back and forth," I pointed out. "I'm sure you wouldn't put your own employees in danger. So it must be safe." I got to my feet and held out my hand. "We'll just go help them out."

"You do, and I will have you both arrested for trespassing."

"Then I'll get a court order compelling production of the documents, and I'll go in with a sheriff and seize them."

"A little overeager, aren't you, Jack? A lot of people might find that pretty suspicious - throwing your weight around, trying to take things over when your father isn't even cold."

Not the most tactful way of describing a man who died in a fire. At least now we were talking to the real Mike Saunders. I was a head taller than he was, and when I leaned forward, he stepped back. "Well, I think it's suspicious that you don't want anyone to look at the mill's records," I said. "You gotta think, what's he trying to hide?"

I drew out the last words carefully, giving myself plenty of time to gauge his reaction. I needn't have bothered. You couldn't miss the muscle that twitched in his cheek, the bulging of his eyes, the bobbing of his Adam's apple. He was such a singularly unattractive man.

"Get the hell out of my office," he said. "And stay the hell away from the mill."

Out on the street, Harmony and I both took a deep breath.

"Well, that was interesting - " Harmony began, but she was cut off by a friendly voice behind us.

"Hey, Jack!" someone said, punching me on the shoulder and slapping something into my hand, "Happy Birthday!"

I looked down, puzzled, into an unfamiliar face, which zigged immediately down the street. Then my gaze fell on the sheaf of papers I was holding, papers with a familiar numbered margin and a caption from the Whatcom County Superior Court.

I had never been personally served before.

"What is it?" Harmony asked, as I flicked through the pages.

I avoided her eyes. "It's a motion by my sisters to disqualify me as trustee of their interests in the mill, based on conflict of interest."

Harmony slipped her hand into mine. "Sarah too?"

I made myself look at the caption again, then looked away quickly, stung.

"Sarah too."

CHAPTER 14

I'm not sure exactly what I would have done at that moment if Betsy had not arrived - *Canis ex Machina* - on the scene. Before I could organize or even prioritize the cuss words that were storming into my mind, I heard her deep and vibrant bark behind me.

I turned just as she crashed into my arms. The pages of my sisters' motion flew everywhere, and Betsy trampled them with muddy paws as she squealed and danced from foot to foot. I gave her a rapturous ear rub, scooped her up in my arms, and hoisted all 95 pounds of her into the air. She licked my face and wriggled like a puppy until I put her down. She immediately rolled over at Harmony's feet, looking irresistibly winsome. Harmony bent down to rub her belly.

"Jack, I am so sorry!" A red-faced Mrs. Anthony chugged into view. "Betsy and I caught sight of you as we turned onto Commercial Street. I rolled down the window to call to you, and suddenly she just shot out of the car. I tried to stop her, but, well, you know. She's incorrigible." She enveloped me in a bear hug, then held me at arm's length and looked me over. "How are you holding up?"

"I'm fine," I said automatically, but with a dull note that I couldn't quite keep out of my voice. Mrs. Anthony's gaze fell briefly on Harmony, and I saw - or thought I saw - Harmony give her the smallest possible shake of her head. Then Harmony bent over Betsy, who was sprawled all over the court papers, eyes closed, the very picture of contentment. "Thanks for bringing Betsy, Mrs. Anthony. I really needed to see her."

The arrival of Mark and Detective Anthony cut off further discussion of my well-being. Betsy greeted them both ecstatically. While I transferred Detective Anthony's luggage from my trunk to his, Harmony gathered up the court papers and tucked them into her purse. "We'll need to respond," was her only comment. I noticed Mark's eyes on her and the motion, but he didn't ask.

"I'm a phone call away, Jack," Detective Anthony said as he got in the car. "If you need me for anything, I'll be up here in 90 minutes. In the meantime, Mark and

I have done our best to talk some sense into the cops up here. I think we made some headway. Just remember: Until this is resolved, you're never alone. If anything else happens, I want to make sure you've got (a) an alibi, and (b) protection. Got that?"

"Got it," I said, and the Anthonys were gone.

"Looks like I'm your shadow from now on. I'll take a couple days' vacation until we can take you home," Mark said, removing Betsy's front paws from his shoulders. They had been standing nose to nose. "So where to?"

After a brief discussion, we headed over to the mill. I couldn't get Mike Saunders' feral, frightened face out of my mind. Whatever he had been up to, I wanted to figure it out, and I wanted to figure it out right then. So the four of us - one nominally on a leash - walked up to the mill just as the sun was starting to dip toward the bay, elongating all the buildings with charcoal shadows.

There was no obvious entrance to the mill itself. We wandered around until we spotted a hand-lettered piece of cardboard tacked to the fence: "Office Temporarily Moved to Warehouse 1. Enter at Your Own Risk." We climbed a couple of flights of concrete stairs and found ourselves in front of a squat cinderblock building with more than a few broken windows. Then we walked around the building, trying to find the door. As we rounded the corner of the warehouse, Betsy balked and Harmony caught her breath.

Before us was the site of the fire. We had driven up from the other direction, where the wreckage had been hidden by the mill. But from the higher plane of the warehouse, nothing blocked our view. We were right over the shell of the building where my father had died. Its ribs and beams were blackened and broken, fallen in on themselves like a clutched, dead spider. A scar of soot shot three stories high on the wall of the nearby plant.

The walkway stopped a few yards before the burnt-out building. There was a sheer drop of fifteen to twenty feet from the level of the warehouse to the belly of the wreckage, and the four of us stood on that precipice and stared. I spotted the cracked remains of the concrete trestle that once had connected the office building to the warehouse walkway. It was listing at an apologetic angle, looking like one of the Lake Washington floating bridges right before it sank. I also spotted bits and pieces of what had been a modern office less than two weeks before. A chair here, wiring there. A banker's lamp. And boxes. Lots and lots of boxes. They were charred and crushed, but they were definitely boxes.

"Hey, get away from there!"

The four of us turned toward a ruddy, bearded man wearing work boots and overalls. He waved his hands at us as if he'd like to box our ears. "What are you, more reporters? A man died in there, you know. It's not some freaking carnival to us. What more do you think you can wring out of it, you -"

His voice stopped suddenly, as if someone had switched him off. He looked from me to Betsy and back again.

I put out my hand. "I'm Jack Hart," I said. I added, unnecessarily, "Mr. Hart's son."

The bearded man was a shade less ruddy than he had been before. He swallowed, deliberated, then shook my hand. "I should have known by the dog," he said. "Your dad brought Pilate to work with him a lot. We used to joke about putting him on the payroll." He hmmmed uncomfortably for a moment. "I'm Dave West. I'm the foreman on the first shift."

After I made the appropriate introductions, Dave gave us a thirty-second orientation to our whereabouts. He pointed out the entrances to the mill and the warehouses. Then he turned around, jerked his head toward the burnt-out building, and said, "That's - well, I guess you've figured out what that is."

We were drawn back to the edge of the precipice. "Where was my dad's office?"

"Second floor," Dave said promptly. "He could see out over the bay." He pointed to something that looked like a claw sticking out of the debris. "That's his chair. Or what's left of it." All you could see was its inverted, twisted, three-wheeled base.

"What was on the third floor of this building?" Mark asked.

"Um, I'm not sure," Dave said.

"What's in all those boxes?" Harmony asked, pointing.

Dave didn't seem to have heard her, so I repeated the question. "All those boxes," I said helpfully, pointing out the ones closest to us. "What's in them? You can see something blue where some of them are torn, but - *Betsy*!"

Her leash burned through my grasp. She was over the edge of the precipice before I could process the sting of my hand and the valedictory wave of her tail. The three of us crowded on the edge of the walkway, trying to coax her back. She paid us no attention whatsoever. She just picked her way gracefully down the broken concrete trestle, skidding a little at the bottom.

Then she wandered over to one of the boxes that Harmony and I had been pointing to. Her tail was wagging furiously, which had to mean she was inflicting some grievous bodily harm on that box. Sure enough, the box split suddenly, and a small blue sea flowed out on the blackened rubble. We were too far away to make out what it was.

Betsy took her time coming back to us, our commands, threats, and endearments notwithstanding. Finally she trotted back up the broken bridge and leapt the last few feet to the walkway. She was sooty and triumphant, and she had something in her mouth. After some negotiating, she let me take it from her.

It was a book. A blue book. On the front cover, an eagle was clutching clawsful of dollars, hovering over the red, white, and blue lettering of the title: The American

Way: Why and How U.S. Business Can Lead the Global Economy. In a less colorful but no less conspicuous typeface were the names of the authors: Michael Saunders and Gary Kendall, Ph.D.

Michael Saunders of the fine teeth. Michael Saunders of the feral face. Michael Saunders, the mill's vice president, who just happened to be running for Congress. Who just happened to be terrified at the thought of my poking around the mill.

Gary Kendall was my sister Marianne's ineffectual-looking but professorial husband. And together they had written a book.

I looked back over the wreckage of my father's office. All the boxes were identical - same size, same shape. I looked at the sea of blue spilling from the box that Betsy had shredded.

If all those boxes were full of Michael's and Gary's book, there must have been hundreds of copies down there.

Thousands.

CHAPTER 15

It just wasn't Dave's day. First he had accosted us without realizing that I was one of the new owners of the mill. Then we had grilled him about Betsy's strange discovery in the burnt-out rubble. Were all those boxes full of Michael Saunders' and Gary Kendall's books? we asked him. And if so, why?

"Look, I really don't know anything about those boxes," Dave insisted weakly, mopping his forehead with his sleeve.

"Had you ever seen them before today?" Mark asked.

"Well, yes," Dave admitted.

"When?"

"I don't know. They were just always there on the third floor of the office building."

"Not ten minutes ago, you told us you weren't sure what was on the third floor of that building," Harmony said. "Were you lying then, or are you lying now?"

Under normal circumstances, I would have felt sorry for Dave. I knew from recent personal experience that it was no fun being questioned by a homicide detective, let alone by a homicide detective in cahoots with two attorneys. But my ears were ringing with Mark's description of how my father died. *It's possible that your dad deliberately set the blaze*, he had said, *that it went up faster than he expected, and that the ceiling came down, hit him on the head, and killed him before there was a lot of smoke.*

Just from where I was standing, I could count about fifty of those big, charred boxes. If the ceiling had come down faster than my dad had expected, I figured we didn't need to look much further to find the reason. Books are heavy. Not only would their extra weight have brought the ceiling down, but they would have crushed anything or anyone below. You might survive being hit by a ceiling tile, or even a beam, but even one big box of books easily could have killed my dad.

I turned toward Dave. I wasn't mad at him personally, but it was impossible to keep the anger out of my voice. "I'm going to assume until proven otherwise that all those boxes are full of this book," I said, shaking the unfortunate volume at him. "And I'm going to assume until proven otherwise that my dad had no idea that he had a whole library hanging over his head if and when he set that fire. Now the only thing I'm not going to assume is who's responsible for there being thousands and thousands of copies of this book stuffed on the third floor of my dad's office building. But if you don't want me to assume that you had something to do with it, then I suggest you tell me everything you know, right here and right now."

Mark and Harmony both looked at me with surprise. I was not, as a rule, a confrontational person, at least as litigators went. Harmony had been my mentor at Piper Whatcom, and she had trained me in her own style: courteous, calm, and persistent. I knew that left to her own devices, Harmony could have wormed every last detail out of Dave, either by giving him a shoulder to cry on or by subjecting him to such unnerving silences and knowing stares that he would confess to anything just to make it stop. But I did not have time for Harmony to weave her magic spell. I wanted to know what was going on, and I wanted to know right then. And I'll confess to the slightest bit of ego as well. If there had been some hanky-panky at the mill - and all my instincts were telling me there had - then I wanted to be the person to root it out. I wanted to be the person to avenge my dad.

I fixed Dave with my most piercing glare. "So what's it going to be?" I said. "You either get on board or you get run over. Because I am not going to let this go."

"Look. I'm telling you the truth. I really don't know anything."

"But you suspect," I said.

"I suspect," he admitted, after a pause.

"What do you suspect?"

"I could lose my job," he said.

"If things keep going the way they have been, everyone's going to lose their jobs."

"Mr. Saunders wrote that book about two years ago. Nothing much happened with it, at least as far as I could tell. He and Marianne Hart's husband - that weenie guy -"

"Gary Kendall?" I interjected.

"Yeah. Mr. Saunders and Gary had a big book signing up here, and all the employees got copies instead of a Christmas bonus, but that was about it. But when Mr. Saunders announced that he was running for Congress, all his fliers and his TV spots said that he was a best-selling author, that that book of his had hit the top of The New York Times' best-seller list. The boxes had been arriving for a while, and that's when people started to put two and two together. Just because someone's buying a lot of books doesn't mean anybody has to read them, you know what I mean?"

I stared into the burnt-out building. There were fifty or so boxes of books down there; a lot of books, certainly, but probably not enough to create a nation-wide best-seller. "Where are the other boxes?"

"Warehouse 1 and Warehouse 2," Dave said, jerking his head toward the buildings behind us. "Everyone's pretty freaked out to go in there. They think if the books brought down the roof in the office building -" He broke off, coughed, and looked away. No wonder the sign to Warehouse 1 said "Enter at Your Own Risk."

"Dave, go get everyone out of the warehouses," I said. "Everyone. Tell them we're evacuating the place until we can have the buildings inspected. And tell the office manager or the accounts payable manager or whoever would have kept the purchase records on these books that I want to talk to him or her pronto - and before he or she calls Mike Saunders for direction."

Armed with invoices and flanked by Mark, Harmony, and a supremely self-satisfied Betsy, I reappeared in Mike Saunders' office. I plopped the offending volume on the desk in front of him, enjoying the sight of Betsy's teeth marks perforating the cover. Mike turned pink, then purple, then a congestive yellow. It was like watching a horrible sunset.

"Invoices for $3 million for 'corporate gifts,'" I said, dealing them one by one across his desk. "All paid to the same small Northwest publisher, to a P.O. Box that just happens to be registered to you." I fanned the photocopied checks. "All for this book, the copies of which you stored at the very mill you were bleeding dry, stacked and stuffed in every spare corner, boxes piled on top of boxes on the unreinforced third floor of a 100-year-old building, just waiting to come crashing down and break my father's neck."

Mike Saunders seemed to have lost the gift of speech. He swallowed several times, then stammered, "So now it's a capital crime to buy books?"

"It is if you killed my dad to keep it quiet."

Mike just gaped at me. I wouldn't have thought it possible for someone's eyes to protrude so far from their sockets.

"How dare you!"

"Mr. Saunders, there's enough evidence on that table to charge you with theft," Mark put in. "In fact, based just on what we turned up this afternoon, there's enough evidence to charge you with embezzlement, money laundering, and violating the election laws by funneling money from the mill into your campaign. So I wouldn't waste a lot of time getting all indignant over your fine moral character right now."

"I don't have to listen to this," Mike spluttered. "Get out of my office."

"Mr. Saunders, this is your chance to help yourself," Mark said. "Don't blow it. If I were you, I'd be trying really hard to think of a way to make these nice people whole."

Mike's face hardened into a sneer. "So that's what this is about. Blackmail. I pay you off, and you don't go to the police."

"I *am* the police," Mark pointed out. "We're just giving you an opportunity to tell us your side of the story before we jump to any conclusions. If there's an accounting screw up here and you always intended to take financial responsibility for those books, then now's the time to correct that error. You pay back the money to the mill, and you explain that you were shocked when you learned of the problem and immediately made it right. If it was just a mistake, there's no intent, there's no theft, and there's no motive for murder. But if you don't pay back the money, well, then it looks like it wasn't really a mistake after all. Doesn't it? And a lot of people might wonder what you'd do - or what you did - if Jack's dad happened to find out."

Mike looked at us with pure hatred. "Your father authorized the purchase of every one of those books -" he began.

"Bullshit," I said.

"It's true. It was his idea. Gary's up for tenure this year, and no one was paying any attention to his publications. Not only did I publish Gary's book as a favor to your father, but I found the money in the mill's budget to buy enough copies to get Gary all sorts of media attention and make him a minor celebrity - and not just in Bellingham. All over the place. I did it because your dad asked me to, and I will testify to that in a court of law."

"No you won't," Harmony said. "It's inadmissible hearsay. The court won't let you put words in a dead man's mouth."

"Well, then, I'll tell the tenure committee, and the university, and the press that Gary Kendall's brilliant publishing record is a pure sham, that his father-in-law had to step in and save his career. You want to break that news to sweet Marianne? Face it, Jack, you try anything, and your family goes down with me."

I detest people who try to capitalize on my better nature. I had no intention of hurting Marianne - or even Gary, for that matter. But Mike Saunders' didn't need to know that.

"Given that they're now suing me, do you really think I give a rat's ass what happens to my sweet sisters?" I got up and paused with my hand on the doorknob. "We're going to notify the Bellingham police tomorrow morning. The only question is what we tell them. So you've got about twelve hours to decide whether or not this was embezzlement or just a horrible, horrible mistake. Sleep well," I said, and slammed the door on his thunderous face.

Throughout the confrontation, I had been dimly aware of a low current of voices outside. I had assumed that Mike's campaign staffers were working late, but the desks were empty, and the offices were dark. Betsy, who had been growling to herself in Mike's office, suddenly let loose with an all-out snarl.

A few steps down the darkened hallway, and I knew why. Through the plate glass windows, I spotted the wavering flames of candles, trailing phosphorescence in the damp night air. Pale and ghostly faces milled around the windows, mouths opening and closing in unison like macabre carolers. Some of the visitors seemed hooded. Others clutched blurred signs; one, a Celtic cross.

Was it Halloween already? So much had happened over the past week that it felt quite plausible that the month had simply slipped away. Much as I was grasping for an innocent explanation, however, the cold reality was that it was only mid-October. That and the smothered mutterings outside - somehow much creepier than screaming, as if a giant were trying to whisper - convinced me that whatever they were, these apparitions were not candy-happy trick-or-treaters. Instinctively, I put myself in front of Harmony and grabbed Betsy's collar.

Mark had already drawn his gun and was motioning for us to follow him. We were backing away from the windows when Mike burst out of his office, said, "What the hell?" and hit the light switch.

In the flood of light, the five us flashed into full view of our outside visitors. They disappeared as the inside illumination turned the windows into a mirror. We could see only our own gaping faces but could hear the hideous whisper rise to a roar outside. The glass shuddered under unseen blows.

"Turn off the freaking light," Mark shouted at Mike Saunders, who seemed too frozen to obey.

Mark leapt for the light switch just as one window shattered. I thought it was a rock. I hoped it was a rock. But in all, I counted three shots.

One that splintered the wood of a doorframe right behind me.

One that tore into my side as I threw Harmony to the floor.

And one that seemed to whistle over me, although by that time I couldn't really be sure of anything.

Darkness rushed toward me, into me, clear through me. Fire raged up and down one side. The other side felt dead and heavy. It took everything I had to wedge my arm between myself and Harmony, to fumble past her hair and turtleneck to her throat.

The last thing I remembered was the feel of her pulse, wild and racing but strong under my hand.

The last thing I knew was that she was still alive.

CHAPTER 16

I opened my eyes once in the ambulance and saw Harmony hovering above me, drenched with blood. I opened them once in the hospital corridor and saw Sarah flying toward me, blonde hair aloft, a perfect circle around her face. I heard Mark say, "He was dead at the scene." And then I passed out, only reasonably sure that he didn't mean me.

He didn't. He meant Mike Saunders. The third bullet had ripped right through Mike's throat. Mark had done what he could to stop the gushing blood, but Mike was dead before he hit the ground.

As for me, this was the second time I had been shot. It doesn't get any easier. I lost a great deal of blood and a large expanse of time to the haunted, twilit sleep of the seriously hurt and heavily drugged.

Through the fuzz, I caught snatches of whispered conversations. I heard Mark reproaching himself for not protecting me better, castigating himself so mercilessly that Harmony begged him to shut up. I heard Mark and Anthony conversing in low tones about the death down by the Kingdome. The dead man had a bus ticket from Bellingham in his back pocket, and even though Mark and Anthony couldn't tie him to my family or the mill, the coincidence concerned them. I heard Sarah's voice, muffled, but definitely Sarah's voice, say, "We really ought to tell him."

There was a mumbled answer. I couldn't discern the words, but the voice was itchingly familiar.

Sarah again: "I think he has a right to know."

Another mumble, closer this time. My heart was pounding. I was even more certain that I knew the speaker. I caught the last few words: "about Beth."

A pause, then Sarah's voice again: "Well, OK, Dad."

Dad. Dad. Dad. He was there. He was alive. He had come down alive from the second floor of my dream and he was alive right there outside my hospital room. I struggled to open my eyes. I struggled to open my mouth. I struggled to see him, to

speak to him, to stop him from leaving me again. In the dark, close vise of pain and sleep and drugs, I arced and thrashed until I could force out the words:

"He's alive. He's here. Dad, Dad, please don't go!"

The pandemonium that ensued was no match for my screaming, which seemed to continue quite apart from me while Mark wrestled me back into bed and Harmony frantically pressed the button for the nurse. "He's burning up," I heard her say. While I begged them - begged anyone - to let me up so I could find my dad, the nurse flashed a needle toward my arm.

Twenty-four hours and several syringes later, I was almost ready to concede that it had been a dream. Neither Mark nor Harmony had heard Sarah's voice or the murmured replies that so inflamed my imagination. As my fever receded, I was able to put on at least a show of normalcy. I read the paper, ate my Jell-O, watched TV.

But periodically I would fall asleep right in the middle of a conversation, or I would start in the middle of a news story and realize that I had been staring at the same word for an indeterminate length of time. In those moments of intense weariness and dislocation, I could hear those murmurs nibbling at the edges of my consciousness. I could hear Sarah's voice say, "Well, OK, Dad."

By my second morning in the hospital, I was focused enough to talk about the shooting.

"They assume the shooter was after Mike, since it was his office and all, but they can't be sure," Mark explained. "Most everyone at the mill knew we were heading over there. So just in case, we've got two Bellingham policemen outside your room."

Given how much the Bellingham police seemed to suspect me, I wasn't sure that increased my odds of survival.

"Who were those people with the candles?"

"Protesters from a couple of environmental organizations," Harmony said. "They've been dogging Mike and Gary Kendall for months. That book they wrote is all about the World Trade Organization."

"Pro or con?"

"Pro. The gist is that America grew strong by exploiting its environmental resources." She pointed to herself, never quite comfortable with her family's huge timber fortune. "Exhibit A. Anyway, they argue that we need to allow developing countries the same flexibility if they're ever going to get their foot on the ladder, that we can't impose our mature environmental standards on economies that are just emerging. It's not a new argument by any means, but because Mike bought all those copies and pushed it up the best-seller list, the book has drawn a lot of attention and a lot of fire. The tenure committee met Monday night as well, and there was an identical protest at the university - although there wasn't any trouble over there."

"They think some tree-hugger tried to kill us?" I had heard of environmental guerrillas spiking trees that were set for logging, but I had never actually encountered anyone willing to shed human blood to protect a fish, or an owl, or Bellingham Bay.

"That's Sergeant Lee's working theory," Mark confirmed. "And they took a couple of guns - and a lot of pot - off some of the kids out on the street, but -" He broke off and looked uneasy.

"But?" I prompted.

Mark shook his head. "It doesn't fit. The kids had cheap, lousy little guns. You can't tell if they're planning to shoot you or light your cigarette. The shots were from a rifle, and from the angle, I'd swear they came from above the crowd."

"Bullets from heaven?" I hazarded weakly.

"Bullets from across the street," Mark said. "From the second floor. Detective Anthony checked it out yesterday, and the windowsills and doorknobs have all been wiped clean. Someone could have been up there in the dark, just waiting for Mike - or for us - to walk out the door. When the lights came on and the kids got rowdy, it would have been an easy shot. A spotlight and a distraction - perfect."

I absorbed that with a shudder while Mark and Harmony filled me in on other developments. Even though the angle seemed out of kilter and none of the protesters had a rifle, the environmentalists were the only official suspects of the Bellingham police. Several protesters had been arrested on the drug offenses; at least three were trying to cut a deal by fingering the others as the people who bombed my dad's funeral.

"Underneath two months of accumulated dirt, these are snot-nosed little rich kids who want to grow up to be doctors and lawyers," Mark said. "No offense. When you put a former prom queen from Laurelhurst in a pokey room with Sergeant Lee and Sheriff Mac, she's going to crack pretty fast, even if she does have dreadlocks, an anarchist tattoo, and a bolt through her nose. They're all pointing fingers at each other on the bombing, and Lee's already found traces of potassium chlorate in their apartments. That was the explosive in the pipe bombs. But there's nothing yet to tie them to the shooting."

I heard a familiar voice outside and glimpsed a twitch of waist-length hair through the crack in the door. Without even looking at me, Mark rose and went outside, closing the door behind him before I could protest. I heard a tentative question and Mark's cold reply, "Jack is badly hurt. He can't be disturbed." Then he slipped back inside and shut the door in Emily's face. Her gaze locked on me for just an instant. She dropped her eyes as the door closed.

I turned on Mark in astonishment. "Don't treat my sister like that."

"You can't talk to her," Harmony said.

"Sure I can," I said, momentarily forgetting that I was now adverse to my sisters. Ethics rules forbid attorneys to talk to opposing parties. "Well, I can if I get someone to represent me and don't appear *pro se*."

"It's not just that," Harmony said, then stopped. She and Mark exchanged a look.

"What else?"

"Emily works for one of the organizations that was protesting the night you were shot," Mark said.

"So? She wasn't there, was she?"

"No," Mark admitted. "But she's dated - or is dating - one of the guys Lee arrested."

"Mark, I get the impression that Emily has dated pretty much everybody, male and female. Just because she had a fling with some kid -"

"Not a kid. A forty-nine-year-old former Berkeley professor with a couple of drug convictions and a Glock semiautomatic. He's a founding member of RIOT: Resist International Oppression Today. Most of the protesters were college students, but Emily's friend seems like he was the organizer."

Mark looked at my frankly disbelieving face and sighed. "I'm not saying she did anything. But all of them have a motive to get rid of you. They all want to keep their house; they don't trust you with the mill; Marianne doesn't want Gary to be exposed or lose his chance at tenure; and Emily was or is sleeping with someone who brought a semiautomatic to what was supposed to be a non-violent vigil to redeem the 'soul of the earth,' or whatever. I just want to make sure she doesn't have another crack at you if she was behind it." He suddenly leaned forward, and I started at his stricken face. "I'm not going to screw up again."

It was more than a relief to return to Karen's lace-curtained bed and breakfast on South Hill. While Mark and Betsy patrolled the perimeter and Karen and Harmony plied me with soup and tea, I amused myself by watching Ben and Bart. Our hostess's twin nephews were into dominos, and they arranged hundreds of them around the living room as I cheered them on from the puffy floral couch.

Their engineering was ingenious. With great ceremony, Bart flicked the first domino, and a blur of black collapsed across the mantle. The last one tumbled off the fireplace, hit a seesaw of balsa wood arranged below, and jerked away the tether holding a windup whale. The whale paddled across a water-filled roasting pan and set off a chain reaction of white dominos when it hit the other side. The white dominos cascaded with a satisfying clack across a bookshelf, the last one knocking over a precariously poised Milk-Bone. Bear the Rottweiler, who had been waiting patiently for the treat, looked up at just the right moment and snapped the biscuit as it plummeted from the shelf.

I applauded furiously from the couch while Ben, Bart, and Bear took their bows and Ben and Bart started gathering up the dominos.

"Come on, kids," their aunt Karen said, picking her way through the wreckage. "Jack needs his rest, and you need your lunch. There's macaroni and cheese on the table and I want to see that you've eaten at least three carrot sticks each." She put a steaming tray in front of me. "You too."

While Bart and Ben scrambled to the kitchen, Karen and Bear settled down for a chat. Karen sank into a magenta armchair while Bear snuggled next to me on the couch, his nose suggestively close to my lunch.

I dug into the bright orange macaroni. "Karen, thanks for letting us come back here to your B&B after the shooting. Are you sure you're OK with it?" I tried and failed to keep my eyes from the Bellingham Herald on the floor. The front page was emblazoned with a picture of me in a wheelchair, surrounded by police officers, all topped with the stark headline, "Slaying Suspect Released from Hospital."

Karen followed my gaze and smiled. "Somehow, I don't figure you for a killer, Jack."

"My honest face?"

"That and the dog on your chest," she confirmed. "Bear's a discerning judge of character. He never could stand my ex-husband."

I took another forkful of macaroni. "There might be someone after me," I said, feeling a throb of dread as I said the words. "I don't want you and the boys in the way if somebody gives it another shot."

"What, with James Bond on guard out there?" She jerked her head toward the window, just in time to see Mark pass by, eyes roving and mouth grim. "Given that he never stops and never sleeps, I feel perfectly safe, especially with the two dogs. If the boys were here at night, I might be a little concerned, but their mom picks them up right after work." She raised her glass of Kool-Aid to me. "Yet another benefit of being an aunt."

"Do you have any children?" It was a bread-and-butter question, but as the answering silence lengthened and the colors of the room grew colder, I braced myself for a reply I was sure I wouldn't like.

Karen leaned over and handed me a photo of a smiling child I had assumed to be Bart or Ben. He was peeking out from a Scooby-Doo costume and hugging an enormous plastic pumpkin full of candy.

"That's Jake. When he was five. That's his last Halloween. He was diagnosed with leukemia right before that Christmas, and he was gone by the next October."

Five. Jimmy's age. With my own emotions rubbed raw, I was newly amazed at how much suffering there was in the world. "I'm sorry. Karen, I am so, so sorry."

"Me too," she said. "Every day."

We sat in silence for a little while, Bear's nose inching ever closer to my forgotten plate. Karen gave me a nod, and I put the plate of macaroni on the floor for Bear to enjoy. The slurping sounds were oddly comforting. One of us was having a good time.

"He came to see me afterward," Karen said suddenly.

"Who?"

"Your dad. He was my homeroom teacher in high school. My favorite teacher. He'd been retired from the school for years, but when he heard about Jake, he came over and sat right there on that couch. I couldn't cry anymore. I couldn't talk. I was just so tired of saying what had happened, so tired of trying to explain this inexplicable disease."

She fluttered her hands and swallowed hard. "I didn't know what to say to him. I hadn't seen him for fifteen years. But he just sat on my couch with me. And after we'd spent an hour together, he told me -" She trailed off and started again with a great effort. "He told me -"

The strangled feeling in my chest had nothing to do with my bandages. I prompted: "Yes?"

She looked me right in the eye.

"He told me he knew what it was like to lose a son."

CHAPTER 17

I spent the rest of the day looking through Karen's yearbooks. Karen's mother had gone to school with my dad and Virginia, and Karen and her siblings had overlapped with my sisters. After her parents died, and her siblings married and moved away from the big white house on South Hill, the family memorabilia migrated to the attic and stayed there, even after Karen turned the place into a B&B. Mark carried down the dusty box and placed it in front of me on the couch.

"There's a skeleton up there," he said casually to Karen.

"My father was a doctor," she replied.

"It's wearing a hat."

"He wanted to make sure his interns always remembered that Mr. Slim had been a real person. He thought it would make them more sensitive to their patients. I'm sorry. Did it scare you?"

"I'm a homicide cop, Karen," Mark explained, with a trace of condescension. "I see dead bodies every day."

She was beginning to apologize when he interrupted: "Scared the shit out of me. Mr. Slim nearly took a bullet in the hat. I'll go back outside before I start shooting up the place."

Mark and Betsy withdrew to their appointed rounds. Karen gave me a pat on the head - just like a dog - and lured the boys into the family room with promises of a Pokémon game. Bear settled down beside me and started snoring.

The yearbooks were all called Shuksan, one of the high peaks in the North Cascades. I opened the oldest yearbook and started my climb through my family's past.

My father had been captain of the football team – the Red Raiders. In his senior picture, he had a crew cut and serious expression, perhaps inevitable for an eighteen-year-old about to be drafted.

I searched his face for any clues to his character. Did he look like the type of person who would abandon a five-year-old? No, I decided, but really, who does? I craned up on my pillows until I could see myself in the mirror over the mantle. After some struggles imagining myself in a crew cut, I could see why the lady at *il fiasco* had done a serious doubletake when she spotted me. My father and I had the same round faces, thick, straight hair, and tough, muscular build.

Virginia Carlson had been one year behind my father. Her picture revealed the pretty girl I had glimpsed during our tumultuous meeting - huge eyes, dimples, blond hair meticulously curled. She was as delicate as Beth but without Beth's heartbreaking fragility.

A thumb through the yearbook hinted at Virginia's popularity: "What-A-Sho" princess, cheerleader, lead in the school play. One picture placed her in the thick of what seemed to be the school's ruling clique. Arms around each other's waists, the Crystal Belles wore identical sweaters embroidered with their names. Virginia posed regally between Ida - the lady from *il fiasco* - and a stunning dark-haired girl named Mary.

Virginia and Ida showed up again in the chorus, where I also spotted Clark Swanson, one of the mill's VPs. Karen's mom and dad were in the play with Virginia, who looked suitably tragic in her Juliet costume. Mike Saunders had been Romeo. By the time I closed the book, everyone was starting to look familiar to me.

Moving forward in time, I could pick out my sisters without even having to consult the yearbooks' index. Marianne was thinner but had the same sweet face. She had been a cheerleader like her mother, although she was also a member of the Chess Club. She was standing between her future husband and an astonishingly innocent-looking Sergeant Lee. I made a mental note that his first name was Cecil.

In her senior picture, Emily wore the same delighted, suggestive smile she had flashed over the platter of ham. Her choir gown looked positively clingy. Sarah had been a National Honor Society member and a star tennis player. She had a marvelous fluffy hairstyle. It was so unlike her current, unapologetic blunt cut. There were no pictures of Beth.

I turned back to one of Marianne's yearbooks and took another look at Sergeant Lee. He was short and thin and had a pocketful of pens. No wonder he had grown into such a prick. And no wonder he hated me so much. Even stuffed into a suit and tie, I never looked like anything except a football player, and I assumed Sergeant Lee had taken a fair amount of abuse by the jocks in school. I was resolving to be nicer to him when I turned the page from the Chess Club to athletics. And I nearly dropped the book.

It was a picture of my father and mother. It was a picture of my father and mother *together*. I had forgotten that my father would have been teaching while my sisters were in high school. My dad had coached football and basketball. My mom - astoundingly - had been a cheerleader. And they were both in a picture commemorating the basketball team's district victory.

But the difference between them! My dad was still built like a truck, blond, straightforward, and muscular - chin up, eyes level, looking right at the camera. In her current incarnation, my mom resembled nothing so much as a big, red-haired bat, but here she was bewitching, all dark hair and curves, insinuating herself through a miniskirt. She had her hand on her hip, curling toward my dad like a question mark. In the midst of the other cheerleaders' stick legs and bright smiles, she looked like she had strolled in from a porn flick where the thirty-year-olds pretend to be fifteen. She was liquid, languid, and knowing.

I couldn't take my eyes off them. This is where I had come from. This is where it started. This is where *I* started. I scanned my father's face for traces of guilt. Had it already begun? I spotted part of a calendar captured in the upper corner of the picture. The month was March. I was born the next October. It was possible - it was probable - that it had already happened, that I was already on the way, that I was actually present in that picture. That I was sleeping inside her while they smiled for the camera and pretended they were just the cheerleader and the coach, the adult and the child, appropriate strangers.

A wave of revulsion hit me. I had no difficulty understanding how someone hitched to Virginia Carlson might want to stray. Now that I'd seen her as she was, I had no difficulty understanding how enticing my mother would have been to a middle-aged man with marital problems. But even understanding all that: Way to screw up, Dad. My mother had been the same age as my father's oldest daughter. My mother was standing right next to Marianne in the picture. While Marianne beamed and preened with her pompons and her sweater with the megaphone, did she have any idea how bad everything was at home? Did she have any inkling that the girl posing next to her might be carrying her little brother? I shook my head in disbelief. How could they bring a child - how could they bring *me* - into so many lies and so much pain?

I heard the click of the front door. Harmony bent over me and kissed my forehead. Her lips were deliciously cool. As she straightened up, her eyes fell on the offending picture.

"Oh, my," was all she said. Then she took the book from me and studied it.

"That explains a lot," was her next contribution, her fingertip tracing my mother's suggestive spine. I saw her eyes flick toward the calendar in the corner of the picture, and a small line appeared on her forehead. She was monthing my mother, counting backwards from October.

"Yes," I confirmed for her. "It may possibly be my first and only baby picture."

"She's not showing at all, but I guess it would only have been a couple of months. That may be why she looks so -" She groped for a word. "Voluptuous."

"You win the diplomat of the year award." I leaned back against her, enjoying the smoothness of her suit, drinking in her perfume. It took me a second to remember why she was so dressed up. She had been out all afternoon asking for an extension to respond to my sisters' motion.

"I'm sorry; how did it go in court?"

"OK. We have two more days, but the judge is getting antsy. There aren't any factual issues, so he thinks we should be able to respond even while you're flat on your back. I just kept stressing that you had a right to represent yourself, but he's close to ordering you to hire counsel to appear. Unfortunately, he's right. It's hard to justify my appearing for you to ask for the extension while insisting that you want to defend yourself on the merits."

"How's the work going on the incorporation?"

"Good. I've filed new articles, and I'm making sure it all happens simultaneously – the estate doesn't transfer to you until the new incorporation goes through. So you should have as much protection as possible from personal liability for any cleanup costs. But I can't change what's happened before. We're outside the time period for reinstating the original corporation, so there are a couple of years where Virginia and your sisters could have personal liability."

"How about the response to the motion to disqualify me as trustee?"

"That's harder. As long as your sisters face liability – and they do – there's a big question about whether you can adequately represent their interests. You're just on so many different sides of the v. in this. Plus, you're the big city attorney who used to represent American Fidelity, and a lot of people blame the insurance company for the mill's financial troubles. An outsider, coming in here and trying to take over his sisters' business –" She broke off and shook her head. "We're hometowned in a major way, Jack. Even getting shot isn't going to win you the sympathy vote."

"Do you think I should cave?" I asked. I didn't want to cave. If I disclaimed the role of voting trustee, no one would have a controlling interest in the mill. I would have 50% of the shares. The other 50% would be split among my sisters. The mill was struggling, hemorrhaging money. Someone needed to be in charge.

"I think you need to consider it as a back-up plan. If only -" she said, then stopped.

"If only what?"

"If only the mill's lawsuit against American Fidelity would go away. Is there any chance of settlement?"

"None. The mill's reps admitted in deposition that they knew the chemicals were escaping, and the policy excludes environmental coverage if they knowingly released contaminants. If all this hadn't blown up, I was going to file for summary judgment. And I would have won. American Fidelity isn't going to pay a penny."

I couldn't sleep that night. Even though the house was dark and quiet, even though Bear and Betsy snored and snuggled against me, and even though Mark still prowled outside, I could not let myself relax. Every time I closed my eyes, I saw my mother's gloating face, my father's cold stare, the blur of falling dominoes they had set in motion: the affair, the baby, the abandonment. All those long, cold years of fear and pain.

To distract myself, I focused on the response to my sisters' motion. Even there, I felt like the last teetering domino in a long, sad chain. First my father dumped shit in Bellingham Bay; then he filed a frivolous suit against American Fidelity; then he hamstrung me in his will. Harmony was right: I was on a lot of different sides of the v. I puffed out my breath in exasperation.

Harmony had taught me well: When you're stuck, keep moving backward in the chain of events until you find the weak link, until you can interrupt the flow of consequences that led you to that point. The problem was that all the events leading up to this dilemma seemed irrevocable. Bellingham Bay was already polluted. There was nothing I could do about that. The mill had already sued American Fidelity. Nothing I could do about that. And I had already spent months defending American Fidelity. Not a single thing I could do about that, either.

I sat up and rubbed my eyes. I had missed a step. The whole reason the mill needed the insurance money was that the state had ordered it to pay its share of the environmental cleanup. If the state reversed that order, the lawsuit would be moot. No liability, no lawsuit. No lawsuit, no conflict. No conflict, no barrier to my serving as trustee of my sisters' interests in the mill.

I was out of bed. The dogs watched me with curiosity edging on impatience: *what are you doing; come back here; we're getting cold.* I retrieved the newspaper from downstairs and focused on a story that I had just glanced at earlier in the day.

The Department of Ecology was beginning environmental impact analysis on the proposed waterfront hotel. I jotted down the name of the DOE site supervisor, who was scheduled to arrive in Bellingham the next day. Then I stared at the crude map that accompanied the story. I felt the hair rise on the back of my neck.

The new waterfront hotel would be located right on top of my father's mill. There would be a marina where the cooling tanks were now; the hotel itself would take over the plant and the burned-out office building. The warehouses would fall to tennis courts and a nine-hole golf course. Wasn't all this just a tad premature?

As I scoured the story, a familiar name jumped out at me: Clark Swanson. Clark Swanson had been one of my father's pallbearers. He was vice president of something or other at the mill. And he was also a port commissioner, a Northwest office equivalent in ignominy to a corrupt Chicago alderman. Voters in one town once nominated a raccoon for port commissioner. His human opponent eventually triumphed after a long campaign - but it was a squeaker.

This is what Clark Swanson, SPP vice president and port commissioner, had to say about the hotel that someone was proposing to plunk down on his mill: "The plans are very impressive. Clearly the hotel would make Bellingham a world-class city, drawing tourists and conventions from all over. The Port is committed to making this dream a reality."

That last bit was ominous. So ominous that I did what any rational person in my predicament would do. I hobbled upstairs and woke up Harmony.

After five hours of Internet research, four phone calls, and three pots of coffee, Harmony and I had uncovered the bare bones of the plot. Besides his many other roles in this drama, Clark Swanson was a past director and majority stockholder in the company seeking to develop the mill's property into a hotel. The late, unlamented Mike Saunders was a silent partner in the hotel chain itself.

Their audacity was breathtaking. First they had looted the mill to fund Mike's congressional campaign. Faced with crushing environmental liability and the loss of their cash cow, they filed a frivolous lawsuit against American Fidelity to stall for time, cooked up a deal with the hotel developer, and committed the Port to acquire the mill's land at firesale prices when the mill finally had to declare bankruptcy. The Port would buy the land, then lease it to the hotel and developer at rates that were below rock-bottom, especially for a swath of prime waterfront property. Everyone would profit - except my dad, my sisters, me, and the people who worked at the mill. Ever-generous with other people's money, the Port would be using their tax dollars to buy them out of a job.

Gunshot wound or no gunshot wound, by 9 a.m., I couldn't have gone to sleep if you had slipped me a horse tranquilizer. I picked up the phone and started dialing the Department of Ecology.

For the first time since my father died, I knew exactly what to do.

CHAPTER 18

Bethany Walton was a surprise. I'm not exactly sure what I was expecting in a Department of Ecology site supervisor, but Bethany's crocheted vest, hard dark eyes, and goggle-like glasses were not it. Apparently, I was exactly what she expected, however, because she wasted no time on the usual small talk.

"I know why you're here," she said, checking off our appointment in her Day-Timer and snapping it shut. The paper thwacked together like a punch. "You want me to dismiss the cleanup assessment against SPP. No environmental liability, no lawsuit against American Fidelity, and no reason you can't come waltzing in and take over your sisters' business."

I was less nettled by the insult than I was by the fact that she had immediately fingered the idea that had taken me a week to figure out. Bethany Walton was obviously no fool. Before I could open my mouth, she continued:

"Forgive my bluntness, Jack, but I don't particularly like big tough guys who try to steal their sisters' stuff. And I really don't like people who play on both sides of the fence."

OK. At least I knew where I stood. "Ms. Walton, the whole reason I'm here is that I've been on both sides of the fence. And I know that if you and I can't work something out, there's not going to be any business for anybody to run, whether it's me or my sisters."

A sharp light flickered in her bolt-like eyes. It made them look like they were turning. "You seem pretty sure of yourself."

"I am sure." I explained about the admissions in the depositions and the terms of the mill's insurance policies. "American Fidelity's got no obligation to pay, and it's not going to pay. If the mill doesn't get that insurance money -" I held up my hands in a gesture of defeat. "That's it."

"So what do you expect me to do about it?"

I pushed across a folder full of clippings that Harmony and I had copied that morning in the library. "There are a lot of other mills around the state in the same boat as us, but you've come down harder on SPP than any of the rest. In fact, we're the only one where you imposed full cleanup liability."

"The other mills are cooperating in remedial efforts," she said.

"And we're not?"

"Hardly. At first Saunders was falling all over himself to satisfy me, but suddenly he stopped returning my calls. By May, I couldn't even schedule negotiations with him or Swanson. When people won't cooperate, you don't have much choice but to reach for the stick."

"I think I know why they were so difficult," I said. Again, I saw the sharp flicker spin in her eyes. I quickly outlined the plot Harmony and I had uncovered early that morning.

"I suppose you can prove all that?"

"Yes, ma'am, I can." I turned a few pages in the folder and handed her the documents proving that Clark and Mike would profit from the hotel. I handed her the Port's lease agreement that Harmony had obtained that morning from Higuro. Her father's international bank had been among those the hotel approached for financing.

"Ugly," she admitted. For a moment, she looked uncertain. Then she shook her head in annoyance. "Jack, I agree that it seems Swanson and Saunders did a number on your dad. But that's got nothing to do with me, and it doesn't do anything to clean up Bellingham Bay. If you want to go after them, sue them."

"Mike's dead," I reminded her.

"So kill the other one, then, if you're willing to accept the consequences. But either way, there's nothing I can do for you."

"Yes, there is."

"I'm not letting you out of the environmental cleanup. There's too much damage to let you walk away."

"All I'm asking is that you let us go back in time to when things went haywire with Mike and Clark," I said. "They weren't representing the mill when they talked to you; they were just looking out for themselves. Give me a chance to negotiate the same kind of deal you reached with the other mills around the state." When I saw her sour look, I hastily continued, "Ms. Walton, if you don't, there won't be a mill to pay for the environmental cleanup. I know it's unpleasant, but you kind of need to keep the beast alive."

She fixed me with her dark cold eyes. I had a strange feeling that she could see clear through to the back of my head. Finally, I prompted, "Well, what's it going to be?"

She sighed and smoothed her vest. "See, I've got to look at the big picture here. However this came to be, and whatever happened between your dad and these bozos -" she flicked the documents I had handed her - "the fact is that a hotel has less environmental impact than a papermill, even the best-run papermill. I'd rather have pleasure boaters and tourists and idiots chipping balls into the water than I would have SPP churning chlorine and dioxins into the bay. It's better for everybody."

"Not for the people who work there."

"The hotel will create hundreds of jobs."

"Bellhops," I responded. "Housekeepers. Dishwashers. You're taking people with good, solid blue-collar jobs - jobs where they actually *make* something, jobs where they actually make *money* - and busting them down to scrubbing toilets for minimum wage. That's what big developers always do, Ms. Walton. They pit environmentalists and labor against each other, and while we're fighting, they sneak in and steal everybody blind."

I leaned forward. She didn't lean back. "Don't let them get away with it, Ms. Walton. Don't let them win this time."

She studied me for a few seconds. Then she said, "You're a strange advocate for the working man, Jack." She counted out my misdeeds on her fingers: "Big-city lawyer, dating an heiress, only son of a mill owner, and, oh, yes, just came into about a million bucks." She arched her pinkie obnoxiously. "I'd take your spiel a lot more seriously if I thought you had half a clue what you were talking about."

A jolt of anger surged through me. When you've lived the sort of life I have, it's intolerable to be discounted as a spoiled rich kid. If she only knew, I thought. Then I thought further, why shouldn't she know? Why shouldn't the whole damn town know?

I counted to ten to keep my voice absolutely level. I said, "Ms. Walton, I'm not sure how this came to be about me. It shouldn't be. But if what you decide to do with the mill is going to be based on what you think of me, who you think I am, then you better know the whole story." I scribbled a release on a piece of paper and handed it to her. She took it gingerly. "You call the Department of Social and Health Services and ask them for everything they've got on John Boyden Hart. Then you call me and tell me what you want to do."

I thanked her and took my leave. Harmony and I went back to Karen's B&B, where we waited.

And waited.

And waited.

And waited.

Bethany didn't call until the morning of argument on my sisters' motion, which left me and Harmony only a few hours to craft the appropriate declarations, get signatures, and copy them at the library. We slipped into court with five minutes to spare.

The place was packed. My sisters were sitting in a tense row at the front of the courtroom. Except for Beth, they all looked away in unison when I glanced in their direction. I smiled at Beth and thought I saw a small softening of her rigid features. She was wearing a dark blue dress with a white collar edged in tatting. The judge came in, the bailiff called our case, and we were on.

My sisters' attorney gave a concise, straightforward explanation of why I was conflicted. It wasn't rocket science. "Your Honor, we are not casting aspersions on Mr. Hart's character or competence. We are not saying that Mr. Hart would not want to fulfill his fiduciary duties to his sisters. But we are saying that Mr. Hart is simply on too many sides of the v. in *SPP v. American Fidelity.* He can't continue to press the lawsuit without breaching his obligations to American Fidelity. And he can't dismiss the lawsuit without violating his obligations to his sisters. As long as there is a dispute over the mill's alleged environmental liability, Mr. Hart has a clear conflict of interest."

Amen, brother. I couldn't have said it better myself. If he had wanted to - which I was certain he had not - my sisters' attorney could not have given me a better opening.

The judge nodded at me, but there was an edge to his voice. "Feeling better, Mr. Hart?"

I popped up. "Very much so, Your Honor. I appreciate the court's indulgence."

"Since I've postponed this hearing twice at your request, I've had plenty of time to consider my decision. Can you give me a single, solitary reason why I should not grant Mr. Pembers' motion?"

Oooh. Showboating for the hometown crowd. "I can, Your Honor. I agree with Mr. Pembers that there is a conflict of interest so long as the mill and the insurance company are disputing who pays for the mill's environmental liability. But I'm sure Your Honor would agree that if there were no environmental liability, the lawsuit would be moot, and there would be no conflict of interest."

"Mr. Hart, that is a very interesting hypothetical, but up here in Bellingham, we confine ourselves to the realm of reality."

"It's not a hypothetical, Your Honor. May I approach?" At his grudging nod, I walked to the bench and handed him and Pembers copies of Bethany Walton's signed declaration. "This morning I concluded negotiations with the Department of Ecology to reverse the environmental assessment on the mill." Gasps broke out around the courtroom. Except for Beth, my sisters' mouths were open.

"No liability, no lawsuit, no conflict, Your Honor," I said. And I sat down.

A rush of murmurs and exclamations rose from the seats behind me. Harmony squeezed my hand under the table. Pembers was on his feet, objecting to being blindsided.

"Order! Order!" The judge banged his gavel. "Order or I clear this court!"

As the noise subsided, he turned on me. "Mr. Hart, what do you mean by dropping this bombshell at the time of argument? Mr. Pembers has had no time to prepare for this; I've had no time to consider it. I must say that I am inclined to impose sanctions."

Fine. Sanction me, I thought. Just rule the right way. I was rising to pour some oil on his offended judicial dignity when a clear voice rang out behind me.

"I can speak to that, Your Honor." She still wore a crocheted vest, albeit in a different color. "Bethany Walton, Washington State Department of Ecology. Mr. Hart was gravely wounded and unable to make the trip to Olympia to meet with us. He had to wait until I arrived in Bellingham. He has been conscientiously pursuing these negotiations and should not be blamed for any delay. It was literally only hours ago that I received final approval from the Director to rescind the order requiring payment."

I cast Bethany a grateful look. She had been astonishingly nice to me all morning. The judge stared at her, taking in her ramrod posture, her implacable black eyes. Then he glared at me as though I had sprouted horns and a tail right in his courtroom. He looked down at the declaration and read through it slowly and carefully, shaking his head several times.

He straightened up. I held my breath.

"I hope you know what you're doing," he said to me.

Then he shrugged his shoulders and swung his gavel. "Motion to disqualify dismissed."

The courtroom erupted, and this time the judge made no effort to quell the noise. That may be why I didn't hear her shrill cry, didn't hear my sisters' gasps, didn't see her until she was actually upon me.

With a sudden rush of air, Beth launched herself from her seat, sailed over the low barrier before counsels' tables, and attacked me.

ONLY THE GOOD

CHAPTER 19

She crashed into my wounded side, almost felling me with the pain. While I struggled to keep my balance, her small, scrabbling hands fastened on my throat. She was squeezing my windpipe so fiercely that I couldn't breathe. The world darkened and swirled. *This is what happened to Virginia Carlson*, I thought. I thought further that if Beth didn't let go, I was going to die. I didn't want to hurt her, but I had to get some air.

I snapped my arms upward, breaking her grasp on my neck. Her nails tore at my skin as she released me. I enveloped her in a bear hug, pulled her to me, and pinned her arms to her sides. By the time Mark reached me, it was over. I rocked her back and forth and made soothing sounds into her ear. She relaxed almost imperceptibly against me. I could hear the little gasps and hiccups of her breath.

Mark was taking out his handcuffs. I shook my head. I wouldn't release her to anyone - not Mark, not the agitated bailiff, and definitely not Sergeant Lee - until Sarah appeared before me, her face white, and held out her arms. Beth went to her sister without resistance, as though nothing had happened.

Sarah sucked in her breath as Beth turned away from me. Bright red blood spangled my shirtfront. It looked festive, sort of like a Hawaiian shirt. Beth's face was smeared with red; her delicate white collar looked like a dishrag rung in blood. My sisters closed ranks around her in stricken silence. Sergeant Lee wedged himself between us as though I was the attacker.

After a brief and panicked inventory of my upper body - which I thoroughly enjoyed - Harmony was satisfied that I was bleeding only from the scratches around my neck. The wound in my side hurt like a mother, but the stitches held. Mark and Harmony clustered around me while Sergeant Lee and the large policeman escorted out my sisters. With what I considered remarkable presence of mind, I obtained the judge's signature on the dismissal order before we turned to leave.

"Good luck," was all he said, handing it to me by the corner. The page was blotched with blood. The judge shuddered.

By the time we had gathered up our things, Bethany Walton was the only person left in the courtroom. Mark and Harmony drifted a few feet away. Bethany rose as I approached her.

"Thanks," I said, extending my hand. She gave it a hard squeeze. I didn't know how to put the question into words, but she could read it in my eyes: *Why?*

"Bitter Lake Home for Boys and Girls," she said, with the tone of someone describing a tour in Vietnam. "1968 to 1972."

The Bitter Lake Home. I knew that story. After someone died of hypothermia - in mild, maritime Seattle - it came out that one of the home's seasonal disciplines was to soak kids with cold water and lock them in the basement. In the middle of winter. Naked.

"I'm sorry."

"Me too." There was the slightest fuzziness around her bolt-like eyes before they fastened down again. "But don't expect any special treatment from me, Jack. Now that you're in charge of this outfit, you just remember that I am going to be looking over your shoulder and on your back 24 hours of every day."

"I would be disappointed if you weren't," I said, with a little bow.

She stared at me. A sudden bark of a laugh escaped from her mouth, and she jumped as if it startled her. That made her laugh even harder. It was so incongruous to see her relax that I couldn't help joining in. Pretty soon we were both giggling like idiots as we moved toward the door. She fumbled for her coat. I was helping her put it on and holding open the door for her when we were blinded by flashbulbs and the glare of television cameras.

By the time we had fought our way through the reporters and were driving back to Karen's, I was feeling - well, I was feeling like I'd recently been shot. My side throbbed, my knees shook, and my face and palms were slicked with sweat. I couldn't tell whether it was just the exertion of the day or whether I was suddenly feeling the full weight of responsibility for running the mill.

"I hope you know what you're doing," the judge had said to me before he ruled. I had treated it as a rhetorical question because the truth was that I had absolutely no idea what I was doing. I didn't know how to run a paper mill. I didn't know how to run a business. I was just a lawyer, the very definition of which is that you don't actually know how to *do* anything. My only consolation was that I couldn't really screw it up any worse than had my dad.

I took a deep breath and closed my eyes, trying to match my breath to the steady motion of the car. The image of my red blood on that white paper flashed into my mind. I shuddered.

At Karen's B&B, all I wanted was sleep and a snack, not necessarily in that order. But there was a strange car parked outside - a pale gold Mercedes. Mark had his hand on his gun as the door opened - and Sarah got out. She took the three of us in warily but addressed herself only to me: "Jack, may I talk to you a minute?"

"This isn't a good time," Mark answered for me. I noticed that his hand was still proximate to his gun. He added, unnecessarily, "Jack has just been attacked."

"*Please.*"

"Come on in, Sarah." She followed me through the entryway, Mark and Harmony close behind her. Both dogs came thundering down the stairs. Betsy launched herself at me from the fifth step. She caught sight of Sarah and did a 90-degree turn in mid-air to examine the newcomer.

"Manners, Betsy," I hissed, but she ignored me. She was entranced by Sarah. After the formality of hand-sniffing and chin-tickling, Betsy accompanied Sarah into the living room and sat on her feet.

Sarah got right to the point. "Are you going to press charges against Beth?"

"No. But I think you need to get her some help."

She bristled. "She wasn't trying to hurt you," she protested. "She wasn't angry with you. It's just that she likes you, and you had turned your back on her and you were talking to the judge and not to her. She was just trying to get your attention."

"Is that why she attacked your mom?" Mark's voice was even, but his eyes were hard. "Just trying to get attention?"

She took a second to rally. "Beth didn't attack Mama. Beth has never done anything like this before."

Mark reached over and pushed my collar down. The damage was bad enough that Sarah looked away. "Your mom's throat looked just like that, Sarah. Both torn up by small, strong hands." He crooked his fingers at her. "Tatting hands. If Sergeant Lee had really wanted to solve this case, he would have scraped under Beth's nails, and he would have found your mother's blood and your mother's skin. But he's never wanted to solve this case. He didn't want it to be one of your sisters. It was so much easier to blame Jack. It was so much easier for all of you to blame everything on Jack."

She swiveled toward me, her eyes awash with tears. "I told Cecil and Sheriff Mac that you couldn't have done it," she said, with a pleading note that made me sorry for her. "I told them you left at 10:30 and Mama was fine at midnight. I never tried to put any of this on you."

"I know," I reassured her, but Mark was not to be deterred.

"Your sister ever start a fire before this?"

"I beg your pardon?"

"I checked the logs. The fire department's been out to your place quite a bit over the last few years. Is that another way Beth gets attention?"

Sarah turned pink then pale as she realized what he was suggesting. "Don't be absurd. How's Beth supposed to have gotten to the mill and back to set the fire? She doesn't even have a driver's license."

"Hasn't slowed her down before. She's been stopped at least twice - and those are the ones Lee couldn't hush up. She's even gone joyriding in your own car. It's just like her teaching herself tatting. She can imitate anything."

Sarah rose, dislodging an offended Betsy, and gathered up her purse. "This is ridiculous. I should have known not to come here." As she turned to leave, her coat swung open. She caught sight of my face. "Jack? Jack? What is it? What's the matter?"

Sarah's white blouse was sticky with half-dried blood - my blood, I assumed, transferred from Beth when Sarah took her in her arms. The sight brought back Sarah framed in the doorway of her father's palatial house, barefoot, harried, sweatshirt stained from her slashed hand, collapsing in my arms at the sight of blood.

Sarah had sucked in her breath when she saw the blood on me and Beth, but she hadn't fainted. With the sudden click of a key turning in the lock, I realized the things that had been wrong with the picture that confronted me when I stepped over the threshold of my father's house.

Sarah couldn't have been in the back of the house picking up glass from the broken window. The floor was littered with glass; she was barefoot yet unscathed. She couldn't have cut her hand on the glass, not a slash like that clear across her palm. And she couldn't have cut herself then run toward the door. Mark had taught me how to read a blood trail: the tear-shaped blood drops point in the direction you're running, and Sarah's drops pointed away from the door. Someone had slashed her near the front door, probably with a knife, and she had run to the back of the house.

As I stared at her, I realized what had been nibbling at me in my dreams. There was indeed something out of place in my father's house. There was a maple knife block on the granite island with fancy shears, a sharpening steel, and a bread knife all extant, but only an empty slot waiting for a chef's knife. I had had to rummage in a drawer of rusty castoffs for a knife. I stared at Sarah, thinking furiously.

"Jack," she said again, "what is it?"

"You didn't faint," I said slowly, indicating the matching patterns on our shirts.

She glanced down and blanched. For a moment, I thought she was going to faint just to prove me wrong. Then she pulled herself together and gave me a small, self-deprecating smile. "It's only my own blood that freaks me out," she said. "Your blood I can handle."

"You didn't cut your hand trying to pick up the glass from the back window."

This time I saw it. The flash of guilt - and panic.

"You didn't run toward the door bleeding."

She folded her arms across her chest.

"You didn't faint in my arms."

I kept my eyes on hers. She didn't look away, but I saw the anguish churning there. Sarah was not by nature a liar.

"I did faint," she said. "I really did faint."

"Beth was in the coat closet, wasn't she? In the coat closet, waiting for me with a knife. But when you opened it instead, she slashed you, and you chased her down the hall. You didn't even know about the brick smashing through the window until I told you."

Very slowly, Sarah sat back down, as if her legs could no longer bear the weight she carried. "She wasn't lying in wait for you," she said. "She didn't even know you were coming. She was just hiding because she was scared. Daddy was gone, everyone was crying, and all these policemen and neighbors kept coming to the house. Beth needs a routine to feel safe, and when she doesn't get it, she tries to protect herself. She didn't mean you or me any harm, Jack. And she didn't slash me. I just cut my hand trying to take the knife away from her."

I was trying to sort the truth from the lies in that account when Mark spoke up again, gently this time, from bad cop to good cop in seconds. "Sarah, no one's saying that Beth intended to do anything wrong. I don't even know whether she can formulate legal intent. But whatever she means to do, she's hurting people, and it's got to stop. She attacked Jack. She attacked you. She attacked your mother -"

"She didn't. She couldn't have," Sarah interrupted. "I would have heard her. I'm only a few doors down."

I thought of Virginia's tiny, wasted body. Terrified, with the breath rung out of her, she couldn't have made much noise bouncing down those plushly carpeted stairs. Sarah was evidently thinking the same thing, because she waved her hands and protested, "Beth makes cries and grunts when she's upset. I'm used to listening for them. I'm attuned to them, and I would have heard them. And all that smashing in Mama's room. All that damage. I would have heard that, too. I'm sure."

It was Mark who pointed out the illogic. "*Somebody* trashed your mother's room. If you slept through all that smashing, you easily would have slept through whatever noises Beth makes. You're a new mother, you're running the household all by yourself, you're mourning your dad, and you're exhausted. You're just exhausted. It's no wonder you slept so heavily." He placed a comforting hand on her back. "I know how hard this must be for you, Sarah, and we'll do absolutely everything we can to make it easier, but you've got to face up to it before somebody else gets hurt."

She wavered at his unexpected gentleness. When he was challenging her and prodding her, she could at least flare back at him, but she seemed to have no defense against his kindness. Tears flooded her eyes, and she hung her head. "No," she kept repeating. "No, you don't understand. She's not like that. She wouldn't have done that. She wouldn't have hurt Mama or Daddy. She didn't mean to hurt me or Jack."

Mark was leaning forward to give it another try when Harmony, who had been quiet and concerned throughout the exchange, suddenly kicked the last leg from beneath Sarah's denials.

"Sarah," she said, covering Sarah's twisting hands with both of hers, "Sarah, you have a nine-month-old baby."

The cry that broke from Sarah's lips made me shudder. It wasn't even a word, just a formless wail.

"Beth wouldn't hurt Jennifer." She was trembling; she was trying so hard to hold herself together that it hurt to watch her.

"How can you be sure?" Harmony slipped off the couch and put her arm around Sarah. "What if she gets frustrated with Jennifer because she takes up so much of your time? What if she's trying to get Jennifer's attention and gets angry because she crawls away? You can't watch her twenty-four hours a day. You can't watch either of them twenty-four hours a day. You need help, Sarah. Let us help you."

I watched Sarah crumple before my eyes. She sobbed in Harmony's arms while I patted her awkwardly on the back and Mark fetched her cold water from the kitchen. Betsy nuzzled her and licked her cheek.

"What do you want me to do?" she asked, wiping her eyes.

"She needs to be evaluated by a doctor and a psychiatrist," Mark said. "Maybe she needs a change in her medication. At the very least, you need to bring in someone to keep track of her - day and night. You need to lock up or remove anything flammable. And you need to tell the police what happened the night Jack came to see you."

"I already did," Sarah said. "They told me not to tell you about it, Jack. I'm sorry. I'm sorry I lied to you."

I swallowed my irritation, abandoning my resolution to be nicer to Cecil Lee. Dear old Cecil had been trying to frame me for all manner of things ever since I walked into town.

Sarah was calmer but still apprehensive. "So you don't think Beth will need to be committed? That was always Mama's and Daddy's biggest fear."

"We're the last people to want anyone to be in an institution," Mark told her. "If that's the only way to keep her from hurting herself or anyone else, then, yes, it might come to that. But that's a long way down the road. First you need to get the evaluation. And you need to get someone into your house right away to make sure all these accidents stop happening. Will you do that?"

She nodded.

"Good. Do you need any help?"

"No. No. I'm OK." She got up hurriedly, rubbing Betsy's neck as she did so. "I have to get home. Marianne will have the police dragging the Bay for me."

I must have flinched, because she immediately began apologizing. "I'm sorry - I didn't mean - I don't think - I've never believed - you wouldn't - it's not you -" She hiccupped miserably and tried again. "I'm just sorry," she said. "I'm just so sorry for everything."

She shook hands with Mark and Harmony and gave me a quick kiss on the cheek. And then she glided away in her champagne Mercedes.

I was tired to the bone. Over dinner, I tried to process what Sarah had told us, what had happened in court, what I was going to do about Clark Swanson and Mike Saunders, and what the hell I was thinking of trying to take over the mill. Halfway through dinner, I decided I could not survive one more minute if I didn't close my eyes. So I went upstairs, laid down, and worried with my eyes shut. Much better.

I was worried about everything: my sisters, myself, the mill, my dad. My dad. More than anything, I was kicking myself for not asking Sarah the question that had been burning on my lips since that night in the hospital. She had seemed so vulnerable, so crushed; the question, so bizarre that I was afraid Mark and Harmony would have carted me back to the emergency room if I had breathed a word.

More than anything else in the world, I wanted to ask one question:

Sarah, is our father still alive?

CHAPTER 20

This was how I figured it: In the weeks and months leading up to the fire, my father had been in one hell of a lot of trouble. His business was teetering on bankruptcy; he had the government on his back and a bunch of environmentalist protestors dogging him and the mill; and his two closest associates - people he had known since high school - were robbing him blind.

Plus, I flattered myself slightly, he was heading for a reunion with me that he couldn't have wanted. It was only a matter of time before someone I was deposing or someone at court remarked on my curious similarity - in name and appearance - to the owner of the mill. I still didn't have a handle on what my father knew or thought of me, but I was pretty damn sure that he would not have been delighted to meet his only son on the other side of the v. in the case that was going to ruin his business and expose his infidelity - if not his outright stupidity.

My dad was in a fix. And when he had been in a fix before - when he had taken leave of his senses and knocked up my mother, for example - he had split. Just split. No explanation. I couldn't shake the feeling that I was witnessing the latest - but perhaps not the last - magic act by the Incredible Disappearing Jack Hart Senior. My dad wouldn't have been the first guy in the world to commit pseudocide when things got too hot to handle.

I agree that there were holes in my theory. There was, for one, the body. Notwithstanding all the inbred bias I had experienced so far in the Bellingham police department, even the estimable Sergeant Lee probably wouldn't go so far as to fake a fatality. I thought of my father's pallbearers, panting and bowlegged under the weight of the coffin. *Someone* had been in that box. The funeral had been closed-casket, though, which probably meant that the body had been damaged in the flames. Just how sure were they that the dead man was really my dad? Anthony had said that Marianne identified him, but she seemed impressionable. Or, I considered, she could have been in on the plot.

So where was he? I considered and rejected the notion that he could be hiding in the Edgemoor house. It was certainly big enough, but the risk of disclosure was too great. But there was another possibility that had been nagging at me since I read the will. My father had left me a vacation lodge on Orcas Island. What better place to hide than the remote, mist-swathed San Juans? I was still tethered to Bellingham because of Sergeant Lee's ostensible suspicions and my obligations to the mill, but as soon as I could, I was taking the ferry to Orcas to check things out.

First, however, I was going to have a little chat with Clark Swanson. Not that I was looking forward to it. Through no fault of my own, I had had more than a passing acquaintance with a couple of murderers, and I bore a formidable collection of scars as testament to their determination not to be exposed. But someone had shot Mike Saunders right through the throat, and I nominated our fine Port commissioner as the likeliest of suspects. Mike and Clark had both been defrauding the mill, and Mark had taught me that a joint crime is the most dangerous act in the world. We had rattled Mike Saunders. I knew we had. Who had a better motive to shut him up than his co-conspirator?

I wasn't going to confront Clark Swanson alone. And I wasn't going to confront Clark Swanson with Harmony in tow. But if all went according to plan, the three of us - me, Mark, and Mark's gun - were going to pay Clark a little visit. Clark Swanson had a lot of explaining to do.

I didn't care if it was dangerous. I was going to fix this. I was going to clean up everything - from the lawsuit to the mill to whatever was going on with Beth. I was going to make it safe for my dad to come back. With that resolution established, I sank almost immediately to sleep.

I woke the next morning bathed in sunlight, in the momentary disorientation of a Northwesterner deprived of the rain and the grey. Harmony was patting my cheek.

"Jack, Sarah just called. She wants us to come right now. They took Beth to the doctor, and he wants to commit her."

To hell with the beautiful day. Sarah's news rousted me, the covers, and both dogs out of bed in an instant. Trailing bedclothes and shedding pajamas, I dressed, combed my hair, and brushed my teeth while hurtling out of the room and down the stairs. Mark and Harmony stood at the bottom, both looking, as always, impeccably groomed. How did they pull that off? Then I glimpsed the clock on the mantle and realized that it was past 11. The two of them had been up for hours.

The mental hospital did not look anything like I feared. There were no hulking nurses, steel doors, or visible restraints. Nothing was institutional green. Instead, a very nice lady with bouncy brown hair ushered us into a pale peach waiting room where plants bloomed, comfy chairs beckoned, and my sisters were having the catfight of the century.

"Who called *him*?" Emily exclaimed as I hove into view.

"I did." Sarah looked like she hadn't closed her eyes all night, but her voice was calm.

"As if he hasn't done enough damage. First he talks you into committing Beth, and now he's here to make sure you finish the job."

Well, that was grossly unfair. I was about to jump right into the fray when Emily burst into tears.

"This would kill Mama and Daddy," she sobbed. "It would absolutely kill both of them; I mean, it would if Daddy weren't already dead. How could you do this, you -" She suddenly flung herself out of the room. The whole room shuddered as she slammed the glass door.

In tense whispers, under the sear of Marianne's radiating disapproval, Sarah told me what she'd done.

Dr. Lane Kovic was an old family friend. She had called him that morning and asked for an emergency consultation. When Dr. Kovic heard about Beth's recent behavior, he told Sarah he wanted to keep her at the hospital through the weekend for observation. Sarah had told her sisters, and the shit had completely hit the fan.

The situation did not seem as bad as I had feared. I had been dreading straitjackets and shock treatments, and all the doctor wanted was a chance to watch Beth around the clock - which seemed to me like a fine idea.

But then the door opened and I saw Beth herself, tiny - almost translucent - and terrified. She hunched over. She hung her head. She clutched a delicate white handkerchief edged with elegant tatting. She rubbed and twisted the fabric, as if the handkerchief were a magic lamp that could save her, that could somehow take her away.

It was the tatting that hurt the most. It was no big deal for me - for Sarah, for almost anybody else - to spend the weekend in a hospital. But for Beth, it just might seem like the end of the world. She'd probably never stayed away from home overnight, never been away from her family. And now, after she'd just lost her father and maybe even her mother, I had callously set in motion the possibility that she was going to be locked up for two days in a strange place, with strange people, strange food, strange smells, strange sights - nothing comforting or familiar except her tatting. I could have throttled myself. For the guy planning to clean up the whole town, I had managed to make an almighty mess of my first attempt.

The bouncy-haired lady who had welcomed us escorted Beth in from the hallway. A somewhat sobered Emily followed. The lady settled Beth in one of the comfy chairs by a tank of tropical fish, talking to her a bright, syrupy chirp. She never paused to let Beth answer her inane questions. Unlike my sisters, who actually listened to Beth's silences and seemed to understand, Ms. Bouncy-Hair didn't make the slightest effort to determine what Beth might actually want. Her initial pleasantness to us notwithstanding, I was beginning to dislike her intensely.

"There, dear, there you go, you want to watch the fish, don't you?" she prattled to Beth. "Right, there you are with the fish. And you want to put down this pretty hankie, don't you, dear?"

She yanked the handkerchief out of Beth's hands. Beth's fingers flung out, then crumpled in her lap. Before any of us could protest or explain, Ms. Bouncy-Hair turned to us - right in front of Beth - and held out the wisp of cloth and lace. "We don't want her messing up something this nice, do we?"

"It's Beth's handkerchief," Sarah said, in a voice so cold that even Ms. Bouncy-Hair seemed to sense that she had done something appalling. "She made it."

"*She* did?" Ms. Bouncy-Hair eyed Beth uncertainly, nonplussed that a patient could actually do anything besides sit in front of a fish tank. "Well, aren't you the cleverest little thing?" she cooed to Beth.

Ms. Bouncy-Hair edged uneasily from the room. As the door closed behind her, I said, not quite under my breath enough, "Bitch." And I heard, over by the fish tank, a very small, clear, unused sort of voice echo: "bitch."

That startled all of us enough to laugh. For a moment I thought it must have been my mind playing tricks, but my other sisters didn't seem unduly surprised. At our ill-fated dinner party, I remembered, Sarah had said that Beth didn't talk much, not that she didn't talk at all. I hoped I hadn't taught her a new word.

I had learned by now what happened when you turned your back on Beth, so I went over to her, replaced the handkerchief in her hands, and bent and kissed her cheek. I introduced her to Mark and Harmony, waiting politely for her to say hello to them and continuing undisturbed when she didn't. She didn't stir when Harmony gave her hand a warm, kind squeeze, but she raised her head and looked Mark full in the face when he greeted her. Simply more evidence that Mark was irresistible to women. Even Emily, despite her outburst, had recovered sufficiently to cast predatory glances in his direction.

Mark ignored Emily. While Emily and Marianne clustered around Beth, Mark slipped an arm around Sarah's shoulders. "How are you holding up?"

"I'm OK." He cocked an eyebrow at her, and she reconsidered. "Well, not exactly OK. Pretty crappy, actually."

"Everything's going to be all right, Sarah," he told her. "You did the right thing."

Emily glared at Sarah, who seemed buoyed and flattered by Mark's attention. I was debating whether to join their conversation when I noticed two orderlies in scrubs and white coats, staring at us through the glass door. They weren't looking at Emily, which would have been understandable, as she was wearing a black leotard and faded jeans that seemed to have grown on her. They were looking at Beth - tiny, blond, beautiful, vulnerable, fragile Beth, who seemed so delicate she might break if you touched her. And they were nudging each other.

Now this was the mental hospital I had feared. A jolt of fury shot through me. I started toward the door. Mark glanced up from Sarah, appraised the situation, and followed me.

The two orderlies stopped their sniggering as Mark and I shouldered through the door. Mark and I are both big guys. You could have made one of us out of the two of them. To heighten the effect, Mark ran his hand through his hair, raising his leather jacket just enough for them to see his shoulder holster.

We got right in their faces, close enough to note the beads of sweat sprouting above their pimply lips. And I got right to the point.

"You were looking at my sister."

The shorter, balder one tried to weasel out of it. "We weren't looking at anyone, man, we were just -"

"You were looking at my sister," I interrupted. "I love my sister very much. If she ends up spending any time here whatsoever, I will be coming by at all sorts of strange hours. I will show up when you least expect it, and I will be watching for the two of you. And if anything happens to my sister - if I find so much as a tiny bruise on her, or if she seems the slightest bit upset - I will rip off your dicks and shove them up your ass."

I said all this calmly, matter of factly, even patiently, as though I were a teacher explaining a difficult concept to my stupidest pupils. That seemed to scare them even more than if I had screamed at them. They looked wildly from me to Mark - and then to Harmony, who had followed us from the waiting room.

"What he said," she confirmed, with dignity. We let them slither away, and then we turned around and came face to face with Dr. Kovic. He had a thin, quicksilver face and incongruous heavy-lidded eyes, sort of like a cross between a weasel and a frog. But he showed admirable aplomb, especially since he had just overheard me threatening his staff with grievous bodily harm.

"All our staff is licensed and bonded," he said mildly. "And we ensure patient safety with twenty-four-hour supervision."

"By those two creeps?"

"If you are concerned about Tom and Terry, we'll assign other personnel to your sister."

Good start. The doctor himself seemed like a decent guy, but from what I had seen of Tom, Terry, and Ms. Bouncy-Hair, I didn't want Beth anywhere near this place. Now I just had to stop what I had started.

"Dr. Kovic, why do you have to keep Beth here? Isn't there any way we can care for her at home?"

"That may well be possible, but at the moment, I'm not sure what we're dealing with." He stepped closer and lowered his voice. "I understand that Beth has attacked at least two people and maybe more. Added to that her predilection for throwing things and starting fires, and I am very concerned about releasing her without a thorough evaluation, especially given the presence of a child in the house."

"What if we brought someone in to watch over her?" Harmony asked. "A day nurse and night nurse, for example?"

"Well, it will be difficult to find someone, for one thing. And private nursing is expensive."

"But that would address your safety concerns?"

"It would mitigate them, yes, but it wouldn't assist in therapeutic evaluation or diagnosis. I really need to see how Beth behaves when she doesn't know she's being observed. I need to see her in a clinical setting."

"How about if we installed some hidden video cameras?" Mark was a veteran of all sorts of surveillance, wiretapping, and covert operations. "We could bring you the tapes on Monday so you could see how she got along. And we could also rig up some motion detectors so we'd know if she went into the baby's room."

Dr. Kovic nodded slowly. "It's not a perfect solution, but it would give us something to start with." He suddenly gave his head a decisive shake. "All right. We'll see you Monday, then. Good luck."

We turned to Sarah, who was framed in the doorway, expecting her to be pleased. Instead, she looked concerned.

"How much is all that going to cost?" she asked.

"It doesn't matter, Sarah," Harmony said.

Sarah didn't catch Harmony's meaning. She glanced at me with trepidation. "It does kind of matter," she said. "That insurance company won't pay on Daddy's life insurance policy. And since he left everything else to you under the will -" She broke off and rubbed her forehead. "It does matter right now, if this kind of care is going to be expensive. It matters a lot."

Harmony tried again. "I meant, don't worry about it."

This time Sarah understood. She flushed. "Oh, no," she protested. "That's so nice of you, but we couldn't let you do that."

I chimed in to give Sarah genuinely helpful advice. "Sarah, I used to get in arguments like this with Harmony all the time. But now I've learned that I might as well just say, 'OK. Thanks.' The eventual outcome is exactly the same, and it's so much easier on everybody."

Sarah was not up to a fight. "OK. Thanks," she mumbled to Harmony, embarrassed but painfully grateful.

And that was how we all ended up spending the afternoon at my father's Edgemoor mansion. While Harmony worked the phones to find excellent in-home care, Mark and I installed tiny video cameras that looked like anything but video cameras, safety locks on everything from the knife drawer to the garage, and motion detector alarms on all the outside doors and Beth's and Jennifer's rooms. Beth sat and tatted happily, Jennifer crawled around our feet and cooed and gurgled when I picked her up, and even Marianne and Emily seemed to warm toward me.

I caught Marianne throwing away that morning's Bellingham Herald. Splashed all over the front page was a picture of me and Bethany leaving the courtroom the day before. Because I was helping her with her coat, it looked as though I had my arm around her, an impression the Herald emphasized with the banner headline, "Heir Cuts Sweetheart Deal With DOE."

"The Herald prints such trash," was all she said. But it was enough.

Somehow, somebody invited us to dinner - then panicked when it became apparent that all the hams in the refrigerator had been picked clean. So Harmony, who had already secured the services of two highly recommended nurses, slipped into the kitchen and took charge. Soon two chickens were crackling in the oven, onions and tomatoes were sputtering in butter on the stove, and a head of somewhat dejected lettuce was crisping in icy water. Everyone found their way to the kitchen, drawn by some remarkably good smells.

"You all are incredibly useful people," Marianne allowed, peeking into the steaming pot of Harmony's seared tomato soup. Harmony had stumbled over two dusty cans of tomatoes in a cupboard and was putting them to good use.

"You really are," Emily agreed, watching Mark replace the glass panel Beth had smashed on my last visit. It had been covered with a sodden piece of cardboard. "Mark, what do you do in real life? Are you a carpenter? An electrician?"

Mark skimmed off some errant putty before replying. "No, I'm a cop. With the Seattle Police Department."

"You're a policeman?" Emily was aghast. "You don't look like a policeman."

"Homicide detective. Yeah."

Emily exhaled in exasperation and fluttered her hands toward Sarah. "OK. He's yours," she said. Then she flounced out of the room.

"What was that all about?" Mark asked Sarah, who was beet red.

"Oh, nothing. It's just that my husband was a police officer," Sarah explained.

"I thought he worked at the mill."

"He did, but only after he left the sheriff's department. His partner was shot in front of him, and he wanted a nice safe job in a nice safe paper plant doing nice safe boring things. He was foreman for a while - and then he died in an accident just a week after Daddy made him the chief operating officer." Her eyes clouded as she wrenched herself from the memory. "Anyway, Emily used to date Scott while he was still a cop, before we started going out. And it didn't work out too well."

"I can't imagine why," Mark said.

Sarah rose to her sister's defense. "Oh, you've just seen Emily at a bad time," she said. "She's wonderful, really. It's just that Scott had so much going on in his work life that he needed some peace and quiet at home. And Emily's not like that. There's never a dull moment with her. So eventually, Scott and I got together." She blushed and half-smiled. "There are many dull moments with me."

That made us laugh, and some of the sadness lifted from her face. As she and I set the table, we suddenly found ourselves alone in the kitchen. Harmony was rummaging around in the pantry, and Mark was putting the putty away in the garage. Sarah reached for my hand over the table.

"Jack, I am so sorry for trying to stop you from taking over the mill. Especially since you had been with me just that morning. It was cowardly to have them serve the papers on you like that. You must have been so angry."

"It hurt a bit," I admitted. "But I can see why you thought I might try to pull a fast one on you."

She shook her head in protest. "I didn't think you would do anything wrong. But Clark Swanson came over right after you left, and he told us all these things about American Fidelity, and how you'd have to treat us a certain way because you had represented them, and -" She blinked. "What's the matter?"

So it was Clark Swanson who had tried to get me disqualified. And small wonder, given what he had to hide. I wanted to talk to that bastard, and I wanted to talk to him right then. I shook my head at Sarah's worried face. "It's nothing. I just forgot that I was hoping to hook up with Clark today. I've got to ask him some questions about the mill."

"Well, he just lives down the street," she said unexpectedly. I hadn't quite mastered Bellingham geography. "You might as well call him from here."

I didn't want to tip Clark off, but before I could think of a way to stop her, she had dialed his number and was handing me the phone. Fortunately, the line was busy. That meant he was home. I considered, then asked, "How far down the street?"

"About a mile. Do you want to run down there before dinner? He won't mind. He's very nice, and kind of lonely, too, since his wife died. He always likes a chat. Would you like me to go with you?"

I refused a little too hastily. I told Harmony where I was going and watched her brows knit with worry. "We'll be all right," I assured her. "Will you be OK here?"

"Oh, yes, I'll be OK," she replied, with an undernote of sarcasm. "I can take your sisters if they get out of hand. But I wish you'd wait until Detective Anthony gets here to confront Clark Swanson."

"Anthony can't come until Tuesday, and it's better to catch Clark now before he gets the wind up. Don't worry; Mark will be with me. We'll be careful. If we're not back in an hour, call the police."

She didn't say it, but I could read her expression: *A lot can happen in an hour.*

Mark and I discussed strategy during the short drive to Clark's house. He would stay a little behind me, protecting my back. We would start affably enough, asking general questions, figuring out his movements, establishing opportunity. Then we'd move in for the kill. So to speak.

The bright blue October day was flaming to a close. Leaves and gravel crunched on the driveway up to the house, a broad-beamed Tudor affair that was just as ostentatious as my dad's. Warm lights glowed in the mullioned windows. A black Lexus was parked near the door. As we rounded a line of birch trees, we got the full effect of Clark's water view - a sweep of sea and sky. The house was perched before it, like a dark porthole to the Pacific, and the sunset streamed through it, red and refracted in the plump pillows of glass.

Mark put his hand on the hood of the Lexus. "Cold," he said. "He hasn't been anywhere in a while."

We rang the bell and listened. Nothing. We rang again. This time, I thought I heard the smallest noise, although it may have been my overactive imagination or the growing fire in my side. My pain meds were back at Karen's bed and breakfast, and I was missing them. I was also hungry and tired, and beginning to regret this entire enterprise. Mark apparently agreed. He hammered on the door a few times, then shrugged.

"If he's in there, he's not answering. Maybe one of your sisters called him and tipped him off. Probably Emily." He tried the bell again. Still nothing.

"Let's walk around the house and try the back door. And if he doesn't answer then, I say we split." He jerked his thumb toward the cold black Lexus, the massive, brooding house, the thicket of trees screening us from the street. "All this wealth is giving me the creeps."

Pools of light from the windows surrounded the house. We avoided them as we walked. If someone was watching us - from inside or outside the house - it was best to stay in the shadows. But as we rounded the corner, a low stone fence forced us to step close to two French doors.

And we both saw it at the same time.

An open gun cabinet on the far wall, stocked with rifles and pistols - with an empty space gaping in the pistol rack.

A phone receiver swaying slightly by its cord.

A man's hand, flung upwards in a sad, valedictory wave.

That's when Mark kicked in the door, but we were too late.

Clark Swanson was quite, quite dead.

CHAPTER 21

"Well, well, a dead body and Jack Hart. What a surprising combination."

"Spin on it, Lee."

Mark tensed and put a warning hand on my back. Lee stopped and whirled around. "What did you say to me?"

"I said, spin on it - *Cecil.*"

I agree that this was not the smartest move I ever made, but I had had it. I was sick of being accused of things I didn't do. I was sick of being in the wrong place at the wrong time. And I was especially sick of little Cecil Lee trying to pin every crime in Whatcom County on my shoulders.

Lee's face was white with fury. He took a step toward me, and I took a step toward him. Mark threw himself between us and pushed me back; one of Lee's officers tactfully but firmly positioned himself in front of his sergeant. Glaring at me over the officer's shoulder, Lee gestured contemptuously with his thumb. "I want them interviewed separately. And hook him up."

Which is how I wound up handcuffed in the back of a Bellingham police cruiser, watching the cops swarm Clark Swanson's house. Flashes from the police photographer froze the horrible scene in strobe-like relief. Spinning lights played on the Tudor house. Criminalists were dusting and measuring and sketching; everyone was paying particular attention to the open gun cabinet. Someone was busy wrapping and tagging the weapons. They were taking all of them into evidence.

The officer left the front door of the cruiser open so I could "cool off." I was duly freezing, but at least I could hear what was going on. I heard Mark giving his statement - calm, emotionless, and factual, deliberately vague on the reasons for our visit to Clark Swanson. I heard Lee shouting orders like a belligerent major dwarf. And I heard the terrible thud and scrape of the stretcher as the medical examiner removed the body. I shivered as the long black shape jerked toward me. This time, it had nothing to do with the cold.

At least someone had turned off the record player. When Mark kicked in the door, the first thing we heard was the scratching of the needle at the end of a record, a sound at once strangely, cracklingly alive, yet shudderingly, ceaselessly final. The record itself was an old Glenn Miller 45. More than anything else, that convinced me that no matter how carefully the stage had been set, this was a murder, not a suicide. Nobody blows his brains out to the tune of *Chattanooga Choo Choo*.

My manacled hands stuck to the Naugahyde seat. The position was not only undignified but pulled the muscles in my wounded side. Without food or pain medication, I was beginning to feel seriously woozy. I consoled myself with thoughts of suing the City of Bellingham in general, Sergeant Lee in particular.

Another hour clicked by on the clock in the cruiser. We had been gone three times longer than we expected. Harmony would be frantic. I had no illusions that the Bellingham police would have explained the situation. From what I'd seen of Sergeant Lee, their MO was pretty simple: bully your witnesses any way you can. I cringed at the thought of Harmony in some dingy, airless interview room, prodded with questions, pelted with misinformation, not knowing whether Mark and I were alive or dead, murder suspects or murder victims. I ground my teeth with frustration and set off a wave of cramping down my side and through my arms. I mentally added another zero to my eventual damage claim. If they were abusing Harmony, they were going to pay.

All told, I was already in a foul mood when the officer who had cuffed me slid into the front seat. He slammed the door and cranked the heat, ignoring me while he shuffled papers, judiciously picked his nose, and - this was my favorite part - called his wife to tell her he would be home for dinner.

"Yep, this one's pretty well wrapped up," he drawled into the phone. "We got the guy who did it. All that's left is the paperwork. And Lee said he wants to handle that himself. I'll see you soon, sweetie." He made nuzzling noises. "You too, baby doll. Bye now."

He clicked the phone closed and caught my eye in the rearview mirror. "So what's it gonna be, slugger?" he said. "You gonna be good now? You gonna make it easier on yourself?"

I nodded toward the phone. "You know, those things work a whole lot better if you turn them on before you dial."

In his sheepish look, I caught a flash of admiration that I had cut so quickly through his subterfuge. He was blushing, but the smile he turned on me was genuine enough. Removed from Lee's tutelage, this officer might have a future as a real human being. "So that's how you do it," he said, shaking the phone and holding it up to his ear. "Damned newfangled gadgets." He smiled at me again. "Thanks for the tip."

"You're welcome."

"So how did a smart kid like you get into so much trouble, Jack? You want to tell me about it?"

Oh, please. Now he was good cop. Give me a little credit, I wanted to say, but I refrained. I was in no mood for a roasting at the expert hands of Lee or the large, square-faced policeman. I replied politely but firmly: "No. I want to talk to my attorney. Her name is Harmony Piper. She's at my father's house."

"Jack, Jack, Jack." The officer rolled his eyes. "That would be the second biggest mistake you've made today. We're trying to work with you here. If this was an accident, if this was self-defense, no one's trying to make it murder. But you start dragging attorneys into this, Jack, and you can see how that looks to us. Only criminals need attorneys." He turned all the way around and fixed me with a sorrowful, kindly stare. "You trying to tell me you're a criminal, Jack?"

When this was over, I was going to write one hell of a law review article about the *de facto* erosion of the constitutional right to counsel. For the moment, I made do with repeating my earlier request. "I want to talk to my attorney, Harmony Piper. I'm not saying anything to you or anybody else until I do."

The officer snapped off the heat. "It's going to be a while before we can get you two together, seeing as how much work we've still got to do here. And *Ms.* Piper herself is already down at the station, talking to the detectives. She sure is a hot little number."

Well, that was as close to a threat as I wanted to come: *We're going to work over your girlfriend for a few hours while you sit here and freeze your ass off.* My heart twisted at the thought of Harmony alone with these goons, but the best way to get her out was to insist to see her as my attorney. They had to let me see her then; otherwise, they could keep us separated for as long as I was in custody.

The officer was watching me expectantly, waiting for me to crack. I stared back at him in stony silence. Finally he exhaled noisily, said, "Have it your way, asshole," and lurched out of the car, leaving both front doors open to the sharp sea wind.

No, I reflected bitterly, watching his retreating back. No future whatsoever as a real human being.

The cops let me stew for another two hours, while I ran through every possible scenario involving Harmony and a series of hateful Bellingham detectives. I was most worried about her personal welfare, but a small tinge of self-interest nagged at me as well. Harmony was the most composed person I had ever met. She was not one to lose her sangfroid. But Harmony loved me. I was still a little amazed by it, but I knew it to be true. She really loved me. And I wasn't sure how she would react if some bastard told her I was dead, that Mark was dead, that we were the ones lying still and cold in the ME's black van. If she cracked and told them about the plot we had uncovered, about my suspicions that Clark Swanson had killed Mike and my dad

- well, I was going to have a lot of explaining to do. Motive and opportunity, Lee would think.

I stretched again, setting off another wave of cramps. No sense borrowing trouble. There was nothing I could do about it in my current position. I just had to wait and get to Harmony as soon as I could.

I breathed slowly and deeply, trying to dispel the constriction across my chest. I was so cold that I had long since lost feeling in my hands. This was not necessarily a bad thing, as the handcuffs had hurt like hell.

I had worked myself into a Zen-like state of oneness with my pain when Lee himself slid behind the wheel and drove me silently, though with much jerking, jolting, and braking, to the police station. He pushed me in ahead of him. I wobbled on my numb and frozen legs. My hands stung and buzzed in the station's warmth.

The first thing I saw was Harmony. Marianne, Emily, and Sarah were just a blond blur behind her. One look, and I knew that my fears about Harmony's cracking had been unfounded - if not hallucinatory. Harmony's eyes were dry, her chin was up, and even from where I was standing, I could tell that she was furious. Not scared, not cowed - *pissed.*

Harmony saw me, and was suddenly plastered against me. I didn't even see her move. First she was across the room, then she was hanging on my neck. She slid her arms down to my waist, expertly avoiding my gunshot wound, and realized I was handcuffed. I felt the jolt go through her when she touched the cold metal. I felt a second jolt go through her when she touched my colder hands. She turned on the officer behind her, in a thick, adenoidal voice that I was sure was a devastating mimicry of his own: "But Ms. Piper, we just don't know what's happening over there."

The adenoidal officer had the grace to look embarrassed. Then she turned on Lee, with a snake-like intensity I'd rarely seen in her outside the courtroom. "Take off those handcuffs."

"See here, honey -"

"I said, take them off," Harmony snapped. "Right now."

Astonishingly, Lee obeyed.

"Thank you," Harmony said, sounding not in the least grateful. "Where is Mark?"

"Oh, he'll be along," Lee said, just as the door scraped and Mark was ushered in by two beefy policemen. Mark looked disheveled. This worried me. Mark almost never looked disheveled.

Harmony took our arms without a word. She marched us past the startled policemen toward the door.

"Whoa, whoa, whoa," Lee said, stepping in front of her. "Just where do you think you're going?"

"We are going home."

"You may go home if you want to, hon, but those boys there are staying with me. We have a lot to talk about."

"They're not saying anything to you." She tried to step around him, but he blocked her path again.

"Well, then, we'll just have to see about that, won't we?" Lee was taking out his handcuffs. At the mere sight, my wrists began to ache. "If that's the way it's going to be, I'm just going to have to take these two into custody."

"Sergeant Lee, we have cooperated with you fully since the beginning of this investigation. We voluntarily came to Bellingham after Mrs. Hart was attacked. We gave you complete and detailed statements that proved that my client could not have been involved. We agreed to stay in Bellingham until you completed your investigation. You could not compel us to do so. We stayed because we respected you, we respected your authority, and we wanted to assist you in whatever way we could. Instead of making even the barest attempt to investigate this case, however, you have done nothing but try to railroad my client. You have suppressed and ignored exculpatory evidence indicating that it was Beth Hart - not my client - who attacked her mother, you have instructed Mrs. Duncan not to tell us about this exculpatory evidence, and in so doing, you have endangered not only my client but also his sisters and his baby niece. In the short time we have been here, my client has been throttled, shot, and nearly killed. You have done nothing to protect him, you have done nothing to investigate the attempt on his life, and you have done nothing to prevent Beth from inflicting further harm on other members of her family. We are not cooperating with you anymore, Sergeant Lee. You are not acting in good faith, and we do not trust you. Now kindly step aside."

By this time, Lee had begun to suspect that Harmony was not someone you could call "hon." Not if you wanted to survive. "Now see here, Ms. Piper, you don't seem to understand what's happening here. I can toss both those boys in jail."

"Go ahead," Harmony said. "Charge them."

She had called his bluff. The prosecutor didn't have enough evidence to charge us. He knew it. She knew it. They stared at each other for what seemed like a very long time.

Lee played his last card, the one that had kept us in Bellingham even though we weren't under arrest. "I can hold them a couple of days before we charge, Ms. Piper. And a lot can happen to two pretty boys like this during a couple of days in jail."

"Sergeant Lee, the Section 1983 lawsuit that's heading your way is already a doozy. Don't make it worse by threatening my clients with bodily harm. Up to this point, I'm just going to go after you civilly. Just money. The city will pay; you'll get busted down a few ranks, pilloried in the press, generally hounded as a bad policeman, but you probably won't get fired. But believe me, if you put them in harm's way, if anything happens to them, it's a criminal case - and we will press charges. How would you like to be the pretty little boy in jail?"

They were nose to nose. Lee's face was grey and sweaty. Even his eyes looked clammy. His breath came rapidly and in little gasps. I thought he might have a heart attack right there.

Harmony moved a step closer. "Charge them, or get out of my way."

After what seemed like an eternity, Lee slowly moved aside. "Don't leave town," he hissed at me as we filed past.

"We will go anywhere we please," Harmony snapped back. "If you have anything to say to us, you can call David Mann in Seattle. You are not to contact my clients directly."

Lee flushed an angry red. "Any other orders, Ms. Piper?"

"Yes. Zip up your fly."

Then she swept out, shepherding me and Mark and trailed by my sisters, who had seemed transfixed by the proceedings. Once outside, it became clear that Harmony had meant every word she said about going anywhere she pleased. My sisters protested in disappointment and dismay, but Harmony was undeterred.

"I'm sorry, but we need to sleep in our own beds and shower in our own bathroom and eat our own food and live our own lives for a while. We will call you tomorrow morning to make sure everything went OK with the new nurses, and we will come up Monday if you need us to unload the videotapes and talk to Beth's doctor. But right now, we really have to go home."

To my surprise, she hugged each one of them goodbye, even Emily, who ended up chauffeuring us back to Karen's bed and breakfast. The police had seized my car, so the three of us stuffed our things into Harmony's little red Honda. We left Karen a note and a check, gave Bear a farewell rub around the ears, and roused Betsy with some difficulty. She went from grumpy to anxious in a matter of seconds, even insisting on snuggling between me and Harmony in the back seat. I was touched but thwarted. I loved my dog, but if anyone was going to warm me up, I wanted it to be Harmony.

Harmony was almost silent as we filled her in on what we had found at Clark Swanson's house. Around Marysville, she started to cry. I elbowed Betsy out of the way and hugged her as she sobbed. In little bits and gasps, she told us what had happened during the five hours when she didn't know if we were dead or alive.

Two officers had come to my father's house and asked her for our next of kin. They had refused to tell her what was going on, saying only that there had been a shooting and that she needed to come with them down to the police station. They had tried to take her alone, but Emily wouldn't hear of it. She had linked her arm with Harmony's and flat-out refused to let go.

"She said she learned how to hold on like that while she was protesting old-growth logging in Oregon," Harmony said, wiping her eyes. "They couldn't separate us without hurting us, so they didn't have any choice but to take us both. Marianne and Sarah waited for the nurse and Marianne's husband to come to take care of Beth, and then they showed up at the police station, too. They didn't leave me alone for a moment. They kept insisting that the police explain what was going on. Marianne called Sergeant Lee and told him that if he didn't bring you back right away, she'd never talk to him again. They used to date in high school, and now that she and Gary are having problems - well, I guess hope springs eternal. Lee showed up with you not ten minutes after she made that call."

She hugged Betsy, who had managed to re-insert herself between us. In response to my unspoken question, she said, "I didn't tell them anything. I didn't say what we had found or why you went over there. I figured that if you were really dead, they would have just come right out and told me so. I figured they had to be setting me up for something. I knew - at least in my mind I knew - that the only reason they'd be playing games with me was if you were still alive." She drew a long, shuddering breath. "But when I came out of the kitchen and saw those two men in uniform with their hats in their hands -" She broke off. Betsy whined and licked her cheek. "You have to promise not to do that again. You have to promise to take me with you."

Mark and I exchanged glances in the rearview mirror. "We can't do that, Harmony," Mark said. "We can't agree to put you in danger."

"Then you can't put yourself in danger, either," Harmony insisted. When we didn't reply, she pressed on: "You don't understand. If something happens to you, I don't want to be OK. I don't want to be the one who's left behind."

When she put it like that, I did understand. Just a year before, Harmony had driven out of Seattle as the long October sun was coming up, ferrying home some children as a favor to a friend. By the time she returned a week later, almost everyone she cared about was dead: her stepmom, her secretary, and the man who had raised her, the man she believed all her life to be her father. She had never come back to work; she avoided her parents' vast, empty mansion in Magnolia. When she was in Seattle, she stayed with me, watching over me and Mark, sleeping on a lumpy futon in my sunroom. I looked at her tense, tired face in the darkness and understood. Harmony was done with being left behind.

Most reluctantly, Mark and I promised that we would not knowingly blunder into danger without involving her. She accepted our pledges gravely, shut her eyes, and leaned against me. I was still freezing, and she flinched as her cheek touched mine. "Poor Jack," she said, rubbing my hands to warm me up. "We need to take you to the doctor. You could have caught pneumonia out there, especially hurt the way you are. No offense, Mark, but I really hate policemen right now."

"No offense taken, Harmony. Sometimes I hate them too."

I didn't like the sound of that. After much prodding, Mark admitted that the Bellingham police had, as he put it, "pushed him around."

"Did they hurt you?" Harmony demanded.

"No, not really. They slammed me up against the wall a couple of times, and one guy did his best to make me think he was going to work me over. Mostly, they just had a lot to say."

It was past three when we pulled up outside of my modest little house on the poor, flat, no-view side of Green Lake. Betsy scampered in and immediately set about sniffing the perimeter of each room, reestablishing her territory, making sure no one had trespassed any of her sacred boundaries. We unpacked in exhausted silence. Harmony and Mark went to bed; Betsy debated which one of us most deserved her favors, then sacked out with Harmony in the sunroom.

I ate a couple of graham crackers and chased them with my pain meds. For the first time that day, felt the fire in my side begin to wane. Then I looked around my little house, so unlike my father's lush, comfortable mansion or Karen's antique-filled B&B. While I had been surrounded by my father's leather couches and soft rugs and cushioned by Karen's Queen Anne bed, it had occurred to me that it might be a bit of a shock to come home. None of my furniture matched. I had bought some of it at garage sales; a few hand-me-down pieces had stuck around after various roommates moved on to bigger and better things.

Maybe it was the drugs, but I was amazed by the satisfaction that surged through me as I looked around my house. I had lovingly restored the maple floors. The chairs shared no parentage with the sofa, but they were grouped companionably around the fireplace and the TV. I didn't have any ornaments, collectibles, or knickknacks, but I did have photographs on the mantle: me, Mark, Harmony, and Betsy, decorating the Christmas tree; me and Mark at a church picnic when we were foster brothers; me and Betsy at her graduation from obedience school. She was wearing a little mortarboard and glaring at me.

I sat in my bay window and looked out at my garden as it took shape against the lightening sky. It was another startlingly beautiful Northwest morning, all pink and gold and blue. Everything seemed lit from within - the maple floorboards, the mantlepiece, the bed of crisp green hostas - everything the three of us had built and cleaned and polished, everything we had made grow.

I couldn't stop looking at it. I couldn't get enough of it.

It was full daylight when I went to bed. Mark and Harmony were still asleep. Betsy was curled next to Harmony, her nose snuggled under her chin.

My head hit the pillow. I let out a long, slow sigh as my body curved around the familiar hills and valleys of the mattress.

I closed my eyes and just let myself be safe and happy, at peace and at home.

CHAPTER 22

We didn't want to leave. First we thought we'd head back to Bellingham Sunday night to help my sisters remove the hidden video cameras, unload them, and insert new tapes. But Mark talked Sarah through the operation over the phone, albeit with much arm-waving and gesticulation, so we didn't have to go. Then we thought we should show up Monday for Beth's appointment with Dr. Kovic, but it turned out that Beth had passed an uneventful weekend. She seemed to like both of her nurses, one of whom knew how to tat, and the videos showed only two escapades that were out of the ordinary.

In one, she tried to climb out her window. In the other, she stole from her bed about four in the morning and went into her mother's room, where she started going through the closets and drawers. Each time, she was intercepted by the night nurse, who had been alerted by the motion sensor alarm and video cameras.

"We couldn't tell what she was looking for," Sarah said. "Marianne thought it might be tatting cotton, but Mama hasn't tatted since her strokes. We keep all the thread in Beth's cabinet in the kitchen. But anyway, she wasn't upset when the nurse came in. She showed her how to turn on the lights around Mama's vanity mirror, she sat down at Mama's dressing table, and then she started brushing her hair. That's where Mama always got her ready for school." There was a tremor in her voice. "So Emily thinks maybe Beth just misses Mama. There wasn't anything violent or scary on any of the tapes."

So far so good. Then Sarah said wistfully, "Does that mean you won't be coming home?"

Home. I was home. And I wasn't eager to leave any time soon. I explained that we'd come whenever they needed us, and that I'd be coming up to talk to people about the mill. But for the moment, at least, we were going to stay in Seattle. They had a standing invitation to visit.

Sarah's answering "Oh," was freighted with disappointment and something approaching distress. I remembered her concern over the cost of the nurses and video cameras and broached the subject as delicately as I could - which wasn't very delicate. "Sarah, are you guys OK for money right now?"

I could sense her embarrassment over the phone. "Well, not exactly. I have Scott's Social Security and his pension from the sheriff's department. That would be enough for me and Jennifer, but Beth goes to a private school, and it's not cheap. And you wouldn't believe how much it costs to heat this house. It's so kind of you to let us stay here, but we may not be able to afford to much longer. Unless -" She stopped.

"Unless?" I prompted.

"I have no right to ask you this."

"Ask."

"Will you please talk to that insurance company about Daddy's policy? I know they used to be your client, and I'm not trying to put you in a jam, but they just won't listen to me. They keep insisting it was suicide, and I know it wasn't. I know Daddy wouldn't do that to us. But now I can't even get them to return my calls."

Dammit. I had been expecting Sarah to ask for help with the tuition and the gas bill, which I was more than willing to provide - at least until Virginia Carlson died and the girls came into their inheritance. I liked the folks from American Fidelity, but we hadn't exactly parted on the best of terms. I was still smarting over the way they had dumped me when they learned about my less-than-stellar childhood, and I imagined they were probably still smarting over the sticky spot I had put them in, however unintentionally. But Sarah seemed so worried. Before I could stop myself, I was saying, "Sure. I'll talk to them. But I don't know whether they'll listen any more to me than they did to you."

"From what I've seen so far, you're pretty persuasive, Jack. So thanks. Thanks for everything." And then she was gone.

After that, the four of us got back to wallowing in being home. Harmony bought actual groceries and made us fried chicken and mashed potatoes. For dessert we tucked into warm apple pie. Mark was so inspired that he promised to cook dinner sometime that week, which immediately set us to guessing. I'd seen Mark prepare only two things, one of which was margaritas.

On Tuesday, Mark went back to work. Harmony spent hours speaking Japanese into her cellphone, negotiating some settlement for Higuro. I began to sort out my dad's estate and to try to impose some rationality on the mill. Probate was progressing up in Bellingham, but I didn't need to wait for those formalities to take control of the mill, which had passed to us by trust. I drafted a nonsuit dismissing the case against American Fidelity and messengered it to the courthouse and the insurance company.

By Thursday, it had become apparent that I had to go into work. Somehow people figured out I was back in town. Even though I was studiously avoiding my voicemail and e-mail, partners and even clients were calling me at home - undeterred by my phone greeting informing them that I was on indefinite unpaid leave because of a death in the family. It got to the point that I had to either buck up and get back to work, or totally withdraw from my current matters and kiss Piper Whatcom goodbye. I was still undecided about which course to take when Harmony and I showed up at Piper Whatcom Thursday afternoon.

The receptionist's eyes lit up when we stepped off the elevator at the 42nd floor. She ran around her desk and gave us each a little hug.

"Are you back? I've missed you so much. You two were my favorite attorneys at the firm." She considered. "I realize that's not saying much, but really, it's been horrible around here without you."

"We need to pick up some stuff," Harmony explained vaguely. "But we missed you too."

On the way to my office, we encountered Rob Browning, who smoothed his sleek hair and snapped, "I need those repo seminar materials by tomorrow, Jack"; Dan Bradford, who smirked at me and said, "I knew you'd come crawling back"; and Sydney Leath, who exclaimed, in genuine disappointment, "Oh, you're not in jail after all."

Home, sweet home at Piper Whatcom. I shut my office door more decisively than necessary and sank into my chair. Harmony smiled at me from across the desk. "Some things never change."

"Makes my decision easier."

"Really?"

I shuffled the messages on my desk. Two were from one of my favorite clients, for whom I had successfully defended a forfeiture action on his beloved Cessna. One was from an opposing counsel who had to be a hundred and three and who always called me "Tiger," making me laugh even while he tried to slip the most outrageous discovery abuses under my nose. And one was from Judge Brady, the best judge in King County, in his own tiny handwriting: "Stopped by, Jack. So sorry about your dad. Miss you like hell on the Calexton Mining case. Dan Bradford is such an ass."

"Really?" Harmony prompted.

I looked at the messages, at the bookshelf stuffed with binders organizing each of my cases, at the Lucite cube containing a shrunken version of the judgment awarding one of my clients $6 million in damages. It had been my first trial.

"No," I admitted. "No, not when it comes right down to it." I waved my hand around my office. "I've worked so hard to get where I am, Harmony. I don't want to throw it all away."

She leaned across the desk and took my hands. "You're not throwing anything away, Jack. Whatever you decide, you'll still have everything you've worked for.

Even if you leave, you'll still have your reputation, and your experience, and your skills, and your contacts -"

"But not my salary," I reminded her.

"Your dad left you pretty well fixed."

"I'd have to sell the house out from under the girls. The mill may not be worth anything right now. So it's kind of hard to rely on that."

We sat quietly for a while. She told me she'd support me no matter what. I was afraid she meant it literally, so I just said, "I know."

I sighed and stretched. "I can't think here. Let's go for a walk and get some lunch. Maybe that will clear my head. Or maybe I'll just flip a coin."

We ran into Cory Corliss in the elevator well. Cory was the preening little pipsqueak of an associate who had replaced me in defending American Fidelity. As Dan put it, Cory was much more their speed: Harvard grad, son of a UW Regent, member of the Seattle Tennis Club. He never took off his suit jacket - not even on dress-down Fridays - and he always wore a Harvard signet ring. He was looking particularly glossy these days, with his little Caesar haircut and his wee Brooks Brothers suit.

"Monie!" he exclaimed, kissing a suddenly rigid Harmony on both cheeks. I hammered the down button while Cory brayed about their alleged mutual friends and classmates. He had a blaring nasal voice; all by himself, that man could raise whitecaps in Elliott Bay.

At length, he deigned to recognize me. Oh joy.

"So Jack," he drawled, "I got your nonsuit dismissing American Fidelity today. I must say that's the easiest case I've ever won. I wish I was always up against you."

I waited for the surge of anger - I was actually preparing to count to ten - but the flash of annoyance didn't come. I just glanced at him over my shoulder and said, "Oh, hi, Cory. Glad I could work that out for you. By the way, I'm looking for outside counsel for the mill. Got any recommendations?"

I watched in bliss as horrified realization washed over Cory's shiny little face. He suddenly twigged to the fact that I was no longer a fellow associate, no longer a competitor from a school he considered laughably inferior, but instead a potential client, someone he should, by the eat-what-you-kill law of the firm, suck up to until I relented and threw him some work. Then a fresh wave of horror broke as he realized that not only was I now someone who demanded pandering, but that since I was asking for recommendations, I obviously had no intention of hiring *him*.

Resentment, distaste, and venality struggled on his face. Venality won. "You know, Jack," he said, suddenly attentive. "I've got some time now that the SPP case has gone away. And I'm really interested in helping strengthen the manufacturing base across Puget Sound. It's only a matter of time before the dot-com bubble bursts, right? I think you'll find my hourly rate more than competitive –"

"Gee, thanks, Cory," I interrupted. "I appreciate the thought. But remember, *you've* got a conflict of interest."

Then Harmony and I stepped into the elevator, both giving him a cheerful wave. Somehow we waited until we had dropped two floors before we glanced at each other and burst out laughing. We were still laughing as we strolled out of the elevator, out of the lobby, out of the firm where I had spent five years of my life. As the huge arched doors closed silently behind us, I felt a rush of freedom. It was typical grey Seattle weather, the city smothered under a close layer of clouds, but it felt like the very first beam of light on the very first day of spring. The air just crackled with possibilities.

I draped an arm around Harmony's shoulders. "I am going straight to hell for enjoying that so much."

"I'll be right beside you if you do." Harmony was flushed with forty floors of hilarity. "That's the third-best thing about having money: being able to jerk the chain of guys like Cory, who so richly deserve it."

"What's the best thing?"

"Security."

"Second-best?"

"Doing nice things for people that would otherwise be impossible. Whenever I can do a good deed, especially if it's in secret, I think of it as penance for my ancestors cutting down all those beautiful old trees."

"I'll have to start doing penance for my ancestors dumping shit into Bellingham Bay while they stewed those beautiful old trees into pulp and paper." I pulled her closer. "Interesting, isn't it, that you and I ended up together? Timber and paper - a match made in heaven."

"It *is* a match made in heaven."

We were right in the middle of Third Avenue. I mean, literally, right in the middle of Third Avenue, crossing the street at University. With the benefit of hindsight, it was probably not the most auspicious location I could have chosen, but when she agreed that we were meant to be together, hope and joy flooded through me, knocking out my usual reticence and good sense. Her eyes were so blue and so happy.

Before we reached the other side of the street, I stopped, turned to her, took her hands, and said, "Marry me."

"*What?*"

"Marry me."

She was absolutely stunned. A car honked at us, and I added hurriedly, "I'll do it right later. Flowers, candles, dinner, and a ring. But marry me, Harmony. Please, marry me."

She swallowed. I had never seen Harmony so at a loss for words. She said slowly, "I don't need flowers and candles. I don't need dinner. I don't need a ring."

"Singing waiters?" I offered. "Skywriters? A billboard?"

"I just need time, Jack. I need more time."

"How much more time?"

"I don't know. Just more."

"How about a long engagement?"

Another car swerved around us. "Jack, we should not be talking about this in the middle of the street."

I nodded in agreement, walked her to the sidewalk, then turned to her again. "OK, we're not in the middle of the street. Marry me."

"We've only been dating two months," she protested.

"We've known each other five years. We've gone through murder, kidnapping, Betsy, and ten semiannual associate performance reviews. How much more do you think we need to experience before we know each other well enough to get married? Fire? Flood? Pestilence? We've already had a fire, so that just leaves the other two. Hell, with our luck, Harmony, flood and pestilence could happen this afternoon."

"Jack, Jack." She had hold of my arm, trying to slow me down. "Jack, I know what you're trying to do. I had the same reaction when my father died. It's so painful where you are right now that you're trying to make yourself a new family. That's what I did with Higuro - not consciously, but at least part of me was so relieved to go to Japan, with a brand new father and a brand new life, so I didn't have to face what had happened back here. I see you doing the same thing with your sisters. You're getting so enmeshed in their lives, you're getting so enmeshed in the mill, and now you're doing the same thing with me. But it doesn't work, Jack. You have to go through all the pain and the loss and the grief before you can move forward. And you haven't. You can't even admit that your father's dead."

I thought that over. "Maybe part of that's true," I admitted. "Maybe that is what I'm doing with the mill and my sisters. But not with you. I've wanted to marry you since the day I met you, and the only reason I've waited this long is that I didn't have anything to offer you before now. I love you, Harmony, and I want to marry you. And it has nothing to do with my dad."

She stared at me. Just stared at me. Her eyes were deep blue and bottomless. She was scary as hell when she looked at you like that. And then she said, "I can't."

"Can't ever?" There was an ugly incident in Harmony's past, a horrible experience when she had been sixteen, and a virgin, and on her second date. It had kept her locked up in herself for years. I was the only boyfriend she'd ever had, and it had taken her almost a year to risk even that.

"I don't know. But I can't now. If the question is still on the table, the answer is no."

"The question is not still on the table, Harmony." With more crispness than I intended, I spun around and continued down the street.

She caught up with me. Her small hand slipped into mine. "Please don't be mad."

"I'm not mad. But I don't think I can be a grownup with you right now."

She winced, and I felt like a jerk. It wasn't her fault that I had blindsided her when she wasn't ready. "I'm going to court to talk to Judge Brady and wrap up some cases. I'll meet you at the pig in an hour."

"Will that be long enough for you to act like a grownup?"

"No. But I'll fake it."

I started to turn from her, but she held me fast.

"I love you," she said.

"I love you too."

"And I'm sorry."

"I'm sorry too."

We had picked up that exchange from Detective Anthony. Policemen have such a high risk of not coming home at night that he made a point of clearing the air with Mrs. Anthony before he left each morning. He had seen too many new widows agonizing that their last words to their spouse had been over who forgot to take out the garbage. I kissed her quickly, and we squeezed hands and parted.

As I charged up Third Avenue, I reflected that at least I hadn't had a gaggle of singing waiters as the snickering witness to my rejection. I was rehearsing what I'd say to Harmony on the way home when I spotted Leah Batson, general counsel for American Fidelity, just about to enter the Arctic Building, a fine, weird old Seattle edifice with walrus-head gargoyles.

God was clearly punishing me for my cruelty to Cory Corliss. First Harmony, now Leah. I was still pissed at the way American Fidelity dumped me, but I had promised Sarah I'd talk to American Fidelity about my dad's life insurance payment. Here was my shot.

"Hey, Leah, wait up!"

She turned and spotted me. For just a second, I saw apprehension, maybe even fear, cross her face. But that was quickly engulfed by what looked like actual pleasure.

"Jack!" She threw her arms around me and hugged me hard. The drizzly day had pumped her frizzy brown hair to twice its normal volume. "I'm so glad I got to see you. I stopped by Piper Whatcom this morning, but you weren't there."

"What are you doing in town?"

She jerked her head toward the Arctic Building. "Hooking up with the hubby. It's one of our romantic getaway weekends where we both fly into Seattle, stay in a hotel, and try to pretend we don't live a thousand miles apart. His firm just opened up a branch in Seattle, though, so he's in there trying to ingratiate himself into a transfer to this office. Every little bit closer helps."

I made sympathetic noises.

"How about you? How are things going with the mill?"

"Oh, as well as could be expected, given that I don't know what the hell I'm doing."

She smiled at me. "You've already pulled off the coup of the century, getting the DOE to reverse that cleanup order. I still have no idea how you did that."

"Hey, let me represent all sides and sometimes I can do wonders. By the way, thanks for not trying to have my license revoked."

"Dan explained to us what had happened. We felt so bad for you. I'm so sorry about your dad. So sorry about how you grew up - well, sorry doesn't even begin to cut it."

It was the perfect opening. "Speaking of my dad - it's rotten to nab you like this, but my sisters are getting the runaround from your claims department on my dad's life insurance policy. And I'm not getting much further on trying to make a claim for the fire. We don't even know if we have a property casualty policy."

Sudden wariness shuttered her face. "Jack, really, there's nothing I can do on a claims matter -" she protested.

"Please, just point me in the right direction. My sisters can't even get anyone to return their calls."

She hesitated, then nodded. "I'll have someone look into it. If I don't call you back, I'll make sure someone else does." She patted my shoulder with what seemed like genuine affection. "Look, I've got to run. But take care of yourself, Jack. I miss working with you. Cory's a nice enough kid, but he doesn't have your, well, panache. I wish things had worked out differently."

"Me too."

She escaped into the Arctic Building. I took a few steps down the street, then stopped and looked back at the new sign in the window: Triad International. The name niggled at me for a few minutes. I couldn't place it. Then a tiny movement inside the building caught my eye, and I realized with a start that Leah was watching me from the other side of the glass. I had been standing outside staring in at the murky interior; she had been standing inside staring out at the murky day. We both made an embarrassed gesture - half acknowledgement, half apology - and I hurtled down the street.

I spent a productive hour at the courthouse and showed up just minutes late at Rachel, the huge bronze piggybank in front of the Pike Place Market. An extraordinary number of directions to places in downtown Seattle begin with the words: "OK, start at the pig . . . ."

Harmony was already there. One look at her red eyes and anxious face, and I felt like a total jerk.

"I was afraid you weren't going to come back."

"I'm always going to come back, Harmony."

We held hands and wandered from stall to stall. Mark had given us a shopping list for his mystery dinner – all sorts of ingredients we did not usually have in the house, including tequila. Harmony pondered the list.

"Posole, guacamole, and margaritas," she predicted.

"He'll set the place on fire," I protested.

"Oh, he only did that once. And it wasn't entirely his fault."

We passed a tranquil, healing hour at the Market but fell silent on the way home. Just before I turned into my driveway, I looked over at her and said, with all the delicacy I had shown so far that day, "Is it the sex?"

"Is what the sex?"

She was playing dumb. "Is that why you're afraid to marry me? You're scared to sleep with me?"

There was a long pause, then an almost inaudible "yes."

"Harmony." I unbuckled her seatbelt and pulled her close. "Harmony, it's not going to be like that with me. You can trust me."

She didn't answer. She was stiff and cold in my arms. Finally she looked up at me and said, "I do trust you. It's not you. But sometimes when we're together, I can feel his hands on me."

That ended that conversation right there. I couldn't think of a thing to say. I was actually afraid to touch her. We just went into my little house and helped Mark put together his incendiary pork stew.

Harmony was an amazing woman. From her warm, friendly, relaxed demeanor, no one could have guessed what had happened between us that day. But I noticed she kept a more physical distance from me than usual - and that Betsy inserted herself between us when I got a bit too close. So much for man's best friend.

We were washing up when the telephone rang. It was Sarah, bursting with excitement.

"Jack," she said, "Jack, everything's OK. You can come back home now. Sergeant Lee says Clark Swanson committed suicide."

CHAPTER 23

Well, if Lee thought it was suicide, it was a sure bet to be murder. I managed to keep myself from saying so to Sarah, making do with explaining gently that we hadn't left Bellingham because I was afraid of being charged with a crime.

"Oh," she said, sounding crushed. "But you will come back soon?"

I promised, and we said goodbye.

I filled Mark and Harmony in on Sarah's news. Ballistics linked the bullets that had struck me and Mike Saunders to one of the rifles in Clark's open gun cabinet. Phone records showed a call from Mike's office to Clark's the afternoon of the shooting. The way Lee figured it, after we had rattled Mike's cage about the books, Mike called Clark and told him he was going to come clean. Clark shot Mike to keep him quiet, and later shot himself, either out of remorse or desperation. As soon as I was granted control of the mill, Clark must have known that it was only a matter of time before I uncovered the extent of his conspiracy. Lee thought Clark killed himself before we caught up to him.

Somewhat to my surprise, Mark did not vehemently disagree with Lee's assessment. "It could have happened that way, I suppose," he said.

"Oh, come on. Nobody kills themselves to *Chattanooga Choo Choo*."

"Even happy songs can have sad memories," Harmony pointed out. "Clark's wife died not long ago. Maybe that was a song they danced to when they were young. Maybe he wanted to hear it one last time before he joined her."

"It wasn't just the song. The whole thing was so staged. The gun cabinet was open, one gun was missing, there it was on the floor. It was like someone was drawing a connect-the-dots. I mean, Mark, when we rounded that corner, didn't you feel like you'd just walked into a play?"

He made noncommittal noises. I was getting annoyed.

"Mark, can you look me in the eyes and tell me you believe it was suicide?"

Mark considered. "No," he said.

"How come?"

"Lots of little things. From the powder burns, it looked like the gun wasn't flush against the skull. That's unusual for a suicide. You don't hold the gun out here -" he demonstrated with his finger - "where your hand's going to be shaking and you might miss and blow off your nose; you steady the barrel against your head. The angle was strange. The round came out his temple, which means the gun was slightly behind his ear, pointed up on a diagonal. It's hard to hold a gun that way. Most people don't. They either eat it or they shoot straight from ear to ear. And the gun itself was hinky. Swanson had an awesome collection of guns - a Luger, a Walther Kurz, a Colt Python, a Smith & Wesson 59. If you like guns that much, I don't know why you'd pick a dime-a-dozen .38 to kill yourself. I wouldn't. He had a couple of nice little 9mms there, and that's the way I'd go."

"Why?"

"You saw the exit wound in the temple?" I nodded with a shudder. It had been the size of a grapefruit. ".38s take a lot of tissue with them; you know you're going to splatter yourself all over the place. It's a lot cleaner with a 9mm. They've got little Parabellum ammo that goes right through. Maybe it's just my vanity, but even if I were going to off myself, I wouldn't want to be tore up that bad."

He paused while Harmony and I digested that. After I had recovered, I asked, "So why did you say that it could have been a suicide?"

"Well, because it could. Just because something looks suspicious doesn't mean it is."

This was not the veteran cop I knew and loved. He must have sensed my frustration, because he said, quietly but extremely firmly, "Just leave it alone, Jack. Don't go up there and start sniffing around on this. Don't try to make this into a murder."

"Strange advice from a homicide detective, Mark."

"I'm off-duty. I'm not a homicide detective right now. And you're not a homicide detective at all. I don't want you to get hurt. And if you start stirring this up, you're going to get hurt. At the very least, you're not going to like where the answers lead."

I was afraid to ask him what he meant. Deep inside, I thought I already knew. I said, "You think it's my dad."

"Actually, I think your dad's dead. But assuming for the moment that he's alive, then he's got a lot of explaining to do. Three bodies: Mr. X at the mill, Mike, and now Clark. If your dad is still alive, he's got to be suspect number one. He's got motive up the wazoo. And if he's dead, then your sisters are pretty much suspects two, three, four, and five."

Harmony and I both protested. "Mark, I had my doubts about Jack's sisters, too," she said. "But after the way they treated me that horrible night up in

Bellingham, the way they rallied around me and wouldn't let the police mistreat me -" She broke off. "I think they really are sweet."

"I think they *seem* sweet," he countered. "But I also think it's interesting that Emily insisted on going to the police station with you. I wonder what she wanted to find out. I think it's interesting that Sarah brought up Clark Swanson and suggested you go talk to him. I wonder if she slipped away that afternoon while the three of us were busy with other things. I think it's interesting that Beth climbs out of her window at night. I wonder where she goes."

OK, this was the veteran policeman I knew and loved. Suspicious to a fault.

He shook his head at me. "Look, I'm not saying they did anything, but if I were really trying to get the bottom of this case, I would be taking a hell of a hard look at them right now." He paused and leaned forward. "You like those girls. You want to find out something about them that you'd rather not know?"

Harmony and I thought about it. "Aren't we taking an awful risk if we think it's murder and don't do anything about it?" Harmony asked. "What if he - or she - does it again?"

"There's a risk. But this looks to me like a closing crime. Someone went to a lot of trouble to wrap this up tight. They've sort of wrapped themselves up, too. Right now, the official finding is that Clark killed Mike, then killed himself. If there's another murder, that's going to blow that theory all to hell and open up the prior killings to reinvestigation. So in a way, accepting the closure kind of makes it less likely that anything else is going to happen."

"At least not right away," Harmony said.

"At least not right away," Mark conceded.

I groaned, walked into the kitchen, and came back with a shot of tequila. Mark and Harmony were startled. My mom was a drunk, and I had no intention of ending up like her. I drank about a beer a month - for medicinal reasons - and could count on one hand each year's forays into hard liquor. The margarita I had nursed with dinner had been unusual enough. The shot was out of character.

"You feeling OK, Jack?" Mark asked.

I knocked back the booze and felt its warmth and strength surge through me. Only after I swallowed did I consider its likely effect on my pain meds. Too late.

"No. No, I'm not." Everything Mark said made sense. I didn't want to get my dad in trouble. I didn't want to get my sisters in trouble. I personally didn't want to get in trouble. But if my dad was still alive - if he was really out there somewhere - I had to see him. I had to know. I had to ask him why he had messed around with a girl half his age, a girl young enough to be his eldest daughter. I had to understand how he could have left me with my basket case of a mom and taken off. I had to know what he wanted me to do with the mill. I didn't care if he was a murderer. I didn't care if he was a mass murderer. I wanted to see him. I needed to see him.

My head spun with the liquor and the pain pills and the sheer waste of it all. Forgetting the distance she had kept from me all evening, Harmony wrapped her arms around me and held me tight. It was nice to have someone prop me up.

After a while, she said, "Jack, do you still think your dad might be hiding out in the house on Orcas Island?"

"I don't know. I guess so. I guess I think that if he is alive, that's as good a place to hide as any."

"OK," Mark said, "Let's go up and check it out. If he's there, we'll have the drop on him - and if he's not, then you'll let this rest. Agreed?"

He held out his hand. I caved and shook it. "Agreed."

Which is how the three of us ended up the next morning on the ferry to Orcas Island. We didn't tell my sisters we were going. If they were in cahoots with my dad, we couldn't chance their calling him to tip him off.

Orcas is one of the San Juan Islands, a mostly submerged mountain chain that fringes Washington and Canada. Depending on who's counting, there are more than seven-hundred rocks or islands at the lowest tide, half that when the sea unfurls. More than a hundred have names. On a sunny day, the San Juans are the loveliest place on earth: emerald islands, a bright blue sea, whales, seals, and eagles. But as we boarded the ferry, it was grey, and it was raining. Our only wildlife sightings were sodden seagulls. They flapped and squabbled over a hamburger bun someone had dropped at the dock.

I loved the rain. During the summer - during those years when we had summer - I missed it, didn't feel good if it was sunny for days on end. But right then, I wanted a ray of sun, a flash of blue, a sudden patch of opal on the dark, salt sea - anything to lift my feelings of dread and oppression. Maybe it was the names. To our left was Victim Island. Farther into West Sound were Skull Island and Massacre Bay.

The landing at Orcas improved my mood. The ferry terminal had a cheerful red roof, and the streets were right out of a fairytale: Horseshoe Highway, Lover's Lane, Enchanted Forest Road. After a while, there it was: a large gate set back from the road, almost invisible behind hemlock and cedar.

A long driveway turned into a clearing. Before us was a long, rambling lodge - cedar-shingled, supported by huge timbers. It was backed by a swath of beachfront with a view that seemed to stretch all the way to Japan.

I unlocked the door. Mark moved through the house with his gun drawn. He turned on lights and opened doors until he was satisfied that the house was clear. Then we split up and searched from room to room.

The refrigerator was bare except for a box of baking soda, a bottle of ketchup, and a six-pack of beer. Fridge-stocking abilities apparently ran in the family. But the freezer was stacked with vacuum-packed salmon, tidily labeled with dates. I unscrewed the elbow pipe below the kitchen sink. Flaking-off dry.

In the living room, leather chairs lounged around a low table topped with a polished cross-cut of a mammoth oak tree. I ran my fingers over the rings, over the rough bark. On the walls were faded fishing and hunting prints, a stuffed pheasant, a huge painting of a sunset in the San Juans. A stone fireplace took up one corner of the room. On the mantle was a framed photograph of my dad and my sisters, each holding up a sizeable fish. My dad had his arms around Beth, his hands cupping hers, hers cupping the line. Her head was down, as usual, but her cheek was pressed against her dad's, she was looking at her fish, and it seemed like she was smiling. I'd guess she was about ten.

Upstairs in the master bedroom, I peeled back the down comforter and the white sheets. There was no sign that anyone had slept there recently. I opened the glass-doored bookshelf and thumbed idly through some of the volumes: hunting and fishing guides, navigation manuals, an ancient cookbook called *High Adventure in the Kitchen*. There was a signature on the flyleaf. It had belonged to my dad's mom.

I rummaged in the desk drawers. I found a master's thesis, meticulously typed on onionskin. It was an oral history of the oldest residents of Bellingham - what they remembered about Victorian times, what they had been told about pioneer days. I was beginning to read it, and enjoy it, when I noticed that the date on the first page was the year I was born. I stuffed it back in the drawer and pulled out a ratty white photo album. The pages were brittle and yellowed. A shower of those little black corner things dusted the floor as I opened it.

The pictures were mostly of boats. *The Sabbath-Breaker* looked like a shark cutting through the waves. *The Virginia* resembled a floating couch. A faded black and white snapshot toward the back showed my dad, Virginia, and a few others standing by a pretty little sailboat. I recognized a few faces from my perusal of Karen's yearbooks. I could make out just the first part of the name on the hull: *The Mary B-*.

I shivered, shut the drawer, and walked over to the fireplace, a slightly smaller replica of the one below. The living room grate had been empty, but here a fire lay unlit. I knelt and pulled the crumpled balls of newspaper from beneath the logs. Four were dated late August; one from the first week of September - almost two full months ago.

Intense weariness washed over me. No one had been here for months. He was dead. He was really dead. I wished I hadn't come. At least then I could have kept pretending he was alive.

Harmony found me at the end of the pier - drenched, looking out at the immense grey sea. I had no idea how long I had been out there, staring at the water, watching the bizarre black rows of sand dollars standing on edge. They looked even weirder alive than they did when they washed up dead on shore.

Harmony stood with me quietly for a few moments. Then she said, "Did you find anything?"

"No."

"Neither did we."

"No one's been here for months."

"No," she agreed simply.

I couldn't think of anything else to say.

"You know, Jack, when my dad died, I had all these questions no one could answer. All of a sudden, I was a different person - even a different race - than I thought I was. And I wanted to ask my dad what had happened, whether he realized I wasn't actually his daughter, why he kept me if he knew. One day I'd be sure that he couldn't have known; that he must have been blind to how different I looked because he loved me so much. And the next day, I'd be just as sure that he knew I wasn't his daughter, that he just played along with the lie because he wanted to keep control of my money. I spent months going through all his papers, trying to find something he might have said or done that would answer all those questions. I talked to all his friends. Sometimes I felt that I would die - literally die, Jack - if I didn't know for sure. But there wasn't anything. All those nights reading, and rereading, and wondering –" She stopped and rubbed her eyes. "There wasn't anything to tell me the truth."

"So what did you do?"

"Eventually, you get to the end of -" she paused - "the pier, and there isn't anywhere else to look. And then you just decide what you're going to believe, and you let the rest go. Because if you don't, you'll drive yourself mad, Jack. You will absolutely drive yourself mad."

"What do you believe about your dad?"

"I believe he knew early on that I wasn't his daughter, but that by the time my mother died four years later, it didn't matter anymore. I was all he had left of her. I believe he loved her, and I believe he loved me. And when he looked at me, he didn't see Higuro, or my mother's infidelity. He saw my mother, and he saw someone he loved."

Her blue eyes were full of tears. "I don't have any proof. There's no one I can ask. But that's what I believe in here." She put her hand over her heart.

"I don't know what to believe about my dad, Harmony."

"You will. Eventually, you will."

Together we crunched over the beach of shells and pebbles. Mark was waiting for us by the door.

"I couldn't find anything, Jack," he said. "I'm sorry." That was one of the many great things about Mark. He never said *I told you so.*

"I know. Thanks."

"You ready to head home? Is there anywhere else you want to go?"

I considered driving up to Bellingham to see my sisters, then thought better of it. I didn't want to explain to them where we'd been. I especially didn't want to explain why. "No. Let's just get out of here."

And that could have been where it ended - would have been, in fact, if we hadn't decided to go up to Bellingham to pick up my car at the police impound lot. A traffic accident and road work forced us into the wrong lane. For just a moment, we got lost. If we hadn't gotten lost, if Mark hadn't taken a wrong turn, we wouldn't have ended up on Lakeway Drive. I would have gone back to Seattle and gotten on with my life. I wouldn't have looked out the window and seen the white winged crosses of the gate of Bayview Cemetery. And I wouldn't have said, "Mark, please pull in here. I never got to go to the grave. I think it would help if I saw it for myself."

Bayview Cemetery spreads over a hillside, so the world seems to drop away from you as you walk. On that wet October day, humped-top hemlocks and Douglas firs loomed black against the twilit sky. Some of the trees were shaped like giant toadstools.

We were in the older part of the cemetery, where some of the pioneer stones still stood, lichen-bitten and blackened with salt and wind. There was a whole host of Harts, stretching back to the late 1800s, resting together, waiting for me. My father didn't have a headstone yet, but that only made his grave more conspicuous. You couldn't pass the slashed-out rectangle of sod - muddy and browned, thrust up a few inches - without feeling the wrench and disruption of his death.

I stood in front of the fresh grave and thought about my dad: burned, stretched out, boxed six feet below. I was wishing I had some flowers to put on the awful grass when Harmony suddenly clutched my hand, hard enough to make me wince.

I followed her gaze toward a cluster of gravestones about twenty feet away. The Boydens. Well, this was quite the family reunion, with both sides of my family present and accounted for. I was about to turn back to my father when I noticed how intent Harmony had become, almost like a dog on point. Mark had stiffened as well.

A look back at the Boydens, and I knew why. Mark and Harmony were staring at a grey marble stone, engraved with a rose and the legend "Beloved Sister, Teacher, Friend."

The name on the gravestone was Mary Boyden. She had died two months after I was born.

My mother's name was Mary Boyden. She went by Marta because it sounded more exotic, but she had been born plain old Mary. It was there in black and white on my birth certificate. And now there it was engraved in stone.

Mary Boyden, I thought.

The Mary B.

CHAPTER 24

Mark flashed his headlights in my rearview mirror. *You're bear bait*, that meant. *Slow down.*

I slowed, but I was still in an almighty rush to reach Spokane. I felt like I hadn't slept since we saw the gravestone; my briefcase was stuffed with the days and nights of research it had launched. I had brought copies of everything with me, just in case I needed them when I confronted my mom. I knew every word by heart, but if I had to turn up the heat, it wouldn't hurt to deal out the birth certificates, the death certificate, the sour-smelling microfiche of a tiny Seattle Times article published two months after I was born.

"Infant Survives Murder-Suicide Attempt," the headline read. In three sparse paragraphs, the article told how a Mary Boyden, 35, had killed herself with an overdose of barbiturates. Her two-month-old baby, John, had also been given an overdose, but had vomited the drugs and survived. The landlady at the Josephinium Apartments had heard the baby crying. The police had broken down the door.

I pulled up in front of my mom's fiancé's Overbluff mansion at 9:30 p.m. Mark and Harmony parked on the other side of the street, inconspicuous but with a clear view of the house. They had refused to let me go alone.

"Sorry to drop in on you like this," I said to Bill, my mom's comfortable, balding fiancé, when he came to the door. "But I was on this side of the mountains on a case, and I really need to talk to my mom. Is she home?"

Bill waved me in. "Jack, you're welcome here anytime," he said, so sincerely that I regretted my fib. "She's here, but she's resting right now. She, uh, well, she hasn't been feeling so hot today."

Oh, dear. Not only had my mom been hitting the bottle, but she had poor old Bill lying for her as well. I nearly said, "That's OK, Bill. I understand. Just go sober her up," but fortunately, I caught sight of my little brother peeking around the banisters. With a squeal of delight, Jimmy launched himself at me. I swung him up so his hair brushed the ceiling, then down so his hair brushed the floor. He giggled and wriggled in my arms.

"Jimbo! What are you doing up? Your bedtime was an hour ago."

"But Bill, I heard Jack's voice, and I want to show him my Halloween costume. Please let me show him my Halloween costume."

Bill looked torn. He glanced anxiously upstairs. Then he said, "OK, but don't tell your mother."

Jimmy's Halloween costume was a miracle of engineering. Bill had crafted a turtle carapace out of a large packing box, embossed the cardboard so it resembled a shell, and painted it so carefully that it had an organic heft and sheen. The carapace slipped over Jimmy's head. In green footsie pajamas and a green stocking cap, he made the world's cutest - and fastest - little turtle, leaping around, making snapping noises, and pulling in his head and arms because it made me roar with laughter.

It was so much fun to watch the two of them - flushed with justifiable pride, talking over each other, eager to point out all the benefits and elements of the costume - but it also made me think about my dad. My dad never made me a Halloween costume. I was sure of that. He never took me trick or treating. He never talked to me, or played with me, or protected me the way Bill did Jimmy. And Bill was no more Jimmy's father than I was. He was just a nice guy who happened to fall prey to my mom.

I guess it showed on my face, because suddenly Jimmy stopped in mid-cavort and said, "What's wrong?"

I wasn't going to tell him. It was far too complicated for a little boy. But before I could evade the question, Bill put one pudgy hand on Jimmy's blond head and said, "Jack's dad just went to Heaven to live with the angels, Jimbo, like your grandma did last year. So I guess Jack misses him. I guess he's a little sad."

Jimmy was beside me on the couch, immensely concerned. "Are you sad?"

"A little."

Jimmy wrapped his arms around my neck. "Don't be sad anymore, Jack. When I grow up, I'll be your dad."

It was hard to hug him through that turtle thing. I managed to get out, "That would be great, Jim. Thanks."

Satisfied that his work was done, Jimmy bounded off the couch and set about demonstrating how he could slide along with his stomach on his skateboard, making convincing whooshing noises to simulate swimming. "Now I'm a sea turtle," he announced. Then he set off in search of his own pet turtle, Mr. Pokey, so I could be properly introduced and feed him some lettuce.

"So how are things with you and my mom?" I asked Bill, once Jimmy was safely out of earshot. "Have you set a date?"

Bill rubbed his broad forehead. "Well, not yet, Jack," he confessed. "We're still sort of working some things out. You know, your mom, she's a hell of a woman, but -" He broke off and seemed to physically separate himself from thinking about my mom. "Now, that Jimmy, he's such a great little kid. My late wife and I, we couldn't have any kids. Hanging out with Jimbo is just about the most fun I've ever had."

Poor Bill. I saw the problem. I was about to advise him to marry her, adopt him, and divorce her. I would testify on his behalf at the custody hearing. But my mother chose that moment to make her grand entrance.

The last time I had seen my mother, she resembled nothing so much as a big, red-haired bat. Now she looked like a big, red-haired bat who had spent a great deal of time and money at a beauty shop, who had chiseled about an inch of makeup off her face, who had redyed her hair something approaching a human color, and who was wearing a powder blue, designer sweat suit. Stick her behind the wheel of a minivan, and from a distance and at 65 miles an hour, you might actually mistake her for an upper-middle-class suburbanite.

I could tell that Bill was itching to intercept Jimmy before my mom spotted him out of bed, so I said, "Bill, thanks for the chat. It's great to see you. But would you mind giving me and my mom a few minutes alone?"

Bill popped up, relieved. "Of course not. I understand. Sometimes a guy's just got to talk to his mom."

Alone at last, my mom lit a cigarette and blew smoke in my face. "What are you doing here, Jack? Don't you know it's rude to drop in on people late at night?"

"Just raised wrong, I guess," I said.

My mom raised her hand to slap me. She was about to slap me - she would have slapped me - if I hadn't intercepted her arm in midair and pushed her wrist back against the wall. She had hit me plenty of times, even when I was old enough and big enough to stop her. This was the first time I had ever stopped her.

"I wouldn't try that right now if I were you," I said. Her look of surprise was quickly mingled with something else, uncertainty approaching alarm. Then she wrenched her arm away from me, walked over to the fireplace, and took a long drag on her cigarette.

"What do you want?"

"Who's Mary Boyden?"

She sneered at me. "What do you mean, who's Mary Boyden? I am, of course. Don't be stupid."

"Then you've been dead for twenty-nine years, and I've been spending a lot of time lately at your grave."

Again the uncertain look, quickly hooded. "What are you talking about?"

I told her about the Bellingham headstone. She cackled at me. "In case you hadn't noticed, Mary's a pretty common name, Jack. I've got some cousins up in Bellingham. It's probably one of them."

"Did one of your cousins have a little half-sister named Marta and a son named John? Or is that just some unspeakable coincidence?"

Full-fledged fear this time. I was almost impressed that she rallied as well as she did. "Look, I know we haven't always gotten along, and I guess I don't really blame you for wanting to believe you've got a long-lost mother somewhere else. But however much each of us might wish things were different, I am your mom, and you are my kid. So be a good kid, and go home. I have a terrible headache, and I am going to bed."

I blocked her path. "You lying, cold-hearted bitch."

The cigarette fell from her lips. I ground it out under my heel, mentally apologizing to Bill and his hardwood floor. She started toward me again as if to slap me, but this time all I had to do was raise my hand in a warning. Her arm fell to her side, and she shrank from me a little. Then she steeled herself and snapped, "Get out. You little bastard, just get out of here!"

She tried to bluster toward me to push me from the house. I stood my ground.

"I'm not leaving. I want the truth. Or else."

"Or else what?" Her tone was mocking, but her voice was strained.

"Or else I tell Bill everything you've done. I tell him how you beat me, how you abandoned me, how you drink and drug and fuck anything that moves. I get your criminal records from Mark, and I show them all to Bill. You're on thin ice with him already because of the booze. You think he's going to keep you in designer clothes once he knows what you're really like?"

She was a ghastly white under her tasteful beige makeup. She was too stunned to even try to slap me. Panic flashed in her eyes. For a moment, she was blank and dazed. Then a cunning look of triumph crept across her face. "You wouldn't," she said.

"I would. I will."

She shook her head. "You won't. You've seen how much Jimmy loves Bill. You've seen how much Bill loves Jimmy. You won't do anything that would split them up. You don't have the stomach for it."

Yet another person who was trying to use my best self against me. She was right, but she didn't need to know that. I leaned so close to her that I could smell her hair dye. I had her flattened against the wall. "They're going to get split up anyway - not by me, by you. Bill won't be able to stand you much longer, not even for Jimmy's sake. And you're not going to be able to control yourself much longer, not even for the shot at staying here on easy street. He'll find the needle marks on you, and you'll be out on your ass like that." I snapped my fingers in her face. She flinched. "And as much as I don't want to hurt Jimmy, at some point he's going to have to face the truth about you. He might as well start now." When she didn't reply, I leaned even closer and hissed into her ear, "I am sick of having everyone else's welfare taken out of my skin."

She stared at me, testing me.

I stared back, daring her to chance it.

She blinked first. She groaned, sank onto the couch, and said, "Fine. You're my nephew. Mary was my half-sister. She was twenty years older than I was, and she raised me. Our dad and my mom were killed in a car crash when I was just little. When Mary died, I didn't have any money or anywhere to go. I was afraid they'd put me in a foster home. You could get welfare and food stamps and a break on rent if you had a kid. So I took you, I took her ID, I changed her age on your birth certificate, and I told people I was your mom. No one ever checked. You happy now?"

It wasn't a surprise. It was what I was expecting, what I had known since I had researched the official records in Olympia, what I knew in my heart the moment I saw the gravestone. But when she said it like that, so flatly, so matter of factly, it suddenly became real to me. At first, it was a marvelous relief. She wasn't my mother. She was my aunt. My half-aunt, even. Everyone has a crazy aunt. There is no shame whatsoever in having a crazy aunt.

I had spent most of my life afraid that I was going to end up like her, limiting my liquor like a stingy host, fighting whatever biological imperatives might drive me to drinking, stupor, and dishonesty. For the first time, I felt free - free and absolutely alone.

As the exhilaration faded, the gravity of the news sunk in. I sat down slowly. I was an orphan. I had been half-orphaned before I saw my first Christmas, and I had been a full orphan for a month without knowing it. I felt the tidal pull of grief. It seemed to come from an even deeper, colder place than had my mourning for my dad. I was alone. I was really alone.

Motherless.

Fatherless.

Less.

My mom's - aunt's - harsh voice cut across my thoughts. "You got what you came for. Now go away. Just go away and leave me alone."

I didn't move. I couldn't. She poked me in the side, right in the gunshot wound. She had always had an uncanny sense of how to hurt me. The pain unleashed a rage in me, hotter than I thought possible. I struggled to keep from striking her. Instead I sprang up, making sure she was just barely out of reach. "Damn you to hell," I shouted at her. "I wish I could hurt you the way you've hurt me."

Her head snapped up in protest. "I took care of you!"

"You used me. You used me so you could sit around on your ass and cheat the government."

"I didn't want them to put you in foster care."

"News flash, *Mother*, **you** put me in foster care, remember? The only difference is that if you had let them take me as a baby, someone would have adopted me, and I would have had a real family. People want babies. It's battered and broken kids who never get out of the system." I was so angry at her I could barely breathe. "Do you have any idea what you've done to me? Do you have any idea what it was like spending ten years in foster homes?"

She raked her rose-painted nails over the powder blue plush of her pantsuit. She sniffed and said, "I wanted to do right by you. I needed the money to feed you and clothe you and house you. I couldn't make it without the welfare benefits."

"Oh, bullshit. I've talked to Virginia Carlson, you know. She told me all about the money they sent you. Admit it - you're a cheat and a liar and -" The look on her face stopped me cold.

"Virginia told you about the money?" She seemed dumbstruck.

I nodded.

"I can't believe that. I can't believe that she would do that."

"Believe it. She told me everything."

She sat stunned on the couch for a few moments. "All those years. All those years." Then her expression hardened and she put her head in her hands. "Well, while she was telling you everything, did she happen to explain why she's three weeks late this month?"

Wait. Wait just a damn minute here. What did she mean by "all those years"? What did she mean by "late this month"? According to Virginia, my dad had discovered I was no longer with my "mother" sometime around when I was ten. Surely they wouldn't have kept sending her checks for child support after that. Unless the checks were never for child support in the first place.

The back of my neck was pricking. My mother thought I knew more than I did. If she realized how lost I was, she wouldn't tell me a thing. While she thought the game was up, I had a clear advantage. The only question was how to use it best.

I sat next to her and got my voice under control. I made myself touch her. I couldn't bear too much contact with her - just a quasi-pat on the arm. She didn't respond, but she didn't pull away.

"No, she didn't say why she was late this month," I said quietly. "Do you want me to talk to her about it? I've been spending a lot of time up there. She's worried about what I'm going to do and say to her daughters when she's gone, so I think she might listen to me."

It was a gamble that paid off. My mother clearly had no idea that Virginia Carlson was in a coma. She puffed with indignation and importance. "You talk to her all right. You tell her I've still got it, and just because Jack's dead doesn't mean I won't use it. I'll take it to the police; I'll take it to the newspaper. We had a deal, and she has to pay."

I wished I was wearing a wire. I nearly stormed out and brought Mark and his gun into the room. I struggled to keep myself under control, to keep her talking. But it was too much. Even for my mom, this was way too much. My voice was thin as a papercut.

"So on top of everything else, you're a blackmailer. You've been blackmailing them for twenty-nine years."

"She owes me!"

"Oh, right. She owes you. Everybody owes you. Poor, pitiful you."

"She took everything I had."

"Bullshit," I said. "You made your own bed. Nobody forced you to take me on. Nobody forced you to pass yourself off as my mom. What did you threaten them with, telling everyone that my dad had an affair with a fifteen-year-old girl? If even a rumor like that ever got started, the school district would have canned him."

My mother had a strange, convulsed expression on her face. For an instant, she reminded me of Virginia. She raised her head slowly, but with a sudden, incongruous dignity.

"So Virginia only told you half the story. If you're going to stand there and judge me, you should know everything first."

My mother coming clean. Would wonders never cease? I swung back on the couch and shrugged. "Go ahead. Give it your best shot."

"She killed her. And she tried to kill you. I found the handkerchief and I showed it to the police, but no one would believe me."

"Who killed who?"

"Virginia. Virginia killed my sister -" she stabbed me in the chest with that lethal finger - "your mother. Mary was going to tell Jack about you. And Virginia was afraid he'd go back to her. He'd always wanted a son. That's the one thing Virginia couldn't give him. She kept trying and trying - one baby after another. That's why she blamed him for Beth."

I took a close look at her eyes. My mother - or my aunt or whoever the hell she was - was an inveterate liar. I once caught her red-handed taking twenty dollars out of my coat, and she told me she was just checking to make sure I had a Kleenex. But I could usually see the lie in her eyes. They were either mobile and watchful or flat and black. Right then her eyes were still and soft and sad. I was shocked to see the pain there, the welling tears, the regret. I put my hand on her arm. This time I didn't have to force myself to touch her.

"I think you need to tell this to me from the beginning," I said.

She nodded, wiped her nose, and for the next hour, told me what she claimed to be the real story of my mom and dad. Or, more accurately, of my mom and dad and Virginia Carlson. According to her, Mary Boyden and Virginia Carlson had been best friends - right up to the point that Virginia had stolen my dad away from Mary. I remembered the yearbook photograph of them in their identical sweaters: the Crystal Belles. Mary had dated my father all through high school. He had given her a promise ring; they were going to get married when he got back from the Army. But when he was discharged, she was still in her second year of college back East. By the time she returned home for the summer, Jack and Virginia had eloped. Marianne was born seven months later - and so was Mary's little half-sister, Marta.

"Mary used to tell me I was a gift from God," she said. "She was feeling so bad about Jack. And she couldn't even complain to her best friend what a heel he had been because it was her best friend who stole him from her. She used to play with me and babysit me. She used to make my clothes and dress me up. She sewed my christening gown. When my mom and dad were killed in a car crash, she transferred back from Smith. She finished her student teaching in Bellingham, she got a job at the high school, and she took care of me. She was a good mother. She was a great mother." She shot me a look, so mixed with guilt and pride, apology and resentment, that I couldn't even begin to interpret it. "That's what I wanted to do with you," she said. "I wanted to pay her back for taking care of me."

Neither one of us needed to point out that she had failed. We both knew. She swallowed hard a couple of times and continued. Jack and Virginia separated when Beth was a toddler. Jack went back to Mary. Mary rented an apartment in Seattle, and Jack and Mary were making plans for their new life together when Virginia's father died and Beth was diagnosed as developmentally disabled. And that's when my father left my mother for the last time. He left not knowing she was pregnant, and she never told him. She had the baby alone, with only her terrified teenage sister to assist her in the delivery room.

"She was a lot like you, Jack. She always wanted to do the right thing." Somehow she made it sound like a character flaw. "He'd already been trapped once; she didn't want him to think she'd tried to catch him like Virginia had. But when you were a couple of months old, she decided she had to tell him. It was almost Christmas, and she couldn't bear that he didn't know you, that you wouldn't know him. She was very honorable about it, though. She called Virginia and told her what had happened and what she was going to do." She sighed and rubbed her hands over her face, leaving livid furrows in her makeup. "And two days later, she was dead."

"Why do you think it was murder?"

"She wouldn't have killed herself, Jack. She was happy. She adored you. She bought a little Brownie camera and took a million pictures of you. But of course the cops wouldn't pay any attention to what I said. As far as they were concerned, she was an unwed mother, and she was better off dead. I stood there in the freezing rain arguing with them, and all they would say to me was that a lot of people kill themselves at Christmas.

"So when I couldn't get anywhere with the police, I called Virginia Carlson. We struck a deal. She agreed to pay me very well, and I agreed to keep my mouth shut and pretend you were my son. She didn't care if anyone thought Jack had messed around with me. She just didn't want anyone to know that he'd gone back to Mary, that her old competition had given him a baby boy."

"When did he figure out the truth?"

"Not for a long time. The school district got wind of the rumors almost right away and sacked him, but they didn't tell him why. It took a couple of years before someone actually said it to his face. He was down to Seattle like a shot, believe me, demanding to know why in hell I was telling people he was the father of my child. I told him I wasn't, but that I couldn't help what other people said. He just thought I'd gotten myself in trouble and was afraid to tell him who the father was. He tried to be very nice to me - for Mary's sake. He gave us money, and he took you out and bought you some clothes. You looked more like Mary and me when you were little, so he didn't see the family resemblance. By the time he got suspicious enough to order your birth certificate, you were already long gone."

She fell silent. I was filled with so many conflicting emotions that I thought I was going to explode. Part of me felt sorry - genuinely sorry - for Marta. She had been fifteen years old, suddenly and completely alone in the world, and she had coped the best she could - miserably and dishonestly, of course - but probably the best she could.

On the other hand, part of me wanted to strangle her. She had let her sister's killer get away with murder, in exchange for blood money that I was sure had gone in her arm or up her nose. And part of me thought she was lying. Maybe not about everything - maybe even a lot of the story was true - but she lied so easily and so frequently, I doubted whether she could spend an entire hour telling the undiluted, undiverted truth. So the part of me that doubted her and the part that wanted to strangle her decided to put her to the test.

"Mom," I said, laying my hand on hers. "Mom, you are in a hell of a lot of trouble. Someone tried to kill Virginia Carlson a couple of weeks ago. She's been in a coma ever since. The police are still looking for the person who attacked her, and I think they've stumbled over the blackmail angle. There's no other reason why all that money would be coming your way. They think that once Jack died, Virginia balked at keeping up the payments, and you assaulted her. Whatever you've got that would link you to Virginia, you've got to get rid of it. You've got to give it to me. I'll take care of it."

When she didn't budge, I turned up the heat. "Mom, the cops are already outside." I walked her to the window and pointed out the dark shape of Mark's car, parked inconspicuously but with a clear sight line to the house. You could just discern the outlines of the occupants. "Quick, Mom. You've got to get that stuff out of the house right now. We'll put it in my briefcase. They can't open it without a search warrant, and by the time they get one for me, I'll be long gone. They've probably already got a warrant for you."

It worked. With me behind her, worrying her like a border collie and hissing "quickly, quickly" whenever she hesitated, she flustered up to her bedroom and showed me her hiding place. Underneath a chest of drawers were a small satin box and a bag of white powder. I held open my briefcase, and she picked up the box and put it inside. I wanted her prints on it, not mine. Then I jerked my thumb toward the baggie. "Flush that."

I hightailed it toward the door, her voice behind me, beseeching, pleading - so unlike her. As I paused to find my keys, she suddenly thrust her face right next to mine. She looked old and used and scared.

"I can trust you, can't I, Jack?"

I took her hand and squeezed it.

I squeezed harder and harder, until her lips parted in protest but no sound escaped.

"Of course you can trust me," I said evenly. "Just as much as I trust you."

Then I marched down the driveway to my car. As I drove away, she was still standing there on the porch.

Just standing there, looking after me.

CHAPTER 25

Mark insisted that I turn the box over to the police. Not the Bellingham police. That would have been the same as throwing it away. I surrendered the box to Detective Anthony.

Inside was a matted, tatted handkerchief embroidered with the initials "VHC." Underneath was a small, white leather datebook. On the page for the day she died, my mother had written "Virginia C., 7 o'clock." At the back of the book, she'd pasted a faded color snapshot of her little family. She had her arm around Marta, and she was holding me up to the camera. Even in the orangy blur of the old film, her face was radiant. It was the only picture I had ever seen of myself as a baby. I looked sleepy, wrinkled, and wise.

It didn't prove anything. Even if the handkerchief was Virginia's, that didn't necessarily place her at the scene on the night of my mother's death. But along with the note in the datebook, it at least would have given her a lot of explaining to do. And according to Marta, she had been willing to pay a hell of a lot of money to avoid the questions, criticism, and suspicion that the datebook and handkerchief could have - should have - unleashed.

Mark and Anthony pulled police records and autopsy reports on my mother, but the police report was terse and unhelpful; the autopsy simply identified the cause of death as an overdose of barbiturates, probably self-administered.

"My guess is, they didn't exactly bust their butts on this one," Anthony explained. "See, especially twenty-nine years ago, you're going to have a couple of tired, overworked, middle-aged cops looking at an unwed mother dead in a little flophouse apartment," he said "And unless there's a sign of a struggle, they're going to assume she did it herself. They're going to clear it as a suicide and have it off their desks by happy hour."

The lack of information only made me want more. From the time I left Bill's house, I was a man possessed. I had to know more about my mother. It hurt - it physically hurt - to give Anthony the datebook. He had a copy made for me, but it wasn't the same. It wasn't hers. She hadn't touched it, carried it, consulted it, checked the dates on the well-child appointments she had so meticulously logged, turned to the back for no reason except to see my newborn face. I threw myself into trying to fill the void.

The pile of paper on my desk swelled exponentially as I tracked down all the public records I could find: birth announcements, real property transactions, my mother's mother's obituary, the police report of my grandfather's car accident, my mother's transcript from Smith. The faded shavings of their lives sketched only the barest census. I knew they had been born, and walked the earth for a few years, and died. I knew they were buried in Bellingham. And aside from that, aside from the few flashes of color I could find in the public record - my mother studied anthropology; my grandfather was a pilot in World War I - they were as blank to me as strangers. I knew more about the nice lady who handled my dry cleaning than I did about my own mother.

So I went back to Bellingham. I had to know more.

I had a good cover story. The employees at my dad's mill were understandably concerned. They were shell-shocked from the fire; they knew nothing about me; the mill's senior leadership had died under mysterious circumstances; and it was apparent to everyone that money wasn't exactly rolling through the doors. Somebody needed to level with them, and as the guy who had fought a court battle to keep control of the mill, that somebody was going to be me.

The office building had burned to the ground, so we met in the warehouse, dwarfed by enormous rolls of paper. I remembered how Sarah's husband had died and shuddered at the thought of him, splayed and crushed beneath them. Poor Sarah. She was there to support me - they all were - but she didn't even glance at the paper rolls.

I shook hands and introduced myself as people filed in. In my wake I heard a thicket of whispers: *It's a WARN meeting.* My father's employees faced me warily - resentful, anxious, bone-tired. They were expecting their formal notice of layoff under the Worker Adjustment and Retraining Notification Act. They had a heartbreaking air of resignation.

"This isn't a WARN meeting," I began. "I'm sorry if you were worried because I asked to meet with you. It's just that you've all taken some really hard hits lately, and I wanted to say thanks. I also wanted to meet you and let you know how things look to me right now. I'm still learning, and I want to hear your thoughts."

Without lingering too much over the gory details, I spelled out where we were. For at least two years, Mike Saunders and Clark Swanson had put no effort into marketing. Our customer base was soft; our suppliers were drying up. Our cash flow was almost a contradiction in terms: very little cash, purely negative flow.

"I thought you said this wasn't a WARN meeting," someone interjected from the back.

"It isn't. But we're not in good shape. On the other hand, we do have a few things going for us. We've been suffering, uh, large capital outlays for corporate gifts over the past few years. That's not going to happen anymore. We've been facing a big environmental assessment. For the moment at least, that's gone away. So we've got some opportunities."

"How did you get the DOE off our backs?"

"Don't you read the Herald?" I asked. "Wasn't it obvious from the picture that I'm sleeping with them?"

That actually got a laugh. A begrudging, uncertain laugh, but still a laugh.

Another voice piped up, this time from a pugnacious-looking woman in the front row. "What qualifies you to run this place?" she demanded. "Why do you think you can do it better than your sisters?"

"I don't. I don't know why my father wanted me to be in charge. But I guess he figured that sometimes you really need a junkyard dog."

I smiled at her as I said it. I said it quietly. But there was an intensity in my voice that made her blink. Even though she laughed along with everybody else, she laughed nervously - and she backed down.

I capitalized on the moment by whipping out the financial analysis Harmony and I had commissioned for the mill. I passed out copies, introduced Harmony, and sat by Beth while Harmony precisely and concisely outlined our financial situation. We had enough orders and accounts receivable to keep us going through the end of the year. After that, we would have to source new business to keep our doors open. Mike and Clark hadn't bothered. They figured that the Port would have taken us over by then.

As the impact of the numbers sank in, Harmony stepped back while I picked up the thread of the discussion. For the next hour, the employees and I brainstormed about ways to stay afloat while we tried to drag the mill back to solid ground. At first, they were reluctant to admit that there wasn't enough work to keep everybody busy. They still thought I was looking for reasons to lay them off.

"Look," I said. "If I wanted to close the mill, I'd just do it. We're not in great shape. But I think we've got a chance, and I'm willing to take it. But I need a team to work on developing new business. I need a team to analyze Phases II and III of the Cluster rules, look into chlorine-free bleaching and oxygenization, and work every day with the DOE to make sure we run cleaner. I need a team to stabilize our suppliers. Now I can go out and hire a bunch of smarty-pants Harvard kids who know even less about your business than I do, who will just ask you what you think and put it in a pretty PowerPoint for me. Or we can do it ourselves. Who wants to do it ourselves?"

Every hand went up. By the end of the hour, we had unanimously decided to suspend the second shift, at least temporarily. Production would be our first priority. But when people weren't working production, they would devote their time to customer service, marketing, and environmental innovation and compliance. By the time I left the mill, everyone had a job to do. My sisters were going to contact each current customer and try to solidify and expand their business. Harmony and I were going to search for potential investors. We needed an infusion of capital fast, and I wasn't going to accept it from Harmony.

It was kind of fun. Within a couple of days, we had garnered a fair amount of interest from an unlikely coalition: long-time labor advocates wanting to prove they walked the walk, newly minted Internet millionaires eager to own something real, rich liberals impressed by our partnership with the Department of Ecology. We spent a lot of time on the phone, brushed up on the rules for a private offering, and created our own website touting the investment opportunity as "blue-green": blue-collar but environmentally sound.

I knew nothing about pulp and paper. I trusted Dave West, the foreman who had accosted me at the precipice of the burned-out building. But as I became more enmeshed in the business, I found myself growing more and more curious. I stayed up late studying DIP process, fractionation, and fine screening. I made myself a little office in a corner of the warehouse and appropriated all the records that had survived the fire. And when I wasn't in my office, trying to unravel the mysteries of the pulp and paper business, I fanned out across Bellingham, trying to unravel the mysteries of my mom.

Gradually, very gradually, she became alive to me. She was always the smartest girl in the class, one of her friends told me. She won a scholarship to Smith and headed off to the Northeast even though she had never before ventured farther than Spokane. She was a natural athlete, another classmate said, a champion swimmer. She loved to fish and sail. She used to boast that she had kayaked to 112 of the San Juan Islands, and that she and Jack had necked on 85 of them. (Some of them were too muddy.) The two of them would go crabbing up in the clear, cold waters of Mosquito Pass, baiting their traps with salmon-sickles of frozen fish heads and tails, boiling the crabs over a driftwood fire, feasting on the beach with their friends.

"She was so bright," one of her old teachers remembered, over cups of weak tea and damp Fig Newtons in the dining room of her nursing home. "Bright in every way - smart and sparkly. The last time I saw her, she just glowed. She was a couple of classes away from her master's degree. She had big plans to go on some Anasazi excavation down in Utah and Arizona. She was so excited about everything. And the next thing I heard, she was dead. By her own hand." She shook her head. "I just couldn't believe it. It was as if the sun had simply decided not to come up in the morning."

"Do you have any idea why she would have taken her own life?"

"Well, whenever there's a man involved, I guess you have to start there. It had been hard enough on Mary when Jack married Virginia. But when he took up with her own little sister - when he got Marta in trouble -" Suddenly she remembered who she was talking to and patted my hand. "Not that it was your fault, dear. You were the true innocent in all this mess." She patted my hand again. "Have another cookie."

I choked down another Fig Newton to show her I had taken no offense. As casually as possible, I asked the key question: "How did you know that Jack had taken up with Marta and had a child?"

For the first time, she seemed uncomfortable. She ran an almost translucent hand through her almost translucent hair. "Well, I guess it doesn't matter now, after all these years, but I did promise."

"Please tell me."

"Why don't you ask Marta all these questions? She was there, after all."

I groped for a satisfying answer. "That was a really hard time in her life. She doesn't like to talk about it. But I'm trying to do my genealogy and put together a family history, and there just aren't that many people I can ask. I want to make sure I get everything right."

That charmed her. She had taught journalism for forty-five years. Accuracy FIRST. "Virginia told me," she said. "She came to me in a terrible state. Marta had contacted her and told her that Jack had taken her home one night after a football game and - well, that you had come along nine months later. Virginia just didn't know what to do. She didn't want to hurt Jack, she didn't want to hurt her family, but she couldn't stand by while he had access to all those vulnerable young girls. And of course, when she told me, I had a duty to take it to the principal. I didn't want to - I liked Jack tremendously - but I had to. Marta was fast, she was flashy, she was impressed with her wow-power, but no fifteen-year-old girl in the world deserves that. We kept it as quiet as possible, out of deference to Virginia and Jack, but he had to go."

She was quiet for a moment, reliving what had to have been a painful decision. Then she tried to smile. "I guess he showed us, though, didn't he? No sooner was he out the door of the high school than he started up that mill. I think he was a millionaire within three years." She glanced at the loud, shabby furniture of the care center, breathed the hot, stale air heavy with onions, urine, and disinfectant. "Strange how life goes sometimes, you know, Jack."

Over and over, I got the same answer to the key question: *Virginia told me Jack and Marta Boyden had had a child. She asked me not to tell anyone else.* For someone who ostensibly had been trying to keep the story under wraps, Virginia had had a big mouth. The gamble had paid off for her. Everyone in town believed I was Marta's son. Virginia had inoculated them with her gossip. Even if news of the truth reached Bellingham, no one would have believed that Mary was my mother. And the *sub rosa* scandal came with fringe benefits: my dad got canned from the job he loved but that didn't pay well enough to satisfy Virginia. She didn't leave him much choice but to start up the family pulp and paper mill, to make a fortune for her in a business he detested.

I knew less than he had when he had started the mill, but I was finding it increasingly fascinating. Part of it was just my lawyerly weakness for documents. Litigators spend so much time fighting over document production that when the box of paper finally hits your desk, it's like Christmas, your birthday, and the Tooth Fairy all rolled into one. You just know you're going to get something good. I spent hours in my makeshift office, pouring over the papers I had collected from the mill and my dad's house. I sorted and organized, making piles for operations, labor relations, insurance, marketing, finance, and compliance.

It wasn't just idle curiosity. I was figuring out the business, figuring out where the money was coming from and where it went. I couldn't find any of the mill's insurance policies, and if we had property casualty insurance – which any business should – we needed to make a claim for damages from the fire. I made a note to call Leah and ask for copies. I also paused on a $3 million payment from American Fidelity shortly after Sarah's husband's death. The mill must have had insurance policies on its executives. I wondered whether that coverage had survived on Clark Swanson and Mike Saunders. If it had, the mill could use the money. I made another note.

All in all, things were going pretty well. I was settling into my new life as an amateur genealogist and even more amateur mill owner. I was learning about my mother; I was learning about the mill. My sisters seemed delighted to have us around, even insisting that we stay with them instead of at Karen's B&B. Beth seemed to be getting better all the time. Dr. Kovic changed her medication and had her switch schools. She still went into her mother's bedroom sometimes during the night, but she was quiet and peaceful night and day. We made it through two whole weeks without anyone's being shot, slashed, or strangled. We made it through two whole weeks without a death, a fire, or an unsuccessful marriage proposal. A personal best.

So when the scandal broke in Japan, there seemed to be no reason for Harmony to stay. Her father's company, the mighty Yamashita Incorporated, was rocked by allegations of paying bribes to *sōkaiya* - mobsters who threaten to disrupt shareholders' meetings with allegations of corporate corruption. One of Higuro's top guys had been videotaped offering a bribe to an undercover agent. So far, no one had implicated Higuro personally, but as CEO, he was responsible for whatever had happened. He bore the brunt of the shame.

"Some Japanese CEOs have killed themselves when their companies were exposed like this," Harmony explained. "It's a matter of honor. I need to see Higuro. I need to talk to him. I need to remind him that our family is not that honorable. I'm so sorry, Jack, but I really have to go back to Japan."

"Don't worry about it, Harmony," I said, helping her pack. "Of course you have to go to him. And all I'm doing right now is pushing paper and taking tea with nice little old ladies."

"You'll be careful?"

"I'll be extremely careful. Not a single papercut. I promise."

"You won't do anything stupid?"

"You wound me, Harmony."

"You know what I mean. You won't get suspicious of someone and decide to investigate them by yourself? You won't pry into anything? You won't go into the dark basement all alone?"

"No, no, and no."

"Good." She kissed me - more intensely than usual - and then she was gone.

I passed another placid week in Bellingham. I continued assembling and reviewing data on my dad's business. I continued visiting my mom's friends, classmates, teachers, and employers, all over Bellingham. Without exception, they were delighted to see me. Without exception, they had loved Mary Boyden. Without exception, they thought I was Marta's son, not Mary's. I drank more tea in the three weeks I spent in Bellingham than at any other time in my life.

Eventually, even Mark had to admit that the only danger I seemed to face in Bellingham was probable diabetes from all the cookies that had been pressed upon me. So when he and Anthony got their first break on the murder down by the Kingdome and needed to go to Canada to compare notes on a drug smuggler, I told them not to worry about me.

"Just go," I told Mark. "I'll be fine. All I'm doing right now is trying to find out about my mom. Even I can't get in trouble chasing ghosts."

Famous last words.

CHAPTER 26

My dreams came back with a vengeance. Every night I spent in the Edgemoor mansion, I dreamed that my father was alive and well upstairs, while I moved silently throughout the dazzling house, trying not to disturb him. I passed my cold, bloodstained sister, the blood-spattered hall, the parquet floor sparkling with shattered glass. So much glass. And then I woke.

Sometimes the dream would wake me several times a night. Betsy took to sleeping with her front paws firmly planted on my chest, so I couldn't thrash around and wake her up.

As Thanksgiving approached, the dreams intensified. After Betsy abandoned me in disgust at 4 a.m., I decided to call it a night and get up and work. I was already deep in a treatise on chlorine-free bleaching when I heard the muffled sobs, faint and faraway.

Sarah was sitting in the kitchen, crying over a tableful of pictures of our dad. Betsy cuddled beside her, licking her chin. Sarah didn't look up when I sat down and put my hand on her shoulder. "I'm sorry I woke you," she said, her voice thick with tears.

"You didn't. You OK?"

"Yes. No." She pushed the damp tendrils of hair away from her face. "Jack, I miss him so much."

We sat without speaking for a while, petting Betsy, as the night sky thinned to a fretful grey. The birds hazarded their first, uncertain chirps. Slowly, almost automatically, Sarah began to reach for photographs and hand them to me: herself as a baby, Emily as a Brownie, Beth as a fairy one Halloween. Marianne as a cheerleader. That one made me wince. Jack and Virginia, barbecuing in the backyard, surrounded by respectable, well-fed suburbanites - Mr. and Mrs. Middle America at home. Jack and Virginia's wedding photo from the Light of Love Chapel in Las Vegas. That one made me wince again.

We sat together for hours. Photograph by photograph, Sarah was sharing their lives with me, including me in their family. She pointed out the vacations I never took, the Christmas mornings I had missed, as if I had simply been sick that day, as if I had decided not to come. Over and over again, I saw her family - my family - gathered at Disneyland, the Grand Canyon, Hawaii. In the cold skew of the early morning, I could almost see my absence standing next to them.

She handed me a picture of the Orcas cabin. I didn't recognize it. We had seen the lodge closed up, swathed in winter mist, hunkered behind huge trees. It looked completely different surrounded by people. It was a picture of some sort of party, although I couldn't tell the season. The people were wearing coats and caps, but in the Northwest, that doesn't narrow it down.

My attention riveted on a tall woman standing near my father. My mother was in this picture. She was right at the edge of the frame - a significant distance from Virginia - but she was there. And she was holding a baby. A small, sleepy, wise-looking baby.

"Who's the cute kid?" I asked, trying to keep my voice level.

Sarah started a little. It was the first time either of us had spoken in several hours. She took the picture from me and puzzled over it for a moment. "Oh, that's Beth," she said. "Wasn't she darling?"

"She was indeed." I returned my attention to the picture and willed my heart to stop pounding. If the baby was Beth, this picture predated me by several years. I studied the dynamic of the photograph. My mother was smiling at Beth, who seemed to be smiling back. My dad seemed to be smiling at my mom. And Virginia was standing stiffly in the middle of it all, staring blankly at my dad.

"May I have a copy of this?" I blurted, before I could think of a plausible reason why I wanted it.

"Well, sure." Sarah took it from me. A little line appeared on her forehead and almost immediately smoothed as she jumped to the wrong but understandable conclusion. "Of course. You're right. This is the Orcas cabin. It's yours now. When the weather's better, I'll take you over there and introduce you around."

"I'd like that," I said, hoping no one would tell her we had already made an expedition of our own.

"We should wait a couple of months. It's so beautiful over there in the spring. You'll love it. We're famous over there."

"Why?"

"Because Pilate loved to chase skunks. He never actually caught one, but he got close enough that they, well, registered their displeasure in the particular way that skunks do. We tried everything to get rid of the smell: tomato juice, orange oil, even buttermilk. The only thing that worked was Summer's Eve douche. Unfortunately, Pilate weighed more than 150 pounds, and those little bottles didn't go very far. It took 20 at a time to get him clean. Daddy used to beg us - he used to bribe us - to go into Eastsound and buy the stuff for him. And you can imagine how people reacted when my sisters and I would stroll in almost weekly and buy five boxes each of Summer's Eve. Absolutely everyone knew who we were. Cleanest girls on the island."

She laughed heartily, and I joined in. "Pilate liked Springtime Flowers best," she said, still laughing. Then her face grew somber. She reached over and handed me another photograph, this time of a boat. "This is yours, too, Jack. We'll go down to the marina sometime and take you aboard. And there's one or two more docked on Orcas. Daddy loved boats. I guess he figured you would, too."

Sarah mistook my answering silence for discomfort. "It's OK, Jack. We understand. None of us begrudges anything Daddy left you."

I believed her, but I barely heard her. I was just staring at that picture of the boat. I had spent summers in high school as a boat dog at the Seattle Yacht Club, scrubbing barnacles off the bottoms of yachts that weren't nearly as nice as this. It looked like a 45-foot Catalina sloop, gleaming and immaculate, *The Sound Venture* painted on its side.

You could go anywhere in a boat like that. You could sleep six people; you could be gone weeks at a time. If you were hiding from something, you could stay below deck. You could dock wherever you needed to, and you could slip away at the slightest threat of detection. And if you loved boats and fishing, if you had grown up crabbing on Bellingham Bay, if you had kayaked to 112 of the San Juan Islands and made out with your girlfriend on 85 of them, then you would know the local waters and islands well enough so you could disappear - just disappear - for months. For years.

I looked back at Sarah. She was still sorting the pictures. Her eyes were red and wet with loss and memories. I almost asked her about that night in the hospital, the night when I thought I heard her talking to my dad. At the last second, I bit the words away. She was suffering - awash in grief, hoarding the little she had left of her father. I couldn't believe that anyone was that good an actress. If my father was still alive, I decided, Sarah didn't know.

I hesitated, unsure of how to approach the subject. I had to see those boats. I had to check whether they were still moored, search for signs of recent use or occupancy. I asked, "Did you go boating with your dad a lot?"

"Oh, I used to. For my birthday, we used to sail to Victoria and have tea at the Empress Hotel and then go crabbing off Salt Spring Island. But none of us went too often over the past few years. Mama just kept getting worse and worse, so Daddy wanted to be close to home. And after Scott -" she paused - "died and Jennifer was born, no one really had much time. All those boats probably need a complete keelhaul. We hired a guy to keep them up, but you know." She shrugged. So hard to get good help these days.

"Well, I spent four summers as a boat dog, so at least I can make sure they're put to bed for winter," I said. "How about you show me this one today? Maybe we could head over to Orcas tomorrow."

An indulgent smile suffused her tired face: *little boys and their toys*. "That would be fun, Jack," was all she said. "How about a real seafaring breakfast before we go?"

We were in the middle of large bowls of Lucky Charms when the phone rang. It was Dave West, the foreman of the mill. We had a problem. Bethany Walton was challenging our latest discharge reports, and she wanted to see me ASAP. As in that morning. As in right then. So much for spending the day inspecting my vessels. So much for the life of the idle rich.

"Don't worry about it, Jack," Sarah said. "I have a class this afternoon, but we can see the boats tomorrow. And the weather's supposed to be nicer then anyway."

So I finished my cereal, hugged her and Betsy goodbye, and left to do battle with Bethany.

It wasn't much of a battle. She had me waxed before I even walked in the conference room she was using at the Whatcom County Courthouse. Contaminant levels in our discharge waters were unacceptable, she began, not even bothering to say hello. We had been taking measurements too high up the deep-water shunt. We weren't picking up the effluvium that mixed with the discharge farther down the shunt during a later stage of processing. And what was I going to do about it?

I argued with her a while. We were following industry standard, I insisted, hoping that was true. Even with the additional effluvium, we were within striking distance of the DOE requirements and we were planning operational improvements as soon as we could secure some capital. The DOE had okayed a similar measurement process in a competing mill. How could she hold us to a standard she didn't impose on our competitors?

She leaned forward. I saw the flash in her bolt-like eyes. "Your competitors don't owe me big-time the way you do."

I didn't answer.

"I can close you down," she reminded me.

"I know you can."

"I can fine you."

"I know."

"I can reinstate the cleanup assessment. And I can hit your sisters with personal liability."

"I know."

"This isn't a game, Jack. I told you I'd be on your back every minute of every day, and I meant it. And this is what that feels like."

"What do you want us to do?"

"I want you to start taking measurements appropriately. Give me that data every day, starting tomorrow. Once we know what's actually going on, I'll give you a reasonable period of time to take remedial action."

"What's a reasonable period of time?"

"A week."

"Bethany!" I protested. "We're barely making it as is. I've got no money for capital improvements, and until I can get some investors on board, I'm not going to be able to make processing changes."

"Two weeks, then. Call me tomorrow. I want a full report."

OK. At least I knew where we stood. On my way out, I paused and looked back at her.

"Yes?" she demanded.

"I shudder to think how you'd treat us if you didn't like me so much."

She burst out laughing. "I do like you, Jack. Now get out of here. You've got a lot of work to do."

I escaped. On my way back to the mill, I passed the Bellingham marina and almost stopped to search for *The Sound Venture*. Only my promise to Harmony kept me away. I had assured her I wouldn't go blundering off investigating while she and Mark were gone. And if my dad were hiding out on that boat, it was pretty clear that he didn't want to be found.

It was almost 11 when I reached the mill. Marilyn, the pugnacious-looking lady from my first meeting at the mill, passed me as I trudged up the concrete stairs. "I wish I had your schedule," she said.

"Do you wish you had my salary?" I returned, less than cheerfully. My sisters and I had made it very clear that we weren't taking any distributions from the mill - not that year, at least, and probably not the next.

Marilyn mumbled something placating and retreated. I stood on the concrete precipice and stared down at the wreckage from the fire. We had cleared out the most dangerous rubble - the broken beams, the warped floorboards, the wiring. Here and there I could discern the old brick walls of the foundation - blackened and crumbled like a ruin. An idle thought crossed my mind: My mom would have loved excavating this place. It was replaced by an active thought: I needed to call American Fidelity on the property casualty coverage. We needed our payment from the fire.

I hunted down Dave West and broke the bad news about my morning with Bethany. For most of the rest of the day, we scrambled to reposition the discharge monitoring in the deep-water shunt, to plan a remediation effort if Bethany found us out of compliance. I was grimy, damp, and worried by the time I went into my office and sank down in my rickety chair.

There was a smoky box of documents on my desk. "We found another one, Jack," someone called from the back. "Knock yourself out."

They all saw it as a harmless eccentricity, this predilection I had for paper. As we slowly cleared the site of the fire, everyone knew I wanted to see every document that had survived the blaze. There wasn't much - just some formulas for pulping, old bills, purchase orders for chemicals, accounting ledgers kept in a spidery hand. I opened the new box with my pocket knife, careful that the whole thing didn't crumble. A gust of soot greeted me as I unpacked the scorched and stiffened contents.

Just bills and purchase orders this time, I decided, lingering over invoices for chlorine dioxide and sodium hypochlorite, the bleaching agents at the heart of all the environmental havoc. I set about squirreling them away in the appropriate piles. When I reached some bills from American Fidelity, I nearly stacked them unread in my insurance pile. But I was curious enough about any policies for Mike Saunders and Clark Swanson - and eager enough for a payout if the coverage had survived - to slit the crumbling rubber band with my knife and start paging through the bills. They were written in that annoying shorthand common to all insurance companies. Even after five years as a commercial litigator, I still found it difficult, but fortunately, not impossible. At least I could understand what the bills were for, and I couldn't find any sign of a policy on Mike or Clark. I shook my head in frustration. It didn't make any sense that the mill would have purchased a policy only on Sarah's husband and not on the other folks in charge.

I called American Fidelity policyholder services. It took the nice lady on the other end of the line all of five minutes to clear up the mystery. Yes, the mill had purchased life insurance policies on all its executives, she told me. But after a few premium payments, it let all the policies lapse. Scott Duncan's coverage must have been reinstated at some point, as there had been a claim on that coverage, but none of the other policies were in force. Did I need anything else?

I was about to say no when I remembered the missing insurance policies and my sisters' struggles with my dad's life insurance claim. It had been a couple of weeks, and Leah hadn't called me back. "If you could transfer me to Leah Batson, that would be great," I said. And then I fiddled with the stiff old bills while peppy '70s music poured into my ear.

I was in the middle of something that sounded like *Staying Alive* done by 101 Strings when one word of the faded rectangular print caught my eye: "Rider." It was a common enough word, one that normally would not have demanded a first - let alone a second - look. But the extra cost for the extra insurance was on the bill for the mill's General Commercial Liability policy, and if there was one thing I knew about, it was the mill's GCL policy.

I had been litigating the GCL policy for months. I had quoted it in motions. I had grilled people on it during depositions. I had even created giant foam-core blow-ups of it to use as exhibits in my summary judgment argument. I knew that the mill's General Commercial Liability policy did not have any riders expanding coverage. I paged through the bills to see whether there could have been some mistake. Every single one of them said there was a rider.

The phone line clicked in my ear. Leah sounded out of breath. "Jack, I'm sorry, but I'm just heading out for a meeting."

That old dodge. "Oh, you are not," I said, more amused than offended. There was a long pause.

"You're right," she said finally. "I'm not. But I could be."

"I'll be fast. Any news on my dad's life claim and any property casualty coverage for the fire?"

Another long pause. "Jerry said he'd call you back."

"He hasn't. Look, Leah, please just tell me what's going on."

"I haven't heard from Jerry on whether there's still a casualty policy in force on the mill, Jack, but even if there is, I wouldn't get your hopes up. The official finding of the police was that your dad started the fire intentionally. So even if you have a casualty policy, we're likely to exclude as arson."

I hmmed noncommittally. Arson seemed like it should require a higher showing of intent. But until I knew whether or not we had a policy, there was no reason to antagonize Leah.

"Yeah, I'd like to take a look at the arson exclusion. Would you ask Jerry to fax me the policy?"

"I will if your policy exists. Jerry's checking, and it may take some time. There's actual microfiche involved here."

I was touched. "I'm sorry. I really do appreciate all the extra work," I said. "And I hate to press my luck, but –"

"You will?" she finished for me. "Honestly, Jack. You just really do not know when to quit. But on the life policy, the finding of the policy is that your dad either committed suicide or died accidentally. If it's suicide, he's within the exclusion period. All we'll pay is the reserve amount – a couple of thousand at most."

"And if it was an accident?"

"Then he was caught in the blaze while he was trying to destroy documents responsive to our discovery requests. And we exclude coverage when the death occurs in the commission of a crime."

"Destruction of documents isn't a crime."

"It's punishable with contempt."

"*Civil* contempt, Leah, not criminal sanctions. Geez, you must know how thin this is. That's why you didn't call me back."

She let out a long puff of exasperation. "Jack, you asked me to tell you what's going on, and I told you. I don't want to argue with you."

"Then stop arguing and just listen to me. You and I both know it wasn't suicide. No one kills themselves by hitting themselves over the head and then setting a fire. And we both know he wasn't setting the fire to evade discovery."

"Oh yeah? How do we know that?"

I spun around in my chair, fumbling for an answer. Through the smudged glass of my narrow window, the cold winter sun reflected madly off Bellingham Bay. The waves stirred under a brisk November breeze, and the light on the waves made the sea look like a path of shattered glass. It looked just like the glass in my dream. So much glass.

Glass.

Glass.

Glasses.

I had seen them myself when I wound up in my father's bedroom after my eventful conversation with Virginia Carlson: his reading glasses, there on his dresser, in a muddle of breath mints, spare change, and receipts. You can't destroy documents you can't see, can you? If I hadn't had Leah on the line - saying, *Jack? Jack? Are you there, Jack?* - I would have slapped my forehead and kicked myself all at the same time.

As it was, I swallowed, recovered, and said, "We know he wasn't trying to evade discovery because he left his reading glasses home that night. He couldn't have decided which documents he needed to destroy without them."

She was tapping her pencil on her desk. That meant deep thinking. "Not if all the documents were grouped together," she protested. "Not if he intended to burn everything just so it wouldn't look obvious that he was targeting only the documents that were damaging to the mill."

"They weren't, and he didn't. In fact, I've got a box of documents on my desk right now that would have been responsive to our discovery requests. They're smoky, but they're intact. And the weirdest thing, Leah - there are a bunch of bills here for a rider on our General Commercial Liability policy."

"What? You don't have any riders on your GCL."

"Well, that's what I thought, too, but that didn't stop you guys from billing us for it."

A heartfelt groan reverberated across the line. "You know, I liked it a lot better when you were on our side."

"So did I." We were both silent for a moment.

She groaned again. "Look, I really do have to go to a meeting now. I'll have someone look into the rider thing, OK? And - and I'll ask Jerry and Carl if we can reconsider the life coverage. No promises, but I'll try. And if in the bowels of this company there's some tattered old casualty policy with your company's name on it, I'll send it to you so you can see for yourself that any fire claim would be excluded. Since you obviously don't trust my ability to interpret an insurance contract."

"You were always my favorite client, Leah," I said, and she responded "ha ha," and hung up.

It was late afternoon when I put on my jacket and set out to do a little digging on the mother front. I plucked one of the mysterious bills off the pile as I headed out the door. It came from a local address, not the main office in LA. I drove by the building on Commercial Street, but I could see no sign of an American Fidelity agency. Small wonder, really. The bill was 15 years old. I almost parked and went in to look around, but my promises to Harmony intervened. *You won't get suspicious of someone and decide to investigate them all by yourself,* she had demanded. *You won't go into the dark basement all alone.* I stuck the bill in my pocket, merged back into traffic, and set out on my intended errands.

After a few tries, I found the house where my mother grew up, a blue and white Victorian on Utter Street, with a porch swing, an apple tree, and a bright-eyed Husky in the front yard. He bounded over to the fence, barking madly. After a few kind words, he hushed and let me scratch his ears. Then he rolled over and let me rub his belly.

He was deep in doggie bliss when the front door opened and an older woman came out. "Mookie, what are you doing?"

Mookie started, gave me a guilty look - "oops" - leapt to his feet, and rushed toward the house. Then he realized he was in trouble for lying down on the job, turned back toward me, and let out the most unconvincing growl I have ever heard. I burst out laughing, and after a moment, the older woman joined in. Mookie hesitated, one paw in the air, unsure whether his dignity was being compromised. Then his owner chucked him under the chin and said "it's OK, Mook," and he was immediately happy again.

"What can I do for you?" she asked, walking toward the fence.

"I'm working on my genealogy," I explained. "My mother grew up in this house. I just wanted to see it for myself."

Maybe it was Mookie's obvious affection for me, maybe it was my honest face, but she invited me in and served me tea. And she talked and talked and talked. Of course she had known the Boydens, she said. She had been in the same class as Mary and Virginia. She had taught Marta in Sunday School - or tried to. She rolled her eyes and shook her head at me. A lost cause.

She insisted on giving me the grand tour of the house and garden, with a running commentary on how it had looked when she and Mary were growing up. There was the graveyard under the apple tree where Mary had buried her goldfish; there was the porch swing where she and Mary used to play dolls. Mary's bedroom had had a border of cabbage roses; the bathroom floors still were marble. By the time I left - well after dark - I could picture my mother as a little girl, safe and happy, playing in that house.

Emily had a date, Marianne had a PTA meeting, and Sarah and Beth were having dinner with Dr. Kovic and his family. There was no rush to get home. I dropped by Karen's B&B to make sure our account was settled. Karen was entertaining new boarders, so I declined her offer to stay for dinner.

I ended up at the Colophon Cafe in Fairhaven, lingering over peanut soup and blackberry pie while I pored over books of Bellingham history and collections of old photographs. Every now and then, I would glance up and catch someone's eyes on me. I would nod, they would nod, and I would go back to my dinner. The thought struck me as I brushed off the crumbs and headed back to my car: I was rapidly becoming a local character.

It was after 9 p.m. when I arrived back at my father's house. It no longer startled me with its grandeur. Now it just seemed like a nice place to come home. Betsy leapt to greet me as I walked in. I was wrestling with her when I heard a soft cough behind me. Beth's night nurse was keeping a wary distance from Betsy, whose size, power, and overall bounciness unnerved her.

"Jack, your sisters left you some messages," she said. "One of them looks urgent."

There were two messages on the bulletin board by the kitchen phone, each with "JACK" written in large letters across the top. The first was from Sarah. "Leah B. called and said they'll pay on Daddy's insurance!" she had written. "Thank you, thank you, Jack. You are the greatest! Sarah."

The second message looked like Emily's handwriting. "Dave West. Big probs with DOE. Needs you tonight. Meet him in plant - boilers. Sorry, can't wait."

Poor Dave. Poor me. Bethany was going to be spitting fire tomorrow if we couldn't meet her demands. I put my jacket back on and fumbled for my car keys.

Betsy was horrified that I was leaving so soon after I arrived. One look at her injured orange face, and I relented. "OK. Come on. You can stay in the car."

It was a perfect November night. Sharp breeze, bare trees, a faint suggestion of a moon. Betsy was asleep by the time we reached the mill.

I tossed my jacket over her, cracked the window, locked the door, and climbed the concrete stairs toward the plant. I didn't want to look over the precipice at the burned-out hulk of the office building, but it was impossible for me to pass without turning my head. The almost moonless night made the pit look black and bottomless.

The lights were on in the plant. It was wreathed in the steam from the venting system, making it look like it floated a little above the ground. I stepped up my pace. "Dave?" I called, as I made my way toward the fat, gleaming boilers. "Dave? Where are you?"

As I rounded the corner, I heard the slightest noise behind me. For just a split second, I saw his reflection in the fun-house mirror of the boiler side.

Tall, solid, round face, silver hair. No way this was Dave West.

It was my dad. It was really my dad.

Before I could process what I saw, before I could even say his name, he hit me over the back of the head. The force threw me forehead first into the side of the boiler. I sank to my knees. I was grasping the back of my neck and trying to stand up when he hit me again. This time I really went down. This time I really went down hard. The last thing I remembered was the sound of his shoes walking away.

I don't know how long I was out. I don't know how long I laid there, bleeding on the concrete floor. But it was the noise that roused me: not the smoke, not the heat - the noise.

It sounded like a giant was stamping the plant under his feet, breaking the beams, crushing the equipment, tossing the concrete blocks aside like toys.

Dizzy, deafened, I struggled upward and tried to figure out what was going on. Then I got a smothering lungful of the black smoke that was pouring toward me, and I knew.

Fire.

CHAPTER 27

The inside of a fire is the darkest place on earth. It wasn't just the absence of light. It was the complete antithesis of light. I couldn't see the flames. I couldn't see the equipment. I couldn't see the doors, the windows, or any other way of escape. All I could see was black, black that seemed alive - thick, vicious, bent on getting inside me, on blotting me out forever.

I struggled up, disoriented by the heat and the pain and the noise. The choking black smoke billowed into my lungs and forced me down again. Hunched over and gasping, I half-crawled, half-ran from the most intense heat. I made it just a few steps before I collided head-first with a lump of searing-hot metal. I staggered back, stunned, and set off in another direction - only to encounter an even hotter metal hunk.

I was stranded in the middle of a plant I barely knew by sight, fire was raging all around me, and I seemed hemmed in not only by the fire but by the mill itself. Everywhere I turned, it was waiting for me.

I shrank down to the ground, my sweater over my head, my nose on the concrete floor. I could barely breathe - but I *could* breathe. As a little oxygen seeped into my brain, I inched forward, hesitantly patting the ground until I encountered metal. I canvassed the shape of the obstacle with my hands and tried to picture my surroundings. I figured I was by the calendering rolls. If I was right, there was a straight shot to a door about 100 yards away.

I struck out blindly, retching through my sweater, keeping as close to the ground as possible. Ten steps, and I could feel my skin begin to singe. Five steps more, and the blasting heat drove me back. Doubled over with coughing, I staggered back toward the calendering rolls. The huge sheets of stretched paper began to spark and crackle at my approach. Soon everything would be in flames.

Panicked, I fled from the calendering, toward the Fourdrinier belt. Once again, the intense heat forced me back. I was right in the center of the fire and rapidly losing ground. The horrible noise came closer and closer, deafening as it approached. I could hear the screech of metal as the equipment warped and groaned, the crack of the beams as they splintered and sagged. The roar of flames, the shatter of glass, the rumbling groan of the mill as it fell, piece by piece, to the fire: It was the sound of utter destruction.

I hunched in a hopeless heap. The concrete floor radiated heat. I could no longer even begin to filter the smoke with my sweater. It was too thick, too hot, too solid.

I was going to die. I was absolutely going to die.

And it was my father - my own father - who had done this to me, my own father who had killed me. If there had been a drop of water left in my body, I would have put my head in my hands and cried.

A drop of water.

Water.

If there's one thing a paper mill has, it's water. The only question was whether I could get to it.

I had one last shot. With all the energy I could muster, I hurtled toward the deep-water shunt that drained the processing water out to sea.

Stumbling over pipes and bashing into beams, I finally slammed into the shunt. I wrapped my hand in my sweater and forced down the latch of the sampling station. I couldn't quite fit through the opening, so I kicked desperately at the steaming metal until it gaped. I hurled myself inside and sank to my knees in the foot or two of standing water. I could swear that my clothes and skin hissed as they met the liquid.

Splashing water over my face and hair, I slipped and skidded down the slimy shunt. Soon I would be going under the paper mill. Soon I would be halfway to the sea. The water cooled as I descended. The air was rank and sour, but I gulped it gratefully.

The burning in my chest began to fade to a sharp, cindery ache. When the water was to my waist, I heard muffled booms behind me. I barely had time to process what had happened - the water tanks must have ruptured in the heat - when a wave of hot, caustic water knocked me off my feet and washed me down the shunt. I went down foaming and choking in the stinging water. Another wave lifted me and slammed my head against the ceiling.

Stunned, I sank beneath the surface. Water rushed into my lungs. I managed to claw upward and gasp in the few inches of air between the water and the ceiling. Then another wave of water hit me, and I went down again.

I would have stayed down, too. I had no strength to stand against the current, no strength to find and fight for whatever air remained. The awful water turned red, then black before my eyes. I squeezed them shut. My chest felt like it was going to explode.

I heard splashing coming toward me. Broken and amplified by the rushing water, it sounded like the giant was stomping through the shunt. One faint thought flickered through what was left of my brain. It was my dad. My dad was back, coming to finish me off.

When he seized me by the collar, I was sure he was going to strangle me. But he pulled my head above the water, held it there while I choked and spluttered and gulped in air. When I had coughed up water, he began dragging me back up the shunt, keeping my head above the current all the way. As the water fell away from me, I had the strange, exultant feeling of rising.

My father pulled me up the shunt until the water was just over my thighs. Then he let me down so I slumped against the side of the shunt. He was fussing over me, making small sounds of concern. Then he started licking my face.

OK. That was wrong. I forced my eyes open and looked right into Betsy's frantic, deep brown eyes. Her muzzle was smeared with blood, she was drenched, and patches of her fur looked burned away. She was the most beautiful dog in the world. When my eyes opened, she almost whinnied in delight. Her tail splashed a wet tattoo.

She lay down on top of me, keeping me warm, easing me into the water so most of my body was submerged. I put my arms around her, pulled her into the water, and held her tight.

The two of us lay there in the water, while the fire raged above and around us, while my father's mill melted, flamed, writhed, teetered, and collapsed.

I hugged Betsy and listened to the soft, sweet pleading sounds she was making in my ear. I closed my eyes and sank deeper into the water.

And I let the darkness take me.

CHAPTER 28

"Good morning, Sunshine."

I blinked, blinked again, and looked up into another pair of dark brown eyes. This time, they were Mark's. I didn't even need to ask where I was. From the smell alone, I could tell I was back in the hospital. Maybe I could get a special rate on the room.

"Where's Bets?" My tongue felt far too large for my mouth. The roar of the water still rang in my ears.

"At the vet's. She's OK. She's like you - cut up and scorched and half drowned, but she's Iron Dog. She barked and barked until the firemen found you. They couldn't believe that anyone survived that blaze - man or beast."

"How did she get out of the car?" Betsy weighed 95 pounds; I knew she couldn't have slithered through the crack in the window.

"Right through the windshield. As far as we can tell, she had some help. We dug a bullet out of your front seat, and there's human blood around your car and smeared all over her teeth. We think she was barking when the guy who set the fire came back to the parking lot. He must have shot at her to shut her up. The bullet shattered the windshield, she went right through the glass, and she attacked him. She probably would have killed him if she hadn't decided to go in after you instead. As it was, there's a hell of a pool of blood there by your car. Whoever he was, he's torn up pretty bad. We've checked all the hospitals within a hundred miles, though, and no one's come in with dog bite wounds."

It was impossible. I could believe a lot of things about my dad - I had to believe a lot of things about my dad - but I couldn't make myself accept that my father would shoot a dog. I had seen the pictures of him with Pilate. I could sense their ease, their affection, their mutual respect.

"No way." I said, only half-aloud. "No way would he have shot at Betsy. My dad wouldn't hurt a dog."

Mark's jaw tightened. "What's your dad got to do with this?"

"It was him, Mark. He hit me over the head. He must have set the place on fire. He's alive, Mark. He's alive - and he tried to kill me."

Mark just stared at me. "I think you'd better start at the beginning," he said.

I told him, in a thick, lisping voice that improved only slightly with frequent sips of water. When I got to the part about seeing my father's face, he shook his head in disbelief.

"It was only for a second. His face would have been distorted by the curve of the boiler. How could you know who it was?"

I explained about the boats, the possibility that my dad could have been hiding out on board. He shook his head again.

"I saw him, Mark," I insisted. "I know it was just for a second, but I saw him."

"You'd been thinking about him and looking at pictures of him. You'd been thinking maybe he was hiding out in the marina. You were hoping to see him. You were expecting to see him. Your mind was playing tricks on you."

"I wasn't hoping that he'd hit me over the head," I protested. "I wasn't expecting that he'd try to set me on fire."

It was too much. I thought I had been chasing a kindly ghost - someone who adored his daughters and granddaughters, someone who loved my mother, someone who might have loved me. Harmony had assured me that eventually things would seem clear to me, that eventually I would know what to believe about my dad. All I could believe right then was that he wanted me dead. Maybe he always had.

A terrible thought trickled into my conscious, a thought so awful that I scrabbled to push it away. What if I had had it backwards from the start? What if *my father* had poisoned me and my mother, intent on ridding himself of obstacles to his reconciliation with Virginia? What if, all this time, Virginia had been covering up for *him*?

Mark began to talk to me, very quietly, about nothing in particular. He told me that the Seahawks, the Huskies, and the good old Franklin High football team had all lost miserably over the weekend. He told me that one of Detective Anthony's champion Rottweilers, Peanut, was expecting puppies. He told me about the Kingdome case that he and Anthony were working on. It had started out looking like a drug deal that went bad, he said. As they pulled the plot apart, it turned out that the victim was a Bellingham bartender who supplemented his income by making book for one of the drug gangs in Vancouver. The guy got greedy and started skimming. He started his own little business on the side, taking the long-shot bets himself and walking away with the profits. It was a gamble he lost. The gang had gotten suspicious and done its version of an audit. The cause of death had been a single bullet at the base of the skull.

In spite of myself, I was getting interested. I opened my eyes. "Did you catch the guy?"

"No, not yet. We know the when, the why, and the how, but not the who. We're working with the Vancouver police on it. By the way, Anthony and I ran into David Mann while we were in Vancouver. He's started working out. He's put on about ten pounds of muscle. He challenged you and Harmony to an arm-wrestling match. If you win, you get to join his firm."

David Mann was the best criminal defense attorney in Seattle. "What does he get if we lose?" I asked.

"You *have* to join his firm."

Mark continued like that for a while, distracting me with news about people we knew from home, pointing out the gifts on the bedside table. My sisters had brought me flowers; Karen had dropped off a thick book on Bellingham history that I had admired at her B&B; the little old ladies I had visited over the past few weeks had inundated me with prayer cards and cookies.

We both had a cookie. "Are you feeling better?"

I did feel better. It was amazing what Mark could do to a person. I tried to nod, but the cervical collar was too stiff. "Yeah, I'm OK."

"Good." He leaned forward. "Because now I'm going to yell at you." He smiled at me, but there was real hurt in his eyes. "When we got the call about the fire, Anthony and I came screaming back from Vancouver. We used the lights and the siren the whole way. And then we stood outside that mill for seven hours. The firemen wouldn't go in and search for you until the flames died down. When a building's a total loss, they won't risk their lives to retrieve a body. We just stood there and watched the roof cave in. We watched everything fall apart, piece by piece.

"When they got the fire under control, they sent a team in after you. They brought in a cadaver dog. They kept coming over to me and Anthony and saying, 'We haven't found it.' Not *him*. '*It*.' Jack, I stood there for seven hours and waited for the body bag. Whatever was left of you, I was going to be there when they brought you out. I was going to see it through."

He stopped and rubbed his eyes. "I know you were lured there. I know you just thought you were going to work. But Jack, you've known for two months that you've been playing with fire. Whatever's buried up here, someone wants it to stay buried, and someone wants it bad. And when you take risks like this, when you take your life in your hands, you're not just messing with your life. You're messing with my life, and Harmony's life, and the life of everyone who cares about you. Maybe your dad is worth all that. Maybe knowing what happened to him and figuring out who he was - or is, or whatever - is worth it. But I doubt it."

He paused. "I could just kill you," he said, straightening up and brushing himself off. "If someone else wasn't trying so hard to beat me to it, I probably would."

I started to apologize, but Mark was done. That was another great thing about Mark. He never lingered. His change of subject was dizzyingly abrupt. "I'll tell Detective Anthony about those boats. We'll check them out."

As he turned to go, I saw the source of the gurgling noise that had nagged at me since I opened my eyes. Behind him was a small fountain, about two feet high. Water gushed out of a bamboo shoot and splashed over smooth black river stones. I shuddered. The sound reminded me of the water rushing down the shunt to drown me.

"Where did that come from?"

"Higuro sent it to you. It's for your energy or something. I think the water is supposed to help you heal from the fire."

"I can't believe Higuro would send me a fountain." The man didn't even like me. In fact, given that he absolutely did not want me to marry Harmony, I was pretty sure that Higuro would have been immensely relieved if I had died in that fire. I was about to say so, when Mark's voice cut across my thoughts.

"That's not all he sent you."

He pulled the curtain separating me from the next bed. Harmony was curled up asleep, her black hair across her beautiful face.

"How'd she get here so fast?"

"You've been out almost two days. She's been here a couple of hours. And I don't think she's going anywhere anytime soon." He shook her gently by the shoulder. As she stirred, he gave my good arm a fierce squeeze and headed out. "I think you two probably want to be alone."

Harmony was warm and smooth and exquisitely soft. I was trying hard not to breathe on her, but she seemed oblivious to the effects of my two days of unconsciousness. She kissed me, hugged me, kissed me again. She stroked my hair. I tried to explain to her how I'd kept my promise to her - how I didn't go to the marina alone, how I was tricked into going to the mill - but she shushed me. "It doesn't matter, it doesn't matter," she kept saying. "As long as you're all right, then nothing else matters."

She kept apologizing. She was so sorry she had gone to Japan, she said. She was so sorry she had left me behind. She would never, ever leave me again.

I looked up at Harmony, next to me on the narrow hospital bed, propped up on one elbow and stroking my face with her free hand. Her tears fell onto my face, slipped over my cheeks and into my eyes. She had dark circles under her eyes, her hair was all over the place, and she was crying and murmuring in small broken gasps that she thought she'd lost me, that she thought she'd never see me again.

That's when I did the most unethical thing of my life.

That's when I asked her to marry me.

And she said yes.

CHAPTER 29

I kept waiting for her to back out, but she didn't. Even after she had washed her face and regained her composure, she didn't try to revisit what had happened between us. Even when I introduced her to the nurse as my fiancée, she didn't flinch. She even talked to me seriously and calmly about picking out a ring.

A small flicker of hope tingled through my chest, but I was still wary and realistic. Harmony was the exact opposite of a fair-weather friend. When I was in trouble - especially if I was incapacitated and in trouble - you could not pry Harmony away from me. It was when I was up and around and full of myself that she got scared.

Right then, she had nothing to fear. I had whiplash, second-degree burns, and a broken wrist. I had respiratory damage and chemical scalding, and I was thoroughly concussed, casted, and catheterized. The most I could do was hold her hand. But when the tubes came out, when my wrist, skin, and lungs healed, when I regained my strength and wanted more than her hand, would Harmony still want to marry me? I watched for signs of flight.

None thus far. She snapped open her cellphone and took charge. Speaking a shifting mixture of English, Japanese, and something that sounded a whole lot like high school slang, she wheedled, dealed, and debated until she had obtained at-cost paper products to cover our existing orders. She sensed that Higuro's fountain freaked me out and made a gracious gift of it to the nice lady who changed my dressings. She called each of our customers and suppliers to explain what had happened and to make alternate arrangements to meet any existing obligations or expectations. "We don't know when we're going to reopen," she kept saying. "But your business is important to us, we want to preserve the relationship between us, and we're committed to making sure you're taken care of while we're rebuilding. What can we do to prove that to you?"

During a rare pause while she looked up a phone number, I reached over and took her hand. "Why are you working so hard, Harmony?"

"To keep good will with your customers."

"Why?"

"So if you want to rebuild, you won't have lost your base."

"Harmony." With my good arm, I fished around in the newspapers by my bed and pushed one toward her. The whole front page of the Herald was crammed with pictures of the fire - during and after. The flames had shot three stories into the night sky. The mill itself was a total loss, a melted, broken ruin of twisted metal and charred beams. Both warehouses had been torched and burnt to their concrete shells. Everything in them had been destroyed - even the huge, 900-pound rolls of paper had burned away, exposing the empty, tilting skeletons of their metal frames. The panoramic pictures of the aftermath were chilling - a blackened swath of utter destruction against the blue sea and bright sky. "It's gone, Harmony. It's all over."

"It doesn't have to be. If you want to, we can just bulldoze it under and build a new mill right on top."

I shook my head the best I could. "No one but an idiot would start a pulp and paper business right now, Harmony. Timber supplies are too tight, the environmental liability is too huge, the market's too soft - and too confusing. Everyone wants clean air and clean water, but they also want their paper - even their toilet paper - dazzlingly white. You can't get wood pulp that white without bleaching it. Oxygenization just doesn't cut it. We'd never recoup the cost of the mill, and I don't think we'd ever meet environmental standards. Even with Bethany trying to work with us, we weren't running clean enough. I don't want to be an industrial polluter, Harmony. And I don't want to be a failure, either. Not even a glorious failure."

"You're not a failure, Jack." She was quiet for a moment. "It's not that I want you to do anything you don't want to do. It's just that you've seemed so dedicated to that mill. For the past three weeks, every night we talked on the phone you spent at least twenty minutes teaching me about fractionation or the DIP process or the new Cluster rules or chlorine-free bleaching. It's seemed so important to you. I don't want you to lose that."

I thought about what she had said. With her usual accuracy, she had touched ever so lightly on a place that hurt far more than my crushed wrist or bashed head.

"Well, it has been important to me," I said carefully. "And the people are still really important to me. I made a commitment to them, and I'm going to carry it through. We'll get what we can from the property and the insurance, and we'll put together a retraining program and a good severance package. I still need to talk it over with Bethany, but we might even get them some help from the state. But other than that -" My voice trailed off.

"Other than the people there, I guess I don't feel the same about the mill anymore. It was like my dad gave it to me, like he wanted me to have it, to take care of it. And since my dad just tried to kill me, I guess I don't feel like there's any reason to take care of it anymore." I thought for a moment. "I feel like the mill was just bait, like he used it to catch me in a trap."

"If it wasn't your dad who attacked you, would you feel differently?"

"It *was* my dad."

She raised her hands. This was not an argument she or Mark relished. "I'm just asking. If it wasn't your dad who attacked you, would you feel differently about rebuilding?"

I was so tired. I hurt everywhere. I was so tired of hurting everywhere. "I don't know, Harmony. Right now, I really just don't know."

"OK." She pulled out her cellphone again. "I'm going to keep working with your customers. But I'll also start putting together a contingency plan for a retraining program and a severance package, in case you decide you want to sell the property. Do you want me to start researching the market value and investigating the bids? We've had a lot of offers."

That was an understatement. The news coverage of the fire had flashed nationwide. Far from finding it horrifying, America's investment community had taken one look at the mill's waterfront location - its sweeping, unobstructed views of the beach and the sea - and cheered in unison: *development*. They wanted to stick big ugly condos or big ugly hotels or big ugly yacht clubs on the land where my dad's family had made pulp and paper for more than 100 years. I hated the idea. But we couldn't afford the taxes on the property unless we were making some money off it. "Yeah, I guess so," I said. "We might as well hear what they're willing to offer."

I closed my eyes. Harmony was punching numbers into her cellphone and starting the long, elaborate dance of real estate negotiations. I was almost asleep when I heard her say, "Vancouver, please. Do you have a business listing for Triad International?" For reasons I couldn't place, the name reverberated in my head. Where had I heard it before? I was still searching my memory when the pain and exhaustion pulled me under, and I fell asleep.

I woke in the cold blue twilight of the hospital. My room was dark, but the glow of the hallway seeped under the door. I listened for Harmony's breathing, felt for her beside me. Nothing. This worried me. Mark and Anthony had promised that Harmony and I would never be ten feet from a trusted police officer.

As if on cue, the door cracked, and I saw a familiar shape peer around it. "Detective Anthony!"

"Hey, Jack. Mark took Harmony to see Betsy at the vet's and shower and change clothes at your dad's house, so I'm your babysitter for the evening." He swung himself down in the chair beside me. "Back from the dead again, I see."

"Thanks to Betsy."

He nodded. "It was one of the spookiest things I've ever heard - her barking from inside that metal pipe. You guys were all the way under the mill, and it sounded like she'd been buried alive. She must have picked up the scent of the cadaver dog they brought in to find you, and she wouldn't stop barking until the other dog sniffed her out. It's a miracle you're alive, Jack. They'd already passed the tape around the department."

"Excuse me?"

"When an officer dies, we stick black tape over our badges - to honor him and remind us what we face every day."

"I'm not an officer."

"You're kind of a mascot. You're well worth the tape." He leaned back in his chair. "So who did it, Jack? Mark says you think it was your dad."

"Yeah," I said, bracing myself for the inevitable argument.

It didn't come. "That must really be a bitch," he said quietly.

I waited for him to tell me that it couldn't have been my dad, to point out that I had only seen my attacker for a second, to insist that my dad was dead and buried, blah, blah, blah. But he didn't. In the inviting, intervening silence, I started to tell Detective Anthony just how much of a bitch this was, just how much it hurt to lose my dad over and over and over again. First he abandoned me, then he died on me, then I thought he might still be alive, then I had to accept he wasn't, then I started to come to terms with his memory - and then he materialized *and tried to kill me*. Anthony didn't say a word. He just looked at me and nodded slowly while I ranted about what it felt like to be whipsawed back and forth - over and over again.

I had raved myself into something approaching calm. "I'm sorry," I said. "I'm sorry to go off like that."

"Nothing to be sorry about. Sounds like you needed to tell that to someone."

I tried to nod. I still wasn't used to the cervical collar. "Mark and Harmony, they just don't want to hear it. Every time I talk about my dad being alive, they get nervous."

"That's because they're afraid. They're afraid you're going to get hurt." He waved his hand toward my collar and cast. "And they do sort of have a point. Plus, Jack, you're dealing with two people who may have even more screwed up relationships with their fathers than you do. There's a reason why they can't quite get their minds around what you're saying."

I hadn't thought if it that way. Mark wasn't even on speaking terms with his father, and Harmony was still stranded between Humphrey and Higuro - the man who raised her and the man who fathered her.

"Oh," was all I said. Anthony smiled and let me just think about things for a while.

"OK," he said eventually, pulling out a notebook. "So your dad's a suspect. Because coming back from the dead appears to be a family trait. Any idea where he'd be? The boats he left you are still moored and empty. Where did he use to go?"

I cast my mind back. Everything I had learned about my dad seemed so far away. "He used to take my sister crabbing up by Salt Spring Island," I said slowly. "And he'd take her to tea at the Empress Hotel in Victoria."

"Anywhere else?"

I told him how my father had kayaked to 112 of the San Juan Islands. I told him about the Orcas Island house, and he nodded and said a buddy of his on Orcas was keeping an eye on it.

"You find anything interesting at the house itself?"

"Yeah, a bunch of navigation maps - mainly for around here: Desolation Sound, Rosario Strait, Mosquito Pass. My sister said he loved to sail."

He wrote that down. "Tell me step by step what you did the day of the attack."

"I already told Mark."

"I outrank Mark. And I'm older. And better looking."

I started to laugh, then realized he might be serious and tried to turn it into a cough. He smirked at my discomfort. "Just kidding. I know no one's better looking than Mark. But go through it again."

"Well, I met in the morning with Bethany Walton," I began, but he stopped me. He wanted to know absolutely everything I'd done that day - beginning with my dream that my father was still alive. Straining for details, I told him - my dream, Sarah, the photographs, the call from Dave West, Bethany, the mill, the box of documents, the call to Leah Batson, the visit to my mother's house, the brief chat with Karen at the B&B, the Colophon Cafe, the message from Leah about my dad's insurance, the alleged message from Dave. The rest, he already knew.

He wrote the events on separate pages of his notebook and grilled me on each one. Who said what? Where was I? Who else was there? Could anyone have overheard? Had anything struck me as strange then? Did anything strike me as strange now?

I was getting tired. There was a strange buzzing in my ears, and it was increasingly hard to talk with that collar around my neck. My chin kept hitting it. But I struggled to concentrate. The picture with my mother holding a baby at the Orcas house was strange. Sarah thought it was Beth, but if it wasn't - if it was me – then everything Marta had told me was a lie. It was strange that the mill had dropped its insurance on its executives right after it had collected $3 million under Sarah's husband's policy. It was strange that the insurance company had billed us for years for a non-existent rider. It was strange that no one seemed to know or care whether we had fire insurance on the mill. And now that I thought about it, it was strange that Emily wouldn't have recognized Dave's voice.

"That's it," I said.

"That's enough," Anthony replied, taking notes. "Mark and I will stay in Bellingham for a couple of days. We've still got stuff to do in Canada, so we'll drive up from here each day. Unless one of us is with you, you and Harmony stay in the hospital. You are not to go anywhere without a cop. If you do, I'm going to shoot you in the foot. You got that?"

"Got it," I promised. "Thanks, Detective Anthony. Thank you for everything."

He was saved from answering by the arrival of Mark and Harmony. He and Mark ducked into the hall.

Harmony put her arms around me and recounted the adventures of the evening. She and Mark had dropped by the vet's with Betsy's blanket and toys, only to find Sarah there feeding Betsy cubes of tenderloin steak. Betsy was getting better. She was wearing protective shoes – Betsy boots – because of the burns on her feet. The vet wanted her to stay in the hospital about a week while the skin healed. But other than that, she was her usual wonderful self. She ignored all the other dogs, she flirted with the vet, and when the Herald photographer stopped in to take her picture, she reared up in so imposing a pose that the guy ventured, "She can't get out of that cage, can she?" To which Mark had replied, "She went right through somebody's windshield. What do you think?"

"Did he take the picture?"

"He took one. And then she started barking, and he got the heck out of there. So there may be nothing more than an ominous orange blur on the front page of tomorrow's Herald."

Harmony calmly helped the nurse get me ready for bed. She held me up while I brushed my teeth, she washed my face, she tactfully busied herself on the other side of the room while the nurse assisted me with a few bodily functions that do not bear enumeration. And then she started unbuttoning her shirt.

My sudden and not in the least unwelcome surge in blood pressure came to an abrupt halt when I saw the blue flannel underneath. She must have put her clothes over her pajamas when she took her shower at my father's house. Then - even more disappointingly – she headed over to the other bed.

"Don't sleep over there, Harmony," I said. "There's plenty of room here."

She shook her head. "You're hurt."

"I'm not that hurt. Come on."

That, of course, was the problem. I was insufficiently hurt. As weak as I was, I was not incapacitated enough for her to feel safe slipping between the covers with me - especially while I was wearing nothing but an immodest hospital gown. I offered her a compromise: "Bring the blanket over here and stay with me."

She hesitated, flicking her eyes almost imperceptibly across my cast, collar, and tubes. "OK," she said. She very carefully laid her head against my good shoulder and her arm across my chest. "Am I hurting you?"

"No." She felt great, but I was afraid to tell her that. "You're not hurting me. Good night, sweetheart."

She kissed me very softly. "Sleep well," she said. And that's how we spent our first night together as an engaged couple.

I woke the next morning to the sounds of the hospital stirring. Soon somebody nice would be bringing us something appalling for breakfast. Because of the collar, I couldn't see Harmony, but I could hear her breathing, and I could feel her. She was deliciously warm.

I stretched as much as I dared. The skin under my cast had started to itch. I longed to scratch it. Something else was itching at me as well. I was suddenly uncomfortably aware that I had forgotten my earlier concern about Triad International. I had fallen asleep listening to Harmony search for their phone number. The name had struck me immediately, but I couldn't place it. I couldn't remember where I had heard it before.

It took almost an hour, lying there in the dark, listening to Harmony breathe, before the recollection jostled into my mind. It was the day of my unsuccessful marriage proposal, when I had run into Leah Batson on my way to the King County Courthouse. We had discussed my dad's policy with American Fidelity, she had headed into the Arctic Building, and I had been about to go on my way when the name on window had caught my eye: Triad International. She was going to visit her husband, she had told me. He was an investment banker in Vancouver, and twice a month, they met in Seattle and pretended they didn't live a thousand miles apart. The firm had just opened a new branch in Seattle, and she was hoping he would get transferred there.

My mind flashed back to the all-nighter Harmony and I had pulled when we had discovered that Mike Saunders and Clark Swanson had been plotting to steal my dad's land for a new waterfront hotel. The name had meant nothing to me then, but I remembered reading the investment prospectus for the hotel chain, and I was sure that Triad International had been providing financing for the new hotel before Harmony and I blew the lid off the coverup. I knew Leah's husband had been an investment banker, but until that day in Seattle, I hadn't known for which firm. I hadn't known he worked for Triad International.

I felt a familiar clutch of discomfort. It all seemed a little too coincidental that Leah's husband's firm had been backing the hotel, while Leah's insurance company had been withholding the insurance payment that would have saved the property from the auction block. The whole Northwest's pretty much one big small town, but that small? Did the whole region have a conflict of interest?

I tried to force the discomfort away. I liked Leah. She had given me a break, and I didn't want to jump to conclusions about her. But the unease kept niggling back. Leah had been in Bellingham the night of the first fire. I had had dinner with her myself before I left to head back to Seattle. I had run into her in Seattle a few days after Clark Swanson allegedly killed himself. I thought back to the meeting; when she first saw me, I thought I had spotted apprehension, maybe even fear, on her face. And I had talked to her the day of the last fire, that very afternoon. She would have had plenty of time to fly up from LA if she had heard something she didn't like during our conversation. Or, I reflected, her husband could have flown or driven down from Vancouver. That made a lot of sense. It definitely had not been Leah reflected in the boiler, but I didn't know what her husband looked like. Maybe he looked like my dad.

What had I said to her? I thought back. I couldn't remember saying anything that suggested I suspected her, anything related to Triad or the hotel Mike and Clark had been planning to build on my father's property. I had told her about the strange mistake on the bills from fifteen years ago, but Leah was too young to have been involved in that. I hmmmed over all of it in the dark.

Then, with a sudden lurch of my stomach, I knew what it was. I knew what might have set her off. It was the argument we had had over my dad's policy. I had been so insistent that it couldn't have been suicide. I had been so insistent that he hadn't been caught in the fire trying to destroy documents.

If my dad died in that fire, it had been murder. And if Leah - or her husband - had killed him, if they had staged that death to look like suicide or an accident, the last thing they'd want was someone like me sniffing around saying it wasn't. I remembered Sarah's note on the fridge. Leah had called within hours to say that American Fidelity would pay on my dad's life insurance policy. No insurance company makes decisions that fast. I wondered: Was the payout to keep my sisters from pressing the issue? Had she decided to silence me even more permanently?

Half of me couldn't believe I was thinking these things about someone I admired and respected, someone I truly liked as a friend. The other half was starting to wind up with rage and suspicion. It was one minute after 8. Being careful not to wake Harmony, I reached over her to the phone and dialed American Fidelity's main number. The receptionist transferred me to Leah Batson's secretary. I hung up three minutes later and just stared at the ceiling. I almost wished I didn't know what she had told me.

Unexpectedly, Leah Batson had decided to take a week off. She was supposedly camping somewhere up in Canada, and no one was able to reach her. She had left early on Friday, and no one had heard from her since.

Friday, I thought.

The day of the fire.

CHAPTER 30

"So what's her motive?"

The two large cops crammed into my hospital room had listened silently and gravely while I outlined my sudden suspicions of Leah Batson. Now they were politely trying to tell me I was nuts.

"Money, probably," I said. "The hotel deal was worth hundreds of millions of dollars. The investment bank would have gotten a big whack of that."

"The bank would," Anthony objected, "but not Leah's husband himself."

Harmony shook her head. "Actually, he might have. Investment banks don't bill like lawyers. Business lawyers bill by the hour, for services rendered. Investment banks charge part of the deal. If Leah's husband was the primary partner on the deal, he would have brought home a huge bonus."

"Hundreds of thousands?"

"Easily."

"Millions?"

Harmony shook her head. "Possibly, but unlikely."

"Two well-paid, white-collar professionals," Anthony said. "Three murders, two arsons, one attempted murder. That's a lot to risk for a payout that might be less than their combined annual salaries."

"Unless one of them popped Jack's dad during an argument, and all of the other murders were to cover up what they'd done," Mark pointed out. "If they're desperate - and what happened to Jack does look desperate - then they might be killing out of sheer panic."

Anthony shrugged. "Maybe. At any rate, we'll look into it." Anthony scribbled himself a note. "We'll find out Leah's husband's name. Mark, try to get a lead on where they're camping - if they're camping. How do we find out whether Leah's husband is the primary partner on the land deal?"

Harmony held up her cellphone. "I call and ask." Mark and Anthony immediately objected.

"It will be a lot more suspicious if you call than if I call," she pointed out. "And since you've got both of us on ice for the duration, we'll be safe even if it does make them nervous."

After much grumbling, the policemen assented. Harmony made the call, then snapped her phone closed with a thoughtful expression.

"Well?" Mark asked.

"No one named Batson's working on the account, but both the primary partner and the vice president in charge of the proposal are on vacation. Rob Wickers is the primary partner; Maury Rao is the vice president. They said Maury's reachable at home if it's an emergency, but that Rob won't be available until Monday. He left last Friday - and he's camping."

Too close to be a coincidence. That was also Leah's schedule, Leah's story. Rob Wickers' name went down in bold letters on Anthony's list of suspects. We were moving on to the topic of the phantom insurance rider when Anthony's phone rang.

"It's Lee," he said, snapping it open. Anthony was the only one of us still on speaking terms with Sergeant Lee. I braced myself for my next arrest. If anyone could blame me for being bludgeoned and set on fire, it would be the energetic and creative Sergeant Cecil Lee.

Or maybe not.

"You're positive? It's not him?" Anthony was saying into the phone. That sounded promising. "No relation whatsoever?"

But it turned out that for the first time, Lee wasn't focusing on me.

"The blood in the parking lot, Jack – the person Betsy mauled. It's not your dad," Anthony said. "No relation to you or your sisters."

I didn't trust myself to look at Mark or Harmony. Right then, I didn't trust myself to do anything.

"I'm sorry, Jack," Mark said. "I guess."

It had been hard to know what to hope for in the days since the fire. Which was worse: learning that your dad was alive and wanted you dead, or having to accept, after everything, that he was really, completely, irrevocably gone?

Harmony bent her head close to mine. "Jack, would you like to be alone?"

"No. No. Please don't go. It's just that -" I grasped at the last straw - "It's just that Sarah was talking to him. I heard her. I heard her talking to him the night I was shot."

"You were delirious," Mark said.

"You had a fever of a hundred and three," Harmony pointed out.

"I heard her. I know I heard her. I heard her talking to him, and he was alive."

Mark and Harmony exchanged helpless glances. "Have you asked her about it since then?" Harmony asked.

I shook my head.

"Why not?"

"Because no matter what the answer is, I lose one of them. If Sarah was talking to him, then she's been lying to me all this time, and she must have been in on some kind of plot to get rid of me. And if she wasn't -" I paused. "If she wasn't, then it means he's really dead. It means there isn't any reason to hope."

"Jack, it's your call," Anthony said. "But I think you've got to talk to Sarah about this. You've got to get to the bottom of it once and for all."

His phone rang again. "Look, kid, Mark and I have to go. Just think about it."

As if I could think about anything else. The rest of the morning, while Harmony and I talked about inoffensive topics and pretended to watch TV, I kept rehearsing potential conversations with Sarah. What if she denied it but I didn't believe her? What if she admitted it and I couldn't forgive her? What if she laughed at me? What if she cried? I swung between certainty that I was going to broach the subject with Sarah and equal certainty that I wasn't. When she actually walked in that afternoon, I still hadn't made up my mind.

"You're awake!" Sarah gave me a beaming smile and bent and kissed my cheek. Emily was right behind her with a huge bouquet of turkey-shaped balloons.

"Every time we stopped by yesterday, you were sleeping," Emily said, kissing my other cheek and giving Harmony a hug. "Do you like the balloons?"

"I love the balloons."

"We're postponing our Thanksgiving for a couple of days, until you're out of the hospital," she said. "So pay no attention to the slop they'll feed you here tomorrow. As soon as you're released, we'll have a real, old-fashioned Thanksgiving dinner with all the trimmings - which Harmony will cook."

"I will?" Harmony asked.

"It would be a humanitarian gesture." Emily plumped herself down on the bed. "None of us can cook worth a damn."

I turned to Sarah. "I hear you've been cooking for Betsy, though. That's so nice of you."

"Actually, we've been going to restaurants and ordering steak dinners to go every night," Sarah said, reddening. "We figured you'd be pretty mad if we accidentally poisoned her after all she's been through. Besides, she deserves the absolute best. Mark said if it wasn't for her, you would have died in that terrible fire."

"I would have. She saved my life."

"Then tonight, she's going to get a double order of carpaccio from *il fiasco*," Emily announced. "That's the best place in town. You ever been there?"

"Once," I said, reflecting on my fateful dinner with Leah Batson, Jerry Franks, and Carl Moore. And once was enough, I added to myself. If I hadn't stopped for dinner with my clients, if Virginia's classmate Ida hadn't recognized me, if she hadn't told the police, none of this would have happened. American Fidelity would have filed for summary judgment and won, the fire would have pushed the mill into bankruptcy, my dad's death would have been dismissed as suicide or accident, and the hotel chain probably would already have knocked down the hundred-year-old mill and gouged a huge foundation hole for its waterfront resort. Rob Wickers would have gotten his bonus, Clark and Mike would still be alive. I would never have met my sisters. I would never have known that my dad was dead.

If he was.

Emily was still talking about *il fiasco*, saying maybe we could go there for a somewhat delayed Thanksgiving dinner. She broke off in mid-sentence. "Jack, are you OK? Are we wearing you out?"

"I'm OK, Emily." I took a deep breath. "But do you think you could give me and Sarah a moment alone? There's something I've got to ask her in private."

Both Emily and Sarah looked surprised, but Emily rose without a fuss. At the door, she stopped and looked back at me. "I really am sorry about leaving you that note, Jack. It didn't even occur to me that it might not be Dave West on the phone. I've never spent much time with the people who work at the mill. I guess I just suck at being a Socialist."

"Yes," I said. "You suck." Then I winked at her to show her I was teasing, and she stuck her tongue out at me, hmphed, and left. Harmony got up to follow her. She squeezed my hand for luck as she slipped off the bed.

Sarah seemed simultaneously curious and alarmed. "What is it, Jack? What's up?"

I looked her right in the eye.

"Sarah, is our father still alive?"

"What?"

"I heard - I thought I heard - you talking to him while I was in the hospital. In the hospital the last time, I mean."

Her look of complete confusion stabbed my heart. "I was way under the drugs," I babbled. "But I could hear you talking to a man about telling me something about Beth. And at the very end, I heard you say, 'Well, OK, Dad.'"

Realization washed over her face. For just a moment, my heart leapt - then crashed when realization was followed by pity.

"Oh, Jack, oh, you poor thing." She took my hand and held it tight. "Jack, I did say that, but I was talking to my father-in-law. I was asking him if I should tell you about some of the things Beth had done - how she had the knife the night you came to visit, how she smashes things, how she's set some fires. Sheriff Mac - Sheriff Mac Duncan - is Scott's father. I call him Dad. But I always call my father - our father - Daddy. Oh, I'm so sorry. You must have been so confused. You must be so upset."

That was it. That was the last nail in my dad's coffin, the last shred of hope that he was still alive. I lay still and let the loss wash over me. So long as there had been a possibility that Sarah had been talking to him, I had been able to keep the worst of the grief at bay. Now there was no stopping it, no way to block the dark, grasping tide that threatened to pull me under. I felt like I was back in the deep water shunt. Only this time, there was no heroic Betsy to rescue me, no one to hold my head above the current of the awful water, to tug me back to solid ground. I squeezed my eyes shut and forced myself to keep breathing, forced myself to take in the air and push it out. It was a pointless, ridiculous, hopeless act. It seemed impossible that just a few moments before, I had done it without thinking.

Sarah offered me water, asked me if I was all right. I couldn't muster a voice to respond. She whispered: "I know, Jack. I know. I know what it's like."

Sarah had to leave to pick up Jennifer. Harmony came back and sat with me - just sat with me. I began to explain what had happened, but she had overheard through the door.

I kept replaying in my head the conversation I'd had with Sheriff Mac Duncan the morning after Virginia Carlson was attacked. I kept reliving the moment when he had walked into my dad's living room: when he sat on my dad's coffee table, positioned himself under his picture, and asked - in as gentle a voice as could come from a great big barrel-chested guy - whether I'd ever thought about hurting my dad. I replayed the first time I'd seen Mac Duncan - the sudden movement in a crowd of cops, the dizzying, unforgettable second when I glimpsed him from the corner of my eye and thought he was my father.

Harmony said what I was thinking:

"Sheriff Mac looks a lot like your dad."

CHAPTER 31

"For Pete's sake, I'm a cop."

"I'm a cop too," Mark said. "It didn't keep your boys from accusing me of killing Clark Swanson."

Sheriff Mac Duncan puffed in exasperation. He had stopped by at Sarah's insistence, and he was clearly regretting it.

"You gotta admit, it looks suspicious," Mark said. "We've been sharing information with you since day one of this case. But somehow you just neglected to mention that you were Scott Duncan's father. Somehow you just neglected to mention that you were Sarah's father-in-law."

"I didn't think I needed to draw such smart big city cops a family tree."

"But you didn't even tell us your real name," Anthony reminded him. "As far as we knew, your last name was Mac."

"Everyone calls me Sheriff Mac."

"Still looks like you were hiding something," Mark insisted.

"Bullshit," Mac Duncan said.

"Well, if it's bullshit, you've got nothing to worry about." Anthony was growing impatient with Mac Duncan's evasion and indignation. "Where were you the night Jack was attacked?"

"How should I know? Probably home watching television."

"What was on?"

"I don't remember. Some ballgame."

"Was anyone with you?"

"My wife's dead, my son's dead, and you ask if there was anyone with me?"

"Was anyone with you?" Anthony repeated in exactly the same tone as before.

Sheriff Mac glared at him. "No, there wasn't anyone with me," he snapped. "Now are you done with your little game of shifting suspicion, Jack? Anyone else you'd like to accuse while we're at it?"

Anthony leaned forward. I sensed a sudden shift in the room. "You know, you're a damn good cop, Mac."

"Why, thank you, Anthony. I am so grateful you think that. I am so relieved that I can sleep at nights knowing that the great Detective Anthony C. Anthony thinks I'm a good cop."

"Which is why I can't understand how you managed to fuck up this case so bad."

"What? Fuck you, Anthony."

"Geez, it's like a training video. I mean, everything that could have gone wrong has gone wrong. Three people have been killed on your watch. And heavy hitters, too." Anthony counted off the dead on his fingers. "One port commissioner, one congressional candidate, one rich old businessman. Four buildings have burned to the ground, a little old lady got thrown down the stairs, and someone almost simultaneously drowned Jack and fried him to a crisp – which, I admit, is pretty impressive. And you still don't have a clue who did any of it."

"I know exactly who did it." Mac Duncan looked at me with such loathing that I felt I must be guilty of something.

"See, there you go again," Anthony continued. "You've been so wrapped up with Jack that you haven't given yourself a chance to figure out what actually happened here. And when I see a cop - a good cop - so fixated on one theory that he can't even see what an ass he's making of himself, I figure there are only three possible explanations." He paused for dramatic effect. Mac bit.

"Which are?"

Anthony again ticked them off on his fingers. "Incapacitation, corruption, or emotion. I really don't want to believe the first two. I don't think you've been hitting the bottle. I don't think you shed all this blood yourself."

Mac made a disgusted noise, the kind of noise that conveys in shorthand any number of expletives.

"So I'm figuring there's something really eating at you, Mac. Something that's hurting you so bad you can't see straight."

Mac Duncan blustered and hmphed. "Anthony, they'll be giving you a daytime talk show any minute now," he sneered - but not before I saw the anguish in his face. His jaw loosened; his eyes fuzzed; and deep, sad lines creased his cheeks and forehead. He looked as blasted and hopeless as I felt.

The flash of vulnerability had not escaped Anthony and Mark. Anthony's voice was quiet. "So what happened, Mac? You blame Jack Senior for your boy's death? You two have an argument that got out of hand?"

Something snapped in Sheriff Mac. He flushed dark red. Even his scalp shone an angry crimson under his sparse white hair. As the color drained from his face, he turned on me. There was such hatred in his eyes that Mark and Anthony put their hands on their guns.

"It's not Jack Senior who killed my boy. I know who killed Scott, and he's right there." He stabbed his thumb at me. His hand was shaking.

I was mystified. At no time had Sergeant Lee or Sheriff Mac included Sarah's husband's death in the list of my alleged misdeeds. But if they suspected Scott had been murdered - and suspected me of doing it - that explained why they had been so dead against me from the beginning. And it explained why Sheriff Mac might have lured me to the deserted mill, hit me over the back of the head, and set the place on fire.

"What do you mean, Mac?" Anthony's voice betrayed no hint of triumph or excitement. "I thought Scott was killed in an accident."

"It looked like an accident. Except no one could explain why someone who was just promoted to COO would have been messing around in the warehouse after midnight. No one could explain how the paper roll came unhitched from the frame. No one could explain exactly how he died. His neck was broken, but the roll was only on his legs." His voice cracked. He turned his face away. "I was the first officer on the scene the next morning. I went in there and found my boy."

Anthony reached over and patted him on the back. Mac shifted away as if it hurt. "Sarah was hysterical, the baby was on the way, and for her sake more than anything I was willing to believe it was an accident. I wanted to believe it was an accident. But then I met that little bastard, and I knew what he'd done."

He suddenly lunged toward me. Harmony threw herself across my chest, Mark stepped in front of the bed, and Anthony grabbed Mac from the side. He tried to shake him off.

"You son of a bitch," he shouted at me. "I knew Scott was planning on meeting with the insurance company's lawyer, but I didn't put it all together until I saw you at your father's funeral. I didn't put it all together until I realized that that lawyer was you."

He made a motion as if to reach for his gun, but Anthony and Mark were too quick for him. They pinned his arms behind his back. They half pulled, half pushed him out the door. "Come on, Mac. Outside."

I could hear Mac Duncan shouting outside the door. My father and Scott had been so close, he said. He was going to leave Scott and Sarah the mill. Scott loved the mill so much and worked so hard. He had been starting to unravel the environmental shit and working with the DOE and insurance company when he died. Mac insisted that I killed Scott so my father wouldn't leave the business to him. And then, he said, I killed my father - and tried to kill Virginia - so I could come into my full inheritance.

I shuddered. Mac's voice was high and tight. He seemed incapable of stopping. He kept repeating, "Scott was going to meet with the insurance company's lawyer the week he died. And *that's* the insurance company's lawyer" - I imagined him pointing back at me - "and *that's* the prick who killed him."

To my horror, I heard Sarah's voice out in the hallway. "Dad, what is it? What's the matter?"

"Get out of here! I keep telling you to stay away from him, but you won't listen! Just go home. Don't let him near Jennifer or the other girls."

Sarah protested, but Anthony intervened.

"Sarah, I think right now it would be best if you went home. We'll call you and explain. Come on, Mac."

With that, all the voices began to fade. It sounded like Anthony was pulling Mac down the hall. Finally, it was quiet outside. Inside, though, my room still rang with the pitch of Mac's anguish and accusations. I felt as though he'd tossed around the furniture, kicked over my antibiotic drip, pulled out all my tubes. I felt slashed and scalded with his hatred.

Mark slipped back into the room. He put the chairs back where they were, repositioned my bedside table. At least physically, order was restored. He took a deep breath. "Well, that's a hell of a motive."

I just nodded.

"You think it was him? The guy you saw in the mill?"

I considered. I had been scrutinizing Mac Duncan as closely as I dared. He was tall, solid, square-faced, white-haired. My impression had been of someone with a round face and silver hair. "It could have been. I don't know. I only saw him for a second, and his face was distorted by the curve of the boiler." I swallowed. "It sure sounds like he *wants* to kill me."

"Yeah, I picked up on that, too. What do you think, Harmony?"

She didn't answer right away. At length she said, "He's certainly angry, and he certainly seems to think you killed his son. But if he's the person who attacked you, I don't see why he waited this long to try. He's had plenty of opportunities before."

"He could have just snapped," Mark said.

"Y-e-s." Harmony did not seem convinced. "But there would have preparation for the attack on Jack: making the phone call, getting all the gasoline for the fire. It seems more calculated than passionate. And if it was calculated, then it seems strange that Mac wouldn't have arranged an alibi. At the very least, he would have been able to tell you what he watched on TV."

"Real life isn't always that logical, Harmony."

"I suppose. But even if Mac is the prime suspect for the attack on Jack, it doesn't sound like he had any motive for killing Jack's dad or Mike and Clark."

"Yeah, there we're still dealing with Leah Batson. And along those lines, what Mac said about Scott meeting with the insurance company's lawyer was very interesting. Jack, were there any other lawyers representing American Fidelity?"

"Well, Dan Bradford is the Piper Whatcom partner on the case. And Leah's boss was on a couple of the first conference calls. But other than that, it was pretty much just Leah and me."

"Would Leah have had any reason to meet with Scott one-on-one?"

"Maybe. The mill sued American Fidelity a year ago September. American Fidelity hired us in October. So she might have come up here for one last shot at avoiding litigation." I paused. "But she never mentioned it."

Mark was already on the phone, talking to some cops in Seattle who were helping with legwork. "Any leads?" he asked each one.

He snapped the phone closed and handed it back to Harmony with a sigh. "We're not turning up much," he said. "It is the day before Thanksgiving, after all. All the government offices seem to have closed at noon, so we haven't even been able to find her marriage license. We don't even know whether Rob Wickers is her husband."

Harmony smiled at him and started punching in some numbers. "It's not Thanksgiving in Japan. Maybe we can approach this another way."

For the next hour, Harmony called her finance contacts in Asia about the reputation of Triad International in general, partner Rob Wickers in particular. She listened a long time, then said goodbye with many thanks and the humblest of apologies. "Well, that's interesting," she said.

Mark and I could barely contain ourselves. "What's interesting?"

"The consensus is that Rob Wickers is brilliant, ruthless, dedicated - and gay."

"Come again?"

"When I asked if they had ever met Rob's wife, they said, 'Well, you know, Harmony, he's *dôseiai*.'"

"He might be bi," I said.

"Maybe. But a couple of them said they'd met his partner, Todd, who also works at Triad. Todd does loan workouts."

Mark groaned and stretched. "This case," he protested. "Every time we get a lead, it doubles back on itself."

"It does seem to keep circling back to American Fidelity, though." Harmony made a spiral with her finger. "Jack, who else at the insurance company was involved with the SPP litigation? Business people, anybody. Scott might have told his dad that he was meeting with a *representative* of the insurance company, not someone who was legally *representing* the insurance company. And actually, that would make more sense. By the time a company's in-house counsel gets involved, it's usually pretty much 'have your lawyer talk to my lawyer.'"

"Jerry Franks and Carl Moore were my primary contacts. Jerry's the claims manager. Carl Moore's the senior VP of the division."

"What do you know about them?"

I reflected. All I knew about Jerry Franks was that he and his wife had conceived their twin daughters during the 1962 World's Fair. All I knew about Carl Moore was that he had moved from Seattle to LA sometime in the 1980s. I said as much.

"Were either of them ever agents?" Harmony asked.

"I don't know. Why?"

"That phantom insurance rider," she mused. "It still bothers me."

The three of us sat quietly for a few minutes, thinking. I was trying to concentrate on the matter at hand, but it had been a long, difficult day. The pain and the weariness threatened to overwhelm me, and my mind kept wandering. For some reason, all I could think of was the story Mark had told me about the bet-skimming bookmaker in Bellingham. Eventually, I just gave up.

"I'm sorry, but I need to take a nap. Every time I try to work through this, I end up thinking about that guy who got whacked for taking the best bets from that gang up in Canada. I'm not at my sharpest right now."

"What guy who got whacked?" Harmony asked.

Mark explained the story - how the Bellingham bartender he and Anthony had found dead by the Kingdome had been operating his own little bookmaking business on the side, pocketing the most lucrative bets. He broke off as he saw her startled look.

"Oh," was all she said. And then, "Oh. Oh." And then a long, drawn-out "Ohhhh."

Mark seemed simultaneously amused and concerned. "Harmony, it doesn't have anything to do with this case. Honest. Don't even go there. Anthony and I checked it out, and there's no link between that Canadian gang and the mill."

"It's not that." Harmony drew her knees up to her chin. Her eyes were so dark blue they looked almost black in the harsh hospital lights. "It's not that they're linked. It's that they're parallel."

She glanced at our puzzled faces and tried again. "The insurance business is basically a big legal gambling operation. They're betting that something won't happen to you - that your house won't burn down or that you won't die - until they've had a chance to recoup in premiums all the money that they'll pay out. And if someone was going to try to skim that business, like that bookmaker did up in Canada -" She stopped and thought for a moment. "If someone was going to try to skim those bets, he'd write all the most lucrative policies himself. He'd sell riders of coverage that didn't exist. He'd pocket the extra money."

Mark suddenly stiffened. "The County popped a guy for doing that a couple of years ago. He was an insurance agent, and he sold all these homeowners' policies to a bunch of folks over on Bainbridge Island. But he just kept all the premiums. He never told the insurance company about it, so they never issued any coverage. For a while, he just paid whatever claims he got out of the premium money he had collected - like he was his own little insurance company. When we had the floods a couple of years ago, and people's houses started sliding down the hill, he couldn't swing it anymore. He tried to cover it up with rubber checks, but eventually they nabbed him."

"Maybe in this case, he tried to cover it up with murder," I said. "If that phantom rider was an environmental rider, there'd be no way he could cover the cleanup liability. He'd have a damn good reason for trying to make sure the mill never tried to collect on that additional coverage. He'd have a damn good reason for killing Scott and my dad, and setting the mill on fire. The first fire wiped out all the mill's insurance policies. American Fidelity is having a hard time laying their hands on our property casualty policy – even on microfiche. So that could mean that it just doesn't exist. And the second fire took all the bills that had the extra amount for the rider. So he may have sold us a fake property casualty policy and a fake environmental rider on a CGL."

"You're sure you told Leah Batson about the rider?"

"I'm sure. She said she'd have someone look into it. So even if she's not personally involved, she may have tipped off someone else who was."

"Tell us again what you remember about those bills."

I screwed up my eyes and described them as best as I could. I was telling them about the return address on Commercial Street when Harmony interrupted. "What building? What was the address?"

"I don't remember. When I'm up and around, I think I could find the building again, but I don't remember the address. I was looking for signs that said American Fidelity; I wasn't really paying attention to anything else."

Harmony glanced at her watch. It was almost 5:30. "American Fidelity will be closed for the day, but the library's still open. Mark, will you take me over there? I want to find old phone books, old newspapers - anything with ads. I want to look at anything that might say who sold American Fidelity insurance fifteen years ago in Bellingham."

Mark called Anthony to take over as my babysitter. While we waited for Anthony, Harmony packed up her cellphone and laptop and searched unsuccessfully for her coat. It was apparently at my dad's house.

"Take my jacket, Harmony. At least put it around you until you get to the library. It's cold out there."

She hesitated, then slipped on my brown leather jacket. More accurately, she disappeared within my leather jacket. As she was pushing up the sleeves and trying to tuck the folds of leather around herself, she thrust her hand into a pocket - and pulled out the only remaining bill from American Fidelity. I had completely forgotten that I had taken one of the bills with me so I could find the building on Commercial Street. I had forgotten that it would have survived the fire.

Harmony looked at the bill for what seemed like a long time. She handed it to Mark.

"This is the building across from Mike Saunders' campaign headquarters," he said, and I could hear the sudden excitement in his voice.

"Judging from the angle and everything, this is where the guy was standing when he shot you and killed Mike. This is where he was standing when he tried to kill you - the first time."

CHAPTER 32

It was like sharing a kennel with greyhounds - when the races had been rained out. They had the scent. They knew it. They wanted to be on the chase. They wanted to be digging into the mystery of who sold my father that phantom insurance rider. They wanted to find the owner of the Commercial Street building; they wanted to identify anyone who would have had access to the second floor. But the rest of the country was busy celebrating Thanksgiving, and we couldn't get anyone to talk to us.

American Fidelity was closed for the holiday. All the government offices were shut up and silent until the next Monday. The local library tossed out Mark and Harmony before they had a chance to review the old microfilms of the Bellingham Herald. Thwarted, Harmony hunched over her laptop, eventually eliciting the only leads we seemed likely to get until everyone else finally stopped being thankful and let us get back to the business of murder.

According to American Fidelity's web page, Carl Moore, Jerry Franks, and Leah Batson had all once been agents for the company. Anthony's contacts at the LAPD cruised by their California homes, only to report that no one was there. That, by itself, didn't mean anything. It was, after all, Thanksgiving Day. All across the country, people were heading home to their families - hugging their grandparents, taking pictures of their nieces and nephews, sitting down to gleaming tables.

Except for those of us spending the holiday at St. Joseph's Hospital. On this Thanksgiving Day, we crammed into my tiny room and picked at our feast: voodoo turkey, pasty gravy, and instant mash. The turkey looked particularly re-engineered and embarrassed in the clinical overhead lights. Still, Mark, Anthony, and I ate every bite. If nothing else, growing up as a ward of the state teaches you there is no such thing as bad food.

We were in the initial stages of investigating our desserts - brick-like orange confections touted as "Plymouth Surprise" - when my phone rang. The voice on the other end was so familiar that at first I assumed it was one of my sisters. But it wasn't.

"Jack! Oh, my goodness, Jack! It is true. I just didn't believe it when I saw the paper."

Leah Batson. The very person we were trying to find. The very person who had suddenly decided to go camping with her husband on the very day someone tried to burn me to death in my father's mill. The very person who had been an agent for American Fidelity, who was married to an unnamed investment banker, who might have profited from the mill's going out of business.

"Hey, Leah." Every head in the room swiveled in my direction. Anthony shot outside. I knew he would try to get the Bellingham police to trace the call. Mark dropped his Plymouth Surprise. Harmony graciously handed him hers.

Leah babbled on. "It was such a shock to pick up the paper and see the pictures of the mill on the front page. Roy and I -"

I put my hand over the receiver and mouthed *her husband's name is Roy.*

"- have been camping the last couple of days. We hadn't seen the news. My gosh, Jack, are you all right?"

"I'm fine, Leah."

"The paper says you nearly drowned. How did you nearly drown in the middle of a fire?"

"It takes real talent."

"Seriously, are you OK? The nurse wouldn't tell me how you were doing."

"I'm OK. Just a little scorched."

"The paper said someone attacked you in the mill. Who was it? Have they caught him?"

My stomach twisted. She was trying to find out whether I had identified the man who tried to kill me. That meant she had to have been part of the plot. I longed to fling the phone away in revulsion, but Mark rotated his index finger in the universal *keep her talking* gesture. They were scrambling to trace the call. I steeled myself and tried to turn the conversation around.

"Leah, I can barely hear you. Where are you?"

"Oh, Roy and I are over on Salt Spring Island. We're spending the week at the Green Rose Farm. I'm on his cell. Here, let me go into the living room. Is that better?"

"A little better. But I thought you said you were camping."

"We *are* camping."

I was amused despite the context. "Leah, the Green Rose is a bed and breakfast. Staying at a bed and breakfast does not qualify as camping."

Her response dripped with offended dignity. "Jack, I was born in Manhattan. Whenever I don't have a bathroom to myself, it's considered camping."

I laughed out loud. Mark and Harmony were startled. Then I stopped laughing and swallowed hard. I liked - had liked - Leah so much. The thought that she must have tried to hurt me - tried to kill me - didn't just appall, infuriate, and rankle. It stabbed at me.

"Jack, you still there?"

Mark circled his finger again.

"Yeah. Sorry. So did your husband ever get transferred down to Seattle?"

"No. No, he's still up in Vancouver."

"What's he do again?"

"Oh, he's an investment banker. M&A."

Mergers and acquisitions. Not real estate development after all. "Can't he do that in LA?"

Her explosive laugh reverberated over the line. "Well, *I* think so." Her voice faded as she turned away from the receiver. "Roy, Jack agrees with me. You should move to Los Angeles."

In the background, I heard an amiable growl: "Jack, don't you be giving her ideas."

Leah chuckled. "Actually, it is better for him to be in Vancouver. Most of Roy's business is on the Pacific Rim, and Vancouver's still the place to be."

"Really? You know, my fiancée's company is headquartered in Tokyo. She's been doing a lot of M&A work lately. What's Roy's last name? Maybe they've run into each other."

"Yakahara," Leah said.

Yakahara, I mouthed to my rapt audience. My mind was spinning. Unless Roy was adopted or something, or unless I was mishearing his name, he was not the person who smacked me over the back of the head. True, I had caught only a glimpse of the man. But it had been a long enough glimpse to determine that whatever else, he was not Japanese.

Leah interrupted as I was trying to process that information. "You know, Jack, I'm glad I've got you on the line. There's something I've been wanting to ask you."

"Shoot," I said.

"We've got a couple of new Washington cases. Big breach of contract/bad faith lawsuits. Dan Bradford wants to staff them with Cory Corliss, and I'm not comfortable with that. Cory's OK, but well -" She seemed to be groping for a kind way of describing Cory. "He's a twit," she said, using the kindest possible word I could have come up with. "And Dan himself is a great guy to go out drinking with, and he's good in front of a jury, but these are subtle cases. I think we can win on summary judgment, but only if the deps are done carefully and our briefing is absolutely solid on the law. Dan and Cory can't pull that off. So the long and the short of it is that we're pulling our work from Piper Whatcom."

I almost whistled. Losing any client is a big deal. Losing a huge corporate client that gets sued all the time is exponentially worse. Piper Whatcom would be pulling the tassels off Dan's and Cory's loafers over this one.

More out of surprise than loyalty to the firm, I protested. "You don't have to do that, Leah. Piper Whatcom's a huge place. Even if you don't want to work with Dan and Cory anymore, there are plenty of other commercial litigators who can take on cases like that."

"But I want someone good and nice. I'm sick of dealing with outside counsel who make me feel I need to wash my hands."

That did narrow it down. I hmmmed for a while. "There are nice litigators at Piper Whatcom," I said uncertainly.

"Name one."

"Um -" I looked over at Harmony. She shrugged helplessly.

"See? You can't. You're gone, Harmony Piper is gone, and I'm not comfortable with any of the other litigators I've worked with over there. That Sydney Leath is a viper. The last time I had a case with her, I found out that she was lobbying my boss to get my job."

OK. I was licked. "Well, do you want me to recommend some other firms? I have some law school classmates over at Farber & Fairchild and Reinhardt Wall. They're good people, and Farber and Reinhardt are both good firms."

"They are good firms, but we've got conflicts with both of them. But anyway, I don't want any recommendations. I already know who I want to work with."

"Who?"

"You."

"But -"

"I know. I know you're Mr. Mill Person now. But especially now that the mill is, well, gone, you might have some time on your hands. We'd hire you at your Piper Whatcom hourly rate. We'd agree to give you all our Washington cases for at least a year. Then we'd get together and assess whether the arrangement's working for both of us. What do you think, Jack? How about I stop by Saturday on my way back from Salt Spring so we can talk it over? I'd really love to see you."

I couldn't believe it. She was trying to get another shot at me. She was trying to finish what she'd started, and she was playing on my ego to give her the opportunity. I put my hand over the receiver and mouthed *she wants to see me*. Mark gave me the thumbs up. "Tell her to come here," he whispered.

I did as I was told. "I'll still be in the hospital on Saturday, so you'll have to check in at the desk. They'll tell you where I am."

"Great. I'll see you then. I hope we can work something out, Jack. Everyone at American Fidelity likes you. Everyone's really excited at the thought of working with you again."

"Everyone?" I had met only a few key people at the company.

"Well, me and Jerry Franks. I talked it over with him, and he was thrilled at the idea. And Carl Moore likes you too, although I didn't get a chance to bring him into the loop."

"Why not?"

"Oh, he's been out of the office awhile. You know, it's the weirdest thing, Jack. Carl said he was taking a few days' vacation a week or so ago. He was supposed to be back last Monday, but I called in and talked to my secretary yesterday, and the whole office is wondering about him."

She paused. I could hear her drinking something in the background.

"No one's seen or heard from him for more than a week."

CHAPTER 33

They arrested Carl Moore in Idaho. His car had gone off the road near Lewiston, just over the Washington state line. Before someone spotted his bumper sticking up, he had slumped in a gully for almost a full day, racked with fever and infection from the dog bites that riddled his face, neck, and arm. One bite had gone right through his cheek.

By the time the police got to him, his hands and feet were almost black with frostbite and infection. He had lost so much blood that he couldn't move. He had just lain there in the wreckage and waited to die.

In the days between Leah's revelation and Carl Moore's arrest, the police had scrambled to flesh out the motives and opportunities of their sudden star suspect. Before the Lewiston motorist ever spotted Carl's bumper, before the paramedics started the first of the four units of blood they would slam into his veins just to stabilize him enough to transport him, Mark and Detective Anthony already knew the bare bones of what had happened.

They knew that Carl had lied to me that night at *il fiasco*. He wasn't from Seattle after all; he was born and raised in Bellingham, a few years ahead of my father in school. They knew that he had dropped out of college and started his career as a struggling American Fidelity agent, selling homeowners' insurance and automobile coverage to the residents of what was then a solidly middle-class, working-class town.

And they knew that somewhere along the line, Carl Moore had started skimming. He sold and issued enough insurance to keep American Fidelity happy; he pocketed the premiums on the rest. Whenever there was a claim on one of his non-existent policies, he covered it with the premiums he had invested. He had a particular fondness for diverting paid-up, single-premium policies, which meant he didn't have to bill on the phantom coverage. But as his scheme flourished and he got greedier, Carl started branching out. He sold false commercial liability policies; he sold phantom riders on existing policies.

He sold fake policies to my dad. First Carl sold my dad a fake property casualty policy. No wonder Jerry hadn't been able to find any trace of coverage – even on American Fidelity's venerable microfiche. Then he sold my dad an environmental rider on his general commercial liability policy, extending coverage for all but intentional pollution. The mill's representatives testified during deposition that they had been aware of chemicals escaping accidentally during processing, but there was no evidence that the mill had set about to intentionally pollute the bay. Under the apparent terms of the rider my father thought he purchased, there would have been coverage for at least a large portion of the state-ordered environmental cleanup of Bellingham Bay. No wonder my dad had sued American Fidelity. At the very least, the mill had a hell of a lot better argument for coverage with the rider than without it. With a rider like that in place, we would have been talking settlement, not summary judgment.

As the government offices reopened, as people came back from their holidays, bit by bit the story fell in place. Carl Moore owned the Commercial Street building across the street from Mike Saunders' campaign headquarters, where Mike was killed and I was shot. He had easy access to the second floor, the location indicated by the angles of the bullets. For years, Carl ran his American Fidelity insurance agency out of that building. All billings came directly from that office; all payments went directly to that address. Carl had kept two – at least two - sets of books: one for real policies, one for his phantom coverage. The Lewiston police found the records stuffed in the trunk of his car. Among Carl's non-existent customers were a great many of the little old ladies I had visited over the past few weeks.

That was what had triggered Carl's attack on me. Even though the Lewiston police Mirandized him, he babbled out a rambling confession on the way to the hospital. He had been hiding out in Bellingham, watching me. When he saw me calling on his customers - customer after customer - he didn't realize that I was trying to find out more about my mother. He thought I had stumbled on his deep-buried insurance fraud. And when Leah left him a voicemail telling him that I had called with questions about the billings for the mill's non-existent GCL rider and coverage under its non-existent casualty policy, that clinched it in his mind.

He was stunned that any evidence of the phony rider had survived the fire that killed my dad. He thought I had unraveled his plot, that I was going to expose him. He knew Dave West's name from the mill's lawsuit against the insurance company. He bought gasoline, lured me to the mill, hit me over the head, and set the place ablaze. He had to burn both warehouses and the plant because he couldn't be sure where I had put the incriminating billings.

I was not his first victim. He had also killed Sarah's husband, Scott Duncan. Scott had just been elevated to Chief Operating Officer when the Department of Ecology hit the mill with its share of the costs of the cleanup of Bellingham Bay.

Scott submitted the claim to American Fidelity for indemnity and defense. When American Fidelity, unsurprisingly, refused to pay on a rider it had never issued, Scott had taken the matter straight to the top. He called Carl Moore, American Fidelity's senior vice president of corporate claims, and asked whether they could resolve the matter short of litigation.

There was no way Carl could cover the cost of the environmental cleanup from his personal funds. He couldn't buy off this claim the way he had all the others. Terrified that a lawsuit would expose his years of embezzlement, Carl came to Bellingham and tried to bribe Scott to drop the matter. He hadn't realized that Scott had married into the Hart family. He hadn't realized that Scott was a former police officer. He definitely hadn't realized that Scott's father was the Whatcom County Sheriff. But he learned pretty quickly that Scott wasn't just uninterested in a bribe - that he was royally pissed.

Carl swore that Scott had jumped up and lunged at him. Carl swore that he thought Scott was trying to attack him. He swore that when he picked up a brass banker's lamp and swung - blindly, he said - he did so in self-defense.

The impact had snapped Scott's neck. Carl said he had dragged Scott's body into the darkened warehouse. He staged the accident with the paper roll and slipped away - but not before Mike Saunders spotted him leaving the warehouse.

And that's when the blackmail started. Carl told the police he had paid Mike Saunders $3 million to destroy any evidences of the fake rider and casualty policy and to keep quiet. It was American Fidelity's money; Carl just ordered his claims department to reinstate the coverage that the mill had let lapse before Scott's death. American Fidelity paid the mill, and Mike laundered the money through the books the mill bought from him and his publishing company. Mike used most of the money to fund his congressional campaign; the rest went to Clark Swanson to convince him that the Port should acquire the land and lease it to the developer and hotel chain in which Clark and Mike had a respective interest.

It was a great scheme. Mike and Clark made a tremendous show of vindicating their fiduciary obligations to the mill. They pressed the lawsuit against American Fidelity, even though they had destroyed the phony rider that was the only basis for the coverage. Far from benefiting the mill, the lawsuit only further sapped its reserves and edged it toward the bankruptcy that would let the Port acquire the land at fire-sale prices. Every day, the mill's land lost value as it hemorrhaged money for attorneys' fees and became less and less able to meet payroll. Through it all, Mike and Clark assured my father that the case was proceeding well. Mourning Scott's death and caring for a dying wife, a new grandchild, and a widowed daughter, he just believed them. He didn't have the time, the energy, or the inclination not to.

It wasn't until the mill was on the brink of bankruptcy - on the brink of losing its land at auction - that Dave West finally pleaded with my dad to get involved.

And when he did - when he called Clark and Mike, when he called his old agent Carl and asked them all why in hell there wasn't coverage under the environmental rider Carl had sold him – my dad walked into his own death. This time, all three of them had a scheme to keep hidden, a secret to protect. This time, none of them could afford for my father - for anyone - to uncover what they had done.

Clark called my dad and asked him to come to the mill. Mike arranged an alibi for Clark in case he was ever questioned. And the very night that he sat with me at *il fiasco*, the very night that he broke bread with me, praised me, asked about my family, Carl hit my father over the back of the head and set the fire in the mill's office building. They wanted it to look as though my father was caught in the blaze while he was trying to destroy documents that would have been damaging in the litigation. And it damn near did.

"Had you met Carl before that night at *il fiasco*?" Mark asked. We were home from the hospital. My sisters had ensconced me and Betsy on the leather couch in the living room. Whenever one of them walked by, Betsy opened her mouth and craned her neck, like a baby bird waiting to be fed.

"No. If he paid any attention to the pleadings at all, he would have seen just my full name: John Boyden Hart. We met for the first time during those three days of depositions. And he did look a little stunned when Leah introduced me. He told me later that he had been concerned about Dan's delegating work to a senior associate, so I just thought he was worried about whether I could pull the case together. But it must have been a nasty surprise for him. He asked me about my family during that dinner, so I guess he was trying to figure out whether I was related to the man he was planning to kill." I scratched Betsy under the chin, avoiding the thin black line of stitches on her lip. Her tail thumped against the pillows tucked around us. "Now that I think about it, Carl didn't eat much at dinner. I guess he was gearing up."

"Why didn't you recognize Carl when you saw him at the mill?" Sarah asked. She sat down on the other side of Betsy, tickling her ears.

I made a curving motion with my hands. "The boiler side was like a fun-house mirror. Carl's as tall as our dad, but pretty lean. The mirror made him look rounder. I really did think it was our dad."

"What's going to happen to him?" Emily perched herself on the arm of Mark's chair. Mark - who had only reluctantly decided that Emily was not, after all, a murderess - shifted as far as possible to the opposite side.

"If he pulls through, they'll extradite him and charge him before Christmas," Anthony said. "Now that Sheriff Mac's come to his senses, he can't wait to pull this case together. He'll stand trial in state court, although the feds have expressed some interest as well. There's a hell of a lot of mail and wire fraud that went on here. They might go RICO on him."

"Will he get the death penalty?"

"He'll try to plead it down. His attorney will try to exclude the confession. He'll say he wasn't in his right mind, didn't understand the Miranda warnings. But there are aggravating circumstances, and he may well be sentenced to death."

Emily was silent for a little while. Except for her choice of seating, she had been remarkably unflirtatious all morning. "I was part of a hunger strike at Walla Walla before the Dodd execution," she said. "I wrote this long article about how barbaric the death penalty is, and how no civilized society can justify it. But I hope they kill him. I hope he fries." She rubbed her eyes, caught her breath, and darted from the room. Sarah went after her.

I thought of all the blood Carl had shed. After he had killed Scott and my dad, murder became Carl's answer to everything. He shot Mike Saunders when Mike got scared and threatened to expose Carl to save himself. He shot Clark Swanson to keep him quiet - and to make it look as though Clark had murdered Mike. He told the Lewiston police that he wasn't aiming at me that night on Commercial Street, but I didn't believe him. Mike and I were both there illuminated in the plate glass window. By then he knew who I was, knew I was a threat. And it was an easy shot.

I didn't mourn Mike and Clark at all. They were thieves. They were liars. They were accomplices to murder. But they had left families out there reeling with the double loss. It's crushing to lose your father - your grandfather, your husband, whatever - to death. It's annihilating to lose him to the wrenching realization that he was not the person you thought you knew, the person you thought you loved. I had seen a clip on the news that made me sick: Mike Saunders' widow, pursued by a pack of photographers, swathed in black, old and shrunken, searching for escape with haunted, restless eyes. Six weeks ago, she had been the proud, chic, adoring wife of a congressional candidate. A month ago, she had been the grieving but dignified widow of a promising politician cut down in his prime. Now she was tabloid fodder, hunted by reporters everywhere she went, shunned by her society friends, terrified that I was going to sue Mike's estate to recoup the money he had stolen from the mill. I had tried to call and set her mind at ease, but her phone was disconnected.

Jennifer crawled over, pulled herself up, and hung onto my knee. She lifted one foot, then the other, then the first, in a sort of rapturous baby dance that her father would have loved, lived for, videotaped over and over. I picked her up and smiled into her beaming face. When she realized she had my full attention, she broke into chuckles - impossibly loud and deep for such a small body.

It was intolerable that Scott wouldn't be able to watch his little girl grow up - that he had never gotten a chance to hold her, even see her. It was intolerable that Sarah was a widow at thirty-six. It was intolerable that I never got to see my dad, to say goodbye to him, to let him explain himself to me, apologize to me. The last thing my dad knew about me - maybe the only thing my dad knew about me - was that I was defending the lawsuit he had brought against American Fidelity. The people I had deposed had told him about our strange resemblance - in name and appearance. He had walked into his mill for the last time, thinking his son was on the side of the people who were trying to cheat him.

"No more talk about murder or Carl Moore," Marianne declared, sweeping in from the kitchen. "Gary just pulled up with Tess and Nicky, and I don't want them scared. Besides, Thanksgiving dinner is served."

We seated ourselves uncertainly around the long, gleaming table. It was a big group - my sisters; Marianne's husband and little girls; me, Mark, and Harmony; Detective and Mrs. Anthony; Sheriff Mac Duncan. Sarah had asked him only with my permission. No one sat at the head of the table. Marianne settled her little girls on either side of her. "Fold your arms," she instructed them. Everyone - even Detective Anthony - immediately obeyed. She glanced around. "Sorry."

Since she was obviously the voice of authority, Marianne said the Thanksgiving grace. She thanked God for letting them have their father as long as they did. She thanked God for preserving their mother's life, and asked that if it were possible, she would wake from her coma. She thanked God for Harmony and Mark. She thanked God for me. That bit particularly stuck in my mind: "We thank Thee for sending us Jack when we needed him so much - and please, God, watch over him and keep him safe and out of trouble." Around the table, there were some almost insultingly heartfelt "amens."

Harmony had outdone herself on the Thanksgiving feast. We started with salmon - which my father had caught and smoked himself - and icy, briny raw oysters. Then we had wild mushroom soup, roast turkey, mashed potatoes, vats of gravy, assorted veggies, and three different kinds of stuffing. For dessert, there was pie - apple, pecan, and pumpkin - warm from the oven and topped with ice cream.

We were lounging around the table, flushed and groaning, when the telephone rang. No one moved. It had been the kind of dinner where it's just too much trouble to push yourself away from the table. Finally, Sarah stood with great effort and wobbled into the kitchen. We heard her say hello, and then we all heard her low, tremulous cry. Emily and I jumped up. *Not today, not today*, I thought. *Please, no more bad news for this poor little family today.*

But it wasn't bad news. At least, not for my sisters.

Emily and I met Sarah at the dining room door. Her eyes were wet, but her face was radiant.

"It's Mama," she said. "She's awake."

CHAPTER 34

One look at her, and I almost lost my nerve.

She was already half dead. One side of her face sagged. The corner of her mouth dragged down; her eye drooped. Blue-black bruises mottled her arms. I couldn't tell whether they were from the hospital IVs or her fall down the stairs. Probably both.

If Virginia Carlson hadn't come out of her coma claiming I was the monster who threw her down the stairs, I wouldn't have confronted her. She looked so weak, so beaten. I would have let her go to her grave with the secret of whatever happened between her and my mom. I wouldn't have had the heart to force a sad, sick old lady to defend herself against an accusation of murder.

But she had, and I did.

Not that anyone had believed her. Not even Sergeant Lee thought I was guilty anymore. Ever since we had identified the person who actually killed his son, Sheriff Mac had been completely on our side. He and Lee had explained gently but firmly to Virginia that I had a rock-solid alibi for the night she was attacked. And then they told her they had arrested the man who killed her husband and set the fire. They assured her that the suspect was a disgruntled business associate with no connection whatsoever to the family.

When she learned that I had an alibi, and that an outsider - not Beth, not Emily, not any of her daughters - had been responsible for Jack's death, Virginia changed her story. No, of course I hadn't been the person who threw her down the stairs, she said. She had had an argument with me earlier, certainly, but the man who attacked her had been, had been . . . . There she faltered. She couldn't give a description of the alleged attacker. She told Sheriff Mac that it was because she was confused, that everything from that night was fuzzy. He graciously accepted her excuses to her face, but to Mark and Anthony - now trusted fellow cops - he was blunt.

"She's covering up for Beth," he said, shaking his head sadly. "The bruises on her neck match the span of Beth's hands. I tried to explain to her that Beth wouldn't face any charges for the attack, but she wouldn't listen. She just said she was too tired to talk anymore." He sighed. "If she wasn't Jennifer's grandmother, I'd say she was a stubborn old bitch. But she is, so I won't."

Jennifer's grandmother or not, I had no trouble calling Virginia an old bitch. But I wanted to keep my powder dry. Until I had exhausted every possible avenue of finding out what happened to my mom, I was going to keep myself completely under control.

Probably.

I knew that Mark, Harmony, and Anthony were all outside in the hospital hallway - most likely with their ears pressed against the door. But all the same, I felt a stab of fear as I entered the room and saw her there. I couldn't tell whether it was fear of myself or for myself. If Marta had been telling even most of the truth, the tiny woman on the hospital bed had killed my mother and had tried to kill me. I didn't know what I was capable of doing. I wasn't going to know until after I had talked to her.

Her eyes were barely open - watery slits of blue against her wasted face. Was she asleep? No, her eyes were tracking me. She was watching me, biding her time.

I swung myself down in a chair beside the bed, putting a safe distance between us. After a moment, she pretended to stir. She blinked.

"Sarah said you wanted to see me."

She nodded. "My girls told me everything you had done for them. I wanted to thank you." Her speech was soft and slurred.

"You're welcome."

She swallowed. "I'm sorry I told Mac Duncan that you were the one who attacked me. I've been so confused. I wanted to make sure you wouldn't hold that against my girls."

"I won't."

"Because they're going to need you, Jack. They're still going to need you." Her voice was almost pleading.

It was an opening. "I'll do whatever I can for your daughters," I promised her. "I'll make sure Sarah and Emily have a place to live until they get back on their feet. I'll watch out for Jennifer and Beth. If Marianne decides to leave Gary, I'll help her out with the divorce. I know some good family law attorneys, so she won't have to worry about losing custody of Tess and Nicky -"

"Thank you," she interrupted.

"- But I want something in return."

Her sagging mouth turned petulant. "Jackie and I already divided our property, Jack. You're already getting half of everything we owned."

"I don't want money."

Petulance veered into suspicion. "What, then?"

"I want the truth. I want the truth about what happened between you and my mother."

I barely caught and couldn't read the flicker in her eyes. "Nothing happened between me and Marta."

"I said 'my mother.' I want to talk about Mary Boyden."

This time the flicker in her eyes was unmistakable. "The last time we talked, you said Mary Boyden went by Marta now."

"Last time we talked, you asked me all sorts of questions to see whether I knew that Marta wasn't my mother," I pointed out. "Back then, I didn't. Now I do. Now I know that my mother was Mary - and that she's dead."

"So what does that have to do with me or the girls?"

"You tell me."

She sighed in exasperation and fumbled for the nurse call button. "Jack, I am too old and too sick and too tired to play games with you. Thank you for looking after my girls."

I leaned forward. Her cheek suddenly twitched convulsively, as if she knew what was coming. "I have your handkerchief," I said. "Your lost handkerchief, with your initials and your beautiful tatting."

Her finger stopped inches from the call button. "I've lost a fair number of handkerchiefs in my life, Jack."

"You lose a lot of them at murder scenes?"

"I don't know what you're talking about."

"I've got the datebook. I've got the appointment she made with you the last night of her life."

She just stared at me.

"I've got your bank statements, too." Mark had done wonders in resurrecting decades of financial transactions. The records showed a steady flow of funds from Virginia to Marta, increasing over time. There were also two lump-sum payments: $5,000 when I would have been around five; $15,000 right before Marta put me in foster care. I had wondered why my father stopped coming around when I was five. I had wondered why Marta surrendered her cash cow to foster care when I was eight. Looking at those bank statements, I figured that Virginia first bribed Marta to keep me away from my dad before he could realize I was Mary's son - then paid her to lose me in the foster system when he started to get suspicious.

"I know you lied to me. You said my dad sent Marta money every month for me, but you were the one who signed those checks."

"Jackie asked me to. I was the one who handled the money. We both agreed that we should send Marta money to take care of you."

"If you really had been sending the money for my welfare, you would have stopped as soon as you realized Marta had put me in foster care," I said. "But you didn't. You started two weeks after my mom died, and you didn't stop until you fell down the stairs."

"It's a crime to be generous?"

"It's a crime to kill."

Silence. She was stonewalling me. I decided to switch gears. Maybe I'd take her off guard.

"Look," I said, with the air of someone coming clean, "I'm not trying to hang you here. It was a long time ago. You'd just lost your father. You'd just found out that Beth was disabled, that she was going to need care for the rest of her life. When you split with my dad, you'd thought your folks were wealthy, that they could look after you and the girls. When your father died and you realized all he had were debts, you were desperate to get your husband back. You couldn't support the girls all by yourself."

"He wanted to come back to me!" She was struggling to sit up. A clot of saliva formed in the corner of her mouth. "I didn't ask him to; I didn't even tell him that my father had lost all his money. He left Mary for me!"

"And you were terrified he'd leave you for her - that you'd lose him for good - if Mary told him about me. You knew how much he wanted a son. You tried over and over, but that's the one thing you hadn't been able to give him."

She squeezed her eyes shut, but not before I saw it - not before I saw the flash of triumph. My dad, after all, had never gone back to Mary. He had never had the chance.

"Look at me." My voice was harsher than I intended. I struggled to keep myself under control. After a moment, her eyes reopened into their watery blue slits. "Tell me what happened. I'm willing to hear it from your perspective."

"Nothing happened."

"If you don't tell me, I'll have to keep digging. And that means I'll have to keep asking questions of all your friends. I'll have to start searching for answers that you've paid a fortune to keep buried."

"I see blackmail runs in the family."

I ignored the gibe. "It will be a huge scandal. I know that you went around town spreading lies about my dad and Marta. If I start digging into this seriously, everyone you talked to will know you were lying. And they're going to wonder why a respected, upper-class lady like you would rather have everyone think her husband had an affair with a student instead of knowing that he just went back to his old girlfriend and had a son." I paused. "They're going to remember that his old girlfriend died right around the time you were whispering to everyone that your husband had been messing around with Marta Boyden. And then they're really going to wonder why you lied to them about my dad and Marta. You want to do that to your daughters? After everything else they've been through, you want them to worry that their mother might be a murderer?"

"You wouldn't do that to them. You adore my girls."

Where had I heard something like that before? Virginia and Marta had an uncomfortable amount in common. I had absolutely no intention of even hinting to my sisters that their mother might have harmed me or my family. I wanted to do everything possible to spare them any more pain. But Virginia didn't need to know that.

"I like your daughters a lot," I admitted. "But my first loyalty is to my own family - to my mother. If I can find out what happened to her without involving the girls or anyone else, I'll let it go. But if I can't -" I broke off and shrugged. "There's no limit to what I'll do. If I have to exhume her body, I will."

"That won't tell you anything."

"*And just how would you know that?*"

Her eyes spat blue like the base of a candle flame. I was suddenly, ridiculously relieved that this tiny, frail old lady was tethered to the bed with the swarm of tubes and IVs. I was suddenly, ridiculously relieved that I had chosen a seat that was out of reach. At length, she licked her lips and said, "That's my understanding from the way she died."

"And on what do you base that understanding?"

She didn't answer.

"I'm offering you an out here. I'm not wearing a wire. Even if you didn't have Sergeant Lee in your pocket, the cops aren't interested in prosecuting a terminal cancer patient for a 30-year-old murder. You give me what I want, and I give you what you want. I get information. You get peace. We both get peace."

"And what's to stop me from making up a story just to get rid of you? If you think I'm such a liar, why do you think anything I tell you would be the truth?"

"Because I don't just want an admission. I want to know everything. I want to know how she contacted you. I want to know what she said to you. I want to know whose idea it was to meet, why you met in Seattle, when you bought the barbiturates. I want to know how she looked that night, what the apartment was like, what she was wearing. I want to know everything you said to each other; I want to know where I was; I want to know the exact moment when you decided to kill her. I want to know how you gave her the poison - how you gave it to me. Did you hold me and feed me a bottle you knew was deadly? Did you leave before the drugs took effect on her? Did you stand there and watch her die?"

She was silent.

"I want to know how long it took, what it did to her. I want to know whether she suffered." My voice cracked on the last word.

Contempt flickered across her face. Her voice was dry and hard. "I take it I have Marta to thank for putting these wild ideas in your head."

"She told me what happened."

"Has Marta ever lied to you before?"

It was a grossly unfair question. Marta had done nothing but lie to me since I was a baby. "Of course. Of course she has."

"Have I ever lied to you before?"

"I'm sure you have."

"So when I told you that I wouldn't let Jackie bring you up to Bellingham, when I confessed that I was the reason you stayed in foster care - you think I was lying then?"

"It sounds like something you would do. I don't know whether it's true. I think you told me that because you thought it would keep me from digging into what my dad knew about me, keep me from finding out about my mother. And I think you were trying to goad me into striking you. You were worried that Beth might have set the fire, and you wanted to deflect suspicion onto me. You trashed your own bedroom - so quietly that Sarah didn't even hear you two doors down. I don't know whether you lost your balance as you were trying to ease yourself out of your wheelchair, or whether Beth actually flew at you and knocked you down the stairs, but I'd lay money that you staged at least 90 percent of that 'attack.' If I had laid a hand on you earlier that night, not even my iron-clad alibi would have kept Mac and Lee from arresting me."

"My, but you do credit me with an incredible imagination."

She was proud. *Proud*. The old bitch was *proud* of what she'd done. She was having a ball talking about it. I swallowed the rage that stung my throat and tried to turn it to my advantage. "I credit you with a lot more than that, Virginia. You got your best friend's man, and you kept him. You pushed him to make a success of himself. You raised four of the nicest girls I've ever met. Your granddaughters are all cute as a button." I stopped to let all that flattery sink in. "And you killed my mother, and you got away with it. Now tell me how you did it."

I lobbed one more attempt into the maw of the ensuing silence. "You've got a couple of months at most. You really want to go to your grave with this on your conscience?"

She sighed and rubbed her mouth. Her eyes were far away. She seemed to be thinking something through. When she shifted and looked up at me, I held my breath.

"Mary called me right before Christmas the year you were born," she began. "She said she had had a baby, that she hadn't told Jackie yet. She sounded terrible. She was trying to take care of you and Marta - who was being a little brat as always. Mary was trained as a teacher, but she got fired when she got pregnant. That's how it was in those days. She was working as a waitress at night, when Marta was supposed to be home tending you. Marta kept skipping out at night, though, so Mary had to miss work to look after you. She was this close to losing her waitressing job, and she was desperate.

"She cried and cried. She didn't have any money, she was so tired, and she was considering putting you up for adoption." She lingered over all three syllables of the word, seeming to relish the effect it had on me. "I told her I'd send her some money, that she was just going through the postpartum blues. She asked if Jackie and I wanted to adopt you. She knew that after Beth, I was afraid to try for any more children, and she knew how much Jackie wanted a son.

"I didn't know what to think. I talked it over with Jackie, and he was stunned to hear Mary had had a baby. He didn't think you were his son. He said he and Mary had been together only once right after we had separated, and the timing wasn't right for him to be the father. I told Mary I'd come to Seattle so we could talk it over. We set up an appointment, but at the last minute, I couldn't go. Beth had a seizure. She couldn't breathe, and we had to rush her to the hospital. I had to call Mary and tell her I had to break our date. She was very quiet, very resigned. That should have tipped me off; normally she was a real firecracker. But I was so worried about Beth."

She daubed at her dry eyes. "It was a week or so before we heard that Mary had killed herself that very night - and tried to kill you. Marta called and said she had taken the baby. We told her she was too young. She was only fifteen; you both should have been in foster care. I told her I was going to call Child Protective Services, and that's when she started threatening us. First she said she would tell everyone Jackie had forced himself on her, and that you were her baby. We pointed out that your birth certificate said Mary was your mother. Then she said she'd tell everyone that I had killed Mary. She had some old handkerchief that I'd given Mary, and the appointment in the datebook. It didn't add up to anything, but Marta was such a sneaky one that I was scared of what she might do. Jackie had already lost his job in cutbacks at the school. We were trying to start up the papermill, and we couldn't afford a scandal. So we started paying Marta."

She looked me square in the eyes. "Marta's been lying to you your whole life. She's blackmailed us with a lie for the last twenty-nine years. Your mother killed herself. I know that's hard for you to accept, and I feel very sorry for you. But it's the truth. You need to face up to the truth, Jack." Then she settled back against her pillows and closed her eyes.

I was so cold I thought my joints would break. Virginia's story was calculated to hurt me as much as anything could. The hateful phrases rang in my mind - "putting you up for adoption," "didn't think you were his son," "tried to kill you." Not only had Virginia cast me as the cause of my mother's misery - she was desperate because she couldn't take care of me; her inability to get rid of me drove her to suicide - but she ground my face in being abandoned. Marta's story - however harrowing - had at least quelled some demons in my mind. If my mother was murdered, she hadn't left me voluntarily. But in Virginia's version, no one wanted me. No one had ever wanted me. I was the upshot of a one-night stand; my mother was trying to give me away; my father wouldn't even admit I was his son. And according to Virginia, my own mother had fed me the drugs, my own mother had tried to kill me.

Logically, I knew it was bullshit. My mind was already starting to deconstruct all her lies. Emotionally, it was a different matter. I couldn't talk. I could barely breathe. I just sat there and tried to pull the shattered pieces of myself together.

I saw the glimmer of blue under her eyelids. She was gauging the damage, considering how badly she had hurt me. It was all I could do to keep from striking her.

"What are you doing, Jack?" Her voice was solicitous, but there was a mocking undernote that sent a bolt of fury through me.

I stared at her for a good long time. She blinked. She shifted uneasily. "What are you doing?" she repeated.

"I'm deciding which lie to believe," I said. I stood up, turned around, and walked out of the room.

It was the last time I saw her alive.

CHAPTER 35

That rainy day on the rocky Orcas beach, with my father's lodge behind me and the roiling, pewter Sound before me, Harmony had promised me that eventually I would know what to believe about my dad.

"Eventually, you get to the end of the pier," she had said, "and there isn't anywhere else to look. And then you just decide what you're going to believe, and you let the rest go. Because if you don't, you'll drive yourself mad, Jack. You will absolutely drive yourself mad."

As always, she was right. After my confrontation with Virginia, I spent the next few months driving myself mad. It was like I was writing a brief against her, against everything she had told me. One by one, I undercut her allegations:

Virginia had said my father lost his teaching job because of cutbacks at the school. But I knew from talking to one of my mom's old teachers that my father had been fired because Virginia spread rumors that he and Marta had an affair. One down.

Virginia had said that my mother was struggling to support herself as a waitress and was desperate for money. But I got her work history from Social Security. At the time she died, my mother was a teaching/research assistant for a UW anthropology professor. Her salary was modest, but it was enough to live on. She had money in the bank from the sale of her parents' house. She left no debts when she died. Two down.

Virginia had said she and my father meekly submitted to Marta's blackmail threats because they were trying to get the mill off the ground and couldn't afford a scandal. But she also said that she and my father had had to rush Beth to the hospital the night my mother died. If that was true, they would have had an unimpeachable alibi for Mary's death. There would have been no scandal - certainly not a scandal justifying the hundreds of thousands of dollars Virginia had paid Marta to keep quiet. Three down.

It went on like that. Every morning I rose smarting from something Virginia had said. Every day I exhausted myself - and Mark, and Harmony, and Detective Anthony, and David, and frankly, anyone who would listen - trying to prove that she was lying. I made lists of her allegations. I opened files. I cross-referenced. I searched for anyone in whom my mother might have confided. I identified her landlady, her professor, and the cops who broke down her door - and traced them to their graves. Quite simply, I drove myself mad.

Slowly, very slowly, the fire burned itself out. Slowly, very slowly, my own story coalesced. I no longer argued every point with myself. Blocks of time fell into place. I could see the links between events. Slowly, very slowly, I knew what to believe. So at the end of it all, at the end of the pier, this is what I believe:

In the phrasing of the day, I believe that Virginia trapped my dad into marriage. I got Marianne's birth certificate, and she was indeed born only seven months after their wedding. I believe that the young couple struggled. My dad was fresh out of the Army and going to school at night, and his teaching salary didn't stretch far.

I believe that four daughters and five dogs later, Virginia was regretting the life she had chosen. She threw my dad out and went back to her wealthy parents. My dad went back to my mom - his high school sweetheart, the girl he had always loved. But before my mother knew she was carrying me, Virginia's father died, leaving nothing but debts, and Beth was diagnosed as developmentally disabled.

I believe that my dad went back to Virginia to support her and the girls - and that my mother had me alone. But my mother was going to tell my dad about me, and Virginia just couldn't stand it. I don't know whether Virginia truly feared my father would leave her, or whether her pride just couldn't bear the thought that Mary had a son, and a claim on her husband she would never have. But I believe that Virginia went to see Mary and slipped her something laced with a fatal dose of barbiturates. And I believe that as Mary fell into a never-ending sleep, Virginia picked me up and gave me a bottle calculated to kill me. Anthony had the tatted handkerchief analyzed. It was stained with barbiturates and milk.

I believe that my mother loved me, was delighted with me, would never have hurt me. I believe my father loved my mother - would have loved me, wanted to love me, was preparing for a reunion with me when he died.

I don't have any proof. There's no one I can ask. But that's what I believe inside.

At least, I *didn't* have any proof.

CHAPTER 36

Virginia Carlson Hart died the last week of February. I hadn't seen my sisters all those intervening months. Virginia's doctors had sent her home to die, and much as I loved and missed the girls, I couldn't bring myself to go to my father's house while Virginia lurked upstairs like a grim, white spider. My sisters could not understand why I stayed away, why I refused their entreaties to come for Christmas and New Year's.

"I'm not up to traveling yet," I told Sarah.

"But you said you were feeling better."

"I am. But I still get really tired."

Silence.

"Jack, have we done something wrong? Are you mad at us?"

I assured her that they hadn't, that I wasn't.

"So why won't you come see us?"

"I can't go up there right now, Sarah. I just can't. But you and the other girls are always welcome to come here."

She accepted that and thanked me, although we both knew they wouldn't be leaving Bellingham until their mother died. But we called each other a lot. They sent me e-mail and funny cards. On Christmas Eve, the postman delivered a box marked "Open Immediately." Inside were a pair of plaid flannel pajamas for me, a black silk nightgown for Harmony, and a heart-strewn pair of white satin boxers for Mark.

"Daddy always gave us new pajamas on Christmas Eve," the note read. "He never actually gave us boxer shorts, but we figured, what the hell, Daddy probably never met anyone like Mark. Hope you like them! Send us a picture!"

We duly sent along a snapshot - of the PJs pinned to the clothesline in the laundry room.

Emily responded with a one-word e-mail: "Spoilsports."

I missed them. I wanted to see them. When Sarah called to tell us Virginia had died, I didn't hesitate. "Do you need me to come?" I asked.

"Yes. We need you," she said immediately. "We need you so much, Jack." Three hours later, Betsy and I were back in Bellingham.

My sisters looked pale and spent. From a whispered conversation with the nurse, I surmised that Virginia's had not been a peaceful parting. The day before she died, Virginia started to talk - even when no one else was in the room. She squabbled, she screamed, she sobbed. Her rigid fingers splayed into claws, shriveled into fists. At the moment of her death, she opened her eyes, looked at the door, and said distinctly, "No."

The hair pricked on the back of my neck. "Who was she talking to?" I asked the nurse.

She shrugged. "No one was there."

"No, I mean, did she say who she thought she was talking to? Did she call them by name?"

"No names. Whoever it was, though, it sounded like they were angry at her. She kept saying she was sorry."

"For what?"

"Just sorry," she said, shaking her head.

Virginia's funeral was scheduled for Friday. I spent the days before it helping my sisters get things under control. The house was a mess; I cleaned it up. They'd been living on pizza, Tab, and take-out chicken; I warmed one of the funereal influx of hams. They were suddenly jumpy that I would want them to move out of the house now that Virginia was gone. I sat them down and hammered out a deal: Sarah, Jennifer, Emily, and Beth could stay rent-free in the Edgemoor mansion. If Marianne left Gary, she and her daughters would be welcome as well. They would be responsible for the utilities, maintenance, insurance, and property taxes. If I wanted to sell the house or move in myself, I would give them three months' notice - plenty of time to find another place. Even though the fixtures and furnishings also passed to me under the will, all I wanted from the house right then was my dad's desk - the magnificent rolltop in his bedroom. My sisters quickly agreed. Emily settled me upstairs with a couple of boxes so I could sort out the drawers and the cubbyholes.

"Daddy was a packrat," she said. "Yell if you need another box."

Daddy was indeed a packrat. I skimmed quickly through what looked like ten years of gas station receipts and twenty years of accumulated Kleenex. As I cleared the detritus, however, the pathos soon emerged. There was Scott's funeral program, creased as though my father had crumpled it in his hand, then smoothed it with infinite care. There was a bundle of birthday cards from his daughters and granddaughters, decorated with stickers and glitter. A picture of his mother as a young girl with a high forehead and an unsuspecting gaze. A snapshot of Sarah and Jennifer in the delivery room. Pilate's collar - which would have fit around my thigh. A postcard of the world's tallest Christmas tree, towering over downtown Bellingham. Clippings about the town's pioneer history. A stack of articles about autism and developmental disabilities, swarming with underlines and notes. He had been trying to help Beth.

I tried to shake a sense of disappointment as I turned to the last cubbyhole. I hadn't expected to find anything dramatic in my dad's papers - a letter to me, an explanation of his behavior: anything like that would be too much to expect. But I had expected - had hoped, at least - to find some evidence that my father knew about me. There wasn't anything. I checked my birthday in each of his datebooks, searching in vain for any check or circle, anything to show he set that date apart. Nothing. On the other hand, there weren't any special markings on my sisters' birthdays, either. Maybe my dad just wasn't a datebook type of guy.

I was feeling sorry for myself when I thrust my hand into the last cubicle - and came out with a fistful of dog-eared receipts and a folded vellum rectangle. Even after I glimpsed the flash of purple, even after I recognized the logo of the UW law school, I wasn't sure what I had. I didn't remember seeing the program from my law school graduation. I was keyed up for my speech; I was a ball of nerves. But I opened the rectangle and read my name: John Boyden Hart, salutatorian, law review editor, Order of the Coif. My father had underlined it twice. Next to my name, there were three exclamation points.

I couldn't form rational thought. I couldn't really see the paper I held in my hands. I brought it close to my eye, examining it millimeter by millimeter, making sure that it existed, that it actually bore my name.

At length, in the vortex of emotions that substituted for my mind, one clear sentence emerged: *He knew.*

After another pause, that was followed by: *He was there.*

I couldn't move beyond that. He was there. He was there. He was there as I leaned over the rostrum in Meany Hall, giving my speech, suddenly acutely aware of how alone I was in the world. As I looked out on the sea of proud families - all searching for their son, their daughter, their sibling, their spouse in the graduating class - I had thought that no one out there was looking for me. But I was wrong. My father had been there. He had come to see me graduate. At the time I thought I was most alone, I wasn't.

Through the next few days, I kept the program tucked in my breast pocket, right over my heart. Even though I was bursting with it, I couldn't bring myself to show it to my sisters. It was too private, too much mine. I worried that they would discount it, that they wouldn't realize what it meant to me. I also worried that it would hurt their feelings or disturb their memories of their father. So I just kept it in my pocket and waited for Mark and Harmony to arrive the morning of the funeral.

As it turned out, by the time Mark and Harmony arrived, I had a lot more to show them than that.

CHAPTER 37

A muffled cry roused me at five the morning of the funeral. I leapt out of bed and charged down the hall, steeling myself to enter Virginia's room. Betsy sat down at the door. She refused to go in.

It was like we had gone back in time. The room was destroyed. All the drawers were pulled out; all their contents dumped on the floor. Clothes were strewn out of closets, sheets wadded in the corner, curtains torn down. It looked almost exactly the way it had the day after Virginia claimed to have been attacked. Only this time, Beth was sitting on the bed, fists bunched under her chin, grim-faced and hollow-eyed.

Sarah, who normally bore her sister's misdeeds with extraordinary equanimity, stood beside her, crying.

"Beth, how could you?" she was saying. "Today of all days. We thought you were getting better. How could you do this *again*?"

I couldn't stand to see Sarah in so much pain. It was the morning of her mother's funeral. Sarah was supposed to give the eulogy. She had agonized all week - never satisfied with what she had written, struggling to make it through these first, horrible days without her mom. And now there she was standing in the middle of the wreckage of her mother's bedroom, in the middle of the wreckage of her mother's life, and she was losing it.

I put my arms around her quieted her, comforted her, and sent her back to bed with the assurances that I would take care of everything. Much as I loathed being in Virginia's room, much as I detested the thought of touching her things, of breathing the air still rank with her death, I could not leave that wreckage unaddressed. It was too visible a symbol of the destruction she had wrought on my life. And I was going to clean it up.

I approached Beth cautiously. I knew what she was capable of. I sat gingerly on the bed beside her, hating the contact with Virginia's mattress. I put my arm around Beth's stiff, thin shoulders.

"You missing your mom, babe?"

She didn't respond. She gave no sign that she heard me.

"You trying to find her?"

The slightest possible shake of her head. I couldn't tell whether it was a yes or a no. Or a nothing.

"Come on, Beth. It's still dark out. You can sleep a few more hours."

I swung myself off the mattress and stood before her. I held out my hand to help her up. She inspected my open palm like a fortune teller and slowly and deliberately pressed her palm against mine - pushed something small and cold and round into my hand.

I pulled my hand away and stared at the ring she had given me. It was a narrow platinum band, studded all the way around with tiny stones.

I picked it up and noticed the inscription inside. Worn letters read "Jack and Mary, Together Forever." At the end was added, in newer carving, "At Last." And then there was a date, the year before I was born.

It was the promise ring he had given her before he went in the Army. It had to be. They must have added the "At Last" and the date when they were reunited. I remembered the snapshot at the back of my mom's datebook. She had been wearing a band on her left hand, but in the police report, there had been no mention of a ring. My head swam.

Virginia must have stood there watching as my mother died. Virginia must have slipped the ring off her finger and taken it away. Mark had told me that killers keep trophies. This must have been Virginia's trophy, all these years. This must have been her symbol that she had won.

I fought to stay upright and lucid. I put my arms around Beth and pulled her close. "Beth, please, I need to know where you found this ring."

She showed no sign of having heard me.

"Please, please," I said brokenly. "Beth, I've got to know."

Her head was bent, her shoulders slumped. "Please," I said over and over again. "Please, please, Beth. Please try to tell me."

Gradually she raised her head. Lines creased the soft delicacy of her cheeks and forehead. Before my eyes, she became increasingly defined, like a face surfacing through murky water. It was as though she was struggling to return from somewhere far away, to break through layers of fog and confusion.

She spoke in the clear, unused voice that I had heard only once before.

"It's yours," she said, nodding toward the ring.

"How do you know?"

She fought to keep focused on me. "Mama talked in front of me. She thought I didn't understand." There was a sudden blaze of fire in her eyes. Each word was separate and measured. "*I understand.*"

We clung to each other in the shattered bedroom. I could sense her fading, feel her slipping back behind the barriers that kept her so very far away. "You knew she had my mother's ring," I said urgently. "After you met me that first night, you wanted me to have it. You were searching for it, and you woke her."

A tiny bob of her head. This time, I was sure it signified acquiescence.

"Did you push her down the stairs?"

A tiny shake of her head. The light was dimming in her eyes. But she forced the words out. "Didn't mean to. Just surprised her."

"And then after your mom was in the hospital, you kept looking for the ring. And tonight you found it. Where, Beth? Where?"

I asked over and over, but she was gone. Her head listed at its usual angle; she leaned against me as if she was exhausted. I surrendered. I hugged her and shepherded her to her bedroom - where the night nurse, bless her heart, was sound asleep.

I tucked Beth into bed and sat beside her until her eyes closed and her breathing deepened. Then I went back to Virginia's bedroom - the ring warm in my pocket - and went through every bit of the wreckage until I found what had to be the hiding place.

Under the bed was a three-inch piece of wood with a depression in its center. After some experimenting and crawling around on the floor, I figured out that it snapped into place underneath Virginia's dressing table. For years, Virginia had brushed her girls' hair at that dressing table - inches away from the ring she had taken from a dead woman's hand.

By the time Sarah roused at 8, Virginia's room was perfect. I had hung the clothes in the closets, replaced all the drawers, and folded the sheets and curtains on top of the bed. I had also done two-hundred push-ups and washed my face so many times that Sarah and Emily didn't suspect a thing as we sat down to breakfast.

Harmony and Mark were another story. They had barely crossed the threshold - laden with the comestibles Harmony had prepared for the post-funeral gathering - when they caught a glimpse of me and stopped. They smuggled me outside on a pretext and clustered around me in concern. "What is it?" Harmony demanded. "What has happened?"

I slipped the ring on her left hand. She looked at me in confusion, then twisted it off, examined it, and read the inscription in disbelief. She handed it to Mark. They both started talking at once. I held up my hands to stop them. I could not muster the words to explain. Not then.

"I'll tell you everything later. I promise. I'm OK. Everything's OK. But right now we've got to go to the funeral. We need to look after the girls."

They relented, although their faces were still tight with worry. With some reluctance, Harmony agreed to wear my mother's ring for safekeeping. I couldn't tell whether her hesitation stemmed from the burden of its history or the fact that I had placed it on her wedding finger. Probably both. She had managed to avoid picking out an engagement ring.

The funeral itself was an eerie echo of my father's service. We pulled up at the same desperately spooky Victorian mortuary, complete with a new, nightmarish Cadillac hearse. The same black-suited, brilliantined man met us at the door. The mortuary had fixed the bomb damage in the entryway, replacing the gold-flocked wallpaper with a veneer of stone. It was like being inside a spanking-clean crypt.

But even though the setting was the same, Virginia's service was much different from my dad's. For one thing, there was no doubt this time that I was a member of the family. I tried to escape the viewing, which required standing with the family around the open casket, but Sarah and Emily ignored my protests, linked their arms with mine, and bore me off. They made it clear that I was going to stand with them, sit with them, ride with them, and stay with them. We made a seamless family, standing there in a semi-circle. I had positioned myself as far from Virginia's corpse as possible, but over and over again, people shook my hand and told me how sorry they were about my mom. I pretended they were talking about Mary Boyden.

The other difference was more profound. At my dad's service, the grief in the room was palpable. It wasn't just the masses of flowers. It wasn't just the tears of the speakers, my sisters' shattered hearts. People - all sorts of people - loved my dad. They missed him; they grieved his loss. People were polite at Virginia's funeral. They spoke of her warmly; they praised her beauty and intelligence. But mainly, they were there not to mourn Virginia but to support and comfort my sisters - and, weirdly enough - to support and comfort me.

I was amazed by the number of people who came to talk to me, hug me, make sure I was recovering from the fire. Pretty much everyone from the mill was there. They all wanted to tell me about their job retraining, their new careers. One guy was opening a bookstore over in Fairhaven; more than a few were retraining as computer engineers; a few had chosen to retire. They wanted to tell me how things were going, to let me know that they were making good use of the mill's generous severance packages, that they were going to be OK. "We miss you," people kept saying. "When are you moving up to Bellingham?"

All the little old ladies I had visited about my mother patted my cheek and asked when they would see me again. Karen told me we were the most interesting guests she had ever had at her B&B. She gave me a picture of Bear enjoying the dog treats we had sent him for Christmas. Sergeant Lee and Sheriff Mac both shook my hand solemnly, muttering something that sounded vaguely like "no hard feelings," and turning away before I could reply. Mike Saunders' widow - whom I had finally reached - hugged me nervously, as if she was afraid I would change my mind about not pursuing her family for the money Mike had stolen. Bethany Walton was there, reminding me that we needed to talk about what to do with the scorched swath of beachfront property. Leah Batson came too, offering me yet more money if I would take on American Fidelity's Washington litigation. I think the insurance company was worried that my sisters and I were going to sue them over Carl Moore's misrepresentations and misfeasance. Every time I talked to Leah about the job, she put more money on the table.

Sarah's eulogy went well. She told stories about her mother: her running battles with my father's dogs, her elegant tatting, her amateur acting, her life with her girls. "When we were growing up, we somehow got ahold of a copy of Valley of the Dolls, which we hid from Mama," she said. "I didn't find out until I was married that Mama also had had a copy of Valley of the Dolls, which she hid from *us*. And Mama's copy was underlined." Her eyes filled with tears. "Mama always tried to protect us from anything she thought might hurt us. It didn't matter what it was. You know, I really believe - I truly believe - that Mama would have done anything for us."

Beth shifted next to me. I put my arm around her, and she bent her cold cheek against mine. Beth understood. Of all my sisters, Beth was the one who understood. I squeezed Harmony's hand and felt the smooth, cool pressure of my mother's ring.

After the service, my sisters impressed me into the long black limousine. Mark and Harmony followed in her little red car. There was room for them in the limo, but they had brought something I needed from home. After my sisters left the cemetery, there was something I had to do.

My sisters protested when I told them I would catch up with them back at the Edgemoor house, but after a searching look, Sarah turned to go. "We'll see you in a few minutes, Jack," she said. Beth slipped her little hand in mine for just a second before Marianne settled her back in the limo.

As the hearse and the limousine headed out of the cemetery, Mark retrieved the wreaths from the trunk of Harmony's car. He had cut switches from the flowering cherry trees in our yard, and Harmony had woven them into wreaths. I put the first one on my mother's grave, stooping to pull the weeds that had grown around her grey marble marker. I laid the second at the foot of my father's new headstone. The slab of granite was rough on top. Flecks of quartz and mica shimmered in the wet stone.

"John Henry 'Jack' Hart," the stone read. "Devoted husband to Virginia Carlson Hart. Loving father to Marianne, Emily, Sarah, Elizabeth, and Jack Junior."

I stepped back so I was no longer standing on the artificial turf that cloaked Virginia's open grave. Even though my mother's grave was about twenty feet away, the identical wreaths linked it to my dad's, the pale flowers fluttering in the stiff spring breeze. Jack and Mary. Together forever. At last.

I stood at the top of the hill and looked out over the cemetery. I was surrounded by Harts. I was surrounded by Boydens. The day was dazzling after the morning rains. Below me was the burnt-out papermill I owned. In front of me was blue, polluted Bellingham Bay, dead and heavy with the chlorine and mercury that had given my dad his good living, his good life. Farther out was Lummi Island, farther still, Orcas, where I owned the vacation lodge and a boat or two. I stood there a long time and thought about all the things I had never had but that were mine.

When I finally turned around, Mark and Harmony were standing by the car, watching me, waiting for me, willing to stay as long as I needed, until I was ready.

I took one last look at my dad's gravestone - his name, my name, and the dates.

I walked back to Mark and Harmony and held out my hand.

"Come on," I said. "Let's go home."

- The End -

BOOK CLUB QUESTIONS

Spoiler: Some of these questions may reveal elements of the story.

Thank you for featuring *Only the Good* at your book club. Here are some questions to get you started. Enjoy your discussion!

1. When were you sure you knew the identity of the murderer(s)? Why?
2. To whom does the title refer? Why do you think so?
3. How does the Bellingham setting affect the story? Share examples.
4. Jack's father is presumably dead from the beginning of the book. How is his character developed?
5. How is the character of Jack's mother developed?
6. Discuss Jack's sisters. Do they seem like people who would be related to Jack? In what ways?
7. What is the symbolism of the polluting papermill? How is that developed throughout the book? Share examples.
8. What is the primary mystery in this book? Why do you think so?
9. Identify two of the ethical dilemmas Jack confronts in this story. How does he resolve them? What values are most important to Jack? Why do you think so?
10. What does the grand, empty house on Orcas Island represent? Why do you think so?
11. Compare Jack's interactions with Marta and Virginia. Who has more leverage? What interview/negotiation tactics does Jack use with both?
12. Jack decides whom and what to believe about his past. Are his beliefs well-supported? Why do you think so? Is there contrary evidence that Jack does not take into account? What?
13. Discuss Jack's discovery of his dad's other family and attempts to develop relationships with his sisters. What are the hurdles to these new relationships? How do the characters try to overcome them?
14. How does the retro timeframe affect the story? Share examples.
15. Would you like to read more books by this author?

If you have a question for me, you can reach me at:

https://www.goodreads.com/goodreadscomrosemary_reeve

Thank you for reading my book!

If you enjoyed it, please leave a review online, and please look for other Jack Hart mysteries on Amazon and the Kindle Store.

Your feedback is very important to me, and I appreciate the time you take to let other readers know your thoughts.

All the best,

Rosemary Reeve

The Jack Hart Mysteries:

All Good Things
No Good Deed
Only the Good
Dead Weight

amazon.com/author/rosemaryreeve
https://www.goodreads.com/goodreadscomrosemary_reeve

CPSIA information can be obtained
at www.ICGtesting.com
Printed in the USA
LVHW042001270219
608932LV00003B/717/P

9 781982 989217